ELDRENOIRE

ELLE WILDES

HOUSE OF INK & RUIN

Book Cover by Rachel Bostwick
Map illustrations by Melissa Nash
ISBN: 979-8-9990226-4-6
First edition published in the United States by House of Ink & Ruin
http://www.ellewildes.com

For every woman who was caged and still kept her crown.
And for my Mathieu-
who never tried to tame the storm, only stood steady inside it.

The Sea Remembers

(Sung in taverns near the western coast, forbidden in Belmara's court)

They say a queen ruled by the sea,

With crown of moon and voice of flame—

But silence fell where song should be,

And none who knew her speaks her name.

Her castle sleeps in silver thread,

A hall of mirrors, trapped in time.

She walks where even ghosts would dread,

A lullaby without a rhyme.

Some say she waits. Some say she weeps.

Some say she dreams of what was torn.

But still the tide its promise keeps:

The sea remembers those forlorn.

So drink and hush, and mind the shore—

The lost are not as lost as lore.

CAELVARRA

CHAPTER 1

Mathieu

T he jungle swallowed him whole.

Mathieu pushed through the tangle of vines, his breath ragged, his side slick with blood. The wound was not fatal—not yet—but each step sent a fresh bolt of fire through his ribs. The Rothgar soldiers were behind him. He had heard their voices, their sharp, guttural commands, and the crackle of branches snapping under their boots. They wanted him dead. Needed him dead.

And yet, the deeper he ventured, the quieter the world became.

The jungle should have been alive with sound. Chirping insects, rustling leaves, the distant call of some night-stalking beast. Instead, silence pressed in, thick and unnatural. The air itself felt weighted, heavy with something unseen, something watching. The moment he crossed into the clearing, he knew he had stepped beyond the world he understood.

A castle loomed before him.

Massive and dark, half-consumed by ivy and time, it should not have been here. There were no maps that spoke of a fortress on the edge of Ziraveen's jungle, no whispered rumors of a kingdom long forgotten. It was a relic of a past he did not know, a ruin untouched by war but still claimed by something far worse.

His breath came slower now, his pulse a steady drumbeat against the quiet. He should turn back. Should take his chances in the jungle with the men who hunted him. And yet, there was a pull to this place, a whisper just beneath hearing. He stepped forward.

The moment his boot met the stone of the castle's outer curtain wall, the jungle behind him vanished.

Gone. As if it had never been there. No trees, no path, no trace of the world he had come from. Only the castle remained, stretching out before him in eerie silence, its massive iron gates yawning open like the mouth of some great beast.

"Reckless bastard."

The voice was sudden, slipping into his mind like a blade through silk. Low, unimpressed, and with the faintest hint of amusement. He turned sharply, instinctively reaching for his sword, but saw no one. Only the flicker of torchlight against the stone.

His eyes landed on a sleek, white cat perched on a crumbling pillar.

Mathieu blinked. The cat stared back, its eyes a piercing shade of grey. Something about the way it watched him, still and knowing, sent a ripple of unease down his spine.

"You've wandered too far, stranger," the voice murmured again.

Mathieu's grip tightened on his sword. His pulse ticked against his ribs as he turned sharply, scanning the ruins. The voice had been close. Too close. Yet there was no one else in sight.

A trick of the wind?

He let out a measured breath, forcing himself to focus. "Who's there?"

The cat didn't move. Mathieu's jaw tightened. His eyes flicked over the trees, the crumbling stone, the shifting shadows. Nothing. No one.

"Show yourself," he commanded, taking a step forward. His voice came out rougher than intended, a warning wrapped in steel.

Silence.

Then, "I am right here."

Mathieu pivoted sharply, his grip flexing around the sword hilt. Still nothing.

Only the ruins. The wind. The cat, sitting motionless on its perch.

He swallowed against the strange coil of tension in his gut. "If you mean to frighten me," he muttered, "you'll have to try harder than whispers in the dark."

A beat of stillness.

Then the voice—smooth, unimpressed. "I don't need to frighten you."

Mathieu stilled. The sound had been... off. Not carried from the trees, not rolling from the ruins, but close. Too close.

He turned again—sharply, deliberately. Nothing. Nothing but the cat. A flicker of unease crawled along his spine.

He exhaled through his nose. "Enough games."

"No game."

Mathieu's fingers twitched. The voice was coming from the same direction as before. The same impossible place.

His pulse beat heavier now, a slow and deliberate warning. He eyed the stones, the shadows, his mind cycling through every trick he knew—hollow pipes, enchantments, something hidden just beyond sight. Anything but the creeping thought taking root in his mind.

"I won't ask again," he said, voice low. "Where are you?"

The cat tilted its head.

And then, "I am right in front of you."

Mathieu froze. His breath slowed. The silence thickened. And then it hit him.

The voice hadn't echoed. Hadn't traveled. Hadn't come from anywhere but—

His gaze snapped back to the cat.

His grip tightened on his sword. It took him a moment to realize the truth.

Wounded, half-delirious, and now apparently speaking with a cat, he still felt the stirrings of irritation and intrigue. "I assume you're the welcoming party?"

The cat leapt gracefully down from the pillar, landing soundlessly at the base of the steps. It sat, curling its tail around its paws with deliberate ease, as though entirely unimpressed by the wounded man before it.

"Hardly. That would imply you are welcome."

His lips twitched despite himself. "That's unfortunate," he said. "I was hoping for a warm meal and a softer bed than the one I've been running through."

"You'll find neither here."

Her words—because it was her, the cat, speaking directly into his mind—should have been a dismissal, but she did not turn away. Instead, she studied him with the keen patience of a predator waiting to see if its prey would falter. There was something unreadable in her expression—not quite hostility, not quite interest. A test, perhaps.

Mathieu had failed enough tests in his life to recognize one when he saw it.

He took another step forward, his body protesting the movement, and forced himself to meet the cat's unblinking gaze without flinching. "What is this place?"

The cat's white tail flicked once, slow and deliberate. "A prison. A graveyard. A gilded cage."

She tilted her head, watching him. Waiting. Then she said as if to herself, "Which will it be for you, I wonder?"

The cat turned without another word, stepping lightly through the open gates and onto the stone path beyond. Mathieu hesitated only a moment before following. What other choice did he have? Behind him, the jungle no longer existed. Ahead, the castle sprawled in eerie stillness, its looming towers disappearing into the mist.

The path led through what must have once been a grand garden. Even in the dim torchlight, he could make out the remnants of beauty—twisting archways, vine-covered statues, fountains long since dried. Roses climbed in tangled clusters along the stone walls, their petals dark as spilled wine. A strange sense of peace lay over the place, but beneath it, something more insidious lurked. This was not an abandoned ruin: it was a mask, a carefully cultivated facade meant to conceal whatever festered beneath.

Mathieu's boots crunched against the gravel as he followed the cat, his fingers brushing the hilt of his sword. "A prison, you said?" he mused. "And yet, you don't seem particularly concerned about keeping me from leaving."

"You assume you have a choice."

The response was lazy, almost bored. The cat padded ahead, weaving through the remnants of the overgrown courtyard with the ease of one who had walked these paths for centuries.

Mathieu narrowed his eyes. "And what if I don't care to stay?"

The cat leapt onto a low stone wall, tail flicking once. "Then you are welcome to try the gates."

Mathieu glanced back. The iron bars still stood wide open, the jungle—

Gone. Just mist and endless dark.

A chill slid down his spine. He had seen magic in his lifetime, but never like this. A trick of the eye? An enchantment? Or something far worse?

"So that's how it is," he murmured. "I walk in, and the door vanishes behind me."

"The door does not vanish," the cat corrected. "It simply ceases to lead where you expect."

His jaw tightened. "And you? Are you my warden?"

A low, rumbling sound that might have been laughter echoed in his mind. "I am no one's warden." The cat leapt down and continued walking. "But you are my guest, whether you like it or not."

Mathieu didn't follow. Not immediately.

His jaw tightened, his gaze flicking toward the gates—their iron bars still yawning open to the world beyond. Or at least, to where the world had been. A trick. An illusion.

He turned sharply on his heel, moving toward the threshold, shoulders squared. He had never been the kind of man to accept a locked door without testing it.

Cool air ghosted over his skin as he stepped forward, boots crunching against gravel, closing the distance to the open gate. Just beyond, the mist curled, shifting in slow, lazy tendrils, waiting.

Mathieu steadied his breathing and stepped through. The air changed. Not violently. Not in any way he could name. But one moment, he was crossing the threshold—
And the next, he was not.

He halted. Stiffened. Looked up. The castle loomed before him, dark and vast. The gates still stood open. And he was still inside them.

His pulse ticked once, slow and measured. He turned. Took another deliberate step through the gate. And again—he did not pass.

No jolt of magic, no invisible wall barring his way. But the world shifted, impossibly smooth, like a card trick performed by unseen hands. Every step forward led him nowhere.

Mathieu's fingers curled into fists. A muscle feathered in his jaw as he inhaled deeply, re-centering, adjusting. This wasn't panic. It was strategy.

He tried again. This time with focus. A careful, measured step toward the gate, his mind tracking each movement. But again, with an ease that defied reason, he remained where he had started.

He tried angles. Circles. Timing. Nothing mattered. Every step brought him back to the same place, as if the castle had no interest in letting him leave.

A soft sound drew his attention.

Mathieu turned his head sharply. The cat perched on a low stone wall, tail flicking in lazy amusement, watching.

Mathieu huffed, nostrils flaring. "Enjoying yourself?"

"A little." Her voice curled through his mind, the faintest note of amusement beneath the purr. "Most take longer to test the limits."

His lips pressed into a thin line. So, this was a game to her.

His grip flexed on the hilt of his sword. "And if I ran?"

The cat's tail flicked again. "You could try."

Mathieu *did* try.

Not blindly. Not recklessly. But as a man trained to track terrain, note patterns, search for the weak points in any structure. He moved sideways, testing different angles. Stepped out, then back in. Walked a slow circle around the courtyard, recalibrating, searching for any shift in the way the space responded to him.

But the castle did not care. The rules were not his to define.

The mist remained. The doors stayed open. But every attempt to leave only led him back to the stones beneath his boots, trapping him in the same moment, over and over.

It was the effortless nature of it that unsettled him the most. A prison without walls. A leash without a chain.

At last, Mathieu exhaled sharply and turned back toward the cat.

She blinked at him, slow and self-satisfied.

"You done?"

He rolled his shoulders, pushing down the irritation clawing at his ribs. Better to let her think he was unbothered. "For now."

"Hmmm." The cat stretched luxuriously before hopping down from the wall, padding away without a backward glance. "Then keep up."

Mathieu's fingers twitched at his sides before, finally, he followed.

The cat led him through the courtyard, past broken fountains and shadowed alcoves, toward the massive arched entrance of the castle. The moment they stepped beneath its stone threshold, a strange warmth settled over him—an unnatural, cloying comfort, as though the air itself sought to keep him.

The cat paused just before the grand doors, glancing back at him. "You are bleeding."

Mathieu looked down. The dark stain spread further along his tunic, sluggish but persistent. He had lost more blood than he realized.

"I've survived worse."

"That may be." The cat's silver eyes flickered in the dim light. "But Eldrenoire is not kind to the wounded."

The massive doors groaned as they swung inward, their blackened iron and ancient carvings depicting long-forgotten battles. They stood tall, oppressive in their weight and history, as if they had sealed away something meant to remain undisturbed. And yet, as they parted, they revealed a world that did not belong inside this cursed fortress.

Sunlight streamed through high windows, pooling golden light across gleaming marble floors. Lush tapestries lined the walls, embroidered in gold and deep sapphire. The scent of blooming roses and fresh parchment lingered in the air. Voices echoed softly—human voices.

Servants moved with quiet efficiency, dressed in elegant yet practical garb. Some carried silver trays, others busied themselves lighting ornate candelabras or tending to the fresh flowers arranged in crystal vases. Amidst them, creatures roamed—foxes curled in window seats, a great stag standing at the base of a grand staircase, birds perched along gilded railings, watching.

Mathieu stopped short, his hand still resting on the hilt of his sword. "This," he said slowly, "is not what I expected."

The cat padded ahead, pausing only long enough to glance back at him. "Eldrenoire is many things," she murmured. "But it is never what one expects."

All at once, hands stilled over silver trays, steps faltered mid-stride, conversations died on the air. Eyes, too many eyes, turned toward him, wide with unreadable expressions. And then *he* stepped forward.

A massive dire wolf, dark-furred and thick with muscle, prowled toward them, his golden eyes locked onto Mathieu with unnerving intelligence. He moved with slow, deliberate purpose, not a single sound from his heavy paws as he closed the distance.

Mathieu stiffened. The deference in the room shifted, and for a brief, breathless moment, he thought it was for him. That they had recognized him. That they had been waiting for him.

A sick feeling coiled in his gut. He had been found.

Rothgar's men had set a trap. He was the fool who had walked straight into it.

Mathieu stopped short, his hand instinctively tightening around the hilt of his sword. He could feel the weight of their gazes pressing down on him, studying him. His pulse quickened.

What did they see? A vagabond in torn, bloodstained leathers? A desperate man on the run?

Then, as one, the room bowed. Servants, noble-looking figures, even the beast that had stalked toward them—all lowered their heads in solemn deference. The dire wolf crouched low on its front haunches, golden eyes never leaving Mathieu's.

His breath stilled. His stomach twisted—had he walked into a carefully laid trap? Had Rothgar's reach extended even here? Were they mocking him?

Mathieu's panic surged, his instincts screaming that he was in danger. His sword left its sheath in a single, fluid motion, the blade gleaming in the unnatural sunlight. But he barely had time to brace before the dire wolf moved.

One moment the dire wolf was lunging—the next, where the beast had stood, a man towered before him. Mathieu staggered back; his sword wrenched from his grip before he could even blink.

Silver-haired, broad-shouldered, with sharp eyes like burnished gold. His stance was military-perfect, his hand still curled around the hilt of Mathieu's stolen sword.

A jolt of instinct hit—tightening his stance, coiling his muscles. *Shifter.* And not just one.

His gaze flicked around the cavernous room, tracking the subtle, unnatural stillness in the surrounding animals. Not beasts. Not pets. A castle full of shifters.

His pulse hammered as his eyes circled back to the cat—the one that had spoken to him.

A slow smirk curled the man's mouth. "Now, now," he said smoothly, his voice carrying a deep timbre. "Is that any way to greet your host?"

A sharp, sardonic laugh echoed through Mathieu's mind. The white cat, still perched elegantly nearby, flicked her tail with clear amusement. "Oh, you poor, deluded creature," she purred. "Did you think they were bowing to *you?*"

Mathieu's breath hitched, his grip tightening on empty air where his sword had been. The slow, creeping heat of embarrassment curled in his gut, battling with the lingering panic. His jaw clenched. "I—"

She cut him off, voice rich with scorn. "What an ego you must have." Her silver eyes gleamed with something between mockery and boredom.

Mathieu opened his mouth, searching for a retort—something sharp, something that would mask the sudden fog creeping into his mind. He needed to stay alert, to stay present. Instead, his vision swam, a low hum growing in his skull.

The cat turned to the man still gripping Mathieu's stolen sword and released a long-suffering sigh. "Renaud, shall we continue this conversation after our guest has finished bleeding all over the newly mopped floor?"

Mathieu looked down. The wound at his side had reopened, blood pouring onto the polished marble floor. The room spun violently. He barely registered the wolf's reply over the dull roar in his ears as he fell to the floor.

The man raised an eyebrow and peered down at Mathieu as he lay bleeding on the ground. "What shall I do with him, Your Highness?"

The cat released a sigh steeped in centuries of disdain, "Another man in need of my help. How tiresome."

The last thing Mathieu noticed before his vision darkened was the mirrored ceiling above him, casting reflections of the room—the strange gathering of humans and creatures alike. But his gaze caught on one impossible detail.

Where the white cat should have stood beside him, the mirror's reflection showed a woman.

She was tall, regal, draped in the deep, elegant hues of midnight and storm. Her dark chestnut hair cascaded over her shoulders, her silver-grey eyes sharp as a blade's edge. A scar curved over her collarbone, half-hidden by the fabric of her gown. There was something ancient in her beauty, something untouchable.

Mathieu blinked.

His pulse stuttered—just for a moment.

That wasn't right.

He had expected to see the cat's reflection. And yet, reflecting back at him from the mirrored ceiling, there was no feline silhouette. No sleek white fur. No glinting grey eyes.

Just her.

A trick of the glass. Or magic.

Maybe he was imagining things—his body was still wrecked with exhaustion, his mind still sluggish from pain. Maybe this was another strange enchantment of the castle, one of the many things he was beginning to suspect lurked beneath its walls.

But the woman in the reflection didn't waver.

His breath slowed, unease curling in his chest. Was this a hallucination?

He didn't have time to dwell on the answer.

The world tilted. The edges of his vision blurred. Then, darkness.

CHAPTER 2

Améliane

The rogue was still breathing. The fever had set in quickly. He'd been unconscious for nearly an hour, but already the bandages were slick again.

Améliane watched the slow rise and fall of his chest, arms folded as she leaned against the marble pillar near the hearth. The firelight flickered over him, casting sharp shadows across his features—the hard planes of his cheekbones, the faint lines at the corners of his eyes, the scar that cut across his forearm. He looked like a man who had fought one war too many.

And yet, he was young enough. Not yet old, but far from untested.

She had expected him to be crude, brutish—a common sellsword who had wandered where he should not. But there was a controlled stillness to him even in sleep, an ingrained discipline beneath the grime and blood. Not just a warrior. Something more.

"He'll live," came Sabine's voice, dry and dispassionate. "Unless he's as reckless as he looks. In which case, I'll be seeing him again soon."

The older woman blew an escaped grey hair out of her face as she knelt beside the divan, tightening the last of the bandages around his side. Her sharp, practiced hands moved with the efficiency of a healer who had seen too many bodies broken before her.

At the foot of the bed, Renaud stood sentry, arms crossed as he exhaled a sharp breath. *"We should have let him bleed out. He could be a spy. Or worse, an idiot."*

Élodie, reclining elegantly in a nearby chair, smirked. "How fortunate for him that you do not make such decisions."

Améliane did not respond to the dire wolf's grumbling. She rarely did.

Instead, she continued to study the man on the bed, cataloging the details of him. The faint bruising along his knuckles, the roughness of his hands—a man who had worked and who had fought. A man who had likely also taken and lost. His breath remained steady, despite the fever creeping into his skin. He had survived this long. He would survive this, too.

Élodie shifted in her chair, green eyes glinting with amusement. "Interesting, isn't it?" she mused, smoothing an invisible wrinkle from her gown. "You brought this one to a guest chamber instead of the dungeons. That's rather generous of you. The last unfortunate soul to stumble into Eldrenoire was not so lucky."

Améliane did not take the bait. It was true that the last man who had come uninvited had met a much colder reception. And yet, he had not been like this one. He had not intrigued her. But she would not give Élodie the satisfaction of acknowledging it.

Before anyone could press the matter further, Mathieu stirred.

It was barely a movement—just the slightest furrow of his brow, the slow tensing of his fingers. But it was enough.

Renaud was already moving, shifting his weight forward in a silent, predatory motion. His golden eyes sharpened, his stance tensing in preparation for whatever the stranger might attempt.

Améliane, however, did not move. She simply watched.

She watched as Mathieu's lashes flickered, as his body registered the pain before his mind fully woke.

Mathieu stirred again, a quiet sound escaping him, something between a breath and a groan. His fingers twitched against the silk-covered divan, his brow drawing into the faintest crease. The fever was pulling at him, keeping him under, but some stubborn part of him fought to surface.

Améliane tilted her head slightly, watching as his lashes fluttered against his skin. Golden firelight cast shadows across his face, sharpening the edges of his jaw, the line of his mouth—firm even in unconsciousness. There was a strength in his features that had nothing to do with brute force.

His breathing hitched. Then, slowly, his eyes opened. Not fully—just a fraction—but enough for her to see the color of them in the dim light.

Hazel. Not a single hue, but many, shifting with the flickering gold of the firelight. There was green there, gold, the deep brown of aged oak. For the briefest of moments, the focus in them was sharp, searching—trying to place where he was, who he was looking at.

And then his gaze found hers.There was no fear in his eyes. No immediate tension, no sharp recoil. Just awareness, muddled with exhaustion. He saw her, but he did not know her.

She didn't move. But something in her, something she hadn't named in years, did. Then the moment shattered.

Renaud stepped forward, a looming shadow at Améliane's side, golden eyes sharp and predatory. His presence was a warning in itself—a silent promise that if the man so much as shifted the wrong way, his life would be forfeit.

Mathieu's gaze flickered, briefly, toward him. Then, as if the effort were too much, his eyes slid closed once more.His breath evened, drawn back under by fever's grasp.

Améliane sighed, quiet and measured.

"See that he does not die," she murmured over her shoulder to Sabine. "For now."

Améliane turned on her heel and left the chamber without another glance.

Her steps echoed through the corridor, satin slippers whispering across cold marble as she left the firelit room behind. She had seen all she needed. The stranger posed no immediate threat.

And yet, something in the way he had looked at her—not with fear, not with reverence, but with simple, sharp-eyed awareness—unsettled her more than it should have.

The corridor ahead was dark and cool, the flickering sconces casting long shadows against the high stone walls. She had only taken a few steps when the rustle of wings disturbed the quiet.

A soft gust of air brushed past her as a dark shape swooped down from the balcony above.

By the time Laurent's boots hit the marble, his transformation was already complete—golden feathers dissolving into the deep navy of his open-collared tunic, the sharp curve of his beak smoothing into the amused quirk of his mouth.

"Now that, Queenie" he drawled, straightening, "was interesting."

Améliane did not slow. Laurent fell into step beside her with ease, his movements fluid and unhurried, as though he had simply appeared at her side rather than descended from the night like some too-clever specter.

His icy blue eyes flicked toward her, curiosity sparking beneath his usual, insufferable amusement. "And here I thought we had enough lost souls wandering these halls. Tell me, Liane, how do you intend to keep this one hidden should Edric decide to visit?"

"If I required your counsel on the matter, Laurent," Améliane murmured, her tone dry as parchment, "I would have summoned you before you threw yourself dramatically from the balcony."

Laurent grinned. Unrepentant. "Dramatic?" he echoed, pressing a hand over his heart. "I much prefer *graceful*. Or *elegant*. Perhaps even—"

"Predictable," she cut in.

His laugh was a soft, knowing thing. "Ah, Liane, you wound me."

She did not slow her stride, nor did she dignify that with a response. Laurent rarely needed encouragement.Still, he pressed on, keeping pace with her as though he had nowhere better to be.

"You know," he mused, "I passed Alaric on the way here. Or rather, I found him in the *Mirror Hall*, staring into his *very empty* book and muttering about how nothing ever changes in Eldrenoire."

That made her pause—just slightly. Laurent noticed, of course. He always did.

"Then, of course," he continued, voice light, "he sighed dramatically and whispered something about *'fate shifting'* before walking straight into a mirror."

Améliane exhaled sharply. "And?"

"And?" Laurent feigned offense. "You don't find that *the least bit* interesting? The last time Alaric noticed a shift in anything, the moon nearly fell out of the sky."

That was an exaggeration. Mostly.

The Mirror Hall was a place few lingered long. A long corridor lined with mirrors that did not show true reflections—some whispered of the past, others hinted at things that might be. No one trusted what they saw there.

Laurent tilted his head, blue eyes dancing. "Come now, Liane. Even you must admit, a stranger appearing out of nowhere, a castle that never changes suddenly *noticing* something—" He leaned in slightly, voice almost conspiratorial. "Something is happening."

She did not like that truth.Not one bit.

Laurent watched her closely, waiting, but Améliane did not take the bait. She kept her expression impassive, kept her steps measured, kept her thoughts her own. Whatever Alaric had seen—or thought he had seen—it did not matter.

Laurent must have sensed her decision to drop the subject, because he sighed in that long-suffering way he always did when she refused to entertain his whims.

"Fine, fine," he relented, rolling his eyes and tossing his golden hair over one shoulder. "I'll let you keep your secrets—for now."

She hummed. "How gracious of you."

They walked in silence for a moment, their footsteps soft against the marble, the air thick with the scent of night-blooming flowers curling through the open corridors.

Then, as if the thought had only just occurred to him, Laurent stretched his arms behind his head and sighed. "*Not that I don't love being trapped in this cursed estate with you,*" he mused, "but one day, I'd like to stretch my wings somewhere that doesn't come with a blood price."

Améliane's gaze flicked toward him.

Laurent had never been subtle about his dislike for being caged. It was in the way he moved, the way he perched on railings instead of chairs, the way his shifter form was always ready to take flight at a moment's notice.

He was always watching the world beyond Eldrenoire's borders.

Améliane turned away. "And yet, you are still here."

Laurent grinned, unrepentant, tossing his long golden hair over his shoulder, "Where else would I find such riveting company?"

Something in his expression shifted, some hidden thought passing through his mind that he did not speak aloud. Then, just as quickly, he smirked.

"I could leave, you know."

Améliane raised a brow. "Could you?"

Laurent flashed a sharp, white-toothed grin—the kind he wore when he was lying to himself. "Of course."

She let the silence between them speak the truth.

He could not.None of them could.Not yet.

Laurent took a deep breath, rolling his shoulders as if shaking off the weight of the moment. "One day, though," he murmured, almost to himself. "One day, I'll fly so far even Eldrenoire won't be able to pull me back."

Améliane did not answer. She reached out, her fingers curling around his forearm—not to stop him, not to restrain, but to steady.

Laurent stilled.

"Careful, Laurent," she murmured, her voice softer now, the sharp edge dulled by something closer to sorrow. "Dreams do not survive here."

For a moment, something flickered in his icy blue eyes. Regret. Resignation. Something neither of them spoke of.

Then, just as quickly, he flashed a careless grin, stepping back, slipping just out of her reach as easily as always. "And yet, you still indulge mine. If I didn't know better, Liane, I'd think you had a soft spot for me."

She sighed with a smile, shaking her head. "I must be cursed."

Laurent chuckled, low and warm, before turning on his heel and vanishing into the shadowed corridor with all the ease of a man who had never been caught against his will.

Améliane watched him go.

Then, with one last glance at the candlelit hallway stretching before her, she turned the other way and walked alone down the dimly lit corridor.

CHAPTER 3

Mathieu

He woke slowly, pulled from the depths of unconsciousness by the weight of something unseen. His body felt heavier than it should, his thoughts sluggish as he surfaced from the fevered haze that had claimed him.

Warmth pressed against his skin—the softest sheets he had felt in years, the faint scent of gardenia curling through the air. Somewhere distant, the rustling of fabric and the muted chime of wind through an open balcony door whispered to him, coaxing him further into wakefulness.

He pried his eyes open.

The chamber around him swam into focus—ornate, sunlit, nothing like the damp, cold places he had grown used to waking in. Golden light pooled on the polished floors, spilling in through sheer curtains that billowed lazily with the breeze. The walls were draped in dark tapestries, embroidered with sigils he did not recognize, their patterns shifting in the flickering candlelight.

He shifted slightly and immediately regretted it. Pain flared up his side, sharp and searing, the memory of steel meeting flesh slamming into him all at once. A grunt left his lips before he could bite it back, but it was the flash of movement in the corner of his vision that made him freeze.

Someone was watching him.

Not someone. Something.

A small, golden fox lay curled near the open balcony doors, its fur so pale it nearly disappeared into the golden light. Only its eyes—a striking, unnatural shade of blue—betrayed its presence. They fixed on him with an intelligence that sent a prickle of unease down his spine.

Mathieu swallowed, blinking hard, trying to shake off the fog still clinging to his mind. He had seen shifters before—had fought beside them, against them. But in the moments between sleep and waking, he could not tell if the creature before him was merely an animal or something more.

His throat was dry when he spoke. "Are you real?"

The words felt ridiculous even as they left his lips.

The fox did not answer. It only continued to stare, unblinking.

Mathieu exhaled, the barest edge of frustration creeping into his exhaustion. "You're not going to make this easy, are you?"

The fox's head tilted, something like amusement flickering in those too-sharp eyes. Then, without a sound, it rose to its feet, its movement as fluid as a wisp of smoke.

Before he could say anything else, it turned and darted through the balcony doors, vanishing over the railing down into the sun-drenched gardens beyond.

Mathieu stared after it, frowning. His fingers twitched toward the bandages wrapped tightly around his ribs, the only proof that his wounds were more than just another fevered dream.

He drew in a slow breath, pressing his palms against the mattress as he forced himself upright. His body protested—ribs aching, limbs stiff, and the bandages around his side pulled uncomfortably with the movement. A dull throbbing settled behind his eyes, remnants of fever and exhaustion clinging to him like a second skin.

Still, he was awake. That counted for something.

The chamber around him was unlike any place he had rested in years. It was too *luxurious*. The high-vaulted ceiling was painted with some intricate, gilded design that gleamed softly in the afternoon light. Sheer curtains framed the balcony doors, their deep blue hue shifting with the breeze. A fire crackled in the hearth, its warmth stretching toward him in lazy waves.

And there—set on a low wooden table near the fire—was a silver tray of food.

His stomach twisted painfully, reminding him how long it had been since he had eaten anything more substantial than stale bread and whatever dried rations he could scavenge.

Swinging his legs over the side of the bed was an ordeal in itself. His muscles protested, and a fresh spike of pain shot through his ribs, forcing him to grit his teeth. But pain was something he had learned to push through. He let it ground him as he staggered to his feet, bracing himself against the edge of a nearby chair until the dizziness passed.

One step. Then another. By the time he reached the table, sweat pricked at his temple, but the scent of warm bread and roasted meat chased away any lingering hesitation. He collapsed into the chair and reached for the nearest thing—a piece of crusty bread still warm from the oven.

He tore off a bite, chewing roughly, and let his head fall back against the chair.

The bread disappeared too quickly. So did the rest of the food. He ate with the single-minded focus of a man who had gone too long without a proper meal, barely tasting the roasted meat and ripe fruit before it was gone. His body needed it—*craved* it—more than his mind could keep up with.

By the time he sat back, exhaling a slow breath, the warmth of the fire had seeped into his bones, loosening the tension coiled deep in his muscles. For the first time in what felt like *years*, he was no longer running.

He ran a hand down his face, the roughness of his unshaven jaw a stark contrast to the opulence around him. None of this made sense. A gilded cage was still a cage, but this was a far cry from the dungeons or executioner's block he had come to expect when captured.

Pushing himself upright, he turned toward the far end of the chamber, where a second door stood slightly ajar. The faint scent of lavender and something sharper—like crushed herbs—drifted through the opening.

Curious, he shuffled forward, his bare feet silent against the cool marble.

The door swung open with the faintest creak, revealing a bathing chamber unlike any he had ever seen.

Soft candlelight flickered across the polished stone walls, casting golden reflections against a massive, sunken tub carved directly into the floor. Steam curled lazily above the water's surface, and a neat stack of folded towels rested atop a small bench nearby.

His brows lifted.

This was... unexpected.

Not just the bath itself but the *fact* that it had been drawn for him—and, in a rare stroke of good fortune, it was still warm.

Mathieu sighed, rolling his shoulders. He was not one to question a gift when it was presented, and at this moment, the thought of sinking into that heat overpowered any lingering doubts about his circumstances.

He reached for the bandages wrapped around his torso, hissing through his teeth as he unwound them. The fabric peeled away slowly, revealing the wound beneath—a raw, angry gash along his ribs, though it had been cleaned and stitched with a care he had not expected.

A healer's handiwork, no doubt.

Shrugging out of the rest of his clothes, he lowered himself into the bath. The water burned at first, a biting heat against the raw edges of his wound, but he forced himself to sink lower, letting the warmth do its work. The ache in his muscles dulled, the weight of exhaustion settling into his bones like an old companion.

His head tipped back against the edge of the tub, breath steadying, and for the first time since waking, he allowed himself to *think*. A soft breeze drifted in from an open window, carrying the faint scent of roses and something older, something *earthy* beneath the sweetness. The cool air ghosted over his damp skin, a sharp contrast to the heat of the bath, grounding him in the present.

He was alive. That was the first miracle. He had no right to be.

The last thing he remembered before the castle was *running*.

Not from battle—those days were long behind him—but from the hunters who had been on his heels for weeks. Rothgar's men. He had heard their voices in the jungle, the sharp bark of orders, the snap of branches under boots. He had been bleeding, the gash along his ribs slowing him down when he could least afford it.

He should be dead. He *would* be dead, had he not stumbled upon this place.

His eyes cracked open, scanning the candlelit chamber.

This was no war camp, no outlaw's hideout. This was something else entirely, something far removed from the world he knew.

Even now, the details of his arrival clawed at his mind. The way the jungle had swallowed itself whole behind him. The castle, looming where no map had ever placed it. The moment he had crossed its threshold; the world had *shifted*.

And then, of course—*the cat.*

His fingers traced absently along the rim of the tub, his mind conjuring the last thing he had seen before darkness took him. The mirrored ceiling. The reflection that didn't match reality. A woman where a cat should have been.

He exhaled slowly, dragging a wet hand down his face. Whoever she was—whatever she was—she had let him live. That alone was more than he had expected.

Still, questions gnawed at him.

Why *had* they spared him? Who *were* these people? And more importantly—What the hell had he just walked into?

His fingers curled against the stone lip of the tub, his jaw tightening.

It didn't matter. He had survived worse. And until he figured out what this place was and how to get out of it— he would survive this, too.

A rustle of wings stirred the quiet.

Mathieu's eyes flicked open, his muscles tensing instinctively. On the wide stone windowsill, bathed in the glow of the setting sun, perched a golden hawk.

It watched him with unsettling stillness, its sharp eyes catching the light, glinting like frozen ice.

Mathieu huffed, sitting up straighter. "Let me guess," he muttered. "You're not just a bird."

The hawk did not answer, but something in its gaze felt too knowing, too focused.

He huffed a quiet laugh, shaking his head. *First a talking cat, then a vanishing fox, and now a bird that looks like it's judging me.* He had clearly lost his mind.

"Well," he drawled, gripping the edge of the tub. "Unless you plan on handing me a towel, I'd suggest you find another perch."

The hawk cocked its head, as if considering. Then, with a sharp beat of its wings, it pushed off the sill and vanished into the darkening sky.

Mathieu chuckled under his breath, shaking his head. "Right. Didn't think so."

Mathieu pushed himself upright, water sluicing off his skin as he stepped out of the tub. His ribs ached, but the bath had done its job—he felt steadier, less like a man on the verge of collapse. Reaching for a towel, he wrapped it around his waist, then caught sight of himself in the tall mirror across the room.

For a moment, he simply stared.

The years had carved themselves into him—faint lines at the corners of his eyes, a silvering at his temples that had begun before its time. His body bore the evidence of a life that should have been softer, a life that should have belonged to a king who ruled from the safety of a throne. But the man in the mirror was no king. Not anymore.

His chest and arms were marked with the ghosts of old battles, each scar a memory he had no use for. A long-healed slash across his ribs, a jagged line at his forearm—proof of the wars he had fought, the kingdom he had lost, the years spent running. He lifted a hand, dragging it through his damp hair, watching the way his reflection moved with him.

Forty-two. He had lived long enough to know that was an achievement in itself. Long enough to know that some wounds never faded, no matter how much time passed.

Exhaling slowly, he turned away from the mirror and strode back into the bedchamber. He stopped short.

By the door, standing with his arms crossed over his broad chest, was the man who had disarmed him earlier—the dire wolf, Renaud.

Beside him stood a small, ancient woman, her face as lined and weathered as old parchment. Despite her slight frame, there was something solid about her presence, something immovable. The air of a woman who had seen too much to be impressed by anything anymore.

And at their feet, sitting perfectly still, was the white cat.

Mathieu's fingers twitched against the towel, instinct screaming at him to brace for whatever came next. But none of them moved. They only watched.

The cat's silver eyes flicked over him, slow and assessing. There was no shyness in her study, no pretense of modesty. She took in the damp strands of his hair, the beads of water still clinging to his skin, the bare expanse of his chest and arms—before her gaze flicked back up to meet his.

Mathieu pressed his lips into a thin line, eyes narrowing. *Is it her?*

The image from the mirror swam in his mind—the dark-haired woman, regal and distant, her expression unreadable even as she stood where the cat should have been.

The thought made his skin prickle, a strange awareness creeping along his spine.

He met the cat's gaze evenly, unwilling to be the first to look away.

If this was the woman from the mirror, she was doing an exceptional job of pretending otherwise.

The older woman let out a long-suffering sigh, the kind that suggested she had lived too long to be surprised by the foolishness of men.

"Well," she said, voice as dry as brittle parchment, "I was right. You are as reckless as you look. I do hate to be wrong."

Mathieu arched a brow, but before he could respond, she took a step forward, gesturing impatiently toward his side.

"I'm Sabine, the physician here at Eldrenoire. Since you're already up and parading around half-drowned, I might as well take another look at those wounds before you tear my hard work apart."

She tilted her head, eyes narrowing as she scrutinized him with the sharpness of a hawk.

"Unless, of course, you'd rather bleed dramatically again on the nice clean floors?"

Mathieu resisted the urge to roll his eyes. Instead, he exhaled through his nose, shifting his stance as he loosened the towel enough to give her access to the bandages wrapped around his ribs.

Sabine peeled back the bandages with deft fingers, muttering under her breath about men who never knew how to stay still long enough to heal.

Mathieu huffed a quiet breath, biting back a retort. The truth was, he *had* survived worse. But something about the way she worked—efficient, unflinching, as if she had done this a thousand times over—kept him quiet. He didn't need to make an enemy of the only person keeping him from bleeding out.

Renaud, still standing with his arms crossed, made a low, unimpressed sound. "It's a miracle he hasn't managed to tear the wound open again entirely."

Mathieu shot him a sidelong glance. "Disappointed?"

Renaud only raised a steely brow. "Assuredly."

Sabine clicked her tongue, cutting off whatever response Mathieu might have made. "Enough," she said. "You can measure swords later." She pressed against his side with firm fingers, testing the stitches. "You're lucky," she mused, eyes narrowing. "The stitches are holding, but if you keep throwing yourself around like a fool, I *will* be seeing you again. And I do *not* enjoy repeat work."

Mathieu clenched his jaw against the sting. "Noted."

Meanwhile, the white cat remained seated, silent, watching. Unreadable.

Sabine gave a final, sharp nod, clearly satisfied with her work—or at least as satisfied as she ever would be. "Try not to get yourself killed before the stitches come out," she muttered.

With that, she turned on her heel and disappeared through the door.

Mathieu stretched slowly, rolling his shoulders, testing the stiffness in his side now that Sabine's prodding fingers were gone. He barely had time to settle before the door opened again.

A woman entered, moving with a quiet, measured grace. She was slight, her frame deceptively delicate, with golden-blond hair neatly braided over one shoulder. She did not look at him immediately, her focus instead on the tray of empty dishes left by the fire.

Mathieu watched as she knelt to gather the tray, her movements precise, efficient. He might not have paid her much mind—another servant, another ghost flitting through this strange place—except for one thing.

When she finally turned, her eyes met his.

Striking. Unnatural. The same shade of ice-bright blue that had locked onto him from the foot of his bed earlier.

His breath slowed.

For the briefest moment, he considered speaking. Asking. But what would he say? *Were you the fox in my room?* It sounded ridiculous even in his own mind.

So, he said nothing.

Neither did she. The moment stretched—her gaze unreadable, his filled with quiet speculation. Then, with the barest tilt of her head, she turned, lifted the tray, and walked from the room without a sound.

Mathieu let out a breath, his fingers drumming idly against his thigh. This place was crawling with secrets.

Mathieu flexed his fingers absently as the room settled into silence, save for the low crackle of the fire.

Renaud had not moved from his place near the door, still watching him with the careful patience of a predator at rest. Not tense, but not at ease either. He was waiting—though whether for Mathieu to speak or for an excuse to put him through a wall, it was difficult to say.

Mathieu didn't care to test it. Instead, his attention flickered downward.

The white cat was still there. She sat, tail curled neatly over her paws, steely eyes locked onto him with quiet intensity. Waiting. Calculating.

Then, without a single shift of her expression, her voice slipped into his mind like a blade through velvet.

"Who are you?"

Mathieu's breath stilled for half a second before he forced himself to relax. It wasn't the first time she had done this, but that did not make the sensation any less disorienting.

He let out a low breath. "My name is Mathieu Duran. Of Valmont," he murmured, rolling his shoulders.

"Your name and kingdom of origin tells me nothing. I asked who you are."

Mathieu arched a brow. "That depends on who's asking."

A quiet amusement brushed against his thoughts, feather light. "Clever."

"Not particularly. Just cautious."

The cat's tail flicked once.

For a moment, she said nothing. Then, a pause— "What were you running from?"

Mathieu stilled.

He had expected questions. Had prepared for them.

Mathieu schooled his expression into something easy, something careless.

"You make it sound so dramatic," he said, stretching his fingers against his thigh. "Perhaps I was simply out for a leisurely stroll and took a wrong turn."

The cat's ears twitched. "Through a cursed jungle?"

He sighed. "I got lost."

"You're lying."

Mathieu tilted his head, giving her an unimpressed look. "And you're a talking cat."

The sensation of amusement ghosted through his mind, feather light. "A strange place to draw the line, considering the circumstances."

His jaw tightened. This game of words was a dangerous one, and he had played it too many times before. But something about the way she studied him—the unwavering patience, the quiet expectation—made it clear she had no intention of letting him slip past this unscathed.

The silence stretched.

Finally, he exhaled, looking away.

"I was being hunted," he admitted, keeping his voice even. "Some mercenaries had been trailing me for weeks."

He reached for the towel at his waist, adjusting the knot absently. "I thought I lost them in the mountains, but they found me again in Ziraveen." His fingers curled against the fabric. "And then I found this place."

The words were simple, factual. But they did not touch the why of it. Why Rothgar wanted him dead. Why he had been running for so long.

The cat's silver eyes gleamed in the firelight. "And do they still hunt you?"

Mathieu's mouth flattened into a thin line. That was the real question, wasn't it?

He had vanished. No trail left to follow. The jungle had swallowed him whole. If Rothgar's men had any sense, they had already assumed him dead.

But the Rothgarian emperor himself was another matter entirely.

Mathieu lifted his gaze, meeting the cat's unreadable stare. "They will not find me here."

For a long moment, she said nothing. Then, "Perhaps."

Something about the way she said it sent a prickle of unease down his spine.

A muscle ticked in his jaw as he ran a hand through his damp hair. "Are we finished playing twenty questions, or would you like to interrogate me further?"

The cat blinked. Then she rose gracefully to her feet.

"For now," she said.

Mathieu watched her turn to leave; tension still coiled in his limbs. His fingers twitched at his sides before he spoke again.

"Do I get to ask you a question now?"

The cat paused. A flicker of amusement ghosted through the air between them. Then, slowly, she turned her head just enough to glance back at him.

"You may ask." A deliberate choice of words. Not *I will answer.*

Mathieu huffed a quiet breath, unsurprised but undeterred. "What is this place?"

Something shifted in her gaze, something measured.

"You already know the name."

Mathieu huffed a quiet breath, unsurprised but undeterred. "The name tells me nothing," he smirked as he said her own words back to her, "I asked what this place is."

A beat of silence.

Then, she moved—not toward him, but toward the firelight, where the glow painted long, wavering shadows along the stone walls. She did not sit, did not sprawl in that lazy feline way. Instead, she stood, poised and still.

"This is Eldrenoire," she said at last, her voice slipping into his mind with the quiet certainty of an undeniable truth. "A kingdom that is no longer a kingdom. A home that is no longer a home." Her eyes gleamed, reflecting the fire's restless flicker. "It is a prison, and those who enter do not leave."

Mathieu frowned. "Why?"

The fire crackled.

"The Black Keep is bound by an old magic," she continued, her tone even. "A curse woven into its very stones. The walls do not merely stand—they hold. The gates do not merely open—they choose. And those who step beyond them do not merely stay." Her gaze flicked to him, cool and knowing. "They become part of it."

A chill crept over his skin, a sensation separate from the warmth of the room. He had known there was something unnatural about this place. He had felt it in the way the jungle had disappeared behind him, in the way the halls seemed to breathe with a life of their own. But hearing it spoken aloud, the confirmation that Eldrenoire was not just a fortress but a trap, sent unease curling low in his stomach.

Still, he forced himself to keep his voice steady. "And you?"

The cat blinked, her tail flicking once.

"I have been here longer than most."

It was not an answer. Not truly.

Mathieu narrowed his eyes, watching her carefully. "And you're still here."

Something like wry amusement passed through her expression. "As I said." A pause. Then, softer— *"No one leaves unless Eldrenoire allows them to leave."*

Mathieu exhaled slowly, rolling his shoulders. "You expect me to believe that? That there's no way out unless an old castle grants permission?"

She studied him for a long moment.

Then, with quiet certainty, she said, "You are welcome to try. Again. You wouldn't be the first to do so."

The words settled over him, heavier than he wanted to admit.

How many others had walked this path before him? How many had stood where he stood now, convinced they could break what was unbreakable? And by the gods, what had happened to them?

Mathieu clenched his jaw. He had escaped worse.

She watched him for a moment longer, as if she could hear the shape of his thoughts.

Mathieu hesitated. The weight of her gaze, steady and knowing, pressed against him like an unspoken challenge. He could let her leave. Let the conversation die here, take what little answers he'd been given and sit with them in silence.

But something gnawed at him. Something he had seen—not imagined, not dreamed, but *seen.*

His fingers flexed absently, the sensation of damp stone and warm candlelight bleeding together in his memory. The image had stayed with him, burned into the backs of his eyelids every time he closed them. The mirror. The reflection. The woman.

His voice was quieter when he finally spoke.

"I saw something," he said. "In the Grand Hall. In the mirror on the ceiling."

The cat did not move, but the air between them shifted—subtle, like a thread pulled too tight.

Mathieu studied the creature, watching for even the slightest flicker of reaction. "I should have seen you," he murmured. "But I didn't." His jaw tightened. "I saw a woman."

Renaud shifted.

A small movement but calculated—his weight shifting forward onto the balls of his feet, his stance subtly adjusting. A soldier's instinct. A warning.

Mathieu's fingers twitched toward his side on instinct before he realized he was still wrapped in nothing but a bath towel.

"Did you?"

It was not a denial.

Mathieu's pulse ticked against his ribs. "Was it you?"

For the first time since she had started speaking to him, she did not answer right away.

Instead, she regarded him for a long, careful moment. Something unreadable passed through her grey eyes—not surprise, not fear, but something quieter, something considering.

The silence stretched between them, taut as a bowstring. The flickering firelight carved deep shadows along the walls, casting long, wavering reflections across the polished floor. The air in the chamber seemed to shift, charged with something unspoken.

The creature did not blink. Did not move. And yet, Mathieu felt the weight of her scrutiny settle over him like an unseen hand pressing against his ribs.

Mathieu's nostrils flared. "It was you, wasn't it?"

The cat's silver eyes gleamed, but she remained silent.

His jaw tightened. He didn't know why it mattered—why it needled at him like a thorn beneath his skin. He should have left it alone. But something about the mirror—about the woman who had looked back at him instead of the creature before him—unsettled him more than he cared to admit.

His fingers curled against the damp fabric at his waist. "Why hide?" he asked. "Why not just—"

The cat moved. Not much. Not even a full step. But the flick of her tail, the subtle tilt of her head—something in it held the weight of a warning.

She still did not deny it. She did not try to weave some elaborate misdirection. She said nothing.

A chill curled beneath his ribs. This place was a prison. She had said as much. But he was beginning to realize he had misunderstood the nature of its captivity.

Mathieu dragged a hand through his damp hair, exhaling sharply. He was too tired for riddles, too raw for careful games. "I take it you're not going to explain."

A quiet hum brushed against his thoughts, something like amusement and something like regret. "You have enough to occupy your mind, I think."

It was a dismissal. He recognized it for what it was. Mathieu clenched his jaw, but he let it drop—for now.

The cat turned, stepping lightly toward the door. The evening wind stirred the sheer curtains, sending ghostly ripples through the fabric. She moved through the shifting light, her form dissolving into shadow of the corridor, and for a fleeting moment, he could almost convince himself she wasn't real at all.

But then, she paused in the threshold, her tail curling neatly around her paws. Her eyes flicked to his, unreadable in the dim glow of the firelight. A beat of silence.

Finally, soft, quiet, barely more than a breath in his mind, "Rest while you can, Mathieu Duran."

And then she was gone. The balcony doors swayed open in her wake, the cool night air curling into the chamber.

Mathieu released a breath he hadn't realized he'd been holding. He had walked into something far more treacherous than he had realized. And for the first time since stumbling through the cursed gates of Eldrenoire, he was no longer certain he was the most dangerous thing here.

Chapter 4

Mathieu

The night passed fitfully, his body demanding rest even as his mind refused it. Sleep had never come easy, but this place made it worse. It was not the comfort of the bed that unsettled him—though it was too soft for a man like him. Nor was it the lingering ache in his ribs, the dull throb of half-healed wounds reminding him that he was still flesh and blood.

It was the silence. A silence that did not belong in a place as vast as this.

Even the grandest castles held echoes of life—the murmuring of voices in the halls, the distant clatter of dishes from a kitchen, the low drone of wind through stone corridors. But Eldrenoire was different. The quiet felt deliberate. Weighted. Like something unseen was waiting for him to acknowledge its presence.

By the time the first pale threads of dawn bled into the horizon, Mathieu had had enough of it. Pain or no pain, he would not stay in this gilded cage and wait to be summoned.

He swung his legs over the edge of the bed, rolling his shoulders, only for a sharp pain to lance through his ribs. A hiss escaped through clenched teeth before he caught himself. The slow ache grounded him as he dressed.

His own clothes were gone, replaced by neatly folded garments laid at the foot of his bed—fine but simple, a tunic and trousers in deep charcoal, the fabric surprisingly well-fitted. It was an accommodation, perhaps, or a test. He didn't like either option.

Mathieu moved quietly, listening, and studying. He had spent years navigating places he did not belong—enemy fortresses, unfamiliar war camps, cities that had long since turned against him. This should have been no different.

But it was.

The corridors of Eldrenoire were... wrong.

Not in any overt way. Not at first. The walls were smooth stone, lined with sconces that burned low in the dim morning light. The air carried the faintest trace of old parchment, aged wood, and something floral lingering beneath it. At first glance, the halls stretched in predictable patterns—archways leading to corridors, stairwells winding toward unseen destinations.

It was only when he tried to leave that he noticed.

The first time he reached for a door, it was instinct—testing, nothing more. The heavy wooden frame groaned slightly as it swung open, revealing a long, dim corridor beyond. He stepped forward, tracing a slow path down the empty hall, following the faint pull of fresh air drifting from somewhere unseen.

The corridor should have led him deeper into the castle, or perhaps to a courtyard beyond. But when he reached the far end, another door waited for him, identical to the first.

He opened it and stepped into the same hallway he had just left.

His pulse ticked once against his ribs. His fingers flexed at his sides.

Another step. Another door. Again, he stepped through. Again, he was where he had begun.

A flicker of something cold curled at the back of his mind. This was no simple trick of architecture.

He exhaled through his nose, rolling his shoulders as if shaking off the weight of something unseen. Then, without hesitation, he turned sharply and strode back through the door he had just entered.

The same hallway greeted him.

Mathieu let out a quiet huff, not quite a laugh. "Clever."

The castle was toying with him. He had seen magic before—runes etched into steel, whispers of power bound into weapons, healers who could mend wounds with a breath. But this was different. This was not power wielded by a hand. It was the castle itself. It breathed. It shifted. It watched. And it did not intend to let him go.

He turned, pacing back toward the center of the hall, pressing his fingers against his temples as he considered his options. If this place had been built as a trap, there had to be rules. Even the strongest enchantments had limits.

A test, then. He let his instincts guide him, taking an unfamiliar path, one chosen not by sight but by defiance. He turned left when instinct said right, chose descending stairs over the promise of open-air balconies. Each step sent a dull pulse of pain through his ribs, but he forced himself to keep moving. To push through it. Weakness was a liability.

Then, a shift. A set of doors, taller than the rest, loomed at the end of the corridor.

Mathieu hesitated. They were different from the others—etched with sigils he did not recognize, their surfaces dark with age. A threshold, perhaps, or a boundary. He pressed a hand against the wood. It was cool beneath his palm, unnaturally smooth. The moment he pushed, the doors opened without resistance.

Beyond them, a vast chamber stretched outward, its high vaulted ceilings swallowed by the dim glow of candlelight. Mathieu's breath slowed. A library.

It was cavernous, its towering shelves vanishing into the dimness above. Books lined every inch, their spines gilded, inked, and weathered with age. A fire burned low in the grand hearth, casting long shadows between the tables and chairs scattered throughout the space.

And there, standing beside a long wooden table stacked with books, was a woman.

She had not looked up when he entered, her attention fixed on a heavy tome, its pages open beneath her fingertips.

Something in his chest went still.

Mathieu knew her. Not by name, not by introduction—but by the sharp lines of her face, the regal stillness in the way she carried herself. By the image burned into his memory from the mirrored ceiling in the Grand Hall.

His pulse ticked against his ribs, measured and slow. This was the cat. The one who had led him here. He was sure of it now.

She turned a page, utterly unhurried. "You're persistent," she murmured, voice cool, untouched by surprise.

Mathieu let out a breath that was almost a laugh. "And you're real."

Finally, she looked at him.

The weight of her gaze settled over him like silk and steel, assessing, unreadable, "Were you expecting otherwise?"

He had expected confirmation. Instead, something in him twisted. Because for the first time since stepping into this cursed place, he knew. She was not just the cat. She was something more.

His lips curled faintly, though there was no humor in it. "Would you believe me if I said I wasn't sure?"

The firelight caught in the dark waves of her hair, in the gleam of gemstones at her ears. She was exactly as he had seen her before in the reflection of the mirror, yet different now—solid in a way that made his earlier doubt seem foolish.

She did not answer immediately. Instead, she studied him, the flicker of something thoughtful passing behind her eyes. Then, with the barest tilt of her head, she closed the book before her and placed one hand lightly atop the cover.

Mathieu held her gaze, unmoving. He had spent enough time in courts and war camps to recognize when he was being measured.

His fingers twitched at his sides. His body was still stiff, but he ignored it. Pain was secondary. He needed answers.

He blew out a sharp sigh. "I have some questions."

Her brow arched, the movement slight. "Oh, please ask away. I have nothing better to do than answer questions at random."

His jaw tightened. That mocking tone grated on him.

"You told me last night," he said, voice steady, "that no one leaves this place unless Eldrenoire allows it."

Améliane lifted a brow, unhurried as she set her book aside. "I did."

His fingers curled against the back of the chair. "Then tell me this—does it ever allow it?"

A long pause. She tilted her head slightly, silver eyes reflecting the fire's glow. "Not often."

The words struck something uneasy in his chest. He had expected evasions, half-truths—but not that.

His jaw flexed. "So that's it? I crossed some invisible line, and now I'm just—what? A prisoner?"

Améliane did not blink. "Most who enter do not leave."

Something about the phrasing made his skin prickle.

"Most," he echoed. "But not all."

She studied him for a moment, gaze flicking over the tension in his shoulders, the careful control in the way he stood. Then, at last, she inclined her head slightly.

"There have been... exceptions."

Mathieu exhaled sharply, running a hand through his damp hair. A sliver of hope lodged itself in his ribs—but it was brittle. If exceptions had been made, then there was a way. There had to be.

His voice was steadier when he spoke again. "And what about you?"

A flicker of something crossed her face—gone before he could name it.

"You already know the answer."

His grip tightened.

"No," he said, stepping closer, his voice low but edged with something sharp. "I don't."

She lifted her chin, gaze unwavering. "Then let me simplify it for you."

The fire crackled, shadows shifting.

"I was here before you. I will be here after you. And no matter what path you take—no matter how many doors you try to open—you will always find yourself exactly where the castle wants you."

Mathieu's pulse ticked sharply against his ribs.

"If there were exceptions," he pressed, "then why not you?"

This time, she did not look away. The silence stretched, long enough for him to understand. She had no answer. Or worse—she had one, and she didn't want to say it.

A slow tension unfurled between them, something not quite spoken, not quite avoidable.

Améliane turned slightly, reaching for the book she had abandoned. Her fingers had just grazed the book's cover when the library doors slammed open.

Mathieu turned instinctively, already assessing, already bracing, but he did not reach for a weapon that was no longer there.

Renaud filled the doorway, a storm wrapped in a soldier's frame. His chest rose and fell sharply, his expression dark as his gaze swept the chamber—searching, ready for battle.

"Your Highness, the stranger is miss—" He stopped short as his eyes landed on Mathieu.

Mathieu barely heard the rest. The title lingered, threading itself through his mind with the weight of something significant.

Your Highness.

His gaze flicked toward her, reevaluating.

He had known she held power. He had felt it in the way the others deferred to her, in the way the castle itself seemed to pulse with her presence. But royalty? That was another thing entirely.

Mathieu had seen queens before—some ruthless, some fragile, some little more than pretty ornaments sitting on borrowed thrones. But Améliane carried herself differently. She did not wield her title like a weapon, did not cling to it as a shield.

A slow, wry smirk pulled at the corner of his mouth.

"Well," he murmured, shifting his stance. "I suppose I should have guessed."

Renaud scowled. "Show some respect." His next words came like a blade drawn in warning, "You are supposed to be in your chambers."

Mathieu leaned one hip against the chair, utterly unbothered. "Am I?"

A muscle ticked in Renaud's jaw. "You were injured."

"I'm feeling better," Mathieu replied nonchalantly with a half shrug.

"You—" Renaud took a sharp step forward, fury crackling beneath his calm. He cut a glance toward Améliane, as if seeking confirmation, as if waiting for her to demand an explanation from the intruder before them. But she said nothing. She only regarded the scene with quiet, unreadable patience.

Mathieu noted that.

Renaud huffed through his nose, sharp and controlled. "You should not be wandering the castle alone."

Mathieu tilted his head, feigning curiosity. "And yet, here I stand."

Renaud's fists flexed at his sides. "The castle does not take kindly to strangers."

Mathieu arched a brow. "I noticed."

Something in his tone made Renaud's expression darken further, but before he could speak, Améliane's voice cut through the room, cool and even.

"Renaud."

The single word halted him.

Slowly, he turned toward her, his jaw still tight, his stance still bristling with the tension of a man used to solving problems with steel and blood. But he did not argue.

Améliane, to her credit, did not look at him as if he were overreacting. If anything, there was something knowing in her expression, something almost tired, as if this moment had been inevitable.

She sighed softly, fingers tapping once against the book's cover before she finally turned fully to face them both.

"He is not the first to test the castle's boundaries."

Renaud's scowl deepened. "Perhaps not. But the last one who did was found two days later, still lost and barely alive in the west wing."

Mathieu hummed, unimpressed. "You're saying I should be grateful, then."

Renaud's gaze snapped to him, golden eyes sharp as a drawn blade. "I am saying you should be cautious."

Mathieu held his stare, unflinching. "And if I don't like being caged?"

The silence that followed was thick, weighted. It was Améliane who broke it.

"Then you will struggle here, more than most."

Mathieu's gaze flicked back to her, studying the way the firelight played against her features, the way she spoke as if she already knew the shape of his defiance.

Suddenly, a sharp rustling of wings disrupted the tension, a gust of air sweeping through the chamber. Mathieu tensed instinctively, tracking the movement as a hawk swooped down from the rafters, cutting through the firelight like a blade of molten gold.

It landed atop one of the high-backed chairs with practiced ease, talons curling against the wood. For a moment, it was still—watching. Then, with a shimmer of movement, the air itself seemed to shift, bending and twisting in a way that defied natural law.

A man stood where the hawk had been.

Lean and graceful, with the easy arrogance of someone who had never once questioned his place in the world, the man adjusted the cuff of his shirt as if stepping out of the sky and into human form was nothing of note. His golden hair was tousled from the wind, falling just past his shoulders, and his sharp blue eyes flicked toward Renaud, glinting with mischief.

"Oh, look," he said, his voice rich with exaggerated delight. "You've found him."

Renaud's breath caught somewhere between a groan and a hum, his fists clenching at his sides. "Yes, Laurent. So it seems."

Mathieu arched a brow, taking in the man properly now that he was no longer an avian blur. Laurent was striking, but not in the way of warriors or kings. There was something unstudied about him—an effortlessness in the way he carried himself, a confidence that wasn't forced, but rather the result of knowing exactly how much he could get away with.

Laurent turned toward Améliane, his expression shifting into something more familiar. He did not bow to her. He did not wait for permission to speak. Instead, he leaned one hip against the chair in front of him and tilted his head.

"Liane, you should really keep a better eye on your houseguest," he mused, as if commenting on a misplaced trinket rather than a dangerous man wandering the halls unchecked. "What if he had gotten lost? Then we'd have two ghosts lurking about instead of one."

Améliane sighed, the sound carrying more patience than frustration. "If the castle wanted to lose him, it would have."

Laurent's grin widened. "And yet, here he is, standing in your library." He cast a glance at Mathieu, as if finally bothering to inspect him properly. "A bit tall to be a ghost. But I suppose we all start somewhere."

Mathieu exhaled slowly. He had met men like this before—charmers, schemers, the kind who could talk their way out of a war if they so pleased. He studied Laurent in return, remembering a similar hawk in his bathing chambers. "Do you always drop in unannounced?"

Laurent flashed a bright, insincere smile. "It's part of my charm."

Mathieu huffed a quiet breath, unimpressed. Still, he noticed something. Unlike Renaud, who bristled at any perceived threat to Améliane, Laurent's presence was entirely different. Familiar. Unapologetically so.

There was a quiet understanding in the way Améliane regarded Laurent, even as she shook her head at his antics. Not indulgence, but something close to amusement.

Renaud, however, was very much not amused.

"I fail to see how you're helping," he muttered, his voice a low growl of irritation.

Laurent waved a lazy hand. "Oh, I'm sure you'd prefer I stand in a corner somewhere, brooding dramatically. But unfortunately for you, that isn't my style."

Renaud's scowl deepened.

Before the conversation could escalate into something sharp-edged, Laurent clapped his hands together lightly, turning back toward Mathieu with a look of mock consideration. "Well, it's almost time for dinner," he mused. "And since you're doing a truly abysmal job of recuperating in your bed, you might as well join us."

Mathieu arched a brow. "Is that an invitation?"

"More of a declaration," Laurent corrected, stretching as if shaking off the last traces of his flight. "I do like to keep things interesting."

Renaud's glare could have set the room aflame. "That is not your decision to make."

Laurent tilted his head, the barest flicker of something mischievous sparking in his gaze. Then, deliberately, he turned to Améliane.

She said nothing at first. Mathieu watched as she weighed the moment, as she glanced between Laurent's easy amusement and Renaud's silent fury. She did not have to allow this. He could see the choice balanced on the edge of her decision, caught somewhere between caution and curiosity.

Finally, against her better judgment—and against Renaud's obvious dislike of the idea—she sighed and said, "Let him come."

Renaud stiffened. "My Queen—"

"I will not have our guest wandering into another part of the castle where he does not belong," she said, her voice calm but firm. "If he joins the meal, at least we know where he is."

It was not a show of generosity. Not even trust. It was a calculated choice.

Mathieu studied her for a moment longer, then inclined his head. "How thoughtful."

Améliane only lifted a perfectly arched brow. Laurent, on the other hand, looked thoroughly pleased.

"Well then," he said, turning on his heel with the flourish of a man quite satisfied with himself. "Shall we?"

The Solar where they dined was a stark contrast to the rest of Eldrenoire. Where the castle halls stretched cold and vast, this room held warmth—if not in sentiment, then in its rich textures and golden candlelight. Heavy curtains framed the tall windows, allowing only a sliver of the evening light to filter in. The dark wooden table, round rather than long, created an intimacy that felt deliberate.

Mathieu noted the absence of an extra chair. His presence had not been expected.

He shifted his weight subtly as he stood, the dull ache in his ribs a quiet reminder that he had pushed himself too far today. He masked the discomfort, refusing to let his stance betray weakness.

Laurent, perched at the edge of the table like a cat too self-satisfied to be shooed away, smirked. "Oh, did we not set a place for our guest? How rude."

Renaud scowled, but Améliane only exhaled through her nose—something too small to be a sigh, but close. At her slight nod, an awaiting servant retrieved a chair from a nearby corner, placing it beside Laurent's with a distinct lack of urgency.

Mathieu took note of the silent exchange. It was not deference Améliane commanded, but something quieter, something that did not require words to be obeyed.

He settled into the chair, taking a measured glance around the table, noting the faces he had yet to place. He knew Renaud and Laurent, but two others remained unfamiliar.

Laurent, ever the opportunist, seized the moment with a languid wave of his hand. "Since our dear Queenie has neglected introductions, allow me." He gestured first to the woman seated across from Mathieu, her dark auburn braid neatly draped over one shoulder, her green eyes assessing but not unkind. "This is Élodie—our Queen's trusted lady-in-waiting, keeper of far too many secrets, and the only person here who can stitch a hem without wanting to stab someone in the process."

Élodie gave a long-suffering sigh, leveling him with a look that suggested she had tolerated Laurent's antics for far too long. "Your introductions are as unnecessary as they are inaccurate."

Laurent grinned. "Ah, but you didn't deny the stabbing bit."

Mathieu laughed a quiet breath, taking in Élodie's sharp, knowing gaze. She was no mere handmaiden. There was something keen behind her calm—an awareness that marked her as more than a courtly ornament.

Laurent then turned to the last of the group—a blonde-haired woman with bright, fox-sharp eyes and a lazy sort of amusement curling at her lips. "And this," he said, tone dripping with faux reverence, "is Margot. The queen's maid. Resident troublemaker. Stealer of pastries. Occasionally useful."

Margot picked up her goblet and took a slow sip of wine before meeting Mathieu's gaze. "Don't listen to anything he says." Her lips curled at the corners. "Unless it's about the pastries."

Mathieu leaned back slightly, taking stock of them all—their easy familiarity, the way they fit together like pieces of a well-worn game. They were not just attendants. This was no court of fearful sycophants. These people were comfortable with their queen in a way he had never seen before.

Which meant, despite the curse, despite the power she clearly held—she had let them be.

That realization sat oddly in his mind, but before he could dwell on it, Laurent exhaled dramatically and leaned closer. "I'm sure you have more questions."

Mathieu's gaze flicked toward Améliane, who had not spoken since he sat. She regarded him carefully, flint-like eyes cool and unreadable. He was being measured, and not for the first time tonight, he wondered what she saw.

After a moment, she gave a single, imperceptible nod.

Laurent's smirk widened. "Permission granted, it seems." He popped a grape into his mouth. "Ask away."

Mathieu didn't take the bait immediately. He reached for his goblet, took a slow sip, let the silence stretch just long enough to make Laurent's fingers drum impatiently against the table. Then, casually, he asked, "How long have you all been here?"

A pause. Margot was the one to answer, swirling her wine. "Too long."

Mathieu arched a brow. "Vague. That's never a good sign."

Laurent snorted. "Vagueness is the only kindness we can afford you, I'm afraid."

Mathieu looked at Améliane, but she gave nothing away.

Renaud, who had thus far remained silent, finally spoke, his voice low and even. "This place is not like the world beyond it. Time does not pass the same way here."

Mathieu frowned slightly, rolling his goblet between his fingers. "That sounds convenient."

"It isn't," Élodie murmured.

Mathieu let the silence settle for a moment, studying the way the words hung in the air, unanswered. The way Élodie's expression remained calm but guarded. The way Margot, so full of wit a moment ago, now focused on the slow swirl of her wine.

The way Améliane had yet to speak.

His gaze flicked toward her. "And you?" he asked, voice steady. "How long have you been here?"

Améliane didn't so much as blink.

"Since the beginning," she said, lifting her goblet to her lips.

It wasn't an answer. But it was enough to confirm what he had begun to suspect—Eldrenoire wasn't merely a prison for those who had wandered in. It was a prison for its queen as well.

Laurent stretched with feline ease. "You'll find, Mathieu, that time is one of the least interesting mysteries this place has to offer." He plucked a piece of fruit from the platter between them, tossing it into the air and catching it between his teeth.

Mathieu tilted his head slightly. "And what would you suggest I concern myself with instead?"

Laurent, as if sensing the shift in mood, leaned back and let out a short, dry laugh. "Oh, enough of this heavy talk." He reached for a platter, slicing into a roasted pheasant with practiced ease. "Tell me, Mathieu, what is it like to be a man on the run?"

Mathieu's grip on his goblet tightened slightly.

Améliane, for the first time in the conversation, spoke. "Laurent."

The single word was not a reprimand, but it carried weight.

Laurent only smiled, entirely unbothered, and passed Mathieu a slice of the pheasant anyway. "Eat. It's better than whatever you've been surviving on, I assure you."

Mathieu took the offering with a slow nod, but the question still lingered in his mind. They had deflected. Had spoken in half-truths and careful omissions. And that told him more than their words ever could.

The meal continued, and Mathieu let himself observe. How Laurent stole from Améliane's plate and received only an arched brow in return. How Élodie ensured everyone's glass of wine was full before tending to her own. How Margot teased. How Renaud watched, ever-vigilant, how Améliane existed at the center of them all—not as a tyrant, but as something steadier. As something that held them together.

Mathieu took another measured sip of wine, letting the conversation shift and settle, filing away the information that might be important later.

Laurent, ever one to keep things moving, sighed dramatically and sprawled against the back of his chair. "Well, this has been a delightfully tense little gathering." He plucked another piece of fruit from the platter and twirled it between his fingers before popping it into his mouth. "But let's not frighten our guest *too* much on his first evening. We wouldn't want him thinking this place is all ghosts and grim omens."

Margot snorted. "Wouldn't we?"

Laurent grinned. "No, no, I'm trying to be hospitable. *You* should try it sometime."

Mathieu leaned back slightly, observing the group, noting the way they danced around certain subjects. And then, with a wry twist of his lips, he said, "And what else should I expect, then? Or is the hospitality only for show?"

Laurent's smile sharpened. "Oh, well, *he* might find you amusing."

The words were light, offhanded—but the shift in the room was immediate. Améliane's hand froze mid-reach, her jaw tightening as Élodie cast her a sharp, knowing glance.

Margot rolled her eyes and took a slow sip of wine, as if already weary of where this conversation was going. Renaud, on the other hand, stiffened, his jaw tightening in a way that suggested *he* had very little amusement to spare.

Mathieu caught all of it.

Améliane lifted her goblet to her lips, took a slow sip, and set it back down with deliberate care. "Enough, Laurent."

Laurent's eyes gleamed with mischief, but his smirk eased as he waved a lazy hand. "As you wish."

Mathieu didn't miss how quickly he backed down. Whoever *he* was, Laurent knew exactly where the line was drawn.

The silence stretched, heavy and lingering in the wake of Laurent's words. The playful ease that had hovered over the meal dissipated, leaving something taut beneath the surface.

Mathieu watched Améliane carefully. Her long fingers curled subtly against the stem of her goblet, the only betrayal of tension. A deliberate press of her thumb, as if reining herself in.

She held there for a fraction too long before exhaling softly and pushing her plate away.

"That is enough for tonight," her voice was calm. Measured. But the weight of her words left no room for debate.

She rose with the same quiet grace she carried in all things, smoothing long chestnut hair with an absent hand. No further glance was spared for Laurent, nor for the others. Whatever tension had been stirred, she refused to indulge it further.

Her pale, metallic eyes flicked to Renaud. "See that our guest returns to his chambers."

Renaud inclined his head. His expression impassive, though as he stood, his stance was as rigid as ever.

Mathieu's lips curled faintly. *An escort. How thoughtful.*

He didn't protest, though. Getting lost in this cursed castle once had been quite enough for one day. He leaned back in his chair, finishing the last sip of his wine before setting his goblet down with deliberate care.

"Good night, Your Highness," he murmured.

It was a challenge, subtle but present.

Améliane did not flinch at the title. She only regarded him with those piercing silver eyes for a breath longer than necessary before turning and sweeping from the Solar without another word.

Mathieu's gaze lingered after her for half a second, then flicked toward the others.

Élodie's expression was unreadable. Margot swirled her wine, unimpressed. Laurent grinned.

Renaud stepped forward, his presence looming like a silent demand.

Mathieu exhaled through his nose and pushed himself to his feet. "Lead the way."

The meal was over, but its ghosts remained. And so did his questions.

CHAPTER 5

Mathieu

The walk back to his chambers was silent. Renaud did not speak, nor did Mathieu try to engage him. There was nothing to be said—not when the meal had ended with unspoken warnings and the sharp shift of tension curling through the room like a tightening noose.

They moved through the dimly lit halls, the sconces flickering with each passing draft. The silence here was not the same as the silence at the table. This one breathed. It settled between the stones, curled through the vaulted ceilings, watching.

When they reached the door, Renaud stopped. His dark eyes flicked over Mathieu, assessing, weighing something. Then, in a voice low and edged with finality, he said, *"Do not wander these halls at night."*

Mathieu arched a brow, fingers brushing against the door handle. "And why is that?"

Renaud's expression did not shift. "Because it does not want you to."

Before Mathieu could press him for a real answer, Renaud turned on his heel and strode back down the corridor, his broad frame disappearing into the shifting gloom.

Mathieu exhaled sharply, running a hand through his hair before pushing open the door.

The fire in the hearth burned higher now, casting long, golden light over the room. A tray sat on the low table before it, a porcelain teapot and a single mug resting beside a plate of something warm and sweet.

Not tea. He inhaled, catching the rich scent curling through the room. Melted chocolate.

He crossed the room slowly, lowering himself into the chair before the fire. The heat licked at his skin, sinking into the sore ache of his ribs, loosening the tension still coiled in his shoulders.

Without thinking, he reached for the mug, curling his fingers around the warm porcelain. He brought it to his lips and took a slow sip. It was thick, dark, richer than anything he had tasted in years. While he wanted to escape Eldrenoire as soon as possible, it wasn't lost on him that his current situation was certainly better than starving in the jungles of Ziraveen hiding from royal mercenaries tasked with bringing his head back to Rothgar.

He turned over the events of the evening in his mind—the weight of Améliane's silence, the way the others had spoken in half-truths, the warning in Laurent's teasing. And then there was the moment the mood had shifted. *"Oh, well, he might find you amusing."*

It had been a long time since Mathieu found himself in the middle of court intrigue, but he was no stranger to veiled threats, power plays, and unspoken dangers. This was different. Améliane had reined herself in at the mention of whoever *he* was.

He took another sip, the warmth sinking into his chest. The fire crackled, the shadows shifting with its restless flicker.

Finally, when the weight of exhaustion began to pull at him, he pushed himself to his feet and stripped down to his trousers. The bed was too soft, but he did not fight it.

The moment his head hit the pillow, sleep dragged him under—deep and heavy.

At first, it was only darkness—thick and heavy, like the kind found in the deepest reaches of the forest where no light dared to follow. Then, slowly, the world began to take shape around him.

A hall. Grand, ruined, and empty.

Mathieu stood at the center of what had once been a throne room, though time had gnawed at its edges. Banners, tattered and faded, drooped from the rafters above. The stone floor, cracked and uneven, was overtaken by creeping vines that twisted through the fractures, reclaiming the space as their own. Dust floated in the air, disturbed only by the flickering torches set into the walls—though no hands had lit them.

The breath left his lungs slow and measured as he stepped forward. There was no sound but his own movements, no echo of life in the hollow vastness of the room. And yet, it did not feel empty. Something lingered here.

Ahead, near the dais where a throne should have stood, lay a crown. Half-buried in dust, the silver and black metal gleamed beneath the torchlight, its shape fractured—a jagged break splitting one side. Mathieu knelt, reaching toward it, his fingers brushing against the cool metal—

Hands shot from the darkness.

*Not one, but many, pale and grasping, their fingers skeletal and clawed. They snatched at the crown, dragging it back into the shadows before he could seize it. The room shuddered, the torches flickering wildly, and a voice whispered, low and urgent, "**She was never meant to rule.**"*

Mathieu's breath came sharp, his pulse hammering against his ribs as he twisted toward the source of the voice. A figure stood at the far end of the hall, half-shrouded in shadows, their back turned to him.

A woman.

She flickered, like a flame caught in the wind—there, then gone, then back again. He stepped forward, drawn by something he could not name, the broken crown forgotten.

"Who are you?" His own voice sounded distant, warped by the vastness of the space.

The woman did not turn.

The air shifted. A mirror stood before him now, tall and gilded, its glass fractured down the center. Mathieu saw himself reflected in its surface—but the image was wrong.

His face twisted, distorted by something unseen. His eyes darkened, his own skin paling, stretched too tight over sharp bones. He reached out, but the reflection moved before he did, fingers pressing against the cracked glass as if something inside wished to escape.

Then the mirror shattered.

*Darkness spilled out, a thick black fog curling around his feet. It rose too fast, swallowing the floor, licking at his legs. He tried to step back, but the more he moved, the heavier it became. **The more he fought, the deeper it dragged him down.***

*Whispers coiled in the mist, voices overlapping in a cacophony of sound, too many to make sense of, yet all speaking as one, "**Not yet.**"*

Mathieu struggled, twisting against the weight pressing against his chest. His breath came fast, shallow, but the more he fought, the tighter the fog coiled—

*A flicker of movement in the darkness. Silver eyes. Watching. **Waiting.***

Then, as quickly as it had begun, the dream shattered.

Mathieu pulled a hand down his face. The dream's weight still pressed against his chest—the whisper, the crown, the woman cloaked in ruin.

He swung his legs over the bed and stood, reaching for the shirt draped over the chair. The chocolate still coated his tongue, cloying and heavy. He needed water.

Without bothering to light a candle, he crossed to the door and pulled it open.

The corridors stretched ahead, silent and flickering in the dim candlelight. He had no idea where the kitchens were, but that had never stopped him before. He moved carefully, tracing his fingertips along the stone walls, following instinct and the distant pull of logic. Surely, kitchens were on the lower floors. He would find stairs.

And yet—He stepped through an archway and found himself in the same hall.

Mathieu ground his teeth, inhaling slowly through his nose. Again, he turned, taking another passage. The sconces flickered. The shadows stretched. And once again, he was exactly where he had started.

The castle did not want him wandering.

But it would not stop him.

He continued forward, ignoring the twisting, endless loops the corridors wove around him. The way doorways changed, halls turned upon themselves, steps leading him nowhere. He did not fight it. Instead, he walked as if it was a game he had already won, letting his mind adjust to the strange rhythm of Eldrenoire's magic.

Finally, after what felt like an eternity, something changed. A turn. A step. A door slightly ajar. A cool draft of air carried the scent of butter and warm spice.

Finally, the kitchens. Mathieu pushed the door open.

The room was vast but comfortable, lined with shelves of dried herbs and gleaming copper pots. The embers in the great hearth still glowed, throwing a dull warmth over the stone floors. A few candles flickered on the central worktable, their wax pooling against worn wood.

And at the far end of the room, standing with one hand braced against the counter, the other holding a silver fork mid-air—was Améliane.

Her eyes went wide, frozen in place. Because that fork had just delivered an absolutely indecent amount of coconut cake to her mouth.

Mathieu stared. She chewed once. Swallowed.

Then, without an ounce of shame, she lifted a brow. "Well," she said, voice dry, "this is unfortunate."

Mathieu huffed a quiet laugh, folding his arms across his chest. "For whom?"

Améliane carefully set the fork down, brushing nonexistent crumbs from the sleeve of her gown. "For you, obviously."

He arched a brow. "I'm not the one caught sneaking sweets in the middle of the night."

Améliane exhaled, and turned back to the cake, slicing off another piece with effortless precision. "Do you want some or not?"

Mathieu tilted his head, considering. "I came for water."

She gestured lazily toward a nearby pitcher. "Then help yourself."

Mathieu crossed the kitchen, pouring himself a glass of water, though his focus never fully left Améliane. The flickering candlelight softened the edges of the space, casting a golden hue over her dark hair, the elegant drape of her robe. He had seen her composed, distant, sharp as a blade in the firelight of the Solar—but here, barefoot in the quiet warmth of the kitchen, eating stolen cake in the dead of night, she was something else entirely.

His lips curled up slightly as he leaned against the counter, watching her with idle amusement. "Sooooo, midnight snacking is your thing, Your Highness?"

She speared another forkful of cake and lifted a brow. "And sneaking through the halls like an unsupervised child is yours, I see."

He sipped his water. "I was thirsty."

Mathieu's gaze flicked over her, taking in the way the soft silk of her robe draped over her frame. It wasn't indecent—not exactly—but the delicate embroidery at the edges, the cinch at her waist, the way it slipped slightly off one shoulder made him think whoever had designed it had not intended for it to be seen by just anyone.

She looked... effortless. Regal, even here, but undeniably, unfairly beautiful. He remembered the voice from his dream—the whisper curling around that shattered crown. *She was never meant to rule.* The words had felt like prophecy then. Now, staring at her in silk and shadows, he wasn't so sure.

She caught him looking.

Mathieu did not look away.

Instead, he set his glass down with a quiet clink and smirked. "Tell me, does royalty always raid their own kitchens, or is this just a special privilege of cursed queens?"

The corners of Améliane's mouth turned up as she huffed a quiet breath, slicing off another bite of cake. "A true queen knows how to get what she wants."

Mathieu arched a brow. "And what is it you want?"

Her frosted silver gaze met his, steady and sharp. Then, deliberately, she lifted the fork to her mouth and took another bite. "At the moment?" She licked a stray crumb from her lip. "Cake."

Mathieu chuckled, shaking his head. "You're surprisingly unbothered by being caught."

"Why should I be?" She gestured lazily with her fork as her grey eyes twinkled in amusement, "You're the one sneaking through my home in the middle of the night, not the other way around."

"You know, you're not wrong," he winked picking up a second fork from the tray and cutting himself a bite.

She tilted her head, watching him as he tasted the cake.

"Good?" she asked.

He gave a slow, thoughtful nod. "Better than anything I've had in years." He glanced at her. "But then again, maybe I'm just enjoying the company."

For the first time since he'd met her, she laughed. Not a sharp, knowing chuckle. Not a quiet huff of amusement. A real, unguarded laugh. And it was the most beautiful sound he had heard in a long, long time.

Mathieu leaned into it, letting his smirk widen. "Ah. So, you do have a sense of humor, Your Highness."

She shook her head, still smiling, her hand lightly pressing against the counter as if steadying herself. "You're insufferable. I should have let Renaud lock you in your room."

Mathieu took another bite, grinning. "You didn't, though."

Améliane didn't answer, but she didn't deny it either.

Instead, she took another slow bite of cake, watching him over the rim of her fork. "You intrigue them, you know."

Mathieu arched a brow, reaching for another piece of cake. "Them?"

She gestured vaguely. "Laurent. Élodie. Even Margot." A beat. "Renaud is another matter."

Mathieu huffed a quiet laugh. "Yes, I got the sense he'd prefer me thrown off the nearest tower."

"He doesn't trust easily." Améliane leaned her hip against the counter, tapping the edge of her fork against her plate. "But he's rarely wrong."

Mathieu chewed thoughtfully, swallowing before replying. "And you? Do you think he's wrong about me?"

She considered him for a long moment, then took another bite instead of answering.

Mathieu exhaled through his nose, setting his fork down. "Alright, Your Highness, your turn."

"My turn for what?"

"To interrogate me." He smirked, resting an arm against the counter. "You let your people ask their questions at dinner. Now it's your chance."

Améliane tilted her head slightly. "And you assume I have questions?"

"You're a queen," he said, watching the way her gaze flickered, as if weighing the truth of it. "I'd be disappointed if you didn't."

She studied him, silver eyes cool and unreadable, then finally, "Who are you running from?"

Mathieu had expected the question, but that didn't mean he liked it.

His smirk barely faltered. "No subtlety, then?"

"Would you have answered if I danced around it?"

He chuckled low, shaking his head. "No."

Silence stretched between them, not tense, but waiting. The firelight cast long shadows over the stone floors, the embers in the hearth glowing like the remnants of a battlefield long burned out.

Mathieu blew out a low breath, running a hand through his hair. "Rothgar," he said simply.

Améliane's expression didn't shift, but something in her gaze sharpened. "The whole empire?"

Mathieu nodded once, rolling his goblet between his fingers. "They don't take kindly to loose ends."

"And you're a loose end?"

"Something like that."

After a moment she said quietly, "Escaping Rothgar's reach is no small feat."

"It wasn't pleasant." He rolled his shoulders, stretching out the phantom ache that always settled there when he thought of that time. "But I wasn't eager to die in a cell."

Her gaze flicked over him, taking in the scars that mapped his forearms, "You've been running for a long time, then."

"And yet, here I stand."

Her lips twitched slightly, but the amusement in her gaze was tempered by something else—something thoughtful. "How did you end up here?"

He tilted his head. "A particularly bad few weeks."

Améliane arched a brow. "That's all?"

"As far as I know." He took another sip of water. "Though if you'd like to tell me there's some grand fate at play, I'd be interested to hear it."

She hummed, considering, but didn't answer.

The silence stretched again, but this time, it wasn't uncomfortable.

Then, Améliane tilted her head slightly, tapping her fork against the rim of her plate. "What did they take from you?"

Mathieu's fingers tightened around his glass. It was not the question he had expected. His smirk faded, not entirely, but enough. "That's an interesting assumption."

She studied him. "That you lost something?"

"That I had something to lose."

Améliane did not look away, did not let the words slip past as casual deflection. "You were a man of standing once."

Mathieu chuckled, low and dry. "What gave it away?"

She gestured faintly toward him. "The way you hold yourself. The way you speak." A pause. "The fact that you still expect to be obeyed, even when you have nothing."

That struck something close to the bone. Mathieu took a deep breath, rolling his goblet between his fingers. "Rothgar doesn't typically take prisoners," he said after a long moment. "Not in the usual kind, anyway."

"Yes. They prefer to erase, not imprison. And yet, they took you."

His jaw tensed. "Briefly."

"And what did you leave behind?"

For a moment, he considered giving her another glib answer, another well-placed smirk and a clever quip to skirt the truth. But he was too tired for that, and she was too sharp to fall for it.

So instead, he said, "Too much."

He could feel her studying him in the quiet that followed. Améliane did not press, did not ask him to define what or who had been left behind.

But she knew, in the way rulers always did, that some wounds did not fade—only settled deeper into the skin.

Finally, she leaned forward, propping her chin against her hand. The sharpness in her gaze softened just slightly. "You're still standing," she said, repeating his own words back to him.

Mathieu nodded, the ghost of a smile returning. "And yet, here I stand," he said again, softer this time.

For the first time, she did not look at him like an intruder.

For the first time, he was not sure who had survived more.

Finally, Mathieu exhaled, reaching for another forkful of cake. "Your turn."

Améliane arched a brow. "For what?"

"I answered your question." He smirked. "Now you answer mine."

She lifted her goblet, considering. "And what do you wish to know?"

Mathieu leaned in slightly, voice lowering just enough to be teasing. "Who taught you to sneak into kitchens in the dead of night?"

A slow, amused smile ghosted across Améliane's lips. "That," she said, taking a sip of wine, "is one secret I will never tell."

Mathieu chuckled, shaking his head. "Figures."

She tilted her head, watching him. "And what of you? Do fugitives often develop a preference for coconut cake at midnight?"

He huffed a quiet laugh. "Not often." He glanced at the cake. "I think I'd forgotten what something so simple could taste like."

A flicker of something passed over her face—too quick to name.

Her voice softened just slightly. "And what else have you forgotten?"

Mathieu hesitated. Not because he didn't have an answer. But because the answer wasn't simple.

He had forgotten a great many things. What it was to wake without fear. What it was to belong to a place, rather than passing through it like a shadow. What it was to sit at a table and not eat like it might be his last meal.

And before tonight, before this moment—he had forgotten what it was to enjoy someone's company.

But he wasn't about to say any of that.

So instead, he smirked, taking another bite of cake. "How to make a proper escape plan, apparently."

Améliane huffed a quiet laugh, shaking her head. "You're insufferable."

Mathieu tilted his head. "You keep saying that."

"And you keep proving me right."

He grinned, setting his fork down. "And yet, you're still standing here."

She didn't reply. But she didn't leave either.

Mathieu reached for his goblet, draining the last sip of water, but his gaze remained on her.

A glint of white caught his eye—a stray flake of coconut, tangled in the loose waves of her unbound hair. Before he could think better of it, he reached out, fingers brushing just lightly enough to pluck it free.

Améliane stilled.

Mathieu twirled the flake between his fingers, then popped it into his mouth with an easy smirk. "Wouldn't want you wearing your midnight crimes, Your Highness."

Her eyes narrowed slightly, though whether it was in warning or something else entirely, he wasn't sure. But she didn't step away.

Instead, she lifted her chin slightly, as if daring him to test his luck further.

Mathieu chuckled under his breath, reaching past her to collect their plates. "You may be a queen, but you still made a mess." He strode toward the basin, placing them in the sink with deliberate care. "I suppose I'll clean up after you—just this once."

When he turned back, she was still watching him.

The candlelight softened the sharp edges of her face, catching in the silver of her eyes, the dark silk of her hair. She looked steadier now, no trace of the careful distance she wore in the Solar.

Mathieu exhaled, rolling his shoulders before offering her a mock bow. "It was an honor, truly—witnessing the great Queen of Eldrenoire engage in an unsanctioned raid of her own kitchens." He let his smirk sharpen. "I'll try to recover from the scandal."

Améliane hummed, tilting her head slightly. "I expect you'll manage."

Mathieu smirked. "You think highly of me already."

She lifted a brow and stepped past him toward the door. Just before she crossed the threshold, she glanced back, amusement flickering in pale metallic eyes, "Try not to get lost on your way back, *fugitive*. Eldrenoire is exponentially more interesting with you around."

Then she was gone, leaving nothing but the lingering scent of warm coconut and the faintest echo of laughter in the air.

Mathieu shook his head as he ran a hand through his hair.

Somehow, for the first time since stepping foot into this cursed castle, he didn't mind staying just a little longer.

CHAPTER 6

Améliane

T he walk back to her chambers was short. It should have been unremarkable.

And yet, the conversation lingered.

She had not planned to stay in the kitchens, nor had she expected him to find his way there. Eldrenoire had kept him trapped in its endless loops before, denying him any path forward—but when he sought something mundane, like a glass of water, the castle had let him through. That was unusual. And so was he.

Her room was just as she had left it—untouched, save for the faint scent of candle wax. She moved through it absently, her thoughts still tangled in the encounter with Mathieu. The kitchen had been too easy. It had been a long time since someone had made her laugh—since she'd felt something as simple, and as dangerous, as the pleasure of company.

Mathieu was a man with nothing left to lose, and yet he smiled as though he had never been broken. That was dangerous.

She turned toward the gilded mirror near her wardrobe, absently running a hand through her hair. Her reflection stared back—steady, unreadable. And yet, she caught it. The faint curve at the corner of her lips.

A remnant of something she had not meant to keep.

Améliane exhaled slowly, pressing her hands against the edge of her vanity, grounding herself in the cool, familiar weight of carved wood. She had no reason to feel so...unsettled.

Then, the air shifted.

A slow, creeping sensation, like the castle had turned its attention fully upon her.

It was subtle at first—a strange weight pressing lightly against her skin, like the change in air before a storm. The candle flames barely flickered, but something was different.

No. Not different. Wrong.

The scent of candle wax and linen faded. Something softer took its place. Night-blooming flowers that no longer existed. Jasmine.

Améliane stilled.

Slowly, carefully, she turned her head—her eyes flicking toward the farthest corner of the chamber, where the shadows stretched just a little too long, pooling unnaturally against the stone floor.

And then—a whisper.

A name. Her name.

It was faint, as if carried by a breath of wind, the syllables stretching through the room, too familiar to be forgotten.

The scent deepened, wrapping around her, pulling at something buried too far beneath years of silence. She had felt this before. Once. But never like this. This was not a dream. This was not a memory.

This was Eldrenoire remembering.

Améliane's breath slowed. She turned back to the mirror.

The reflection was no longer her own. The mirror betrayed her—reflected not who she was, but who she had once been.

Herself. But not now. Before. Before the curse. Before the fall. Before she became the thing that lingered in the ruins of her own kingdom.

The woman in the glass was a queen in her prime, draped in silk and sunlight, a crown resting lightly atop waves of dark hair. Her grey eyes were bright, untouched by shadow, by loss, by the weight of an unbreakable curse.

And she was not alone.

A man stood beside her. A presence just behind her shoulder, tall and golden-haired, smiling with a quiet kind of certainty.

Edric. Her chest tightened. The sight of him—unchanged, untouched by betrayal—was too sharp. A memory unasked for. A wound dressed in gold.

Her breath hitched. It was not real. Not real.

But it felt real.

The warmth of it, the light, the way his hand hovered just near her own, close enough to touch. Her throat tightened. Then—the glass cracked.

The shattering was silent, but she felt it.

A single fracture split down the center of the reflection, splintering between them, severing the past from the present. The light in the mirror dimmed, the scent of jasmine fading, the illusion unraveling before her eyes.

And in its place—her own reflection stared back once more. Cold. Composed. Alone.

Améliane swallowed, forcing breath into her lungs, willing the weight in her chest to settle.

The castle was changing.

Or the curse was.

Sleep did not come easily. Even when exhaustion finally took her, it did not grant her peace.

She dreamed of nothing and everything. Shadows that stretched too long, whispers curling at the edges of her mind. Flickering candlelight in a vast and empty hall. And beneath it all, a voice like the wind moving through the ruins of a forgotten place, *"She was never meant to rule."*

The words slithered through the silence, sinking into the marrow of her bones.

Améliane stirred as the first pale fingers of dawn slipped through the heavy curtains, painting thin lines of gold across the floor. A cool draft from the night still lingered, weaving through the silk canopy of her bed.

She blinked slowly, adjusting to the dim light. The last thing she remembered—the kitchen, the conversation, the effortless pull of something she had not felt in a long time.

Mathieu.

Her lips parted slightly, her breath steady, as she let herself recall the way laughter had come easily, the way he had looked at her in the candlelight. Amused. Curious. Unafraid.

With a quiet huff, she shifted beneath the sheets, rolling onto her side, only to pause—her gaze catching on something that should not be there.

A single white jasmine blossom rested upon the dark wood of her bedside table.

Améliane stilled. The breath she had drawn lingered, trapped in her chest. Eldrenoire did not grow jasmine. It should not exist here.

Her fingers curled against the sheets, but she did not move. She only stared at the delicate bloom, its pale petals untouched, pristine against the smooth wood.

Jasmine. She had not seen jasmine in years.

The castle gardens held nothing so fragile. The air outside was heavy with wild-growing wisteria, with ivy that curled like grasping fingers, with creeping roses that swallowed stone. But not jasmine. Never jasmine.

Her silver eyes flicked toward the chamber door. Locked.

The windows? Latched.

She sat up slowly, the cool morning air pressing against her skin as she reached out, hesitating just before her fingers brushed the petals. She should test it. See if it vanished at her touch. If it crumbled to dust like the memories Eldrenoire tried to keep from her.

A test, then.

At last, she picked up the blossom, turning it between her fingers.

The petals were soft. Real.

But its presence was impossible.

And that made it dangerous.

CHAPTER 7

Mathieu

A sharp rap at the door roused him from uneasy sleep.

Mathieu groaned, rolling onto his back, muscles stiff from a night spent wrestling with half-formed dreams. The ache in his ribs had dulled to something manageable, but the stiffness in his shoulders made itself known the moment he pushed upright. He exhaled through his nose, rubbing a hand down his face before dragging himself out of bed.

The knock came again, impatient this time.

"Yes, yes," he muttered, raking a hand through his sleep-tousled hair as he strode across the room. He hadn't bothered with a shirt, and the cool morning air brushed against his skin as he cracked open the heavy wooden door.

A young woman in a neatly pressed dress stood on the other side, holding a tray of food. Her eyes widened slightly as she took him in—bare-chested, sleep-ruffled, his scars catching in the flickering morning light. A delicate flush spread across her cheeks, and she quickly dropped her gaze to the tray.

"My lord," she stammered, dipping into a slight curtsy. "Breakfast."

Mathieu arched a brow, fighting a grin as he stepped aside. "Come in."

She hesitated, then quickly crossed the threshold, setting the tray on the low table by the hearth. He caught the faintest tremor in her hands as she adjusted the silverware, doing her best not to look directly at him.

She dipped into another curtsy, clearly eager to flee. "If you need anything else, just ring the bell."

With a polite nod she hurried from the room leaving him alone with his meal.

Mathieu chuckled under his breath, shaking his head as he settled into the chair. He lifted the silver lid off the tray to reveal a spread of bread, fruit, and a poached egg, along with a thick slice of ham. Simple, but far better than the dried rations he'd survived on before stumbling into this strange prison.

He took his time eating, keeping an ear trained on the quiet hum of the castle beyond his door. If he strained, he could hear the distant echo of footsteps, the occasional murmur of voices carried through the stone halls. Eldrenoire might have been cursed, but it was far from lifeless this morning.

Just as he finished the last bite, another knock sounded.

This one was brisk, confident.

"Come in," he called, reaching for the linen napkin.

The door swung open, and Sabine strode inside without preamble.

Mathieu barely swallowed a sigh. "Good morning to you, too."

The castle's physician was as sharp as ever—her grey hair pulled into a loose bun, her sharp eyes missing nothing. She moved with the efficiency of a woman who had spent her life tending to the wounded, and she carried her satchel like a weapon.

She arched a brow at the tray beside him. "Good. You ate."

Mathieu smirked. "Touched by your concern."

She huffed. "Hardly." Without waiting for invitation, she set her satchel on the table and reached for his side.

Mathieu stilled as she prodded the bandages. Her fingers were brisk but not cruel, pressing gently along the bruised skin.

"You're healing well," she admitted.

Mathieu rolled his shoulders. "So, I'll be free to leave by tomorrow?"

Sabine froze. Just for a breath—a hesitation so brief that most wouldn't have caught it.

Then she sighed, straightening. "You already know the answer to that."

Mathieu tilted his head, studying her. "That's not a no."

Her expression was unreadable as she tucked her hands behind her back. "It's not a yes, either."

Mathieu huffed a quiet laugh, but there was no real humor in it. "Then I suppose I'll have to settle for pacing my room until I die of boredom."

Sabine's lips twitched. "That's why I came."

He arched a brow.

She reached into her satchel, pulling out a small glass vial of tonic and setting it on the table. "You need fresh air. The sunlight will help your body recover. I suggest you take a walk in the Shrouded Gardens."

Mathieu rolled the vial between his fingers, skeptical. "A garden?"

Sabine gave him a pointed look. "You could use the exercise."

Mathieu exhaled, stretching slightly. "You make it sound like a death sentence."

Her mouth twitched. "You've never been to this one."

That caught his attention.

Sabine smirked, recognizing the shift in his demeanor. "The paths change," she said simply, adjusting the strap of her bag. "The flowers bloom in colors they shouldn't. Some say the garden listens."

Mathieu frowned. "Listens?"

She shrugged. "Call it superstition if you like, but the last man who walked through those paths while lying to himself found them... unkind."

Mathieu studied her. "And what do you think?"

Sabine met his gaze, her expression unreadable. "I think you should take a walk."

She turned toward the door, pausing only to glance back at him. "Don't get lost."

And then she was gone.

Mathieu let out a slow breath, running a hand through his hair.

The Shrouded Gardens. Something about the name made his ribs tighten—not with pain, but with unease.

The air in the Shrouded Gardens was different. Mathieu had expected the usual scents of earth and greenery, the crisp dampness of morning dew, the faint sweetness of flowers—but what filled his lungs was something richer, older. The perfume of roses, the spice of wild herbs, the cool mineral scent of stone kissed by mist.

Sabine had said the paths changed. That the garden listened.

He wasn't sure he believed that, but he felt something as soon as he passed through the iron-wrought gate. A shift in the air. A subtle, unshakable wrongness.

The winding stone path stretched ahead, veiled in the dappled shadows of towering trees. Somewhere beyond, birdsong called in the distance—but it was wrong. Too slow. Warped.

Mathieu rolled his shoulders as he stepped forward. The path forked. He chose the left. Another fork. He went right.

The gardens should not have been this large. From the terrace, they had seemed enclosed, their hedges neat and manageable. But now, the paths bent unnaturally, stretching into mist-covered distances where they should not have fit.

He paused at a crossroad, glancing over his shoulder.

The gate was gone. His jaw clenched. Fine. Let it be a game. He'd played worse.

Mathieu pressed forward, his boots whispering against the stone. The deeper he went, the stranger the garden became. The flowers shifted in unnatural hues—violets dark as ink, lilies burning red as embers, roses that gleamed like pearls in the dim light.

The trees thickened, their canopies twisting together until the sky was nothing but fragmented slivers of grey. And then—

The scent changed. The sweetness curdled. Beneath it, a sharper edge. Iron. Smoke.

Not roses. Not herbs. Blood.

Mathieu stilled.

The air pressed closer, thickening around him, heavy as the weight of old battlefields. He knew this smell. It was the scent of war. Of dying men. Of fires smothering beneath the rain.

And then—

A new path unraveled before him. It had not been there before. A dirt road. Wet with mud, the imprint of heavy boots pressed deep into the earth.

Mathieu's pulse ticked against his ribs.

He knew this road. It led to Valmont.

His feet moved before he could stop them, drawn forward by something colder than memory, heavier than grief.

The trees blurred, the garden vanishing into the past.

The campfires flickered in the night, illuminating the rows of tents, the gleam of steel lined in racks, the banners still wet with the day's rain. The air smelled of damp wool, of leather and oil, of sweat and anticipation. They were preparing for battle.

And there—

Captain Duran.

He stood near the fires, his hands clasped behind his back, his armor streaked with the wear of a dozen campaigns. His salt-and-pepper hair was damp, his strong, weathered face creased with the weight of leadership.

Mathieu had looked up to him. Duran had been his father's right hand, a living legend among the soldiers. And now—

The captain turned. His sharp hazel eyes locked onto Mathieu's, clear and knowing. As if he could see him now.

Mathieu's breath hitched. This wasn't just a memory.

Duran tilted his head. "You're walking too heavily."

Mathieu's mouth opened—but his voice was gone.

Duran exhaled, stepping closer. "You always did that when you were thinking too hard. Not useful for a soldier."

Mathieu swallowed, his throat tight. "I wasn't thinking about battle."

"No," Duran said, watching him carefully. "You were thinking about duty."

Mathieu stiffened.

Duran's voice lowered, quiet but firm. "A man's duty is not to himself."

Mathieu had heard those words before. Long ago. But this time, they rang different.

"Everything worth keeping requires sacrifice. The moment you put yourself above those who need you, you are no better than the men we fight," Duran continued. His hazel eyes narrowed. "You understand that, don't you?"

Mathieu wanted to answer. But the words stuck in his throat. The war had already been lost. Valmont had fallen. Duran had died fighting for it. His throat tightened, hands curling into fists he hadn't realized he'd made.

And now—

Mathieu wasn't a boy at war anymore. He was a man running from his past.

Duran watched him, waiting. Then, softer—

"What will you choose, Mathieu?"

The garden lurched.

The air snapped back into place, the heavy scent of blood and smoke vanishing.

Mathieu staggered, his breath sharp as he found himself standing beneath the trees once more, the shifting flowers whispering around him.

The dirt road was gone.

The camp. The fire.

Duran.

Gone.

Mathieu dragged a hand down his face, jaw clenched against the weight of what he'd seen.

A test. Not just a memory. A warning.

His grip flexed. He turned toward the winding path ahead, his pulse steadying. The garden had shown him the truth. But truth alone changed nothing.

The walk back took hours. Or maybe it only felt that way.

The Shrouded Gardens had twisted around him, keeping him within their grasp long after he should have found the exit. Each turn brought him back to the same ivy-choked archway, as if the garden was laughing behind his back.

Eldrenoire had toyed with him before—but this had been different.

It hadn't tried to keep him out. It had tried to make him see.

Now, standing in the castle's dimly lit halls, his breath steady but his thoughts restless, Mathieu pressed a hand to the cool stone wall and took a deep breath.

Duran's voice still lingered. *What will you choose, Mathieu?*

His ribs ached with the effort of remaining upright for so long, his body reminding him that he was still recovering, no matter how much he wanted to ignore it. He should rest, let himself sleep off whatever trick of magic had dragged his past out of him—but the thought of being alone in his chambers, left with nothing but his own mind, was unbearable.

He needed a distraction.

So, he went to the one place that had called to him since he first laid eyes on it.

The library was as endless as it was strange.

The moment Mathieu stepped inside, he felt the difference—not in the air, not in the scent of aged parchment and wax, but in something deeper, something beneath the skin.

It was alive.

Books whispered against the shelves, shifting without touch. Some appeared the moment his gaze flicked toward them, while others vanished, their spines dissolving into the dust of time. Entire rows of books held only blank pages; their stories seemingly forgotten by the world.

Mathieu took it all in with careful, quiet steps, letting his fingers trail over the nearest shelf, reading the faded lettering on the spines. Languages he recognized. Others he didn't.

He had come looking for Améliane. She wasn't here. So, he kept moving, letting instinct guide him deeper into the labyrinth of books. And then a flicker of white caught his eye.

Tucked into a forgotten corner of the library, something loomed beneath a sheet thick with dust.

Mathieu slowed, drawn forward. He reached out, fingers curling into the fabric. With one pull, the cloth fell away. Dust spun in the candlelight and revealed a portrait beneath.

Massive, ornate, and heavy with time. Mathieu's breath slowed.It was Améliane. But not the way he had seen her before.

Not the sharp-eyed queen trapped in her own cursed castle, not the woman who wielded silence as a shield.

No. This Améliane was young—just a girl. Bright. Alive. She stood tall in the fine silks of a royal house, but she was not alone. At her side was a boy, no older than fifteen. Her older brother, perhaps?

He had the same sharp silver eyes, the same proud tilt to his chin—but where she had always seemed to carry the weight of something unspoken, his face held the ease of a boy who never doubted his place in the world.

Their parents flanked them on either side. The king stood behind his son, his broad frame draped in royal blues, his hands resting lightly on his heir's shoulders.

The queen was seated, her expression softer, more knowing—her hand resting gently on a small child in her lap.

Mathieu's gaze caught on the youngest girl, no older than six or seven, her curls spilling over her fine dress, her face half-hidden against her mother's sleeve. The youngest princess.

Mathieu exhaled slowly. He hadn't given much thought to who Améliane had been before all of this. He hadn't let himself. He had seen her as a queen, a ruler, a survivor—but never as a daughter. Never as a sister.

But here she was. A girl who had once belonged to a family.A girl who had a brother who would have worn the crown before her. A girl who had once been the second-born princess, never meant to rule.

The words whispered through his mind like a phantom. *She was never meant to rule.*

The portrait had been hidden. Tucked away. Forgotten.

As if someone had not wanted to look at it.

Mathieu's fingers flexed at his sides. He wondered—Did Améliane hide this herself?

Or had someone else tried to erase the girl she used to be?

His jaw tightened. He stepped back, gaze lingering on the faces of a family long lost to time. Then, with slow deliberation, he reached for the heavy fabric and covered the portrait once more.

CHAPTER 8

Améliane

The scent of jasmine still clung to her fingers. Améliane flexed her hand absently as she walked, the hem of her cloak brushing the stone floor. Beside her, Renaud walked in sharp, measured steps, his gaze flicking to her more than once. She had told him everything. The dream, the reflection in the mirror, the whisper in the dark.

And, of course, the flower.

He had listened in silence, his expression unreadable. Now, as they neared the library doors, he finally spoke.

"This is a warning."

Améliane exhaled, slowing her pace. "You think so."

Renaud pulled at the ornate handle and the library door groaned open as he ushered her in.

"I know so," he snapped stepping into the library behind him. "There is no jasmine here. There hasn't ever been any jasmine here." His fingers curled into fists at his sides. "And you're telling me it simply appeared on your nightstand? After a dream like that?"

"Yes."

Renaud muttered a curse, raking a hand through his dark hair. "Then it means something."

She nodded. A long pause.

Then, his sharp golden eyes cutting towards her, "What did it mean to you?"

That was the real question, wasn't it? What had the castle been trying to tell her? What had it remembered?

"I don't know yet," she admitted. "But I intend to find out."

Renaud's scowl deepened. "And what if it wasn't the castle?"

She hesitated. She had assumed—hoped—that it was Eldrenoire who had left the jasmine. That the castle had reached into the depths of her past and chosen a memory she had spent years trying to bury: Edric's endless habit of sending her elaborate jasmine arrangements during their marriage.

It would be just like the castle to choose that. A bloom that had once symbolized his affection, now twisted into something cruel.

After all, Eldrenoire was a curse of Edric's making.

She turned to face him fully. "Then what are you suggesting?"

His jaw flexed. "Someone could have placed it there."

She lifted a brow. "Who?"

"You know who."

Her grey eyes narrowed. "You think it was him."

"I know it could have been him."

Améliane let out a slow breath, turning toward the library doors. She didn't want to argue with Renaud—not about this.

"Mathieu arrived only days ago," she said instead. "And now you think he's toying with me?"

Renaud's jaw tensed. "Mathieu? You don't know him."

"No," she admitted. "I don't."

"Then why dismiss the possibility?"

Because she had dismissed it. Because for all the shadows clinging to him, all the questions he hadn't answered, he didn't feel like a man playing games. He watched too closely. He listened too carefully.

Améliane stood with her back to him, her posture regal despite the weariness that clung to her. Renaud, ever the soldier, loomed close—his stance sharp, protective, the golden glint of his eyes betraying his barely contained frustration.

A long silence stretched between them.

Then, with a sharp exhale, Renaud raked a hand through his silver hair. "I won't press you further," he muttered, though there was a bite to his words. "But I will be stationing a guard outside your door from now on."

Améliane stiffened. "That's unnecessary."

He let out a quiet, humorless laugh. "Unnecessary? You woke to a flower that shouldn't exist and heard whispers in your sleep. Even if this was the castle, even if it meant no harm, I will not gamble with your safety."

She didn't tell him she was not asleep when she heard the voices as she turned to face him fully, grey eyes flashing. "Renaud, I do not need—"

Before Améliane could argue, Renaud took a step closer, lowering his voice.

"This is not just about the castle," he said quietly. "It's about the messages."

Améliane's jaw tighten.

Renaud continued. "You know what he's been saying. The last letter all but spelled it out."

Améliane sighed slowly, rubbing her temple. "He wants me to break."

"And if he cannot break you," Renaud said darkly, "he will find another way to get to you."

Améliane sighed. "You are seeing plots where there are none."

Renaud's golden eyes darkened. "No, I am seeing what he wants me to see. He sends these messages to remind you of what was taken. To remind you of who still holds the power. And now? A flower appears from nowhere? A whisper in the dark? I do not trust coincidence."

A long silence settled. She turned away from him, her thoughts churning—and that's when she heard it.

The soft groan of a floorboard.

Her gaze snapped to the far side of the library, narrowing on the shelves tucked in shadow. A figure emerged from between them—broad-shouldered, unrepentant.

Mathieu. Her breath caught, irritation flashing through her. "You."

Renaud stepped forward at once, positioning himself between them. "How long have you been there eavesdropping?"

"I was reading," he corrected, glancing toward the far corner. "Your shelves are terribly disorganized. Though I suppose that's expected when your library rearranges itself at will."

Renaud bristled. "You had no right to listen."

"And yet," Mathieu said, "here we are."

The air crackled between them. Renaud looked moments away from drawing steel, but Améliane lifted a hand, silencing him with a glance.

"What did you hear?" she asked.

Her tone was calm, but her posture had shifted—not defensive but guarded. Elegant. Controlled. Like a queen on unfamiliar ground.

"Enough to know you have a correspondence problem," he said. "And that someone wants to break you."

Her eyes narrowed. "That is none of your concern."

"You made it my concern the moment you decided I might be the one playing games with you."

Renaud bristled. "You don't get to twist this."

"I don't need to twist anything," Mathieu said evenly. "I only asked a question. A rather simple one, actually."

He stepped forward, gaze fixed on Améliane. "Who is sending you messages? The castle doesn't exactly have a postmaster."

She didn't answer immediately. Her eyes searched his, as if weighing how much danger he posed. Or how much truth he could handle.

"You should not have heard that," she said at last.

"And yet," he said again, "I did."

Renaud growled under his breath. "I can escort him out."

"You could try," Mathieu offered, mouth curling slightly. "But it might get awkward for both of us."

Améliane shot him a look sharp enough to flay the ego off a lesser man.

"Must everything you say drip with insolence?"

"Only when I'm being threatened," he said. "Or condescended to. Or, say, accused of floral terrorism."

That stopped her. She let out a breath—not quite a sigh, not quite a laugh.

"You think this is a joke," she said.

"No," he said, voice softening. "I think this place is suffocating. And I think something is happening that none of us fully understand. But I also think I'm not the enemy."

Her eyes flicked over him. For the first time, her posture eased. Barely.

"Then who are you, Mathieu?"

A beat. He was silent for a breath.

"Someone trying to survive," he said finally. "Same as you."

Another silence stretched. Then, Améliane turned to Renaud.

"Leave us," she said.

Renaud's eyes widened. "My Queen—"

"Now."

He hesitated, jaw clenched, then nodded stiffly and exited, the heavy door echoing shut behind him.

Mathieu blew out air, slow and controlled. "Well, that went well."

Améliane stepped closer. "What do you want?"

He met her gaze. "To know what I've gotten myself into."

She tilted her head, considering him.

"And if I told you?" she asked.

He gave her a half-smile. "Then I'd owe you more than witty banter."

For a moment, neither of them moved.

Then, quietly, she said, "Sit down, Mathieu."

They settled into twin armchairs near the library's hearth, where a fire crackled with quiet determination. The flames danced in hues just a touch too vibrant—amber and gold edged with blue—as if even the fire obeyed the strange rules of this place. Above it, a carved mantle twisted with thorned vines and winged creatures, their eyes watching from the stone like silent sentinels.

The chairs were high-backed and worn with use, their velvet cushions faded but comfortable. Améliane removed her cloak and folded herself into hers like a woman born to thrones, spine straight, one ankle crossed over the other. Across from her, Mathieu lowered himself more slowly, his movement betraying the soreness still lingering in his side. He didn't wince, but she saw it anyway.

For a moment, neither of them spoke.

Then, Améliane broke the silence. "I will tell you what I can."

His brows lifted slightly, surprised by the offer.

"But only," she continued, voice cool and deliberate, "if you offer something in return. A show of good faith. No half-truths. No evasions. You want answers, Mathieu? So do I."

His mouth curved, but the smile didn't quite reach his eyes. "So, it's a trade, then."

She inclined her head once. "Of a sort."

He leaned back in his chair, stretching one leg out slightly in front of him, the firelight casting shadows across his jaw. For a long moment, he said nothing.

Then, at last, he gave a slow nod. "All right. Ask."

Améliane studied him from across the flames, the firelight flickering in her silver eyes. "Very well," she said. "Let's begin with the obvious. Who are you, really?"

Mathieu let out a soft breath, eyes drifting to the fire. "That's a complicated question."

"It usually is when men are running from something," she said smoothly.

His gaze flicked back to her, amused. "And here I thought I was sitting."

"Insufferable," she murmured, the corner of her mouth lifting in a half-smile—one that echoed the rare, unguarded laughter she'd shared with him in the kitchen.

Mathieu chuckled under his breath. "Fair enough."

He shifted in his seat, leaning forward slightly. "I'm no one of consequence, if that's what you're trying to work out. I've worn a soldier's uniform. I've commanded men. I've lost more battles than I care to remember—and one in particular that cost me everything."

Améliane's expression didn't change, but she caught the flicker of something behind his eyes. Not shame. Not quite. Regret, maybe. Or something older.

"You speak like a man who once had a great deal to lose."

He shrugged. "That depends on how you measure value. Land? Title? Bloodlines?"

"Those are all very convenient things to misplace."

His lips quirked. "I didn't misplace them. They were taken. Along with my home. My people. All of it."

She went quiet. Not because she pitied him—but because she knew what it meant to speak in past tense about a life that still lived somewhere in your bones.

"Was it war?" she asked.

He nodded once, the faint smile lines bracketing his mouth deepening into creases as his lips pulled into a frown. "The kind that guts everything. Not just cities. Legacies."

"Your legacy?"

He shot a puff of air through his nose, a sharp, bitter sound. "Whatever legacy there was, I didn't inherit it. Not as one would expect."

A beat passed.

"And now you wander?" she asked, voice soft but not unkind.

"I survive," he corrected. "The wandering came after."

For a moment, neither of them moved. The air between them hummed with unspoken things. Améliane studied him—truly studied him—as though the right angle might reveal his secrets. There was something steady in his gaze, something too tired to be false. And yet... trust had never come easily. Not here. Not anymore.

Her fingers curled slightly around the arm of her chair. Then—

A soft thump.

The thick tome that had rested untouched beside her shifted. Its spine cracked, the pages rustling as if disturbed by windless air. When she glanced down, the title had changed.

Truth and Valor.

Her breath caught. The library had spoken. The title hadn't been there before. She was sure of it. Eldrenoire didn't just reflect—it revealed.

Slowly, she lifted her eyes to him once more, and this time, she nodded. Just once. Barely enough to notice.

Améliane leaned back in her chair, draping one arm over the velvet armrest with the grace of someone perfectly at ease. "Not bad," she said. "Evocative. Slightly tragic. Very mysterious."

He smirked. "And yet, you still haven't told me your full name."

"Hmmm," one dark eyebrow raised skeptically.

"I've bled on your floors, been trapped in your halls, and now I'm being interrogated in front of your very dramatic fireplace. Surely that counts for something."

She arched a brow. "Perhaps."

Mathieu laughed, low and warm. "All right, you win, my host-with-no-surname. What exactly do you think is happening here? Why the flower? What is this about a messenger?"

Before she could speak, the door slammed open.

Améliane whirled toward the sound, instinct sharp. Beside her, Mathieu tensed—muscles coiling, jaw set—as if preparing for a fight that had already begun.

Élodie swept into the room without hesitation. Her crimson skirts flared with every step, and she crossed the distance to the queen in a single breath.

Renaud followed close behind, barely keeping his fury leashed.

Élodie dropped to one knee before Améliane, ignoring Mathieu entirely.

"Your Highness," she said, her voice low and taut with urgency.

Her dark auburn curls had been braided back, though a few tendrils clung to her temples—an elegant sort of disarray that only heightened the tension in her expression. Élodie glanced over her shoulder, then she bowed her head.

"He's here," she whispered.

The air in the room shifted.

Améliane straightened, metallic eyes narrowing like a blade drawn clean.

"How long?"

"He just passed the outer gate," Élodie replied, rising. Her fists clenched at her sides. "We don't have much time."

Mathieu didn't know who he was, but judging by the way Élodie's usual smirk had vanished—and Renaud looked ready to draw blood—it wasn't anyone good.

The queen turned to him, her expression unreadable.

"Mathieu, Renaud will escort you back to your room. Stay there."

Mathieu's eyes narrowed, tension bristling beneath his skin. "I don't take orders."

A pause stretched between them—long enough to become dangerous.

Then, softly, unexpectedly, "Please."

The word was quiet. No command, no demand—just that single syllable, stripped bare.

He stilled. Of all the things she could've said, that was the one he hadn't braced for. A queen did not beg. And yet, somehow, it wasn't weakness in her voice. It was control. Chosen vulnerability, sharper than steel.

His jaw tightened. He nodded once. "All right," he said. "But only because you asked nicely."

The corner of her mouth twitched—almost a smile, almost not.

Renaud stepped forward, clearly unconvinced, but Améliane didn't look away from Mathieu until he turned to follow.

CHAPTER 9

Améliane

The corridors of Eldrenoire stretched long and shadowed, the flickering torchlight casting their reflections across the polished stone. Améliane moved swiftly, the whisper of her gown trailing behind her, her steps controlled but quick.

Renaud caught up with them after depositing Mathieu safely to his room. He and Élodie kept pace at her sides, the weight of their shared silence thickening with each step.

"Does he know?" The words slipped from her lips, quiet but sharp, cutting through the air between them.

Renaud didn't hesitate. "No."

Améliane flicked him a glance, searching for any uncertainty in the tight set of his jaw, the steady line of his stride.

"He can't," he added, voice edged with finality. "It's impossible. No one outside these walls could know."

"Unless," Élodie murmured, smooth and knowing, "someone has told him."

The words hovered, a ghost of doubt trailing in their wake. Améliane didn't respond. She didn't have to. The thought had already buried itself in her mind.

Edric was here. Now. That was no coincidence.

Améliane's pace did not slow, but her voice was steady when she spoke. "No one says a word about our guest."

Renaud gave a single, sharp nod. Élodie's expression flickered with amusement, but her golden eyes held something sharper beneath the mirth.

"You think he matters," she said, almost idly, though her gaze was too assessing for the comment to be truly careless. "You don't know why yet. But you feel it."

Améliane did not look at her. "I trust my instincts."

Élodie hummed, noncommittal.

The truth was, she did not know what made this man different. But Eldrenoire did.

She had felt it the moment he crossed the threshold, the way the air shifted, the way the very bones of the keep seemed to exhale, stretching toward him like an old thing roused from restless slumber.

The Black Keep did not react to just anyone.

Its magic had dulled over the years, resigned to its fate as much as those who lived within its walls. Strangers had stumbled into Eldrenoire before—lost travelers, desperate souls seeking shelter where they shouldn't. The castle had never paid them any mind.

And yet, since Mathieu arrived, something in its slumbering core had stirred. If she noticed it, then Edric would too. And that could not happen.

"We don't know what he is," she said finally. "Not yet. And until we do, I want him kept out of Edric's sight."

Renaud's expression remained unreadable, but Élodie's smirk sharpened. "That should be easy enough." A pause. Then, with a tilt of her head— "Assuming, of course, he stays where he's told."

Améliane's breath escaped in a faint snort. She doubted it.

They turned the last corner, the doors of the Grand Hall looming ahead, the weight of the moment settling over them like the hush before a storm.

Edric was waiting.

And they would face him as they always did. But this time, something had shifted. And Améliane did not yet know whether that would be their salvation—or their downfall.

She stopped just short of the towering doors to the Grand Hall, her fingers curling against the heavy silk of her gown. A single breath steadied her. Then another. The faintest tremor ghosted through her limbs—not from fear, not from uncertainty, but from something older. Something colder. She wished she had not left her cloak in the library. Another layer between her and Edric would be more than welcome.

A familiar weight pressed against her ribs, coiling in the space between breath and bone. She had long since learned how to bear it.

She had once thought Edric golden—like the sunlight spilling through the palace gardens in their youth, like the glint of polished steel catching the dawn. He had been her consort, her partner, the man who stood at her side before he stepped behind her back to stab her in it. The man who had loved her, and yet still found it within himself to destroy her.

A fool's love. The kind that came with a leash.

She adjusted the drape of her sleeves, smoothing away the last traces of her hesitation, her expression settling into a mask of cool detachment. The unease curling in her stomach had no place here. It never had.

Behind her, Élodie exhaled a soft, knowing breath. "You don't have to see him alone."

Améliane did not answer. She only lifted her chin, squared her shoulders, and pushed open the doors, stepping into the golden glow of candlelight with all the grace of a queen who had never been overthrown. The air was thick with the scent of burning cedar and something sharper, wine perhaps, or the lingering ghost of steel.

Edric stood near the hearth, as he always did, as if he owned the space. As if he belonged here.

He turned at her entrance, the firelight casting long shadows across the sharp, aristocratic angles of his face. His golden hair, still as perfectly kept as ever, gleamed beneath the flickering glow, not a strand out of place. The years had not weathered him as they had others—no visible scars, no lines of hardship etched into his smooth skin. His hands, still soft from a life spent commanding rather than doing, rested lazily at his sides, the glint of jeweled rings betraying his ever-present hunger for wealth, for status, for power.

And his eyes. Cold, calculating, piercing through her with a gaze that had once held devotion but now held something far more dangerous. Possession.

She met that gaze and smiled, slow and edged with something that did not reach her eyes.

"To what do I owe the pleasure, husband?"

The word was a blade, sharpened just for him.

She watched, waiting, as the corner of Edric's mouth curled—not in amusement, not in irritation, but in something more deliberate.

"Am I no longer welcome in my own home?" he asked, voice smooth, measured.

Améliane stepped further into the room, the train of her gown whispering against the stone. "Your home?" she mused, tilting her head. "Strange. I seem to recall a time when you had to steal your 'home' from someone else."

His jaw tightened. Just a flicker. Just enough.

Good.

She moved toward the hearth, claiming the space between them as if it had always belonged to her.

Behind her, Renaud and Élodie took their places at the edges of the room, silent sentinels.

Améliane did not spare them a glance. She had only one opponent tonight, and he was standing before her, all golden arrogance and coiled restraint.

"Tell me, Edric," she said lightly, "did you simply grow lonely in my absence, or have you finally tired of ruling a kingdom that rots in your hands?"

Edric's expression did not shift. Not at first.

But Améliane knew him too well. She saw the flicker of something beneath the polished exterior—something sharp, something wounded. A momentary tightening of his jaw, a flicker of hurt in his cold blue eyes before he masked it with that insufferable control of his.

He took a measured breath, before stepping closer. "The kingdom rots because it is incomplete," he said, his voice smooth, but quieter and more careful now. "Because you refuse to take your place beside me."

She scoffed, rolling her eyes. "My place."

Edric's gaze sharpened, the edges of his restraint visible now, like a dam threatening to crack. "Yes, your place. At my side, Améliane. Where you belong." His voice dipped, quieter now, almost intimate. "This was never meant to be a war between us."

She laughed, but there was no humor in it. "You made it one."

"I had no choice." The words came too quickly, too desperate for someone like him. He drew another breath, forcing the moment back under his control. "I never wanted this, Améliane. I never wanted you to suffer."

She tilted her head, watching him carefully. "No?"

"No," he murmured. "I wanted a future with you. I wanted to share this kingdom with you. I wanted children with you." A shadow crossed his expression, darkening the ice of his gaze. "But you forced my hand."

Something twisted low in her stomach. Not regret—she would never regret fighting for what was hers. But the weight of his words, the quiet hurt buried beneath them, scraped against something raw.

She schooled her features, letting nothing show.

"You want me to pity you," she said flatly.

Edric shook his head, stepping closer still. "No," he said. "I want you to see. To understand." He exhaled, quiet but deliberate. "If you would just accept what is—if you would stop fighting me—we could end this. The curse would break. You wouldn't have to live like this anymore."

His voice softened; a plea wrapped in control. "We wouldn't have to be like this anymore."

A silence stretched between them, charged and heavy. Améliane held his gaze, unmoving.

For a moment, just a breath, the years fell away. The history between them, the betrayal, the quiet nights when he had held her hand and whispered of a future they would build together—it all pressed in around her, a ghost of something that had never truly existed.

But then she remembered the truth. The reality of the man before her. Her expression hardened.

"You ask me to stop fighting," she murmured, voice like steel wrapped in silk. "But you forget, Edric—I was quite literally born to rule."

Her silver eyes gleamed in the firelight, unyielding as tempered steel. "This throne was mine before you ever laid a hand upon it. My bloodline built Belmara My ancestors shaped it, protected it, ruled it for centuries before you ever set foot within these walls. My family died for it. And I, their daughter, their queen—I was raised for this. Trained for this. Meant for this."

Her voice remained soft, but there was no mistaking the power beneath it. "And you?" Her lips curled, something razor-sharp slipping into her expression. "You were nothing but a consort."

She saw the flicker of something dangerous in his eyes—the flash of temper beneath the calm exterior.

"Do not—"

"But that wasn't enough for you, was it?" she continued, voice quiet but relentless. "It wasn't enough to be at my side, to share in what was already yours in name, if not in blood." She took a slow step forward, watching the muscles in his jaw tighten. "No. You wanted it all. So, you stole it. You conspired behind my back, schemed in the shadows, whispered poison into the ears of those I once trusted—and for what?"

Her breath was steady, measured, even as something dark curled at the edges of her voice. "For a crown that was never yours to wear? For a throne that was never yours to claim?"

A pause.

Then, quieter— "For a kingdom that will never truly be yours?"

Silence pressed between them, thick and suffocating.

Edric's fingers curled at his sides.

His jaw clenched.

She saw the moment he realized there would never be an answer that satisfied him. That she would never submit.

And he hated her for it. Almost as much as he still loved her.

Edric's lips parted—just slightly—before pressing into a thin, measured line. A flicker of something passed through his sharp blue eyes—guilt? Regret? No. That would have required acknowledgment.

Instead, he slowly tilted his head, his golden hair catching the firelight in an almost too-perfect display of control.

"You speak as if I had a choice," he said smoothly. "As if this kingdom had a choice."

His voice was measured, deliberate—the same way it always had been when he wanted her to listen, to see reason, to stop fighting.

"You and I both know Belmara could not survive under a queen alone," he continued, stepping forward as if closing the distance between them would lessen the divide carved by his betrayal. "Our people would have torn themselves apart—half bound to tradition; half bound to you. I did what I had to do to keep this kingdom from collapsing in on itself."

He let his gaze drag over her, softening just enough to make it convincing. "And yet, you speak of me as if I were some villain instead of the man who did what was necessary—for Belmara. For you."

His voice dipped lower, edged with something quieter, something dangerous. "Tell me, Améliane—would you have rather let them tear you apart? Would you have rather watched your birthright turn to ruin, just to cling to a title that was never meant for you?"

He shook his head, something like disappointment flickering behind his gaze. "I spared you that fate."

He dared another step closer. "I have only ever spared you."

The doors to the Grand Hall closed, and the quiet shuffle of footsteps echoed through the arched ceiling signaling the arrival of the rest of her court. They moved into place without a word, forming a silent wall at her back—Renaud, Élodie, Sabine, Laurent, Margot, the others—all of them standing behind her, their presence an unspoken show of loyalty.

Some stood as men and women, clad in elegant but simple attire, their gazes sharp and unreadable. Others... did not. Creatures in their animal form crouched in the line, as well. A silent reminder of what Edric had made them.

Edric did not acknowledge them.

His gaze remained fixed on her.

He stepped closer, his fingers brushing against hers before taking her hand fully. It was a careful, calculated touch—not forceful, not demanding—just possessive enough to remind her that he still could.

Améliane let him take it. Let him thread his fingers through hers and guide her forward, toward the far end of the hall where the throne stood in solemn silence.

Her stomach twisted—not with grief, not with longing, but with something colder, something tightly leashed.

The throne was the one piece of her kingdom that remained untouched, a gilded relic of what had been stolen from her. She never sat upon it. Not once, not since Edric's betrayal.

But he did.

Every chance he got.

They reached the dais, and just as he had done so many times before, Edric released her hand only to take his place upon the throne—casual, comfortable, like a man returning to his rightful seat.

It was meant to provoke. She did not give him the satisfaction of reacting.

Instead, she withdrew her hand swiftly before he had the chance to grasp it again.

His lips quirked—half amusement, half indulgence. Then, as if nothing had happened, his gaze dragged over her—slow, assessing, unashamedly thorough.

Not with the eyes of a king measuring a rival. With the eyes of a man who had once made love to her.

A muscle in Améliane's jaw twitched, but she remained still.

Edric exhaled, low and contemplative. "There is something different about you today."

His tone was too casual.

He did not say what he truly meant. Did not press, did not accuse.

Instead, he leaned forward slightly, hands clasped over his lap. "Has anything... changed?"

The words were a trap.

The ghost of a knowing smirk toyed at the corner of his mouth, as if he were testing the waters, watching for the slightest ripple of unease. As if he already suspected.

And yet, Améliane's expression remained perfectly unreadable. She had played this game with him for too many years. She would not start losing now.

Améliane did not flinch.

"Nothing has changed," she said, her voice smooth and deliberate. "I am exactly as you left me. The castle is exactly as you cursed it to be."

She let the words settle, let them sting the way she knew they would.

Edric's expression did not shift, but something in his posture tightened, just for a breath—so fleeting it could have been imagined.

Then— "Hmm."

A quiet, considering sound. His gaze flickered—not to her, but past her. To her court. To the silent, waiting figures standing behind her, their watchful eyes betraying nothing.

But it was enough. Though his glance was a fraction of a second, it was enough to make Améliane's stomach coil with unease.

Edric was not just testing her. He was looking for something. Or someone.

Her spine straightened, her fingers twitching against the folds of her gown, though she willed them still.

If there was a spy among them... if someone had whispered of Mathieu's arrival...

She did not let the thought fully form. Not yet. Instead, she tilted her chin ever so slightly, allowing the faintest arch of her brow. "Satisfied?"

Edric's mouth curved—not quite a smile.

"Oh, Améliane." His tone was almost fond. "I did not come just to admire your prison."

She said nothing, waiting.

He let the silence stretch—just long enough for it to settle under her skin—before exhaling through his nose, as if indulging in something bittersweet.

"I came to bring you good news," his eyes gleamed as he spoke. "You are an aunt."

The words struck harder than she would ever let him see.

Aunt. A title she had never expected to hold. A child she would never meet.

Edric smiled, slow and deliberate. "Your sister and her husband welcomed a daughter last night. A healthy girl."

The air in the hall seemed to still.

Améliane did not react. She would not react. Not to the knowledge that her own sister—the woman who had once clasped her hands as a child and whispered secrets in the dark—had betrayed her.

That her sister and brother-in-law had conspired with Edric to steal her throne, to bind her in this cursed place, and now they had a child while she remained here.

Edric watched her carefully, like a man who had just played a winning hand and was waiting to see how his opponent would respond.

Edric tilted his head. "You have nothing more to say?"

Her eyes met his, unblinking. "What would you have me say?"

His mouth curved, but she could see it now—the anticipation. The way he was waiting for the crack—the slip of emotion, the flicker of grief. He was waiting for her to show him that his words had reached her.

She huffed lightly, as if bored. "Congratulations to them."

His expression didn't change. But the way his fingers curled against his palm—just slightly—told her that her flippant response was a disappointment to him.

Good.

Améliane gave him a mocking little smile before sighing dramatically. "As thrilling as this reunion has been, I'm afraid I must cut it short."

She made a vague motion with one hand. "You see, I have an absolutely packed schedule of brooding, pacing, and gazing longingly out of windows. No time for social calls."

Élodie smothered a laugh behind her hand.

Renaud did not laugh. But he looked immensely pleased.

Edric's mouth curved, his expression smooth, but she could see the tightness at the edges, the flicker of something sharp behind his gaze.

Edric slowly stood. The movement was unhurried.

Though he lacked a warrior's broad, battle-forged frame, Edric was still a man built for power—just a different kind.

Where Renaud and Mathieu were brutal strength and rough-hewn resilience, Edric was crafted elegance, his body honed with the precision of someone who valued control above all else.

Tall and leanly muscled, his broad shoulders carried the weight of a stolen crown with ease.

He was a man who had never known hardship in the way warriors did, yet who had still learned how to wield power—through words, through presence, through the careful application of force when necessary.

And right now, that presence was directed entirely at her.

His icy blue gaze swept over her, sharp as cut glass, before his lips curved into something almost indulgent.

"Ah, Améliane," he sighed, shaking his head as if indulging the antics of a wayward child. "Still so willful. Still so untamed after all these years."

Then, before she could step away, he reached for her. His hand curled around her wrist first, firm but unhurried, before sliding to her waist.

She stiffened as Edric pulled her against him as he rose from her throne. He was too close, too intimate—wrong.

The fabric of her gown did little to buffer the heat of him and the possessive way he molded her against his frame as though she still belonged to him.

His hand traveled down her spine to the small of her back before wandering lower.

Too low. Suddenly his fingers were splaying, cupping, claiming.

The other hand speared into her hair, cradling the base of her skull.

She refused to react. This was an act meant to humiliate her in front of her court. A punishment for her sharp retorts and her failure to receive him in her cursed castle as her king.

He leaned in, breath warm against her ear as his lips brushed just beneath it, a kiss that lingered. Not gentle or kind. The kiss was a performance. A warning.

His whisper slithered over her skin like poisoned silk. "It's always so nice to see you, darling." His fingers curled just slightly against her nape, sending a prickle of warning through her scalp.

She swallowed once fighting nausea as she felt his arousal pressing into her stomach.

"Next time..." A slow exhale, his lips grazing her ear. "I might stay the night."

Her stomach twisted, but she did not pull away. She would not give him that.

Instead, she inhaled slowly, deliberately, a measured breath to keep herself from shoving him away and prolonging his wretched visit.

And then—movement.

Over Edric's shoulder, beyond the throne, movement whispered from the shadows near the alcove doors.

Her gaze snapped up—

Mathieu. Watching.

His expression was hard to read, half-shadowed by the flickering torchlight. But she saw the tension in his jaw and the stiffness in his shoulders.

Saw him watching Edric's hands on her, watching the way she did not move. The way she could not move.

A storm brewed behind his hazel eyes that was sharp and unyielding.

Her pulse jumped.

Mathieu saw her. Not as a whisper of power lurking in the shadows. He saw her as she was. As a woman trapped in the arms of the man who had stolen her throne.

The realization sliced through her, sharp as a dagger. For the first time, she felt exposed. Not because of Edric's hands on her. She had long since learned to endure that.

But because this stranger who stumbled into her home was watching.

And she feared—gods, she feared—what he might think. Did he see her—trapped, powerless, broken? Did he think, even for a moment, that she was a queen who had lost her power, a woman who had allowed herself to be caged? She could not allow disruption to the carefully crafted balance of power she had fought to maintain after her exile.

She met his gaze, unwavering, unflinching.

And yet—she saw it. There was a shift in his stance. The tension was coiling through his body like a storm held barely in check. It was the instinctive, chivalrous response of a man who had spent his life protecting those who could not protect themselves.

Her fingers twitched, the only outward sign of her pulse hammering in her throat.

No, she silently implored with her eyes. Don't.

She gave the smallest shake of her head.

He could not fight this battle. Not now. Not against Edric.

She expected defiance. She expected the stubborn will of a man who had fought too many battles to stand by and watch.

But instead—he understood.

Something flickered in his expression—reluctance, frustration, something unspoken and sharp—but he held.

Held, and then moved.

He reluctantly stepped backward, not turning away, but sinking back into the alcove's shadows, letting darkness swallow him whole.

She steadied her breathing, slow and deliberate.

And when Edric finally pulled away, when he stepped back with a smirk and swept toward the doors, she forced her gaze forward—forced herself not to look toward the alcove.

Forced herself to pretend Mathieu had never been there at all.

Chapter 10

Mathieu

Mathieu exhaled slowly, staring at the heavy wooden door like it had personally offended him.

They had locked him in.

He shouldn't have been surprised. Should've expected it, really. He was the one that had agreed to let Renaud escort him back to his room.

He had been a prisoner before. A fugitive long enough to know when someone was trying to cage him. But this? This wasn't a cell. It was a polite imprisonment and a very well-mannered way of saying "stay put".

He had never been particularly good at staying put.

He could, of course, kick the door down. That would be satisfying. More than that, it would make a point—one he had no doubt Renaud, or whoever had locked it, would love to discuss with their fists later.

But as much as he'd enjoy the spectacle, and the release of pent-up frustration a fist fight would bring, it wasn't the smartest option.

Instead, he inhaled, rolling his shoulders. The more subtle approach would serve him better.

Lockpicking had never been his primary talent, but necessity had a way of making men adaptable.

Mathieu crouched, running his fingers along the doorframe, checking for weaknesses in the wood and in the lock itself. It wasn't a complicated mechanism—solid, well-made, but not designed to withstand a determined man with a knack for getting out of places he shouldn't be.

He had broken out of worse.

After fishing a small metal pin from the hem of his tattered tunic that he'd hidden away, he slipped it into the keyhole, feeling for the tumblers. One. Two. Three. A twist, a slow press of pressure, and—

Click.

The lock gave way with a quiet, satisfying snick.

He allowed himself the barest ghost of a smirk. Still got it.

Mathieu straightened, rolling his shoulders as he pressed the door open just enough to peer outside. It was empty.

That was interesting. Where was everyone?

For all the urgency he'd witnessed, he half-expected to find guards stationed outside his room, waiting for him to try something stupid. Instead, the corridor stretched long and silent, flickering torchlight casting shifting shadows along the polished stone floor.

He slipped out, closing the door softly behind him.

"Good thing I didn't kick it down, then", he thought to himself. No one was around to see it.

His smirk faded as he took in the stillness. The silence felt wrong—not like a castle at rest, but like one holding its breath.

Something was happening, something no one wanted him to see. So, naturally, he had to see it.

He stuck to the walls, keeping to the edges where the flickering torchlight couldn't quite reach. His ears were sharp, tuned to the sound of footsteps, whispers, anything.

Then—movement.

Two small, darting shapes slipped across the corridor ahead, disappearing around a corner.

Ferrets.

Not ordinary ones, though. He knew better than that now. Shifters. They were heading in the same direction he was—toward the Grand Hall. That couldn't be a coincidence.

Mathieu adjusted his pace, trailing them at a distance, silently hoping they'd lead him straight to his destination without the castle intervening. He watched the sleek little creatures move with quiet efficiency, slipping into the narrow spaces between stone columns, their bodies almost too graceful, too deliberate to be mere animals.

They knew exactly where they were going.

And now, so did he.

The ferrets rounded a final corner, slipping through a small, almost hidden passage that branched off from the main corridor leading to the Grand Hall.

Mathieu followed, careful to stay out of sight.

The passage led to a narrow alcove, tucked behind the throne's right side. From here, he had a clear, unobstructed view of the hall without stepping into sight himself.

It was a perfect vantage point.

The Grand Hall stretched before him, bathed in golden candlelight. It was massive, lined with towering pillars and banners that had once signified power—now they only whispered of the past.

At the far end, the great double doors stood closed, flanked by tall, solemn guards. The queen's court had assembled before them, a silent wall of figures, their expressions unreadable.

And at the front—Améliane.

Standing before her was a man he had not seen before. Mathieu stiffened. So that's who had arrived.

The bastard didn't look like a warrior, but he carried himself like a man who had never once doubted his own authority.

Mathieu's jaw tightened as he watched and waited for answers.

The ferrets, small and unnoticed, had slipped into the chamber, scurrying across the floor before stopping near the queen's court.

Mathieu stayed where he was—hidden in the shadows of the alcove behind and to the right of the throne waiting to see what he could learn.

Whatever this was, it was important.

Mathieu remained perfectly still in the alcove, watching, listening. He had always been good at that—reading a room, feeling the shift of tension in the air before words were ever spoken.

And this? This was a battlefield. Not of swords and bloodshed, but of words and quiet, sharpened blades hidden behind smooth, honeyed voices.

The man before Améliane was dangerous. Not in the way of warriors, not in the way of killers, but in the way of men who wielded power like a noose and knew precisely how tight to pull it.

Mathieu watched the way he baited her, the way his every movement was calculated. A man who was used to being obeyed.

But Améliane did not bow. She stood, shoulders squared, gaze sharp, her expression unreadable. There was something beneath the stillness.

This was personal.

The court watched in silence. Some in human form, some in their animal shapes, but all of them standing in quiet unity behind her. Even from the shadows, Mathieu could see the way Renaud had tensed, the way Élodie's amusement barely masked the sharp edges of her distaste. The way none of them had so much as twitched when the man seated himself upon the throne. A throne he had no right to touch—let alone sit upon.

Then it happened.

Edric pulled her close.

Mathieu's fingers curled into a fist before he even realized it, his jaw tightening as he watched the way his hands moved over her, possessive, practiced, entitled. The bastard touched her like she belonged to him, like he had the right.

And Améliane... she withstood it.

Not in submission. No, there was no weakness in her stillness. But she allowed it, for whatever reason. Political? Tactical? He didn't know. He only knew it made his blood hot with frustration.

Then her eyes found him hiding in the alcove and for a moment, the rest of the room disappeared.

Mathieu had been expecting—what? Embarrassment? Shame? Instead, he found himself pinned beneath a gaze so sharp, so steady, it nearly made him forget himself.

This was not a woman in need of saving. Even as the man's fingers traced her spine and slid over the rounded curve of her ass, even as his lips brushed the soft skin beneath her ear, she did not plead, did not flinch.

She only looked at Mathieu and gave the barest shake of her head. No.

And somehow, he understood.

He took a measured breath, fists unclenching.

Then, reluctantly, he stepped backward into the shadows, letting darkness swallow him whole.

Frustration thrummed hot beneath his skin as he withdrew, muscles coiled tight with unspent tension. He had questions. More than that—he had opinions.

The way the man touched her. The way she endured it. It didn't sit right with him.

Mathieu had seen women trapped before—prisoners of war, noblewomen sold off in arranged marriages, servants too afraid to speak against their masters. Améliane was not like them. She was not small, not cowering, not broken. She was fire wrapped in ice, steel beneath silk. A woman like that did not submit. Not unless she had no choice.

So, what in the godsdamned hell was this?

His mind churned, turning over everything he had seen, everything he had overheard. He needed to know the truth—why this queen, who seemed anything but powerless, was trapped in this cursed place.

After the man finally left, Mathieu lingered a moment longer.

He watched as Améliane's court moved toward her, their silent support circling like unseen armor. They checked in, speaking softly, watching for any crack in her carefully held composure. But she did not falter. Did not let them see whatever lingered beneath the surface.

She was as much a fortress as the Black Keep itself. And as her court dispersed, he watched her dismiss Renaud brusquely before she shifted in a white blur and fled from the room.

Mathieu exhaled sharply, the tension in his body refusing to settle. He needed answers. So, he turned and slipped away.

He moved swiftly through the corridors, mind racing. He should have stayed and sought out Renaud or Élodie but the sight of the man's hands on her—he had needed to move, to get away before his temper overrode his sense.

His feet barely made a sound as he slipped through the twisting passageways, retracing his path toward the guest chambers. But as he rounded a corner, something made him stop.

A presence.

Not the kind that announced itself with movement or breath. No, this was something older, something that had simply been there, waiting.

Mathieu turned; pulse steady but keenly aware of the weight that had settled over the air.

A man stood a few paces away, partially bathed in shadow. Or something close to a man.

He was tall, robed in black, with mahogany skin and eyes like still water—too calm, too deep. Unmoving, unblinking. Watching. His hands, clasped around a book with no words, did not fidget, did not flex—they simply rested, as if they had done so for an eternity.

His face was sharp with cheekbones casting long shadows beneath the torchlight. But it was his eyes that held Mathieu frozen—dark, bottomless, and knowing.

Mathieu tensed.

"You should not be here," the man murmured, his voice a thread of sound, distant and near all at once.

Mathieu let out a short, dry laugh. "I get that a lot."

The man tilted his head slightly, his long silver-threaded locs swaying. The motion almost unnatural, like a marionette guided by invisible strings. "You are not like the others who have come."

Something cold curled in Mathieu's stomach. "And who exactly are you?"

"I have always been here."

Mathieu's jaw tightened. "That's not an answer."

The man's lips curved slightly. Not a smile. Something else.

Mathieu held his gaze, waiting.

A moment stretched between them, thick with something Mathieu couldn't name.

Then the man took a slow step forward. "Tell me, traveler," he murmured, "have you heard the songs?"

Mathieu frowned. "What songs?"

The man's gaze did not waver. "The ones sung in dimly lit taverns, whispered in the halls of kings. The ones about a queen who ruled the mist-laden coast. A queen whose throne was stolen. A queen cursed to remain in a place that does not let go."

Mathieu's pulse ticked once, sharp and precise.

A queen.

The lost Queen of Belmara.

He had heard the tales. Half-myth, half-tragedy. A powerful ruler cast down by betrayal, trapped in a fate no one could confirm or deny.

It had always been just that—a story.

True believers argued that there had been a queen. They said the queen's consort had simply had her murdered—eliminating her in the most efficient way possible and taking the throne unchallenged. She had disappeared in a single night, leaving no body, no proof—just silence. Mathieu himself had always assumed it was just a story. A queen stolen from her throne, lost to time, waiting to be freed? It was the kind of tragedy that poets loved, the kind of tale that made for a haunting melody in dimly lit taverns.

But standing here, in the heart of Eldrenoire, with the weight of its magic pressing against his skin, with the echo of her silver eyes still burning in his mind—he was no longer so sure.

Mathieu inhaled slowly. "Who are you?" he asked again, quieter now.

This time, the man did not hesitate.

"I am Alaric," he said, inclining his head slightly. "Keeper of Eldrenoire, the Black Keep."

The title settled over Mathieu like a breath of cold air.

"And you?" Alaric continued, his voice softer now. "Are you here by fate, I wonder? Or by folly?"

Mathieu exhaled, his mouth pressing into a firm line. "That depends," he murmured. "Which one gets me out of here?"

Alaric's lips curved again, that same eerie, knowing almost-smile.

"Neither" he said simply.

And then, before Mathieu could blink, he was gone—vanished into the shadows, as if he had never been there at all.

CHAPTER 11

Améliane

The live mouse in the birdcage was tradition.

Not a joke. Not a message. A quiet code born of necessity during the first year of the curse—back when she had spent three straight days in her cat form, mute and unfindable, curled into silence while grief hollowed her out.

When she'd finally shifted back, Renaud had all but snapped. He hadn't yelled—he never did—but the fury in his voice had cracked like a blade against stone. Not because she'd disappeared, but because he hadn't known whether she was alive.

They devised the signal after that.

A live mouse, placed delicately in the empty birdcage near her hearth, meant: *I am alive. I do not wish to be found.*

No one else knew. No one else needed to. And when her court began whispering in confusion after Edric's visit—when they asked where their queen had gone—Renaud simply lifted the latch, opened the birdcage, and released the mouse into the rose garden.

She had not returned to her human form since.

The cat was easier. The cat did not have to explain. The cat could vanish, sleek and silent, into the forgotten corners of Eldrenoire and be left alone.

So, she had.

It had been three days since the throne room. Three days since Edric's hands and his performance. Three days since *Mathieu* had watched.

She didn't want to think about that. Not the way his gaze had fixed on her. Not the storm she had seen in his eyes when Edric had touched her like something owned.

She paced the halls now, paws silent on stone, tail flicking with tension she refused to name.

Eldrenoire did not ask questions. It simply opened doors she wanted open, sealed others shut, and let her roam like a specter through its endless, haunted halls.

Let them wonder. Let them wait.

She would shift back when she was ready.

She spent the days wandering.

Not aimlessly, but without a destination she cared to name. At first glance, newcomers might mistake the castle grounds for a crumbling ruin, but beyond the gate, they found a landscape lush and deceptively serene. Eldrenoire had a talent for looking like paradise while feeling like a prison.

She prowled the gardens at dawn, where silver dew clung to crimson petals like blood that hadn't decided if it wanted to stain. She tested the boundaries of the curse again, nudging her way past the outer hedgerows and through the iron archways, waiting to see if—somehow—they would let her pass.

They never did.

A soft, unseen wall would rise up the moment she crossed the threshold, and the hairs along her spine would lift in silent warning. She'd freeze, ears twitching, and then slowly, with an air of disdain only a feline could manage, she would turn and stroll back as if she hadn't just tried to escape for the hundredth time.

She napped in the sun when it suited her. Not because she was tired—but because rage needed somewhere to go, and she had long ago learned that stillness was one of its sharpest edges.

And when stillness failed—she hunted.

It was not her habit. Améliane did not often indulge the full instinct of her cursed form. She had long since mastered the art of moving through the castle with elegance rather than base predation. But on the second day, after watching a rabbit flit along the outer edge of the rose garden, something inside her snapped.

She pounced.

Clean kill. Swift.

She didn't eat it. She simply stood there, chest rising and falling with tightly controlled breath, the rabbit limp between her teeth, until the fury inside her calmed just enough to let go.

At night she climbed the ivy-covered trellis to her chambers. The balcony doors were left open—always. Renaud made sure of it, his own quiet ritual of trust.

She would shift just long enough to bathe—sinks, basins, and scalding water—trying to scrub away the memory of Edric's hands. Then she would crawl into the massive bed in the center of her rooms and sleep in her human form until just before dawn, when dreams became sharp and real and her body remembered fear.

Each time, she shifted again before the sun could catch her and fled.

By the fourth morning, her claws had dulled from stone. Her muscles ached from disuse in all the wrong places. Her pride throbbed like a bruise beneath her ribs. She was no closer to feeling whole.

She was curled beneath the ivy lattice in the east garden when Renaud found her.

The sun was just cresting the far edge of the keep, gilding the treetops in gold. Her ears twitched before he even spoke. He moved like silence personified, but she'd always known his footfalls.

She did not lift her head.

"I'm beginning to think you've forgotten how to shift back," Renaud said quietly, folding his arms as he leaned against the stone archway nearby.

She flicked her tail once. Deliberately.

"I mean it," he added, glancing at her. "Another day or two and I am going to fetch a very large ball of yarn."

Améliane gave him a long, unimpressed blink.

He huffed a laugh—low, warm, almost fond—but it didn't reach his eyes. "You've made your point."

No response.

"You're angry," he continued, voice still low. "You're humiliated. And you want to be left alone. Fine." His gaze drifted to the trellised wall above her. "But you're not the only one carrying the weight of that visit."

Her tail flicked again. Sharper this time.

"I stood there," he said. "And I didn't draw steel."

That got her attention. Her ears swiveled toward him, her head rising ever so slightly.

"I wanted to," Renaud said. "I wanted to tear his hands from you. I still do."

She sat up then, slowly, regal even as a feline. Her frosted silver gaze met his with something unreadable, something halfway between accusation and gratitude.

"But I held back," he reminded her. "Not because I lacked rage—but because I knew you wouldn't want the blade drawn. And I serve *you*."

Silence stretched.

The wind stirred the ivy. Somewhere in the distance, a hawk cried.

He stepped closer.

"I know what this is, Améliane. I know what this shape means." He crouched, bringing himself closer to eye level with her. "It means you're hurting. It means you're hiding. But you don't get to stay here forever."

Her eyes narrowed.

"You are not a pet. You are not prey." His voice dropped. "And you are not broken."

She let out a slow breath through her nose. A quiet, barely-there sigh. Then padded past him, slipping into the open door of the east wing without a sound.

He watched her go, the barest smile touching his lips. "Welcome back, Your Majesty."

The salon was warmer than usual, the hearth throwing dancing shadows across the inlaid floor. Afternoon light filtered through stained glass, spilling fractured color across the far wall. It was a rare moment of ease in a place that had too few.

Élodie lounged sideways across a velvet chaise, flicking a silver coin between her fingers with practiced ease. Margot sat curled near the fire in fox form, her tail twitching with every toss. And Laurent was winning.

"I'm just saying," he drawled, examining his cards with theatrical suspicion, "if this were a game of actual consequence, you'd be hopeless."

"You say that every time you cheat," Élodie replied without looking up.

"I say that because it's true."

Margot let out a small huff, then shifted mid-stretch—graceful as always—until she was human again, seated cross-legged and scowling. "You palmed the queen of moons."

Laurent clutched his chest in mock offense. "How *dare* you accuse me of such a thing. I am wounded."

"You'll be more than wounded if I find another card up your sleeve," Élodie muttered.

The door creaked open.

None of them turned at first, too caught in the rhythm of bickering and firelight.

Then Margot stilled. Her nostrils flared.

Élodie was already halfway to her feet when Améliane stepped into the room.

No ceremony. No announcement.

Just presence.

Her gown was simple but finely cut, the muted blue silk skimming along her figure as though the fabric itself remembered who she was. Her dark hair was pinned in a loose twist at her nape, a single curl trailing over her collarbone. She wore no crown. She did not need one.

Élodie smiled—slow and sharp. "There she is."

Améliane stepped fully into the room, spine straight, every inch a queen once more. "I see you've kept yourselves busy."

"Laurent's been cheating," Margot offered helpfully.

"I was winning," Laurent corrected, rising with a bow more graceful than sincere. "But only to keep morale high."

Améliane arched a brow. "Ah. How noble of you."

Laurent shrugged. "I do what I can."

She moved toward the hearth, the fire warming her as she approached, and something in her settled. Her court made space for her instinctively—not out of fear, but something deeper. Respect. Recognition.

She didn't sit. Instead, she stood with one hand resting lightly on the mantel, her gaze sweeping over the three of them with quiet calculation.

"So," she said at last, her tone deceptively light. "Did I miss anything useful while I was... elsewhere?"

Laurent leaned against the back of the chaise, arms crossed, expression deliberately casual. "Only the part where your mysterious houseguest has been wandering the corridors for days trying to find you."

Améliane raised an eyebrow. "How tragic. I'm sure he enjoyed the scenery."

Laurent's mouth twitched. "He's starting to take it personally. The castle won't stop shifting the halls on him."

"Then perhaps the castle is smarter than he is," she murmured, turning her attention to the fire.

Élodie spoke next, her voice lower, more measured. "He spoke with Alaric."

That earned Améliane's attention. Her gaze snapped back to them. "When?"

"The day of Edric's visit," Élodie said. "He told me in the garden. Didn't seem to realize what it meant, only that it was strange. But... he suspects. He didn't say it aloud, but he knows. Or he's very close."

Améliane's lips pressed into a thin line. Her fingers curled slightly on the edge of the mantle, then smoothed out again. "Of course he does," she said quietly.

Margot studied her, something sly flickering in her amber eyes. "So... what are you going to do?"

Améliane didn't answer at first. She turned toward the room, her posture once again that of a queen not yet ready to yield her crown—only sharpen it.

"If he guesses," she said softly, "then I owe him some answers."

Then, more clearly, "Until then, let him wonder."

Laurent's smile returned, small and sharp. Élodie said nothing, but her gaze lingered on the queen a moment longer.

A flicker passed through Améliane's silver eyes—barely there.

Let him wonder, yes.

But part of her already knew. He wouldn't wonder for long.

Améliane left the salon in silence, her steps echoing softly against the marble as she made her way through Eldrenoire's long corridor. The air was hushed, the castle unusually still—expectant, almost. As if it were holding its breath.

When she turned the final corner, her chambers stood just ahead. A familiar guard stood outside—Renaud's second-in-command, a lanky, sharp-eyed soldier named Thorne. He straightened when he saw her and gave a shallow bow.

"Your Majesty," he said, then pushed open the door before she could reach for it. "Let me check inside first."

Améliane arched a brow, "I've been sneaking in through the balcony for four days," she said mildly, stepping aside as he swept into the room. "Perhaps check there instead."

He paused mid-step, looking mildly affronted. "You were what?"

"Relax," she said dryly. "I'm rather good at landing on my feet."

Thorne made a choked sound before stalking through the space, checking corners, drapes, under the bed. She folded her arms and waited.

"Well?" she asked when he reemerged. "Any bloodthirsty traitors hiding in my wardrobe?"

"Just a rather sullen looking ballgown," he replied.

She gave him a faint smile.

Thorne stepped aside to let her in. "Door will remain guarded. Renaud's orders."

"Of course it is."

She slipped inside, letting the door fall shut behind her.

For the first time in four days, she wasn't slinking in after sunset to collapse on her bed. She stood in the center of the room, her fingertips brushing the carved edge of the vanity.

This was not the true chamber she had once claimed in Miralys, but a reflection—rebuilt and warped by the curse inside Eldrenoire. The hearth flickered low, the scent of smoke curling gently through the air.

She turned toward it, letting the quiet press in.

And then—voices.

She stilled.

Just beyond the door, muffled but unmistakable, came a low voice. Masculine. Frustrated.

Mathieu.

"I just need to speak with her."

A pause.

Thorne's voice, calm as always, "Her Majesty is resting."

"She's awake," Mathieu countered. "I heard her come in."

"She's resting," Thorne repeated. "Consciousness is not the same as availability."

"Just... tell her I came by."

"I'll be sure to add it to her list of many pressing concerns," Thorne replied.

Another pause. Then footsteps, heavy and reluctant, retreating down the corridor.

Améliane exhaled slowly, crossing the room. She sank into the nearest chair, the hem of her gown spilling across the floor like shadows. Her fingers curled lightly against the armrest.

She stared at the fire for a long while before sliding into her nightgown and crawling beneath the covers of her bed.

Morning came slowly, golden light spilling across the floor in quiet beams that crept past her drawn curtains. Améliane stirred beneath the covers, blinking up at the carved canopy above her bed. For the first time in days she hadn't crept out before dawn. She had slept.

It felt strange. Indulgent.

There was a knock—two sharp taps, then a pause, followed by the soft creak of the door opening.

"Good, you're human," Élodie's voice said, dry as ever. "We brought breakfast. And gossip."

Améliane pushed herself up on one elbow as Élodie swept in, Margot following behind her with a tray balanced on one hand and a linen-wrapped bundle under the other.

"Tell me the gossip is edible," Améliane murmured.

"It comes with pastries," Margot said cheerfully, gliding toward the sitting area.

Améliane sat up fully as the tray was placed on a low table near the hearth. Steam curled up from the silver teapot, and beside it were warm fruit pastries, a selection of cheeses, and a delicate plate of honey-glazed plums. Her stomach twisted—part nerves, part hunger.

"You're spoiling me," she said, though her voice lacked true protest.

Élodie moved to the wardrobe, pulling open the doors with practiced ease. "Renaud said to make sure you were properly bathed and fed. His words, not mine. Personally, I think he's just afraid you'll disappear back into the hedges if left unattended."

"I don't disappear," Améliane said, arching a brow. "I retreat."

"Semantics," Élodie said, selecting a gown and laying it over the dressing screen. "Still, better to keep your claws dulled. In case your favorite consort-turned-tyrant makes another surprise visit."

Améliane ignored that and reached for the tea.

Margot had already slipped into the bathing room. Moments later, the sound of water running filled the air, accompanied by the soft clatter of glass bottles and porcelain jars being arranged along the tub's rim.

"Rose oil or cedarwood?" Margot called out.

"Neither," Améliane replied. "Just hot water. No fragrance."

There was a pause. Then, "No jasmine?"

Améliane's gaze flicked toward the hearth. "Absolutely not."

Margot emerged a moment later with a sheepish smile and a towel draped over her arm. "Had to ask."

Élodie shot her a look but said nothing.

Améliane leaned back in her chair, wrapping both hands around her teacup. The warmth seeped into her fingers, grounding her.

There was peace in this room. Familiarity. The low murmur of trusted voices, the scent of rising steam, the glint of morning sun against polished glass. Her court might be cursed. Her kingdom stolen. But this—this morning ritual—was hers.

Steam rose in delicate tendrils as Améliane stepped into the tub, the hot water lapping at her calves before she sank beneath the surface. The bath was blissfully unadorned, exactly as she'd requested. No petals, no oils. Just heat.

She tilted her head back against the smooth rim, eyes closing for a moment as warmth soaked into bone and sinew. The tension in her shoulders began to ease.

Margot lingered near the edge, humming tunelessly as she arranged fresh linens and a silk robe on the bench.

Élodie, seated on the edge of the vanity, crossed one leg over the other and examined her nails. "You know, if you'd just married a dull provincial lord instead of a power-hungry golden boy, you could be in a sun-drenched villa right now. A glass of wine in hand. Possibly surrounded by handsome footmen who follow orders."

Améliane cracked one eye open. "I did marry a dull provincial lord. He just happened to have big dreams."

Margot snorted.

"Touché," Élodie said, smirking.

The banter settled over them like an old, familiar cloak, softening the silence that had clung to Améliane for days. Here, in this room, she wasn't the cursed queen. She wasn't the woman held in a gilded prison by a man who once called her beloved.

She was just Améliane.

When the bathwater began to cool, Margot offered her a linen towel and turned her back with practiced grace. Élodie busied herself with arranging the gown she'd chosen earlier—a dark plum velvet embroidered with gold thread, understated but imposing. Not quite armor, but close enough.

Améliane stepped from the tub, water slicking down her skin. Margot moved to help her dry, dabbing gently at her arms and shoulders. Élodie handed her the silk robe without a word.

They moved in tandem, familiar and unintrusive. They didn't speak of Edric again. Or Mathieu. Or the fire that still burned quietly behind Améliane's eyes.

Once dried and robed, Améliane moved to the mirror. Her reflection stared back—pale but composed, grey eyes unreadable beneath the sweep of damp lashes.

Élodie approached with a brush. "Hair up, I assume?"

Améliane nodded. "Tightly."

Margot fastened the back of the gown while Élodie twisted Améliane's dark chestnut hair into a sleek coil, securing it with a comb inlaid with mother-of-pearl.

"I hate how good you look when you're barely holding it together," Margot muttered behind her, fastening the final hook. "It's infuriating."

"Tragic beauty is still beauty," Élodie offered.

Améliane met her own gaze in the mirror. The woman staring back at her didn't look like someone clawing her way out of grief. She looked... like a queen.

A soft knock interrupted the quiet. Three measured raps.

Élodie's head turned toward the door. "That'll be Renaud," she said lightly. "And his ominously silent friend."

Margot arched a brow. "I'll see them in." She swept from the bathing room, her steps efficient and soundless, the plum skirts of her gown whispering across the floor.

Améliane remained at the vanity for a moment longer, letting the last traces of steam curl around her face before rising. Her shoulders rolled back into a posture of practiced regality—not forced, but chosen.

By the time she emerged into the main chamber, Élodie trailing a half-step behind, Margot was already waiting in the threshold to the adjoining sitting room.

"They're settled," Margot said with a nod. "Cassien has the usual expression—equal parts reverence and dread. Renaud looks like someone dared him to smile and he failed."

A flicker of dry amusement passed over Améliane's features. "Thank you."

She stepped into the threshold of the sitting room, glancing through the archway just long enough to confirm the men's presence—Cassien standing near the hearth, posture formal, hands folded. Renaud leaned against the mantel with his arms crossed, exuding silent judgment like it was his native language.

They both turned as she entered the room.

"Élodie. Margot," she said calmly. "That will be all."

Neither protested. Élodie offered a shallow curtsy. Margot gave a subtle nod and moved to the door, glancing once toward Cassien with a flicker of curiosity in her eyes before slipping out behind Élodie.

The door clicked shut, leaving only Améliane, Renaud, and Cassien in the firelit quiet.

Cassien bowed low as Améliane sat by the hearth, his spine straight despite the years that had etched silver into his dark beard and deepened the lines around his sharp, watchful eyes. He wore the simple leathers of a traveling courtier—neutral, unassuming, and carefully forgettable.

The kind of man kings trusted to carry delicate truths between thrones.

Edric had never suspected otherwise.

Cassien had always been the kind of man who belonged in the background of important things—an archivist by training, a Seer by birth, and, quietly, a traitor in every way that mattered. To Edric, he was still a loyal servant delivering news to a forgotten queen.

Améliane inclined her head slightly. "Cassien."

He reached into his satchel and drew out a scroll wrapped in crimson velvet, the seal unmistakable—gold wax bearing Edric's serpent crest, its coiled form stamped deep and smug.

Cassien stepped forward and offered it with both hands. "Per His Majesty's instruction," he said, voice dry as old parchment. "The report from Belmara."

Améliane accepted it, eyes scanning the seal as if it might hiss. She cracked it cleanly with a single twist of her fingers.

Behind her, Renaud moved like a blade drawn in silence. He swept the perimeter of the sitting room without a word—checking for eavesdroppers or any magical interference.

Cassien waited until the queen had unfurled the scroll before he began to speak aloud.

"Belmara continues to flourish," he said smoothly, in the lilting tone of one reciting a market report rather than a propaganda scroll. "According to the High Council, an expansion of the healer's wing has begun—funded, of course, by generous contributions from the Crown. Edric personally oversaw the ceremonial blessing of the foundation stones."

Améliane's mouth twitched, but she said nothing.

Cassien continued. "The Ordréan Empress has sent her well-wishes for the kingdom's ongoing prosperity. Trade with Vorskyr has doubled. A new naval contract has been signed with the Mireath 'independent privateers.'"

Améliane gave a soft snort.

"And," Cassien added with a faint sigh, "Edric has declared a week of celebration in honor of the birth of your sister's child. Public games, a naming feast, and a temple offering in her honor. There will be fireworks. Poetry contests. Possibly doves."

"Gods preserve us," Améliane muttered.

Cassien didn't smile. But his eyes gleamed faintly.

He flipped to the final lines, reciting them with the same impassive rhythm, "His Majesty sends his continued hopes for your wellness and spiritual reflection. And reminds you that solitude, properly embraced, can be a mirror for growth."

"Charming," she said flatly. "Did he write that himself, or did he borrow from the back of a wine bottle?"

Cassien bowed his head. "Difficult to say. His penmanship suggests intoxication."

At that moment, Renaud returned to her side. He gave a single, short nod—the room was clean. They were alone.

Améliane turned back to Cassien. The scroll now lay forgotten on the table between them.

"Well?" she said, voice quieter now. "That's the fiction. What's the truth?"

Cassien's gaze sharpened. He stepped forward, slowly, with the weight of something heavier than usual behind his eyes. He did not reach into his bag again. There would be no second scroll. That would be foolish. Dangerous.

He had committed every word to memory.

Cassien didn't hesitate. He remained standing, his voice calm but lower now—no longer that of a courtier delivering pageantry, but of a man bearing the weight of truth.

"The healer's wing is expanding," he said, "but not because Edric suddenly developed a charitable streak. The border skirmishes have worsened—raiding parties from the northern reaches, small incursions out of Rothgar. The soldiers are coming home broken more often than not."

Améliane's gaze sharpened, but she said nothing.

"The deal with Mireath was rushed through in a single night," he continued. "Their fleet now docks at Belmara's western harbors under a mercenary contract. They are not privateers—they're still just pirates. Paid hands with no loyalty, only hunger."

Renaud's jaw tightened.

Cassien went on, folding his hands behind his back. "The Ordréan Empress did send a courier. But it wasn't congratulations she delivered—it was coin. A discreet funding line, masked as a goodwill gesture. Belmara's coffers are thin. Edric's begun selling off Crown lands to hold appearances."

"And the trade with Vorskyr?" Renaud asked.

"Weapons imported under the guise of defense," Cassien said. "But it's more than that. He's stockpiling. Armoring the capital. Preparing for something."

Améliane's fingers drummed once, slowly, on the armrest. "And what do the people say?"

Cassien hesitated, then said, "The unrest grows. Quietly. Carefully. But it grows."

He stepped closer, voice softening. "The Seer population within the city has nearly tripled since last winter. Some... remember things they cannot explain. Others are simply beginning to question what doesn't quite add up. The stories that conflict. The way the castle feels wrong."

Améliane didn't move.

"There is a meeting place now," Cassien added. "Somewhere in the old quarter. I don't know who leads it, but I know what they're calling it."

He paused, letting the words settle.

"The Return."

A silence fell. Not heavy. Sharp.

Cassien did not press further. He knew the queen would ask what she wished, when she was ready.

And Améliane sat perfectly still, a queen who had waited years for a tide to turn.

"There is something you need to know," he said quietly. "Something Edric isn't saying."

Améliane stilled. So did Renaud.

And the fire behind them crackled softly, as if straining to hear what would come next.

Cassien's eyes—sharp, unwavering—met hers. "He suspects something is happening at Eldrenoire."

The words landed with precision, clean and cold.

"He doesn't know what yet. No names, no proof. But he knows the castle is... shifting." Cassien hesitated, as if weighing the wisdom of his next words. "And he knows you're no longer as isolated as he made you."

Renaud muttered a curse under his breath.

Cassien nodded. "He's begun to ask questions. About the castle. About its behavior. He's even sent word to one of his court mages—quietly, off the record. He wants to know if the curse has weakened."

Améliane's hands were still, folded in her lap like marble.

"But he's watching now," Cassien finished. "More closely than ever."

The silence that followed was not one of surprise. It was one of inevitability.

The storm, it seemed, had already begun to gather.

Cassien straightened, the flicker of tension in his frame giving way to quiet resolve. The room felt heavier now—thick with truths spoken aloud, the kind that could not be pulled back.

Améliane rose from her chair and moved toward the carved sideboard near the hearth. She withdrew a velvet pouch, the faint clink of coin muffled by the fabric, and turned to him.

"For your journey home," she said, holding it out. "And for your family."

Cassien's expression tightened with discomfort. "Your Majesty—"

"Cassien," she said quietly. "I know your loyalties. And I know what they've cost you."

He hesitated, the weight of it clear in his eyes. "I serve you because you are the rightful Queen. Not for coin."

"And I accept your loyalty," she replied. "But your children still need to eat."

A beat. Then, reluctantly, he reached for the pouch, tucking it into his coat with a nod of respect.

"I'll be back next week," he said. "If the roads remain open."

Cassien managed a faint smile, then turned for the door. Renaud moved ahead to open it—but before Cassien could step into the corridor, it flew inward with a crash.

A blur of motion barreled into the room—broad-shouldered, winded, and entirely unapologetic.

"I just need to speak with the Queen," Mathieu announced, breathless and defiant, still shaking off the guards who trailed behind him like irritated shadows.

Renaud reached for the hilt of his blade with a snarl, but Améliane lifted a hand—sharp, precise. Enough.

Mathieu straightened, looking like he was bracing for a fight, a retort, anything—

And then he saw her.

CHAPTER 12

Mathieu

H e hadn't meant to crash into the room like a madman. But after four days of chasing shadow corridors, four days of unanswered questions and silent halls, four days of wondering if she was avoiding him or simply gone—he couldn't bring himself to wait another moment.

And now he stood there, breathless, braced for a fight that never came.

Because she was there.

Améliane.

Alive. Whole. Regal and remote, wrapped in velvet and silence.

The weight in his chest eased so suddenly it left him dizzy.

His gaze swept over her, and the awareness hit like a blade unsheathed: she looked untouchable. Dangerous. And so impossibly beautiful that something in him shifted. Not the kind of beauty that begged to be claimed—the kind that warned you to tread carefully or bleed.

Her hair was pinned back, her chin lifted in that effortless way. The woman carried power like a second skin. And she was standing right there, staring at him like he was either incredibly brave or incredibly stupid.

He'd take either. He'd earned both.

Still, some part of him wanted to move toward her. Say something clever. Close the damn space between them and ask the questions that had been tearing at him since the Grand Hall.

But he couldn't move. Not with Renaud glaring at him like he was a rabid wolf who'd just bolted into the nursery.

Mathieu didn't flinch. But he did brace for impact as Renaud launched across the room like a storm given form.

"Are you out of your godsdamned mind?" the queen's personal guard roared.

Mathieu didn't even try to move. He saw the blow coming—could have ducked, countered, broken Renaud's grip—but he didn't. The impact of being slammed against the stone wall was grounding. Real.

Renaud's arm locked across his chest, one hand wrenched behind his back. A clean hold that was painful, yet controlled.

Mathieu grunted but didn't resist. He just let himself be pinned there, like a man who'd been waiting for someone to finally hit him hard enough to make sense of things.

"I should gut you," Renaud snarled, shoving harder. "You do not storm into the Queen's chambers. You do not ignore a guard's post. You do not—"

"I'm sorry," Mathieu said.

The words spilled out unbidden. Quiet. Rough.

Renaud froze.

"I was just..." Mathieu swallowed hard, forcing the rest out. "I was worried."

Silence fell.

Even the guards who had chased him stood still, their hands hovering at their weapons, uncertain whether this was about to become a bloodbath or something stranger.

Renaud eased back a fraction—not letting go but shifting enough to look at him.

Mathieu met his gaze, jaw set. The words still hung in the air, raw and ridiculous. But they were true.

Renaud studied him for a beat. Then his lip curled, equal parts scorn and disbelief.

"It's my job to worry about her," he said coldly. "You can go back to getting lost in hallways."

And he shoved Mathieu once more—just enough to make a point—before stepping back, releasing him.

Mathieu didn't move. Didn't speak.

He just stood there, pulse thudding in his ears, trying to make sense of the fact that somewhere in the span of two ridiculous, cursed, utterly maddening weeks, worrying about her had become second nature.

Which was absurd, of course. But then again, so was everything about her.

Silence reigned for a moment longer.

A heavy, humming sort of quiet—the kind that crackled with all the things no one dared say. Even the fire in the hearth seemed to hold its breath, unwilling to interrupt whatever was about to unfold.

Mathieu didn't look away. He couldn't. Not when she was standing there like judgment in velvet, her silver eyes cutting straight through him.

Then, at last, she moved.

Améliane stepped forward—graceful, unhurried, every line of her posture radiating command. The fabric of her gown whispered with each step, the faint scent of cedar and heat trailing in her wake. She came to a stop just a few paces from him, tilting her head ever so slightly.

"I'm fine," she said at last.

Her voice was cool, smooth—tinged with something that might have been gratitude if it hadn't been so perfectly composed. Her eyes narrowed just slightly, and her lips curved in a faint, bemused smile.

"But thank you," she added, "for your...concern."

It wasn't cruel. Not exactly. But there was no mistaking the amusement laced through her tone—like a queen humoring a knight who'd just tripped over his own sword.

And gods help him, it stung.

Just for a second, the flicker of it crossed his face. A flash of something real, unguarded—something he hadn't meant to show.

She saw it. Of course she did.

The flicker in his eyes hadn't lasted long—barely a heartbeat—but it had been enough.

Améliane's expression shifted. Just slightly. A softening around the mouth, the faintest release of tension in her shoulders. The edge in her voice dulled.

"I know I owe you some answers," she said quietly. "The conversation we started in the library... it was interrupted."

Mathieu's jaw twitched, but he said nothing.

"I haven't forgotten," she added. "And I intend to hold up my end of the bargain."

She hesitated, just long enough to make the next words feel like something carefully chosen.

"I need to speak with Renaud first. But if you're willing... join me for tea this afternoon. In the garden."

Her tone was still poised, still deliberate—but no longer distant.

An invitation, not an order. A thread held out between them.

Mathieu blinked. Their bargain.

He'd nearly forgotten it—lost beneath the weight of worry and stone walls and the sheer relief of seeing her standing in front of him again. But now her words stirred the memory: the library, her challenge, the offer of truth if he asked the right questions.

A corner of his mouth lifted.

"Well," he said, smoothing a hand over his rumpled jacket like a man reclaiming his composure, "it would be a grave offense to decline a royal invitation. Especially one that comes with tea."

Améliane arched an eyebrow.

"Hopefully the garden will be easier to navigate than your charmingly vindictive hallways," he added, voice lighter now.

He offered a quick, fluid bow—more sincere than mocking this time—and turned to go.

As he passed Renaud, he caught the man's gaze—then saw it shift, just briefly, toward the queen. An eyebrow lifted. Not in surprise, exactly, but in something that looked an awful lot like judgment wrapped in disbelief.

Mathieu smirked to himself as he stepped into the corridor.

He didn't know what was waiting for him that afternoon. But for the first time in days, he had somewhere to be.

And yet, even after the door had closed behind him, the moment still clung like smoke.

What in all the godsdamned hells had that been?

He'd stormed in like a man possessed, got himself slammed into a wall by the Queen's guard, and then—just to really complete the spectacle—he'd apologized. Apologized. Like some lovesick errand boy caught trespassing in the stables.

And all because she was standing there—breathing, glaring, real.

He'd never unraveled so fast in his life. He was supposed to be calculated. Controlled. Detached.

Not this.

Not tangled up in a silver-eyed woman with steel in her spine and grief coiled behind her smile.

He just walked—half to clear his head, half because Eldrenoire seemed determined to make sure no one ever left a room the same way they entered.

The corridors twisted again, warping like a slow, living thing. The air hummed faintly. He passed a portrait he was sure he'd seen three turns ago—only now the woman's eyes were following him.

"Not even subtle," he muttered.

He rounded another bend—and nearly walked straight into someone.

A young man stepped out of a narrow pantry, cheeks flushed, hair mussed, shirt half-tucked like he'd just lost a fight with a clothesline.

Laurent followed a second later, smoothing a hand over his perfectly disheveled hair and adjusting the collar of his shirt with casual flair.

They both froze.

Mathieu raised an eyebrow, taking in the scene with an expression that was equal parts amusement and exhausted resignation.

"Please tell me that wasn't the emergency food supply," he said dryly.

Laurent's eyes narrowed while the young man behind him ducked his head before vanishing back through another door, wisely removing himself from the line of fire.

Mathieu didn't look away.

"Shocking, I'm sure" Laurent said, tone light but edged.

Mathieu leaned against the wall, arms crossed. "I've seen a warlord try to seduce a fire mage with a chicken leg. You'll have to try harder."

A beat passed. Then Laurent smiled—slow and genuine, just for a moment.

"Don't look so scandalized. Everyone needs a hobby," he replied, brushing a nonexistent speck from his tunic.

Mathieu shrugged. "Not my pantry."

A beat passed.

Laurent's expression shifted—no mockery, no mask. Just something surprised. And almost... grateful.

"Well," he said, voice returning to its usual purr, "maybe you're not completely unbearable after all."

"Give it time," Mathieu said, pushing off the wall. "I'll wear you down."

Laurent lingered in the corridor, watching Mathieu with a curious tilt to his head—like he was reappraising him, just a little.

"I was just headed to lunch," he said casually. "Élodie and Margot have taken over the kitchen again. Gods help the staff."

Mathieu glanced down the corridor, then back at him.

Laurent's grin widened. "You look like you could use a meal. Or company. Possibly both."

There was no judgment in his tone—just an easy sort of offer, thrown out like a rope across unfamiliar waters.

He lifted a brow. "Coming?"

After four days of solitude—four days of pacing endless corridors, whispering curses at doors that didn't lead where they should, and asking questions that echoed into silence—Mathieu surprised himself by nodding.

"Sure," he said. "Why not."

Laurent flashed a pleased grin and turned without ceremony, leading the way down a side corridor that Mathieu recognized almost immediately. The scent of flour and woodsmoke stirred the memory—warm cake, a flickering hearth, and a queen with frosting on her lip. The hum of activity swelled with each step until the hallway opened into the castle's sprawling kitchen, now vibrant and alive in the light of day.

The room bustled with energy. Servants in plain linen moved like clockwork, some hauling sacks of grain, others peeling root vegetables or kneading dough on flour-dusted worktables. The air was rich with the scent of butter and roasted meat, herbs and yeast, and something tangy he couldn't quite place. Near the center, a towering rack of copper pots gleamed like armor in the firelight.

In the far back corner of the kitchen, tucked around a long, well-worn butcher's table repurposed for more casual gatherings, sat Élodie and Margot. They looked like they owned the place.

Margot had her legs propped on the bench, a half-eaten fig tart in one hand and a wedge of cheese in the other. Élodie sat primly beside her, sipping something from a glass goblet—wine, judging by the color—and occasionally spearing a slice of pear with the tip of her dagger like it was cutlery.

The food on the table looked almost decadent: platters of cured meats, a crusty round loaf of bread already half-consumed, a dish of whipped honey butter, ripe peaches halved and drizzled with cream, and a pile of roasted mushrooms sprinkled with something green and fragrant.

Margot glanced up as they approached and raised her teacup in greeting. "Look what the Keep dragged in."

Mathieu eased into the empty chair beside Margot, who offered a sly smirk but didn't scoot over making him wedge in like he belonged there. Across the table, Élodie arched a brow at him in greeting, tearing off a hunk of bread and popping it into her mouth without breaking eye contact.

Laurent slid into the seat beside Élodie with a theatrical sigh and immediately helped himself to a slice of soft cheese. "You'll all be relieved to know," he announced, "that the pantry remains intact. Mostly."

"I thought I heard giggling behind the barrels," Élodie muttered.

"Unsubstantiated rumor," Laurent replied smoothly. "And even if true, I consider it morale-boosting."

Mathieu, to his own surprise, laughed. Just a low sound—easy, unguarded. It felt... normal. Strange, considering the company.

Margot passed him a plate stacked with crusty bread and thinly sliced smoked meat. "Eat," she said, like it was an order, then added, "You look like a man who's spent four days chasing hallways."

"He has," Élodie said dryly. "Rumor has it he tried to out-stubborn the castle. Bold move."

"Foolish," Laurent corrected. "But bold."

Mathieu shrugged, reaching for the bread. "Boldly foolish," he said. "My specialty."

The group at the table chuckled, and just like that, he was part of it—sitting in the heart of a cursed castle, trading banter with a fox, a flirt, and a woman who could probably kill him with a bread knife. And somehow, it felt like the most natural thing in the world.

As the laughter faded into a lull, Mathieu took a moment to glance around.

He'd been here before, yes—but only in the quiet hush of night, stealing cake with a queen who wasn't quite a queen. In the daylight, the kitchens were something else entirely.

The vaulted ceiling arched high above them, timber beams blackened with age and smoke. Stone hearths blazed along one wall, each one with a cauldron or spit suspended over flame. The scent of roasting meat and fresh bread mingled with herbs, butter, and something faintly sweet. Cooks moved in a rhythm that spoke of long-practiced efficiency, dodging each other with trays and platters, barking instructions and snatching spices off shelves. Beyond the main prep tables, a scullery maid laughed as she tried to wrangle a goose twice her size.

It was chaos, yes—but an elegant one.

"How many people work here?" Mathieu asked, blinking at a trio of bakers who were aggressively arguing about the correct shape of a hand-pie.

Margot arched a brow, mid-sip of tea. "In the castle, or in total?"

"In total."

Laurent gestured with a half-eaten plum. "Last I counted? Just over one hundred and fifty. That's including the stables, the guardhouses, the groundskeepers, and the falconer who refuses to speak to anyone but his birds."

"And the falconer's birds," Élodie added, "are jerks."

Margot nodded solemnly. "Absolute tyrants."

Mathieu stared at them. "You're telling me there are over a hundred and fifty people maintaining a cursed castle that no one can leave?"

"Some of them are illusions. Or echoes. Or possibly ghosts," Laurent said. "But most of them are quite real. Mostly."

"And you feed all of them? How does a cursed castle get supplies? Trade caravans?" Mathieu asked, incredulous, "Invisible delivery goats?"

Élodie smirked. "Don't mock the goats. They're more efficient than half the royal couriers I've met."

Laurent leaned back with a dramatic sigh. "The truth is... Eldrenoire takes care of its own. Supplies arrive. Orchards produce fruit. The game returns to the forest. The larders are never empty for long."

"It's like the castle wants to survive," Margot added, passing him a slice of cheese. "Even if the people in it don't always know how."

Mathieu frowned, a little unsettled. "That's not how reality works."

"Good thing this place isn't terribly fond of reality, then," Laurent said, grinning.

"So... Eldrenoire isn't real?" Mathieu asked slowly, skepticism clear in his voice as he set down his teacup.

The conversation stilled for a beat.

Laurent tilted his head. "That depends on your definition of *real*, doesn't it?"

Élodie picked up a piece of dried fruit, examining it as if it held secrets. "The castle exists. You're sitting in it, aren't you?"

"That wasn't really the question," Mathieu muttered.

Margot leaned forward, elbows on the table, voice low and wry. "You want someone to tell you what this place is. What the curse is. What the rules are. But the only rules here are the ones you figure out for yourself."

"And just when you think you understand them," Laurent added cheerfully, "they change."

Mathieu looked around the table, frowning. "So, none of you know?"

"Oh, we know," Élodie said. "What we've lived. What we've seen. What we've survived."

"But if you want a map of the curse," Margot continued, "or a spell to undo it... no one here can give it."

Laurent smiled without humor. "We can only confirm what you already know."

Mathieu sat back, uneasy. "That's... not comforting."

"Eldrenoire isn't comforting," Élodie said softly, her eyes meeting his. "It's watchful. It listens. It remembers."

Mathieu didn't respond. Couldn't.

Mathieu leaned back in his chair, chewing over the words. "So that's it, then," he said aloud. "You can't *tell* me what you know if I don't already know it."

The group didn't respond. Not with words.

Margot tilted her head just slightly. Élodie's expression didn't change, but she stopped chewing. Laurent set his cup down—quietly.

Mathieu blinked, the realization settling over him like a slow burn. "Right," he said, almost to himself. "Right. It's not about asking."

He looked around the table, a little breathless with the quiet clarity of it.

"It's about *confirming*."

The silence that had fallen over the table wasn't hostile. But it was... watchful. Cautious. Like the castle itself had leaned in to listen.

He glanced between them—Laurent sipping wine too slowly, Margot unusually still, Élodie's expression blank but her fingers tense against her goblet.

No one asked what he meant. No one filled the quiet with another joke or sly remark. They were waiting.

Mathieu leaned back in his chair, one hand resting loosely against the edge of the table. His mind, however, wasn't still.

It moved, fast and sharp, turning over everything he had seen since arriving in this godsdamned place.

A cursed castle that no one seemed to remember.

Rooms that shifted, hallways that looped, voices that whispered through stone.

A queen who ruled without a crown. A court of shapeshifters bound to her service. A kingdom no one named.

The way the castle responded to Améliane—bending, adjusting, almost listening.

The way no one ever said what she was queen *of*....

And then there was Alaric.

That maddening, unsettling creature who carried a book with no words and spoke in riddles like they were prophecy. He had asked if Mathieu had heard the tales. The songs. The stories of the lost queen.

Mathieu hadn't known then—not really.

But now... This was his chance. His test.

He drew a quiet breath, the words forming like a lit match in the back of his throat.

"Is Améliane," he said carefully, "the lost Queen of Belmara?"

The effect was immediate.

Margot's hand froze mid-reach. Élodie's goblet stopped just shy of her lips. Laurent... didn't move at all. Not even a blink. Just stared at him with eyes too sharp to be called amused.

Mathieu felt the air change. No gasps. No theatrics. Just a collective, silent shift. Like a thousand threads had suddenly pulled taut.

No one spoke right away.

Then, finally—Élodie set her glass down with a delicate clink and said, very softly, "You already know the answer to that."

Laurent tilted his head, a slow smile creeping across his face. "Well, look at that," he murmured. "He *is* paying attention."

Margot gave a quiet exhale—something like relief, something like resignation.

He'd asked. And now he knew.

The air around the table shifted—palpable, heavy with something unsaid. Not just confirmation. Not even relief.

Power.

Mathieu had figured one of Eldrenoire's rules. And now they all knew it. He wasn't just another stray the castle had picked up for amusement. He was something else.

A variable.

Margot leaned back slowly, her gaze lingering on him with new weight. "None of the others ever even came close," she said, almost to herself.

Laurent made a sound—not quite a laugh. More a breath caught between disdain and memory. He reached for a plum, examining it like it had offended him. "Bastian came close."

Margot rolled her eyes. "Barely."

"He read poetry to her like it was a spell," Laurent said dryly, slicing into the fruit with a dagger he had just pulled from his belt.

Élodie gave him a look. "We all know you hated Bastian."

Laurent smiled, sharp and a little bitter. "I had good reason."

There was a beat of silence.

Then, softly, Élodie said, "He did love her."

Laurent's jaw tensed. "Then he shouldn't have left."

Margot's eyes narrowed. "He chose to forget."

"And the castle let him go," Laurent said, voice low and edged. "Which tells you everything you need to know."

No one argued.

And across the table, Mathieu sat very, very still.

Because something in Laurent's tone wasn't just bitterness.

Mathieu leaned back in his chair, exhaling slowly. "I'd ask who Bastian is," Mathieu said dryly, "but I'm starting to get it—no straight answers unless I already know them, and cryptic riddles if I'm lucky. Delightful system you've got here."

Margot gave him a mock salute with her teacup. "He's learning."

Élodie's gaze flicked to him, unreadable. "We wouldn't tell you even if we could," she said. "That's the Queen's story to tell."

At the mention of her, Mathieu's thoughts snapped back—like a tether yanked taut.

The queen.

Tea.

His eyes dropped to the table, where the remnants of lunch had long since vanished, dishes cleared away while they'd lingered in memory and myth.

He twisted in his chair, eyes searching the nearest wall—there it was. A gilded clock tucked high on a shelf between bundles of drying herbs.

The hands pointed to a quarter past two.

Shit.

"Well," he said, rising and brushing crumbs from his shirt, "Her Majesty invited me to tea at three, so I'll have my chance. I should probably start now. Last time I was in the gardens, the hedges kept shifting and I spent forty minutes trapped between a statue of a weeping saint and a bench that wouldn't stop moving."

Margot arched a brow. "Do try not to offend her this time."

"No promises," he said. "But I'll aim for charm."

Laurent lifted his wineglass in a mock toast. "May the castle grant you mercy."

"No one else does," Mathieu muttered—and headed for the door.

Mathieu left the kitchens with a half-hearted wave. He was still reeling—half from what he'd learned, half from what he hadn't.

He moved fast, weaving through Eldrenoire's endless, labyrinthine corridors with more instinct than strategy. The castle's mood was always shifting, fickle as a bored cat. Sometimes it opened doors. Sometimes it moved them. And sometimes, it simply swallowed you whole for the sport of it.

But today—today, it didn't fight him.

Corridors unfolded ahead of him like ribbon. Doors opened just as he approached. Even the hedges of the Shrouded Gardens, which had trapped him for nearly an hour the last time, parted politely this time, as if the castle itself had decided—just for now—not to play games.

He emerged into a sun-dappled clearing at the garden's heart, where a wrought iron gazebo stood framed by curling vines and tall blooms swaying in the breeze. Inside, a servant was quietly arranging the tea service: delicate porcelain cups, a silver teapot, tiny sandwiches stacked in meticulous rows. No fanfare. No guards.

The queen was not there yet.

Mathieu slowed his steps, half-expecting the hedges to close behind him, to change their minds and trap him in another maze. But the path remained open.

He crossed the garden and sank onto a stone bench just outside the gazebo, elbows on knees, gaze sweeping across the sunlit petals and climbing ivy. He exhaled once, slowly.

It was the second time he'd noticed it—the strange, shifting logic of the castle. Sometimes, Eldrenoire tried to keep him from where he wanted to go. And sometimes... it let him arrive exactly when he needed to.

CHAPTER 13

Améliane

The corridors leading to the garden were unusually still. No shifting stones beneath their feet. No sudden doors opening into other wings of the castle. Just the steady rhythm of boots on marble, the whisper of silk as her skirts moved, and the ever-present sense that Eldrenoire was... watching.

Renaud walked half a step behind her, as always, but close enough that she could feel the tension in his silence before he finally spoke.

"I still think the jasmine was him," he said quietly.

Améliane didn't look over. "You're still on this?"

Renaud's jaw ticked. "It was him. He's the only new variable."

"He was seen in the east wing that night," Renaud pressed. "Near your chambers."

"And he also wandered into three broom closets, a wine cellar, and a mirror room that led nowhere," she countered, arching a brow. "We've established the man couldn't find a straight hallway in a square room if his life depended on it."

"That doesn't clear him."

"No," she agreed. "But this does—"

She came to a stop just before the garden doors and turned to face him fully.

"He would not know the significance of jasmine," she said, soft but certain, "unless he were working for Edric."

Renaud's eyes darkened, but he didn't interrupt.

"And based on Cassien's report," she continued, "Edric suspects something has changed at Eldrenoire. The only thing that has changed is Mathieu's arrival, so Edric's suspicions make it highly unlikely that Mathieu is working for him."

"Unless he's playing a long game," Renaud muttered.

"Then he's playing it poorly," she said. "And Edric never plays poorly."

A beat of silence passed between them.

"Besides," she added, more quietly, "the castle has been different since Mathieu arrived."

Renaud's head tilted. "Different how?"

"Restless," she murmured. "But not in a way I can explain. Doors shifting when they shouldn't. Rooms I haven't seen in years opening again. Sometimes letting him pass without delay." She exhaled slowly. "It's as if Eldrenoire is... responding to him."

He frowned but said nothing.

"I don't know what it means yet," she said. "But I don't believe he left the flower."

They stood there a moment longer—just queen and guard, curse and consequence—framed by the glass doors that led into sunlight and secrets.

The doors swung open with a soft creak, the scent of warm blossoms and sunlit stone drifting in. Eldrenoire's gardens stretched before them—lush, sprawling, and half-tamed, as if the castle itself hadn't quite decided whether to cultivate or consume them.

Améliane stepped into the light, her slippers whispering against the flagstones. The breeze tugged playfully at her hair, but she ignored it. Her gaze swept the path ahead, taking in the gently shifting hedges, the vines heavy with bloom, the gazebo tucked like a secret into the garden's heart.

Renaud followed at her side now, not behind. After a few paces, he spoke again, his voice low, "How much are you going to tell him?"

She didn't answer immediately. The path forked—two identical walkways lined in flowering hedges—and for a moment she simply stood, watching the way the breeze rustled one set of leaves just a little more than the other.

"The truth," she said at last, choosing the left-hand path without hesitation.

"All of it?"

"No," she said. "Not yet."

Renaud frowned. "Then what?"

"Enough."

He gave her a look—the kind of look that said you are infuriating and brilliant and I'll still die for you in a heartbeat—and she smiled faintly.

"Trust me," she added. "He's not ready for the full story. But he's asking the right questions now. That's more than I can say for most."

They rounded the last bend.

The gazebo came into view, framed in ivy and sunlight, with the tea service already set in gleaming porcelain and silver. And just beyond, on a low stone bench in the shade, sat Mathieu.

They reached the edge of the clearing.

Améliane slowed, one hand lifting slightly to signal Renaud without looking at him. He stopped beside her in the dappled shade, silent as a shadow, his eyes already scanning the perimeter for hidden dangers.

But Améliane wasn't looking for threats.

She was watching him.

Mathieu sat on the stone bench like he'd been there for hours, though the faint tension in his shoulders told her he hadn't relaxed fully—not yet. His elbows rested on his knees, his hands loosely clasped, head tilted just enough to catch the breeze. Sunlight threaded through the canopy above, painting patterns across his broad shoulders and the dark sweep of his hair.

He looked... out of place here. And somehow, not at all.

He wore no finery. No embroidered tunic or polished boots. Just that same worn coat, trousers, and boots scuffed by battle and long roads. And yet, despite the plainness, there was something undeniably commanding in the way he held himself. A kind of quiet gravity—like a man who had once been used to command and had not yet forgotten how it felt.

There were scars on his hands—she remembered that. And more hidden beneath the fabric, carved by time and violence. He bore them like armor. Not flaunted. Not hidden. Just worn.

But it was his face that held her.

There was no smirk there now. No sarcasm. Just thought. Quiet, focused, private thought. His eyes—those strange, changeable hazel eyes—were fixed on some invisible point in the garden, their color shifting in the light like river stones. She couldn't tell if he looked expectant, or wary, or both.

Améliane released a breath she hadn't realized she was holding.

He had the look of a man who had been at war with the world—and with himself—for far too long. And yet... here he was. Waiting for her. In her cursed garden. In her cursed life.

And for one strange, suspended moment, Améliane didn't feel like a queen.

Renaud shifted beside her, just slightly. She gave the barest nod, and they stepped into the light.

Mathieu stood the moment he saw them.

It wasn't stiff or ceremonial—just instinctive. As if something in him demanded he rise when she entered a room. Or in this case, a garden.

Améliane met his gaze evenly as she approached, her skirts brushing the soft grass. Renaud kept pace beside her, shoulders squared and jaw tight.

They were halfway to the gazebo when she lifted a hand and touched Renaud's arm—lightly, but deliberately.

"You do not need to stand guard," she said softly.

He hesitated. Just for a breath.

Then his brows pulled together in a look that was equal parts protest and protectiveness.

"Renaud," she added, her tone still gentle but edged with finality. "I will be fine."

A pause. Then a sharp puff of air through his nose, followed by a brief, begrudging bow. He turned to Mathieu, his gaze positively glacial.

And then—without warning—his form rippled, blurring in a shimmer of pale light and shadow. The tall, grim-faced man vanished, replaced by a massive dire wolf the color of storm clouds and old ash.

Renaud cast one last deliberate glance at Mathieu—heavy with silent threat—then padded off into the clearing.

He curled beneath a shade tree at the garden's edge, paws tucked beneath him, golden eyes fixed on them like twin lanterns.

Mathieu, to his credit, did not flinch.

Améliane sighed loudly and rolled her eyes. "Honestly," she muttered under her breath.

She stepped forward, calm and unhurried, toward the gazebo. Her expression was schooled into something serene—but not distant. She hadn't quite reached him when Mathieu cleared his throat.

"If that's his version of letting go," he said, nodding toward the massive dire wolf glaring daggers from under the shade tree, "I'd hate to see what hovering looks like."

Améliane's lips twitched. "He can eavesdrop better in his wolf form. That's just him trying to be subtle about it."

They both turned to glance at Renaud, who—after holding their gaze for one long, deliberate beat—closed his eyes with theatrical slowness and rested his chin on his paws.

"As I said," she murmured, dry, "subtle."

Mathieu huffed a laugh. "Remind me never to try subtlety in Eldrenoire. Clearly it has a higher bar."

A brief pause settled—quiet, but not tense. Just the sort of silence that lingers between two people who have seen too much of each other, and not enough.

Then, with a crooked smile that didn't quite reach his eyes, he added, "I owe you an apology. For earlier. For... storming in like some kind of underqualified hero."

Améliane tilted her head, regarding him for a beat. The breeze caught a loose strand of her hair, and she didn't bother tucking it back.

"Underqualified?" she repeated, lips curving slightly. "I don't believe that for a moment."

Her voice was calm, almost amused—but not mocking. There was something else beneath it. Something quieter.

"And while I try to make a habit of saving myself," she added, stepping into the gazebo with effortless grace, "I suppose I appreciate the gesture."

She reached for the teapot, her fingers deft and unhurried. "Though next time, perhaps knock first. Or send a flower. Preferably not jasmine."

Her eyes flicked to him over the rim of her teacup—cool, silver, and far too knowing.

Mathieu blinked. "Jasmine?"

He echoed the word like a man turning over a puzzle piece that didn't quite fit. She'd said it casually—too casually. But there was something behind it. Something that tugged at the edges of meaning.

He filed it away.

"Duly noted," he said instead, reaching for a teacup and inspecting it like it might bite. He poured with surprising grace, then glanced at her over the rim.

"You don't seem like a jasmine kind of woman."

Améliane arched a brow. "No? And what kind of woman do I seem like, exactly?"

He set the teapot down with a soft clink, considering. Not joking now—at least, not entirely.

"Not roses," he said first. "Too obvious. Too... eager to impress."

She hummed, amused. "Agreed."

"Lilies are too delicate," he went on. "Tulips too tame. Daisies would be insulting."

"Careful," she murmured. "You're eliminating fast."

He gave her a look. "You don't strike me as someone who settles for what's easy to name."

Then, with a little shrug, "Orchid, maybe."

Améliane blinked.

"Elegant," he said, meeting her gaze. "Rare. Beautiful, but temperamental. You can't just toss one in a vase and expect it to bloom." He leaned back, smirking slightly. "You have to know what you're doing. Otherwise, it dies on you."

Her lips parted, just slightly. Surprise flickered across her face—then vanished beneath something quieter. Not softness, exactly. But interest. And maybe something warmer beneath it.

"Well," she said slowly, "that's either the most perceptive thing anyone's said to me in a decade... or the most well-crafted insult I've ever heard."

He lifted his cup in salute, chuckling softly.

She took a delicate sip of tea, eyes never leaving him over the rim of her cup. "You surprise me, Mathieu."

"That sounds dangerously close to a compliment."

"I said it was a surprise, not a miracle."

He chuckled, low and warm. "You wound me."

"I suspect you can take a wound or two," she said, gaze flicking to the faint scar that curved beneath his collar. "You've certainly collected enough of them."

His smirk faltered just a breath before returning. "Occupational hazard."

She set her cup down, the porcelain clicking softly against the saucer. "And what is your occupation these days?"

"Wandering rogue. Occasional sword-for-hire. Full-time thorn in your side."

"Ah," she said, folding her hands neatly. "So, self-employed."

She let the words hang for a beat, then added, "Though I must say—your knowledge of flowers betrays you. Far too cultured for a mere sword-for-hire."

Mathieu arched a brow, lifting his teacup in mock offense. "Are you implying mercenaries can't appreciate flora?"

"I'm implying you are more than you pretend to be," she said, voice light, but gaze sharp. "A man who speaks of flowers with such familiarity didn't learn that on a battlefield."

"Maybe I had a very poetic weapons master," he offered.

"Or maybe," she said, smile tugging at her lips, "you've spent your life hiding the scholar behind the scoundrel."

He gave a mock-sigh, dramatically wistful. "Ruined. Exposed. My reputation will never recover."

"Good," she said, and took another sip of tea. "I never did care for reputations."

He gave a mock bow from his chair, all gallant sarcasm. "And what, Your Majesty, may I ask is your occupation these days? Trapped monarch? Occasional shapeshifter? Full-time mystery?"

"Only on weekdays," she replied dryly. "Weekends I moonlight as a harbinger of doom."

"Fascinating. You'll have to teach me."

She smiled—an actual smile, small but real—then tilted her head slightly. "I brought you here for a reason."

"I'd hoped it wasn't just for my sparkling personality."

"It wasn't," she said, and for a moment, the air shifted. Not tense—just... heavier.

"You asked for answers," she continued. "In the library. Before we were interrupted."

Mathieu's teasing edge dulled slightly. He nodded, quiet now.

"I haven't forgotten," she said. "And I keep my word. But you need to understand—there are things in this castle, in this curse, that defy explanation."

Mathieu set his teacup down, cradling it between his palms like he wasn't sure whether to drink or think.

"I ran into Laurent earlier," he said, glancing at her from beneath his lashes. "Literally. Walked straight into him outside a pantry. He was... preoccupied."

Améliane arched a brow. "Preoccupied?"

"There was a young man involved," he added dryly. "And a lopsided shirt. I'll let you fill in the rest."

Her lips twitched despite herself. "That sounds like Laurent."

"I thought so," Mathieu said.

She gave a soft huff of laughter.

Mathieu smiled faintly. "Anyway, he invited me to lunch."

That drew a reaction. Améliane blinked, her teacup pausing midair. "He invited you to lunch? With the others?"

"In the kitchens, yes." He leaned back slightly. "Said Élodie and Margot were already there terrorizing the staff. I figured after four days of isolation and magical hallway sabotage, I'd earned a sandwich."

Her expression shifted again—something unreadable in the narrowing of her eyes. Thoughtful. Curious. Maybe even... pleased?

"I didn't realize you'd made such an impression," she said carefully.

"I didn't either." He smiled, but it faded quickly. "They were... welcoming. In their own way."

Améliane nodded once, then waited.

"And during lunch," Mathieu went on, his tone changing—gentler now, more deliberate— "I figured something out."

He didn't look at her as he said it. Just reached for a scone, slathering it with clotted cream and strawberry preserves.

"They wouldn't answer my questions. Not directly. Every time I asked something, they redirected or changed the subject. And then I realized..."

He looked up.

"You can't tell me anything I don't already know."

Améliane froze.

No flinch. No gasp. Just stillness—sharp and immediate, like a held breath.

Mathieu saw it. Registered it. And pressed forward.

"That's part of the curse, isn't it?" he said. "That's why your court speaks in riddles. Why no one ever gives a straight answer. Because you're bound by something that keeps you from telling the truth... unless I already know it."

Her silence was confirmation enough.

He exhaled slowly. "Laurent didn't say it. None of them did. But I could see it. They were waiting—for me to figure it out. And when I did... things changed."

Améliane's gaze didn't waver. But she set her teacup down, quiet and precise.

"And what did you figure out?" she asked carefully.

Another pause. The breeze stirred a strand of her hair, but she didn't reach to fix it.

"That you're not just a Queen in a cursed castle," he said, voice even lower now.

He leaned forward, elbows on the table, eyes locked on hers.

"You're the lost Queen of Belmara."

The garden didn't react. The trees didn't rustle in warning. No thunder rolled across the hills.

But Améliane sat very still. And for just a moment—just one—she didn't look like a queen at all.

She looked like a woman who had been carrying a truth so long, she no longer knew how to set it down.

Then—at last—her lips parted.

"Well, then there's no point in pretending otherwise," she said quietly.

Just a truth, finally spoken aloud.

Mathieu nodded once.

And across the garden, the dire wolf cracked open one golden eye.

Mathieu cleared his throat, his voice low, but edged with something new. Not sharpness. Not sarcasm. Something closer to awe—though he'd never admit it aloud.

"So now that I know who you are..." he said, swirling the tea in his cup as if the leaves might arrange themselves into answers, "can you tell me how much of the stories are true? Half the world thinks you never existed—just some cursed queen made up by tavern bards and half-drunk historians."

Améliane smiled faintly. But it wasn't her usual, calculated smile. It was older than that. Sadder.

"They're not wrong," she said, gaze drifting toward the far side of the garden. "Parts of me don't exist anymore. Not the way they once did."

Her fingers brushed the rim of her teacup, but she didn't lift it.

"The stories... some are close," she said. "The lost queen in the cursed castle, turned to shadow and myth. The court of beasts who serve her. A betrayal born of ambition. A love that broke, and a crown that vanished."

She looked back at him.

"But none of them tell you how it felt to be *forgotten* while still breathing."

Mathieu didn't speak. He didn't move. He just sat there, tea cooling in his hands, as the weight of her words settled over the garden like mist.

"I watched my name fade from ledgers," she went on, voice quiet but steady. "My banners burned. My laws rewritten. I became a ghost while the world marched on."

Her grey eyes caught the sunlight then, glinting like frost. But they didn't waver.

"So yes, some of the stories are true," she finished. "But none of them are enough."

Mathieu watched her for a moment, studying the way her gaze had turned inward—like she was sifting through ashes to find which ones still burned.

He set his teacup down with deliberate care. "The man I saw with you in the Grand Hall," he said quietly. "Was he... part of your life before the curse?"

Améliane didn't answer right away. Instead, she turned her gaze to the garden, where sunlight spilled like gold across the leaves. Her fingers traced the rim of her teacup, delicate, deliberate.

"That man you saw," she said finally, "was part of my life. Once."

Mathieu stayed quiet, sensing the weight behind those words.

"He was not a stranger to my court," she continued. "Nor to me. He came with pretty words and loyal smiles. And when the time came to choose between me and power..." She let the sentence trail off, unfinished.

Mathieu's jaw tightened. "He chose wrong."

Améliane looked at him then. "Many of them did."

A beat passed.

"Not all of them, I'm assuming," he said, eyes cutting to where the dire wolf was still lounging across the garden.

Her gaze softened—just a fraction—but she didn't reply. Instead, she set her teacup down and folded her hands.

"You asked how much of the stories are true," she said, voice lower now. "The tales sung in taverns and scrawled on maps."

Mathieu nodded. "That's the one."

She released a breath, slow and steady. "It's true that there was a queen. And it's true that she vanished."

"But what they don't tell you," she went on, "is that she was betrayed—sold off by those she trusted most."

Her voice was steel wrapped in velvet. The kind of quiet that cuts.

"And the curse?" Mathieu asked, softly.

She hesitated, then gave the faintest shake of her head.

"Some stories must still wait," she said. "Not because I doubt you... but because I've spent too long surviving to offer my trust all at once."

He met her eyes. "Fair."

A breath passed between them, quiet but electric.

Then she added, almost idly, "But you're closer to the truth than anyone else has ever come."

They sat like that for a moment, the air warm with the scent of tea and blossoms, the conversation coiled between them like a thread not yet pulled tight.

Mathieu leaned back slightly, eyes on her—not sharp, not probing. Just... seeing her.

"You're right," he said quietly.

Améliane arched a brow. "About what, exactly?"

"That trust is earned." He paused. "And I haven't exactly given you reason to offer yours."

Her gaze didn't drop. "And yet, here you are. Drinking my tea."

He huffed a soft laugh. "Only because your wolf didn't gut me on sight."

"Don't tempt him. He's still deciding."

Another beat. And then, his expression shifted—just enough to let something real slip through.

"I haven't had a home in years," he said, almost like a confession. "Not since mine was taken."

Améliane didn't move. But something in her stilled.

"I was gone when it happened," he said, eyes drifting toward the distant hedgerows. "At war. Thought I was saving my people by fighting far from them. I came back to ash and silence."

His voice was even. Too even.

"They told me I was the last of my family. That I should run. Disappear." He gave a small, humorless shrug. "So, I did."

A pause.

"I've worn a hundred names since then. But I've never told anyone that."

He looked back at her then.

"I don't expect your trust," he said. "But I'll earn it if I can. You don't owe me your story. Not unless I've earned the right to hear it."

He hesitated—then added, quieter, "I didn't come looking for Eldrenoire. I was on the run. I'd been running so long I forgot what it felt like to stop."

Améliane didn't interrupt. Didn't press. Just listened.

"I hate being trapped," he continued, the words gruff, honest. "But the truth is—I've got nowhere else to be. And to no one's greater surprise than my own, I am happy I stumbled through your cursed gates."

He looked at her fully now, and the flicker of something real—something steady—shone through.

"So while I'm here—or until your charming estate decides to let me leave—I'll do what I can to earn your trust. To be useful, if nothing else."

A small breeze caught the hem of her sleeve, but neither of them moved.

"I'm not asking for anything," he finished. "I just... wanted you to know."

Améliane watched him for a long moment, the silver of her eyes catching the sun.

Then she said with mock surprise, "You just willingly told me a piece of your story without me having to pry it from your lips."

Mathieu gave a crooked smile. "You seemed like the type who collects things."

"I do," she said. "But I never take what isn't freely given."

Their eyes met. And for the first time, the thread between them pulled tight—not with tension, but with promise.

CHAPTER 14

Mathieu

The next few weeks passed in a blur of strange normalcy, the kind that settled over a place when no one dared name how unusual it really was. Mathieu found himself slipping into a routine—not an exciting one, perhaps, but a rhythm that steadied him, nonetheless.

Each morning began with sparring sessions in the courtyard, blades clashing against the grey dawn light as he traded blows with Thorne, Renaud's second-in-command and a man built like a siege engine.

He'd first found his way to the courtyard by following the sharp, rhythmic ring of swords striking a battered sparring dummy—and stumbling straight into Thorne, who hadn't even paused to acknowledge the intrusion.

By midday, Mathieu drifted to the kitchens, where Laurent, Margot, and Élodie made it their personal mission to feed him, mock him, and half-accidentally tell him things they weren't supposed to.

And when dusk fell and the castle's many lanterns flickered to life, he took his place at the long dining table, sharing evening meals with the others—Améliane included, when her duties or moods allowed.

In bits and pieces, he gathered the shape of the story—if not its center. That those cursed alongside the queen were either fiercely loyal or simply in the wrong corridor at the wrong time. That they had been trapped here for seven years while the world outside moved on without them. That Edric—her former consort and current captor—was a first-class bastard so drenched in his own narcissism he believed locking a sovereign queen in a gilded prison was somehow a patriotic act. He hadn't just betrayed her out of ambition—he genuinely believed no woman should rule Belmara.

And though Mathieu didn't quite trust it—didn't quite trust anything yet—he found himself testing the boundaries of the castle less frequently.

He woke one morning well into his seventh week at the castle to the sound of a soft knock and the familiar creak of hinges as someone nudged the door open. A breakfast tray appeared on the small table near the hearth—fresh bread, poached eggs, sliced fruit, and a pot of strong, bitter tea that could probably polish armor.

Mathieu sat up slowly, raking a hand through his hair. The fire had burned low during the night, but the room was warm—one of the castle's many unspoken courtesies. He rose, tugged on a tunic and trousers, and washed quickly at the basin before sitting down to eat. The tea was scalding. The bread was still warm. He didn't know who brought it, and at this point, he wasn't sure he wanted to.

He dressed the rest of the way with the practiced ease of a man who'd spent more of his life in armor than out of it. His coat was slung over the back of a chair, boots neatly tucked beneath. Sword strapped to his hip. Nothing ceremonial. Just functional.

Then he stepped into the corridor—and, as always when he went to train with Thorne, the castle did not fight him.

The route was clear. No sudden dead ends. No shifting stairwells or vanishing doors. The corridor curved gently through a series of arches, tall windows that hadn't been there yesterday, guiding him—without resistance—to exactly where he intended to go.

It wasn't the first time he'd noticed.

Eldrenoire, fickle and fanged, did not tolerate aimlessness. Wander too long, and you'd find yourself turned around, spat out into parts of the castle that didn't exist on any map. But if he walked with purpose—toward a sparring match, or a midday meal with Laurent and the others, or to answer a summons from the queen herself—the castle cooperated.

Not kindly. Not warmly. But with something that could almost pass for respect.

Mathieu crossed the stones of the courtyard and nodded to Thorne, who was already stretching, bare-armed and broad as a battering ram. The man offered no greeting—just tossed him a practice blade and gave a curt.

Mathieu grinned.

The practice blade was heavier than it looked—weighted for endurance, not elegance. Mathieu tested its balance, rolled his shoulders, and gave Thorne a mock salute.

"Try not to cry this time," he said mildly.

Thorne snorted. "Try not to bleed."

They circled once, twice—boots scraping across the stone, the early morning sun slanting over the high walls of the courtyard.

Then Thorne lunged.

The first clash was all brute strength. Steel met steel with a jarring crack, and Mathieu staggered half a step before twisting out of range, letting Thorne's momentum carry him forward. He pivoted, brought the flat of the blade down toward Thorne's shoulder, and was promptly blocked by a low sweep and a brutal upward hook that nearly caught his ribs.

"You fight like a noble," Thorne grunted, resetting his stance. "All precision and footwork. Bet you spent more time at court than on a battlefield."

"I'll take that as a compliment," Mathieu said, breath quickening as they circled again. "But I'll have you know I've bled in every corner of the continent."

"Still bleeding now," Thorne replied, and lunged again.

They locked blades, gritting through the strain, neither yielding. Sweat beaded on Mathieu's brow. His muscles burned. Thorne was built like a fortress—unyielding, practical, relentless. Where Mathieu relied on agility and analysis, Thorne was all brute efficiency.

But Mathieu was faster.

He dropped low, pivoted, and swept Thorne's legs with a move he hadn't used in years—one he'd once seen drop a man twice Thorne's size during a siege in Ilyrios. Thorne hit the ground with a loud oof and a thud that echoed off the walls.

Silence.

Then Thorne stared up at him, eyes narrowed. "That was cheap."

"It was effective," Mathieu said, extending a hand to help him up. "And besides—if you wanted fairness, you shouldn't have brought a sword."

Thorne took the hand grudgingly and hauled himself to his feet. "Next time, I bring two."

Mathieu grinned. "Looking forward to it."

They reset. No ceremony. Just soldiers moving through the familiar rhythm of pain and pride, the bond forged not in words but in bruises. And as they began again—steel clanging in the morning sun—Mathieu realized something odd.

He was enjoying himself.

Not just the fight, but the camaraderie. The way the world narrowed to the present moment. For the first time in what felt like years, he wasn't calculating escape routes or second-guessing the people around him.

They cast their blades aside and the match had shifted into hand-to-hand, all muscle and instinct and bone-deep memory. They circled again, both damp with sweat now.

Thorne feinted left, then ducked under Mathieu's arm and swept his leg.

Mathieu hit the ground with a grunt, the breath leaving him in a sharp huff of air. Dust puffed around him as he landed flat on his back, staring up at a sky just beginning to warm with late morning light.

Thorne grinned above him, offering a hand. "You're quicker with a sword."

Mathieu grabbed his wrist and pulled—not to rise, but to unbalance. Thorne stumbled, and Mathieu used the moment to roll and twist, pinning the younger man with one knee to his chest.

"I'm quicker when I'm not babysitting," Mathieu growled.

Thorne huffed a laugh. "Feeling your age, old man?"

"Feeling merciful." He released him and stood, brushing dirt from his trousers.

Thorne rolled to his feet, stretching his arms overhead in that lazy, catlike way that only made Mathieu more aware of how limber he was. Younger. Less scarred. Still smooth along the ribs where Mathieu had old burns and the faint silvered lines of blades narrowly dodged.

Without speaking, they both removed their shirts. Not out of bravado, but necessity. The courtyard sun was climbing, and the sweat made every movement slick and risky.

Mathieu balled his shirt and tossed it aside, catching Thorne's glance—just a flicker, no judgment, but a moment of awareness. A warrior's inventory. Scars across his side, his shoulder, the brand on his ribs.

Then Thorne's eyes shifted upward.

Mathieu followed the gaze—and froze.

High above, on the terrace of one of the western towers, a figure leaned against the balustrade. Pale skirts caught in the breeze. Metallic eyes focused on the courtyard below.

Améliane. She wasn't even trying to hide it.

For one absurd, unguarded second, heat coiled in Mathieu's gut. Not from her gaze—but from a sudden, ridiculous flare of jealousy. Was she watching him? Or Thorne?

His eyes darted sideways.

Thorne was impressive, in the clean-cut way of soldiers almost to their prime—tall, strong, lean with youth. No limp. No burn scars. No history carved into his skin.

Mathieu felt suddenly aware of his own frame—broader, heavier, more battle-worn. More real, maybe. But older. Marked by every fight he'd won and every one he'd lost.

He glanced back toward the tower.

Améliane hadn't moved. Her expression unreadable. Regal and infuriating as ever. But she was watching.

And that, strangely, was enough to make him straighten his spine and roll his shoulders back before turning toward Thorne.

"All right," Mathieu said, voice low. "Round two."

Thorne grinned. "Trying to impress the queen?"

Mathieu didn't answer.

Thorne lunged again, but Mathieu dodged—barely. Their forearms locked with a crack of contact, muscles straining, feet grinding against the packed dirt. They were evenly matched in this—strength against speed, experience against instinct.

Then something shifted in the courtyard.

A hush, subtle but undeniable, rippled across the space. The kind of pause that meant someone new had arrived.

Thorne disengaged first, stepping back and wiping sweat from his brow with the back of his wrist.

Mathieu turned, breathing hard and noticed Améliane had disappeared from her terrace. At the far end of the courtyard, the main gates had opened—not wide, just enough to allow two figures to enter.

One was unmistakable: Renaud, stone-faced and silent as ever, his cloak shifting with each step like smoke pulled through shadow.

The other—older, leaner, dressed in dark riding leathers with dust clinging to his boots—walked beside him with the casual arrogance of someone who'd been here before and knew the rules didn't apply to him.

The man moved with too much ease for someone entering a cursed castle.

"Who's that?" Mathieu asked, still catching his breath.

Thorne reached for his discarded shirt and tugged it over his head. "Cassien. Edric's messenger."

Mathieu straightened slightly. "Messenger?"

"Mm." Thorne was already brushing the dust from his sleeves, tone casual. "Shows up once a week like clockwork. Brings news from the outside. Orders, updates. Sometimes supplies. Not much else."

Mathieu's brows drew together. "And the queen allows this?"

Thorne shrugged. "She doesn't stop it. He's not a prisoner like the rest of us. Just walks in and out like he owns the place. Castle seems to tolerate him, which is more than I can say for most."

Mathieu watched as the two figures disappeared through the arched corridor leading deeper into the castle.

"Interesting," he murmured.

Because *that* was something no one had mentioned at lunch.

He'd assumed Eldrenoire was sealed—cut off from the world like a forgotten relic. But this? This meant Edric still had a line to her. Still found ways to keep her in his shadow.

And the queen hadn't mentioned it. Not at tea. Not in any of their careful, loaded conversations.

Which meant she had a reason not to.

Mathieu reached for his own shirt, fingers tightening slightly around the fabric.

Thorne clapped him on the shoulder, oblivious to the storm brewing just beneath the surface. "Come on. Lunch will be ready soon, and if we're late, Élodie gets the best of the honeycakes."

Mathieu managed a grunt that passed for agreement, but his mind was elsewhere.

Because now he had a new question: Why the hell was *Edric's* messenger walking freely through a castle that claimed to be cursed? And why did it feel like *he* was the one who was missing something important?

Mathieu didn't move.

Thorne noticed. He turned back, one brow raised, shirt half-buttoned.

"You coming?" he asked, jerking his chin toward the castle.

Mathieu shook his head. "Go ahead. I'll catch up."

Thorne stilled. "Ah."

He didn't ask what Mathieu was planning. Didn't have to.

Instead, he sighed—long-suffering and just a little amused. "You're going to try and eavesdrop on Cassien's report, aren't you?"

Mathieu didn't deny it.

Thorne let out a short laugh. "You've got a death wish."

"Only on Tuesdays," Mathieu muttered.

"Then lucky for you it's..." Thorne glanced at the sun. "Damn. It is Tuesday."

He stepped closer, voice low now. "Don't be stupid. No one's allowed in those meetings. Not me. Not Élodie. Not even Laurent, and that man can break into locked rooms for sport."

Mathieu arched a brow. "And yet, you're still not telling me not to try."

"I'm telling you *you'll fail*," Thorne said dryly. "I'm just curious how badly."

Mathieu gave him a tight, crooked grin. "Guess we'll find out."

Thorne sighed again, already walking away. "I want it noted for the record that I tried to stop you."

"You didn't try very hard."

Thorne didn't look back. "Because I kind of want to know what they say, too."

Mathieu wasn't sure when the corridors had turned unfamiliar. One moment, he'd been marching toward the queen's chambers with determined steps; the next, Eldrenoire had bent around him like a snake, slithering him away from his goal.

He should've expected it by now. The castle didn't like trespassers—especially ones headed somewhere they weren't invited.

Still, it irritated him. Not because he was lost, but because he'd let himself forget. Let himself think, just for a while, that Eldrenoire might actually tolerate him.

Until it didn't.

When he finally stopped, it was because the walls around him had gone mirror-bright. Dozens of floor-to-ceiling panels stretched down a long, endless corridor, reflecting dim torchlight and the warped shape of his silhouette. The air was colder here. He hadn't seen this hallway before, but something about it felt... ancient. Watchful.

The walls didn't just reflect light—they warped it, bent it, turning torchflame into moonsilver and shadow into something sentient.

"You do like to push your luck," came a voice, smooth and ageless.

Alaric stood just behind him, of course. He hadn't been there a moment ago. Now he was.

Mathieu exhaled sharply through his nose. "I take it this isn't the way to the queen's chambers."

"Not unless you intend to pass through seven years of regret," Alaric murmured, strolling lazily past one of the mirrors. "This hall only opens when it wants to. Usually to those who can't help but see what they shouldn't."

Mathieu folded his arms. "Let me guess. You never get lost here."

"Oh, I'm always lost," Alaric said with a faint smile. "But the castle lets me pretend otherwise."

They stood in silence for a moment, the flickering reflections casting ghost-light across the marble.

"You're the only one she toys with like this," Alaric added after a pause, voice suddenly softer. "The only one Eldrenoire bends and breaks for. Everyone else? It either traps, or it obeys. But you..."

Mathieu frowned. "Why?"

Alaric tilted his head. "Because you do not belong to the Black Keep."

That shouldn't have meant anything. And yet—

"The castle protects its queen," Alaric continued, turning to face a mirror that showed nothing at all—not even their reflections. "It always has. It always will. But you... you are the unknown. You are the coin still spinning. And until you land... it will test you."

Mathieu swallowed. Alaric gestured toward a particularly tall mirror, head cocked to the side in amusement.

The blank mirror called to him. Or maybe dared him. He stepped forward, slowly, and raised a hand to its surface.

The glass did not shatter. But the reflection inside it did.

A jagged crack tore through the silver, not through the glass itself but the world beyond it—as if splitting time. And then, in a rush of images, the mirror showed him everything.

A younger Améliane stood in the heart of a sun-drenched courtyard, radiant and unburdened. She laughed without caution, the sound clear and light as wind chimes in summer. Her chestnut hair, unbound and wind-tossed, shone in the sunlight, untouched by crown or care. Her gown flowed like poured starlight, catching the light in shifting waves as she moved among her court—familiar faces, smiling and whole, their laughter echoing hers. They stood close, not as prisoners or protectors, but as friends, vibrant and free. And beside her—just a step too close—stood Edric. Golden-haired and handsome, with a practiced smile and courtier's grace, he watched her like something he owned. His hand rested lightly on her back, fingers curled in casual claim, and she—young, trusting—did not flinch. Not yet.

Alaric's voice echoed beside him, "Some reflections show what was lost—not to mourn it, but to remind you it once existed."

The scene shifted.

Valmont burned. The sky above the citadel roared orange, thick with smoke and the scream of splintering wood. Walls that had once withstood centuries of siege cracked and fell like brittle parchment. Stone turned to rubble. Flame devoured the banners of his house, curling them into ash midair. A younger Mathieu stood in the heart of it—armor scorched, tunic torn, blood slicking the edge of his sword. Ash clung to his skin like a second layer, sweat streaking paths through the soot on his face. His voice cut through the cacophony, hoarse from shouting. Orders. Warnings. Desperate, guttural pleas. Maybe both. But no one answered. The fire didn't care who he was. It consumed everything. Somewhere in the distance, through a haze of smoke and falling embers, a figure emerged—shadow blurred by heat. A woman heavy with child. She was running, golden hair catching the firelight in flashes. His breath caught. Tess. His legs moved without thought. He called out—once, twice—but the words tore away on the wind. And then—

A shriek of collapsing stone.

A flash of flame.

Gone. Swallowed by the inferno.

His breath caught, shallow. The flame in the mirror flickered like it knew the shape of his guilt.

Alaric murmured, "You keep looking for the moment you could've saved them. But some doors were already closed before you reached them."

Then the final vision flickered.

Mathieu and Améliane stood together—older, weathered, bloodied. Crowned. Mathieu's armor bore the scars of a hundred battles, its once-polished surface dulled by ash and time. His crown sat heavy on salt-streaked hair, forged not of gold, but of burden. Beside him, Améliane stood just as proud, her gown torn at the hem, her shoulders squared beneath the weight of a mantle stitched with midnight and fire. Her crown shimmered like forged moonlight—delicate in shape, indestructible in meaning. Their hands did not touch, but they were aligned—shoulder to shoulder, sovereign to sovereign.

Before them stretched a hall that had never existed before—a throne room raised from the wreckage of two shattered kingdoms. Valmont stone and Belmara crystal. War-hardened banners and silken drapes of ancient magic. At the far end of the chamber, above twin thrones forged side by side, hung a great standard: split down the center, one side bearing the black stag of Valmont, the other the moonlit tidelily sigil of Belmara, the line between them stitched in flame.

And yet—the image shimmered. Flickered. The hall wavered at the edges, as if the moment itself were a reflection on rippling water. Too bright. Too still. A vision not yet anchored in reality. A future too fragile to hold. Their eyes met in the silence. Not with triumph, but with understanding. What they had built—what they might build—still teetered on the edge of becoming.

"What you see is not destiny," Alaric said. "It is potential. The kind that demands sacrifice."

The echo of Captain Duran's words surged to the front of Mathieu's mind.

Everything worth keeping requires sacrifice.

He staggered back from the mirror, dragging in deep breaths like a man breaking the surface after nearly drowning.

Alaric watched him with that unreadable smile.

"The castle never shows what will be. Only what might break you."

He turned slightly, voice softening into something more curious—almost reverent.

"Or perhaps... you are the one who might break *it.*"

A hush settled over the corridor. Even the mirrors seemed to hold their breath.

Alaric's gaze lingered on Mathieu like he was seeing him for the first time.

"*Wyrdbound.* That's what the old magic calls you. A fate not chosen, but inherited. Bound to destiny yet not ruled by it."

A beat. "Dangerous things, those. The castle doesn't know what to make of you. Not yet."

Then, with a flick of his coat and a faint hum, Alaric turned and walked into the shadows—vanishing the way he always did: without a sound, without a trace.

Mathieu remained alone.

The mirrors around him flickered dimly, offering no more visions, no clear exit.

He released the breath he'd been holding, slow and steady, the word echoing in his mind like a blade still ringing from impact.

Wyrdbound.

Whatever that meant, whatever the castle thought of him now—it didn't change the simple, irritating truth: He still had no idea how to get out of this godsdamned hallway.

CHAPTER 15

Mathieu

H e had stopped counting how many corridors he'd walked hours ago.

Eldrenoire had swallowed him whole this time—no gentle misdirection, no slyly vanishing door. Just endless turns, halls folding in on themselves like a serpent coiling tighter and tighter around its prey. The air had grown colder. The sconces on the walls flickered with pale blue fire, and the tapestries had changed—no longer Belmaran. No longer anything he recognized.

The castle was watching him. Not passively. Not curiously. But like it was *measuring* him. Studying the weight of his footsteps. The length of his silences. The sharpness of the anger he'd tried to bury after the mirror.

Wyrdbound.

The word hadn't left his mind. It echoed with every step, every twist of the labyrinth. Was it prophecy? A warning? Or just another one of Alaric's riddles, carefully wrapped in myth and thrown like bait into his path?

He didn't know.

And he hated not knowing.

By the time the castle finally spat him out, he was breathless with irritation. Not afraid—he wouldn't give it that satisfaction—but furious. His fists were clenched at his sides. His jaw ached from grinding. Whatever this place was trying to show him, it could go to hell.

He was brimming with rage when the corridor finally opened to a courtyard unlike any he'd seen before. The air shifted the moment he stepped through—warmer, sweeter, tinged with something ancient and clean. Moonlight poured into the space in a cool cascade, pooling like water across the stone.

The courtyard was overgrown but untouched, vines curling lazily along the walls, fragrant blooms unfurling in clusters as if coaxed open by moonlight itself. The stones were pale and cracked with age, and at its heart sat a wide reflecting pool—black as ink, still as glass. It didn't ripple. It didn't move. But something inside it shimmered just beneath the surface, like it was *waiting*.

And she was there.

Améliane stood on the far side of the pool, barefoot on the marble, the hem of her nightgown just grazing the edge of the water. The silk clung to her like mist, pale as starlight, cut low in the back and high at the neck, sleeveless and flowing like poured silver. Her hair spilled freely down her spine in long, wind-blown waves, and her arms were folded loosely across her chest—poised but not guarded.

She hadn't heard him yet.

She looked...

Not fragile. Never fragile.

But *unguarded*. Untouched by her court, her curse, her throne. There was no tightly woven braid on her head resembling her lost crown, no cloak over her shoulders. Just Améliane. The woman behind the queen. The one he'd only caught glimpses of, always veiled in sarcasm and steel.

And she was staring into the pool like it held the answer to something only she could ask.

His breath caught before he could stop it.

She turned.

Her eyes met his across the courtyard—silver catching moonlight, sharp and watchful—and the quiet of the night cracked open like a fault line.

Améliane's eyes narrowed. "What are you doing here?"

No title. No greeting. Just ice.

Mathieu didn't flinch. "I could ask you the same."

Her jaw tightened. She didn't move from her spot near the water, but something in her spine straightened. "This courtyard isn't part of the castle's normal paths. You shouldn't have found it."

"Trust me," he said, voice sharp, "it wasn't on purpose. Your charming little house of horrors had me walking in circles for hours. And then—bam." He spread his arms, mock-grand. "Here I am. Right in your moonlit sanctuary. Must be fate."

Her glare was almost palpable. "This place is private."

"Didn't look like it had a 'keep out' sign."

"No one comes here," she snapped. "Not even Renaud."

"Well," he said, stepping further into the courtyard, "maybe the castle thought it was time for some company."

Her eyes narrowed. "Don't you dare pretend you're here by accident."

Mathieu crossed slowly to the edge of the pool, boots scraping against the stone. "Fine. You want the truth? I was trying to figure out why Edric's messenger is allowed to waltz in and out of your cursed castle like it's a royal errand run."

Something flickered in her expression—guilt? No. Not guilt. Offense.

"You were spying."

"I was *looking for answers*," he growled. "Because you sure as hell weren't offering any."

She stepped closer, silk whispering against stone. "You think you're entitled to every secret I keep?"

"I think I deserve to know there's someone walking freely in and out of this prison while the rest of us are stuck in a time loop. And I absolutely deserve to know what news he brings from the outside world— even if no one remembers my name anymore either."

Her hand twitched at her side.

Bullseye.

"I let Cassien come because he's useful," she said, voice low and lethal. "Not because I take orders from Edric."

"And yet he comes. Weekly. Like clockwork." He took another step. "What does he bring? News? Threats? Love letters?"

Her lips parted in disbelief. "You think I *enjoy* it?"

"I think you haven't denied it."

They were nearly toe to toe now, the space between them stretched tight as a bowstring.

"You arrogant bastard," she hissed.

He leaned in, voice like gravel. "And you are the most manipulative woman I've ever met."

"Oh, *please*. You act like I owe you my whole story just because you've been lurking around long enough to get comfortable."

"You think I *want* to be here?"

"I think you're angry that the castle hasn't bent for you like everything else in your life."

"And I think you like playing the prisoner. It saves you from having to lead."

Her hand rose—whether to shove or strike, even she didn't know—but he moved faster, seizing her wrist with a grip that halted the moment between heartbeats.

He didn't hurt her. He didn't even squeeze. He just held her—trapped her palm against his chest, where his heartbeat thundered hard and fast beneath her fingers.

Their eyes locked.

"That's the difference between us," he said, voice low, ragged. "You turn it off. I never could."

Her lips parted, but no sound came out.

The moonlight shimmered on the surface of the pool, casting twin reflections that rippled—imperfect, fracturing at the edges.

Neither of them looked away.

Her palm still pressed to his chest, caught in his grip. Her breath came faster now—quiet, shallow—but she didn't pull away.

Neither did he.

Mathieu's gaze dropped to her lips, just for a second. He didn't mean to. Didn't plan it. But once he looked, he couldn't seem to stop.

The air between them changed. Heated. Tightened.

One shift. That's all it would take. One inch closer, one moment of madness, and his mouth would be on hers. And gods, he wanted to. He wanted to forget the crown, the curse, the damn mirror, and just *feel* something that wasn't rage or regret.

She didn't move.

Didn't stop him.

Didn't speak.

So he leaned in—slowly, like she might startle. Like he wasn't sure this wasn't another trick of the castle. His free hand hovered near her waist but didn't touch. Not yet. Just a breath away.

And she...

She tilted her chin up.

Her lashes fluttered.

She almost—

Then she blinked.

And stepped back.

Just enough to break the moment. Just enough to leave him standing there, heart pounding and hands suddenly empty.

Mathieu said nothing. He didn't trust himself to speak.

Améliane looked away first, her shoulders drawing back like armor sliding into place. "The castle's already watching us. It doesn't need another reason."

He gave a short, bitter laugh. "And here I thought you didn't care what the castle thinks."

"I don't," she said. "But I care what I think. And I'm not ready to hate myself in the morning."

Mathieu stood there, heart still thudding, every nerve lit like a battlefield flare.

Then—slowly—he dragged a hand down his face, exhaling hard through his nose.

"Right," he muttered. "Fair."

He stepped back, just a half-pace, giving her room. Respecting the space she'd asked for, even if every part of him ached to close it again.

"I shouldn't have come at you like that," he said after a moment. "The yelling. The accusations. That was..." He shook his head. "Not my finest moment."

Améliane didn't move at first. Her profile was lit in silver, cool and composed—but her voice was softer when she finally answered.

"You had a right to be angry."

A pause.

Their gazes met again—not sharp this time, not heated. Just tired. Heavy with the weight of things unsaid.

"I should've told you about Cassien," she said quietly. "But I didn't know how."

"Because you don't trust me," Mathieu said, without accusation. Just fact.

Améliane's lips parted, then pressed into a line. "I trust pieces of you."

He gave a dry huff of a laugh. "That's funny. I was about to say the same thing."

Silence stretched between them again—less hostile now, but no less fragile.

She turned slightly toward the pool, arms folding across her chest, more from habit than defense. "I've been alone in this place a long time, Mathieu. Even when I'm surrounded by people who love me."

He nodded once. "I know the feeling."

Another beat.

"You scare me," she said, so quietly it barely reached him.

He blinked. "What?"

"Not because I think you'll hurt me. But because I don't know what you mean yet. Eldrenoire watches you. Laurent and the others enjoy your company. Even Thorne seems taken with you. And I'm just... tired of not being in control."

That silenced him.

For once, he didn't have a clever response. Just that same heartbeat thudding beneath his ribs.

He took a breath.

"So," he said softly, "what do we do now?"

She looked at him.

A pause.

Then—just the barest curve of her lips. Wry. Tired. Real.

"How do you feel about some cake?"

His brow lifted. "You offering, or confessing?"

She rolled her eyes, but the smile stayed. "I might have hidden a slice in the kitchen. Coconut."

He gave a low, appreciative laugh. "I thought you'd never ask. I've been trapped in that hallway so long I nearly chewed my own arm off."

She turned, already heading for the archway. "Then come on. Before someone else finds it- Margot has the biggest sweet tooth in Eldrenoire."

He followed.

They slipped through the archway like co-conspirators, their footsteps soft against the stone.

Améliane moved ahead of him, barefoot and whisper-quiet, glancing over her shoulder with that same mischievous smile she wore the night he first caught her in the kitchens. Her hair shimmered down her back in a curtain of dark waves, and the moonlight from the high arched windows made her nightgown nearly translucent in places—just enough silk to veil the long lines of her body, not enough to hide the dip of her waist, the gentle curve of her hips, the low sweep of fabric that bared the small of her back.

Mathieu kept his eyes forward.

Mostly.

She didn't speak, and neither did he—not at first. But every time she glanced back, biting back a smile, something in his chest twisted tighter.

They turned down a narrow passage where the sconces were dim and flickering, their shadows stretched long across the walls. Somewhere above them, the castle creaked softly in its sleep.

"Do you always sneak around barefoot like this?" he whispered.

"Only when I'm committing dessert theft," she whispered back, eyes gleaming.

"Is this a regular crime spree, or a special occasion?"

She glanced over her shoulder, grinning. "That depends. Do you plan to report me?"

He smiled despite himself. "That depends. Is the cake as good as I remember?"

She pressed a finger to her lips, mock-serious. "Legendary."

A floorboard creaked beneath her, and they both froze, barely breathing.

When nothing stirred, she took off at a half-run, stifling a laugh. He followed, boots silent against the stone as he trailed her deeper into the quiet heart of the castle.

He was a soldier. A fugitive. A man used to sleeping with a blade beside his bed.

But in that moment—chasing a queen through a haunted castle in the middle of the night—he felt like a boy again.

Just for a heartbeat.

Just long enough to wonder what it might feel like to have a life that wasn't always on the edge of ruin.

They reached the kitchen doors a few minutes later, breathless from laughter they weren't quite letting out.

She turned to face him, finger to her smiling lips again, mischief dancing in her eyes.

And gods help him—he was half in love with her smile.

The kitchen was dim and warm, lit only by a few banked coals in the hearth and the pale glow of a stained-glass lantern swinging gently above the prep table. The space felt cocooned, secret. A place where rules didn't apply—especially not to queens or trespassers.

Améliane plated the cake and grabbed two forks while Mathieu opened a cupboard and peered inside.

"Coconut cake sounds great, but I'm going to need something with a bit more backbone if we're committing late night crimes together."

Améliane leaned against the wall, arms crossed, an eyebrow arched. "Does cake offend your sensibilities, soldier?"

"No, but it's hard to be charming on an empty stomach," he said, already moving. "And if I'm going to be scolded for my emotional outbursts and dragged through magical hallways of existential dread, I at least deserve dinner."

"You *missed* dinner," she said.

He grinned over his shoulder. "Eldrenoire *hid* dinner from me."

She scoffed, but her smile lingered.

Mathieu found bread, thick and crusty, a wedge of sharp white cheese, half a roasted onion, and—blessedly—a jar of something that looked suspiciously like herbed fig jam. He reached for a skillet and stoked the fire with practiced ease.

"You're very confident," she said, eyeing his preparations.

"I'm hungry," he replied. "My confidence is just hunger in a nicer coat."

She snorted, then accepted the chair he pulled out for her with a faint, surprised smile. Her nightgown fluttered as she sat, and she pulled her legs up beneath her, resting her chin on one hand as she watched him work.

He buttered the bread, layered in the cheese, sliced the onion thinner, and spread the jam sparingly on one side. Into the pan it all went, sizzling low and golden. The smell hit them almost immediately—sharp, sweet, and warm enough to make her stomach rumble.

"What *is* that?" she asked, unable to hide her curiosity.

He gave the skillet a casual shake. "It's called 'making do with the battlefield pantry.' We used to make something like this between skirmishes in the Frostlands, though the ingredients were far less quality. We had to melt snow for water, cook over whatever would burn, and pretend the horses didn't look delicious."

She grimaced. "Charming."

"Effective," he said. "Also, the first time I ever got someone to kiss me was after making one of these."

Améliane's eyebrow arched. "Bribery through toasted cheese on bread?"

"Desperation makes it taste better," he said. "But this version's upgraded. I don't serve just anyone onion and fig on toasted bread, Your Majesty."

She laughed—soft and real, like it surprised her. "Well then. I'm honored."

A beat passed, quieter now, as he flipped the sandwich.

"You know," she said after a moment, "I used to sneak into the kitchens when I couldn't sleep. Before the curse."

"To steal cake?"

"To talk to the cooks," she said, lips curving. "Or to sit on the counter and listen to gossip. They always knew everything before I did. And they never treated me like a queen."

He glanced at her, his voice low. "Sounds nice."

"It was." Her tone turned wistful, then she shook it off. "Then Edric banned me from it. Said it was 'unseemly.' Royalty shouldn't linger where flour gets in their hair."

Mathieu made a thoughtful noise. "Seems like your flour-filled rebellion was long overdue."

She smirked faintly. "That, or I was never very good at being the version of a queen he wanted."

Mathieu looked at her then, openly. "Good."

Something in her expression faltered—just for a second. Then he plated the sandwich, sliced it neatly, and set half in front of her.

She took a bite.

Then froze.

Chewed slowly.

And exhaled.

"Divine," she said, mouth still half-full.

"Careful," he warned. "Praise me too much and I'll expect you to name a holiday after me."

"You may have earned it," she said, licking a bit of jam from her thumb.

Mathieu stared at her for a beat too long before clearing his throat and reaching for his half of the sandwich.

They ate in silence for a few minutes, the kind that didn't feel heavy—just settled, like steam rising off a cooling hearth.

Then he leaned back in his chair, chewing the last bite, and said, almost casually, "Since you told me one of your secrets..."

Her eyes flicked to his. Waiting.

"I got lost in the castle earlier."

She gave a very un-queenlike snort, "Clearly."

"No—I mean *properly* lost. The kind of lost where I wasn't sure I'd ever get out." He reached for the jar of jam, turning it in his hands absently. "Eldrenoire pulled me somewhere I've never been before. A corridor full of mirrors."

Améliane froze. Just slightly. "The Mirror Hall."

"You know it?"

"Yes," she said carefully. "It doesn't open often."

"Lucky me."

She tilted her head. "And what did it show you?"

He paused.

Then shrugged. "Visions. Fragments. Nothing I want to revisit."

Her gaze sharpened. "But you *do* remember."

"Of course I do." His voice was quieter now. "I just don't think they were meant for sharing. Not yet."

She didn't press. Which surprised him.

"So," she said instead, "you wandered into one of Eldrenoire's most haunted corners. And lived to tell the tale. Anything else?"

He gave a faint, crooked smile.

"Alaric was there. Waiting. As usual. Said something strange."

Améliane raised a brow. "He always says strange things."

"This one stuck," Mathieu said. "He said the castle didn't know what to make of me. That I was..."

He hesitated, the word still foreign on his tongue. "*Wyrdbound*."

She stilled—not visibly, not quite—but something subtle shifted. A pause in her breath. A silence in her posture.

"Wyrdbound," she repeated, testing the word like it tasted strange in her mouth. "Is that supposed to mean something?"

He shrugged, setting the jar down with a soft clink. "Alaric said it's what the old magic calls someone whose fate wasn't chosen, but inherited. Bound to destiny, but not ruled by it."

Silence settled between them.

Mathieu waited for her to scoff. Or roll her eyes.

She didn't.

Instead, she said, "That sounds like the kind of name that comes with a warning."

He met her gaze. "Yeah. That was the feeling."

Améliane looked down at her plate, then let out a slow, deliberate breath.

"I owe you the truth," she said quietly. "About Cassien."

Mathieu didn't move.

"He brings messages. News from the outside. Curated, of course. Filtered through Edric's vanity. But still—news." Her fingers traced the rim of her plate. "Usually just enough to keep me compliant. A reminder that he's still watching. Still in control."

Mathieu's jaw flexed, but he didn't interrupt.

"This time, he said Valmont has officially disappeared from the Empire's ledgers. Folded into Rothgarian territory with no protest, no resistance, no name left behind. Just... erased." Her voice stayed steady, but her eyes flicked up, watching him.

Mathieu gave nothing away.

"And Rothgar," she added, "has pulled their troops from the Frostlands. No one knows why. The worry is they're preparing for something.... worse."

He said nothing. Just stared at the table, as if the grain of the wood could explain everything he couldn't.

"And Belmara," she went on, slower now, "according to Edric, is thriving. Trade routes are flourishing. The people are 'grateful' for his leadership. The nobility is 'loyal.' The court is 'stable.'"

Mathieu finally looked at her.

Her lips curved—bitter and tired.

"In other words, the usual lies. Wrapped in gold leaf and sealed with his self-satisfaction."

A pause.

"I haven't seen the real Belmara in seven years. But I know her bones. And I don't think she's thriving. I think she's rotting from the inside out." She didn't break eye contact. "And I think that terrifies him."

The words settled between them like dust in sunlight—quiet, weightless, impossible to ignore.

Then, after a beat, her tone shifted. Calmer. Controlled.

"No one else receives the full messages."

Mathieu's brows lifted slightly.

"Cassien delivers them to me," she said. "Renaud is present, as well. But I don't share the details with the others. Not Laurent. Not Élodie. Certainly not Margot."

She let that hang.

"I offer them crumbs. Carefully chosen. Just enough to give hope without stirring unrest."

Mathieu tilted his head. "And you're telling me because...?"

"I don't know yet," she said honestly. "Maybe because I'm tired of shouldering it alone. Maybe because you deserve to know what kind of world is still out there."

A pause.

"Or maybe I just want to see what you'll do with the truth."

The silence that followed wasn't cold. It was *intentional.* Measured. Like she'd placed a key in his hand and was waiting to see if he'd turn it.

She watched him. Not demanding an answer. Just waiting to see who he really was.

Mathieu leaned forward, elbows on the table, fingers laced. The low kitchen lantern cast shadows across the strong lines of his face, softening them just enough to make the weariness underneath visible.

"I know what I look like to you," he said, voice quieter now. "Some wandering rogue with a sharp tongue and too many secrets."

Her lips twitched, but she didn't interrupt.

"And you're not wrong," he added, almost wryly. "I've lied. I've run. I've fought for things that don't even exist anymore. Kingdoms. Flags. People long buried."

He glanced down at his hands, calloused and scarred. Then back up at her.

"But I was raised to be a man of honor. And even now—when I've lost everything that once defined me—I still remember what that means."

His gaze held hers, steady and unflinching.

"You trusted me with this. So I won't use it against you. I won't spread it. And I sure as hell won't forget the cost of you telling me."

A pause.

"I don't know if that makes me the kind of man you need." His voice dipped lower, almost a murmur. "But it's the only kind I know how to be."

Silence.

Not heavy this time. Just... full.

Her eyes were on him, still unreadable—but softer now. Like she was seeing something she hadn't expected. Or maybe hadn't dared to hope for.

The fire crackled quietly in the hearth.

Then, after a beat, Mathieu pushed back from the table and stood.

"Well," he said, reaching for the plates, "if I'm going to be the castle's morally torment-ed houseguest, I might as well do the dishes."

She blinked at him. "You don't have to. You did them last time."

"I know," he said, stacking their plates with practiced ease. "But it gives me something to do with my hands besides hurling myself down enchanted corridors or fighting dire wolves at dawn."

She smiled—small, surprised, but real.

He caught it.

And grinned back, just a little. "Besides, I'm trying to win your favor. Didn't you hear? I make excellent sandwiches, *and* I clean up after myself. At this rate, I might qualify as courtship material."

She made a noise that was almost a laugh.

And for the first time since stepping into that kitchen, the silence between them felt easy.

They didn't speak as they left the kitchen, the only sound their footsteps padding softly over stone and the low creak of the castle settling around them.

The halls were quieter now—still, as if Eldrenoire itself was holding its breath. But not in warning. In watchfulness.

Améliane walked a few paces ahead, her fingers skimming the cool curve of the banister as they ascended a narrow flight of stairs. Mathieu followed, not too close, not too far. And every so often, she glanced back at him.

Once, their eyes met.

She smiled—small, shy, a little disbelieving.

He smiled back.

No words.

None needed.

When they reached her chambers, the flickering torchlight revealed a familiar figure slumped against the doorframe: Thorne, leaning back with his arms crossed, trying very hard to look like he wasn't half-dozing on his feet.

He straightened the second he spotted her—and immediately went wide-eyed.

"My lady—uh—Your Majesty," he stammered, blinking hard like he thought he might be dreaming. "I wasn't expecting—well, obviously, I mean, I *was*, but not... like this."

His gaze flicked to Mathieu, and his expression went from surprised to utterly, comically scandalized.

Mathieu arched a brow. "Relax, Thorne. The queen only stole me away for a slice of cake and mild emotional devastation."

Thorne made a strangled sound that might have been a laugh—or a plea for help.

"See you at dawn for sparring," Mathieu said, already turning away with a half-smile and a wink. "Your Majesty. Thorne."

Améliane arched a brow. "If you two could try to keep your shirts on tomorrow, that'd be appreciated. We're trying to preserve the sanity of the castle staff."

He slowed, turned just enough to throw her a mock bow. "No promises."

"Goodnight, then," she said, voice softer now, but threaded with something warmer.

He nodded once.

Then turned and walked away, the corridor swallowing him in shadow and flickering torchlight.

Thorne turned slowly toward her, eyes still wide.

Améliane just smiled faintly, opened her door, and stepped inside without another word.

CHAPTER 16

Améliane

She awoke slowly, the way one might surface from a long, luxurious swim—no jolt, no gasp. Just a gentle float upward into the golden hush of early morning.

The gauzy curtains stirred in a breeze that hadn't been there the night before. Sunlight spilled in across the floor in soft ribbons, catching the corners of her bookcases, the curve of the writing desk, the pale sweep of the hearth.

Améliane stretched beneath the covers, her body sore in small, forgotten ways—a bruised elbow from bumping the kitchen table, a dull ache in her legs from barefoot mischief.

And then she smiled.

Not out of habit. Not for show.

A real one. Small. Startled.

Ridiculous.

She sat up and rubbed the heel of her hand against one eye, blinking against the warm light. The silk sheets rustled around her as she reached for her robe—midnight blue with silver threading, embroidered with an old Belmaran motif she rarely wore anymore. Too fine for most mornings. But this morning...well.

She slipped into it slowly, her thoughts already drifting back to the night before.

To laughter in the halls.

To stolen cake and toasted cheese on bread.

To the way his voice had gone low and quiet when he spoke of honor, as if it were something fragile he still dared to carry.

Mathieu. The name had settled strangely in her mind—no longer just a label for the brooding soldier who haunted her corridors. It had weight now. Edges. Heat.

And that moment in the Moonlit Courtyard—

Gods. She touched her lips, barely, as if they might still hold the echo of what hadn't quite happened.

It was foolish. Dangerous. And altogether too soon.

But it wasn't like it had been with Bastian.

That had been simpler. A distraction. A choice made in loneliness, when she'd still believed the castle would release her. He'd stumbled in with a cocky smile and a shirt half-undone, and she'd let herself pretend—for a season—that the ache she felt could be dulled by hands and mouths and shared silences.

And he'd fallen in love with her.

She'd known it. Had seen it in the way he'd looked at her, even when she was cold. Even when she offered nothing but her body and a smile that didn't reach her eyes.

When the curse had given him a choice—freedom or a life trapped at her side—he'd left.

And she didn't blame him.

He'd wanted something real. And she had been too broken to give it.

But Mathieu...

He didn't ask for her smiles. Didn't reach for her unless she reached first. He wasn't wooing her or pressing her for softness. He saw her with all her sharp corners and still—

A knock shattered the quiet.

Three sharp raps. Familiar. Stern.

Renaud.

Her stomach flipped, guilt and irritation warring for dominance.

She didn't know what he was here for—yet—but Renaud only knocked like that when something had either gone terribly wrong or exactly as he feared it would.

"Enter," she called, smoothing her expression into something composed.

The door swung open with the precision of a soldier's hand, and Renaud filled the doorway like an approaching storm. Broad-shouldered, jaw tight, steel-grey hair still damp from his morning bath—he looked every bit the sentinel she'd come to rely on.

And he was livid.

"You were supposed to be in your chambers," he said by way of greeting, voice low and clipped, like he was holding back something sharper.

Améliane arched a brow, gliding back to her writing desk without sitting. "Good morning, Renaud."

He stepped fully into the room, letting the door thud shut behind him. "You said you'd be retiring early. That you needed rest. Thorne was posted outside your door all night—until you showed up sometime after midnight with Mathieu in tow."

Ah.

So he *did* know.

"Was he armed with a quill when he reported to you?" she asked mildly, pouring herself tea she no longer wanted. "Or did he sketch us a scandalous little scene for dramatic effect?"

Renaud's mouth compressed into a flat, furious line. "You were barefoot, in a night-gown, walking side-by-side with a man we barely know. *After midnight*. You think I *need* embellishment?"

"Mathieu is not a threat."

"No," he said, "but he's *still* a man."

The teacup hit the saucer with a sharper clink than she intended.

Renaud's voice dropped. "You don't get to disappear, Améliane. Not without telling me. Not in *this* castle. Not with *him*."

"I wasn't in danger."

"You weren't *alone*," he snapped. "And that's the problem."

Améliane's jaw clenched, temper flaring hot and fast behind her ribs. "So, what would you have me do, Renaud? Live the next ten years in shadow because one man betrayed me? Lock myself in at dusk like some cursed maiden from a children's tale?"

"If it keeps you safe," he said, "then yes."

Silence bloomed. Thick and stifling.

And then, cold and controlled, she asked, "Do you not trust me to make my own choices anymore?"

Renaud exhaled hard through his nose, stepping forward. "I trust you to rule a kingdom. To read a man's intentions?" He hesitated, then said it, "Not always."

She stiffened.

It wasn't an accusation. It wasn't even cruel. It was worse. It was honest.

He took another breath, as if trying to cage his temper behind his ribs.

"I know you're lonely," he said quietly. "And I know he sees that. But don't confuse proximity for loyalty. That man is a stranger."

"He's more than that," she said, voice just above a whisper.

Renaud's expression didn't soften, but it faltered—just a flicker.

"I didn't tell you what he said," Améliane added, moving around to face him directly now, the silver trim of her robe catching the light. "Because I needed to understand it first. But you should know. You deserve to know."

Renaud's eyes narrowed, though some of the fury had drained from his posture. "Know *what*?"

She lifted her chin. "He saw the Mirror Hall."

That stopped him. Améliane recounted the story exactly as Mathieu had told it—his journey through the castle's shifting halls, the mirror that showed him too much, and the cryptic figure waiting at the end of it. And then she said it, the word still strange on her tongue, "He said Alaric called him *Wyrdbound*."

Renaud didn't speak at first.

The name hung in the air like smoke, like something half-summoned and not yet ready to disappear.

"Wyrdbound," he repeated slowly, as if testing the weight of it. His steel-grey brows drew together. "What does that mean?"

Améliane nodded. "Alaric told him it was what the old magic calls someone whose fate wasn't chosen, but inherited. Bound to destiny, but not ruled by it."

Renaud's mouth pulled into a thin line. "Sounds like a prophecy."

"Alaric *did* say the castle doesn't know what to make of him," she murmured. "That it bends for him... but doesn't trust him."

Renaud took a slow breath, the kind that usually came right before a tactical plan—or a lecture.

"And you believe him?" he asked. "Mathieu?"

"Yes," she said carefully. "And I believe Alaric gave him that name for a reason."

"That's the part that worries me." Renaud moved to the window, staring out at the mist curling across the gardens below.

She crossed her arms. "Which is why I want to ask him about it directly."

Renaud turned, eyes sharp. "You're going to summon him?"

"I don't think we have a choice."

Instead, she rose from the table in one smooth motion and crossed the chamber with practiced grace, the hem of her robe whispering across the floor. Her bare feet made no sound, but the weight of her intention filled the space like thunder held just behind the clouds.

She stopped at the far wall and opened the drawer of her writing desk.

Inside, nestled between a stack of old letters and a dried moonflower, sat a small leather-bound book. Plain. Unmarked. No clasp. No title. Just aged pages bound in dark thread—and a faint shimmer along the edges, like dust that refused to settle.

The book had no words. It never had. But once, long ago—on the second night of her curse, when the silence of the castle had been so suffocating she thought she might scream—she'd opened it on a whim and written her name. Not as a summons. Not even as a plea. Just to remember who she was, even as the rest of the world began to forget. Within minutes, Alaric had appeared in her chambers like a specter summoned by sorrow.

She'd tested it again, weeks later. Another name, another inked line. No answer.

Only her name had ever worked.

The book was bound to her. Or perhaps... to the castle's idea of her.

She opened it now and turned to a blank page near the middle—though the pages never seemed to run out. Taking the quill from her inkwell, she dipped it once and signed her name in a fluid, looping hand:

Améliane Morvenne.

The ink shimmered—then bled away, vanishing like it had never existed.

She waited, hand resting lightly on the edge of the desk, heart beating too fast for such a small act.

Behind her, Renaud folded his arms. "How long does it take?"

She didn't answer.

Because Alaric never came when called.

He came when *invited*. And he was never late.

The ink had barely dried on the page when the air shifted.

It wasn't dramatic. Just a subtle pressure in the room—like the moment before a thunderclap, when the sky holds its breath.

And then Alaric was there.

Not standing in the doorway. Not appearing in a gust of shadow. Simply there, as if he had always been sitting in the chair across from the hearth, legs crossed, his tattered book balanced in one long-fingered hand. The robes he wore were heavy and flowing, midnight-dark, and somehow impervious to dust or time. Not even the shadows clung to them. He didn't look up from the book. Didn't flip a page.

"You summoned," he said, without inflection. His long locs, threaded with silver, fell over his shoulders in quiet waves, each strand gleaming faintly in the morning light.

Renaud reached for his sword on instinct, the tension in his frame immediate.

Améliane didn't startle. Not anymore.

She stepped calmly toward the hearth, robe whispering across the floor. "How long have you been here?"

Alaric finally lifted his head. His golden-flecked eyes met hers with the slow weight of something ancient.

"Long enough to know your breakfast was underwhelming," he said mildly. "And that your commander could use more sleep."

Renaud bristled. "You—"

"Peace, Commander," Améliane said, lifting a hand.

Alaric turned a page of his book—blank, as always. His finger traced a line that wasn't there. "You've seen him, then."

Renaud stepped forward. "You named him."

Alaric inclined his head. "I did."

"You've never done that before," Améliane said quietly.

"No one's ever worn the title before," Alaric replied. "At least... not in this age."

She crossed her arms. "Then explain it. What is *Wyrdbound*?"

Alaric studied them both, then closed the book with a sound like a whisper being silenced.

"There is an old story," he said. "From before Belmara and the southern kingdoms. From the time when the Veil Isles were still whole, and the gods had not yet turned away."

Renaud rolled his eyes. "There's always an old story."

"And they are always true," Alaric said, his voice sharper now—cutting through the room like a knife through silk.

He stood. His robes did not rustle. Dust did not dare cling.

"There was a queen," he began. "Like you, Améliane. Powerful. Beloved. Cursed."

She flinched—but only slightly.

"Her kingdom fell to betrayal. Dark magic was used to bind her soul to a distant place. A cage of beauty. A curse with no key."

Améliane's voice was barely a whisper. "How was it broken?"

Alaric's gaze turned toward the fire.

"It wasn't."

A long pause.

"But the legend says this: that dark magic, no matter how precise, cannot seal every door. It is always flawed, always hungry. The price it demands always leaves a crack. A hairline fracture."

He turned back to her.

"And into that flaw, fate may slip. Not a hero. Not a savior. But someone bound to the wrong things. To old oaths. Forgotten wars. Grief with no grave. Someone who doesn't want the crown or the story—but becomes part of it anyway."

"Wyrdbound," she said.

Alaric nodded once. "They do not come often. And when they do, they break more than the curse." He looked directly at her. "They break the pattern."

Silence bloomed in the chamber, thick and silver-edged.

Alaric stood still as a mahogany statue near the fireplace, his dark robes barely stirring though the air shifted like it breathed around him. He was tall and lean, but not frail—more like a tree that had stood too long in one place, bearing witness to centuries no one remembered.

His deep brown eyes glinted gold for the barest second as he closed the book in his hands—blank as always—and let the silence stretch.

Renaud was the first to speak.

"So that's it?" he demanded clinching his jaw as he crossed the room in two strides. "You speak in riddles and leave us with prophecy?"

Alaric did not blink. "Prophecies are riddles. That is their nature."

"And you think this man—this outsider who stumbled into our curse by accident—is the Wyrdbound?"

Alaric tilted his head, the barest smile on his lips. "Did he stumble? Or did the castle open for him?"

Renaud stiffened.

Améliane hadn't moved. Her hands rested lightly on the edge of her desk; the summoning book still open beside her. Her gaze was distant, thoughtful. But her voice, when it came, was sharp as a blade.

"You said the Wyrdbound breaks the pattern."

Alaric inclined his head.

"What pattern?" she asked. "The curse? The castle? Or something else?"

A smile ghosted across his face. "Yes."

Renaud let out a low growl of frustration. "If he breaks the curse, then why is he being toyed with? Why not free us all and be done with it?"

"Because the castle does not serve prophecy," Alaric replied, his voice like old stone and wind. "It serves memory. And punishment."

His eyes slid to Améliane. "Eldrenoire was forged to bind her. To protect her, but also to preserve her suffering. And yet, it cannot unmake the loophole left by the dark magic that cursed her."

Améliane went still.

Alaric stepped forward, just once, just enough for the shadows to shift across his face. "The Wyrdbound is not the cure. He is the flaw. The unpredicted variable. The crack in the design."

Renaud's voice was low. "And what happens when something cracks?"

Alaric looked at him, and for the first time, there was no riddle in his tone.

"It either breaks apart..."

He turned to Améliane.

"Or it breaks open."

Another silence.

This time, it was Améliane who broke it. "Is there more we should know?"

Alaric smiled faintly. "You'll know when the castle decides to tell you."

"Of course," she murmured.

And then—as silently as he had come—Alaric faded back. Not vanished. Not disappeared. Just... faded.

The fire crackled again. A page rustled in the book, though no one had touched it.

Renaud let out a slow breath. "What do we do now?"

Améliane stared at the hearth, her jaw tight.

"We watch him," she said. "But we do not cage him."

Renaud's expression was wary. "You trust this prophecy?"

She hesitated. "I trust the castle. And it let him find the Moonlit Courtyard."

Her fingers brushed the edge of the book.

"Mathieu..." she said softly. "He might be the first thing this place has brought me that doesn't seem to want to keep me broken."

Renaud didn't answer right away. He stood beside her in the hush that followed, his gaze fixed not on her, but on the flickering lantern where Alaric had disappeared.

When he finally spoke, his voice was low. Measured.

"Then let's hope the castle doesn't break him first."

Améliane looked down at the blank page in the book still open on her desk.

The ink had dried. But the weight of it lingered.

She closed it gently.

And for the first time in years, she found herself wondering not if there was a way out of Eldrenoire—but if someone might already be carving one.

CHAPTER 17

Mathieu

The courtyard was already hot with morning sun when Thorne lunged at him again, sword swinging in a clean arc that would've taken someone else's head clean off.

Mathieu parried with a grunt, pivoted, and spun out wide to reset. "You always this violent before lunch?" he asked, wiping a bead of sweat from his brow.

Thorne grinned, eyes gleaming beneath his copper hair. "Only when I'm picturing your smug face on a training dummy."

"How flattering," Mathieu deadpanned, circling. "Should I be worried you're working through something? Or is this just your idea of foreplay?"

Thorne snorted. "Please. You're not my type."

"Too tall? Too charming? Too good with a blade?"

"Too loud."

They clashed again—steel ringing sharp in the still air—and this time, Thorne's blade nearly clipped Mathieu's side. Close. He was getting better. Mathieu liked that.

They disengaged, breathing hard, each grinning like boys who hadn't yet learned the cost of bruises. Across the field, another pair had joined them. Mathieu recognized the lean frame of Laurent immediately—fluid, coiled grace in motion as he flipped a short dagger between his fingers like it weighed nothing.

But the other figure gave him pause.

"Élodie?" he asked, glancing sidelong at Thorne. "Since when does she train?"

Thorne followed his gaze, a bit too quickly. "She started the year after we first came to Eldrenoire. Said she got tired of feeling useless." His voice softened slightly. "She's good, though her duties keep her busy most mornings."

Mathieu smirked, already catching the flicker in Thorne's eye. "Ah. I see."

Thorne didn't rise to the bait, but the tips of his ears went pink.

"Oh no," Mathieu said, mock-serious. "You've got it bad."

"I do not."

"You do," Mathieu said, sidestepping a halfhearted swing. "You've been grinning like a tavern fool ever since she showed up. It's adorable."

Thorne rolled his eyes. "Remind me to knock that grin off your face."

Mathieu lowered his sword, just slightly. "Too late. You've got competition now. I've seen her wield a dagger. Sharp, fast, terrifying when annoyed—my dream woman."

"Back off," Thorne growled, only half joking.

Mathieu's smile widened.

Then he heard boots crunching on gravel behind him—heavier, faster, with the rhythm of a man on a mission.

Mathieu turned just as Renaud came into view and instinct had him shifting his stance. Not out of fear. Out of the kind of war-bred reflex you couldn't shake once it was trained into your bones.

Fury was etched into every line of the commander's face. His jaw clenched tight enough to crack teeth. His cloak was already coming off in one rough motion, followed by the deep blue sash at his waist, discarded with the grace of a man who had no time for ceremony. Next went the long outer tunic, stripped and tossed aside as he strode across the field.

The air shifted.

Thorne straightened. "Commander?"

"Move," Renaud barked, voice like a snapped command in a battlefield fog.

Thorne stumbled backward without protest.

Renaud didn't stop. He marched straight into the sparring ring, drew his blade with a fluid snap, and lunged.

Mathieu barely had time to raise his sword.

Steel crashed against steel with enough force to rattle bone.

"What the hell—" he grunted, bracing against the blow as Renaud came at him again, eyes burning with something feral.

"Training," the commander growled. "You said you wanted practice."

Another strike. This one clipped Mathieu's shoulder hard enough to sting through the padding.

He staggered, adjusted, parried.

"I didn't ask for bloodsport," he snapped.

"No?" Renaud said, teeth bared. "Shame. You've already earned it."

Mathieu twisted away from the next attack, dropped low, and came up swinging—only for Renaud to block with brutal efficiency.

"Sir—" Thorne stepped forward.

"Stand down, Lieutenant!" Renaud snapped.

Thorne halted, torn between duty and disbelief.

The clash of blades rang out again. Harder. Heavier. Each blow more punishing than the last.

Across the courtyard, Élodie and Laurent froze mid-spar. They turned as one, daggers lowered, drawn like moths to the fury unraveling in front of them.

Renaud drove Mathieu back with a flurry of strikes—tight, precise, merciless.

Mathieu gritted his teeth. "If you've got something to say, Commander, you could try using your words."

Another swing. Another block.

Renaud's eyes flashed. "You were alone with her. In the middle of the night. And no one knew where you were."

"I didn't touch her!"

"You *wanted* to."

That landed sharper than the sword.

Mathieu's grip tightened. "So what is this then? Some chest-thumping show of loyalty?"

Renaud sneered. "This is me reminding you who she *belongs* to."

And that—*that*—snapped something loose in Mathieu.

He shoved forward, ducked under Renaud's guard, and slammed his hilt into the older man's ribs.

Renaud grunted, stumbled—but didn't fall.

They circled.

Sweat slicked down both their temples. Their shirts clung to them. Dirt smeared their boots and trousers as they moved in that brutal, practiced rhythm of men who had seen real war and never stopped carrying it.

Élodie whispered something to Laurent, too soft to hear.

Laurent didn't answer. He was watching with narrowed eyes, unreadable.

Renaud feinted. Mathieu caught it. Countered.

The next blow came fast and low.

Mathieu blocked. Spun. Slashed.

It was controlled violence, barely kept in check by discipline and pride.

And neither of them was backing down.

Steel met steel again, sparks kissing the air between them as their blades slid apart.

"I didn't go looking for her," Mathieu snapped, circling fast to avoid another blow. "I was lost in the castle for *hours* and it spat me out practically at her feet."

Renaud swung hard. Mathieu ducked beneath it, sweat stinging his eyes.

"And just to reiterate," he added, panting now, "I didn't touch her."

Their blades clashed again—louder this time, more fury behind it.

Renaud snarled. "You think that earns you a medal?"

"I think it earns me a *damn minute* before your sword's at my throat," Mathieu growled, bracing against the next strike. "She's your Queen, not your prisoner."

"You don't know what she's been through."

"No," Mathieu said, shoving back hard enough to make the commander stumble. "But I know this—"

Another strike. Parried.

"She belongs to *no one* but herself."

That landed. Not on Renaud's ribs, not on his sword arm—but somewhere deeper. His next blow was half a breath too slow.

And Mathieu moved.

He twisted in low, hooked Renaud's leg with his boot, and swept.

The commander hit the ground hard, his sword skidding out of reach with a metallic clang.

Silence rang sharper than any blade.

Renaud stared up at him, chest heaving, sweat slicked across his temple. The gravel bit into his back, but he didn't move.

Mathieu stood over him, sword lowered.

And for a moment—just one breath—they were still.

Then Mathieu stepped back, sheathed his blade, and reached out a hand.

Renaud's eyes flicked to it.

The muscle in his jaw ticked.

Then, without a word, Renaud slapped Mathieu's offered hand aside and rolled to his feet, slow and steady, like a man who refused to be helped—even in the moments he needed it most.

He stood nose to nose with him, both of them breathing hard, sweat shining on their skin.

"You may be the *Wyrdbound*," Renaud spat, voice low and biting, "not that I believe in old names and fairy stories—but even if it's true, that doesn't make you special."

Mathieu's jaw tightened, but he didn't speak.

"It doesn't give you liberties with her," Renaud finished. "And it sure as hell doesn't earn you my trust."

He bent, snatched up his fallen sword, then his discarded cloak and sash, his movements clipped and cold.

Then he turned and stalked off across the training grounds without another word, the gravel crunching beneath his boots in time with his fury.

Silence followed in Renaud's wake, heavy and stunned. The only sound was the soft crackle of gravel settling beneath the weight of his departure.

Then, dry as the summer wind, Laurent said, "What the actual *fuck* was that??"

Élodie let out a breath she'd clearly been holding. "Is he always like that when sparring, or did you insult his ancestors in another language?"

Thorne gave a small shake of his head, still processing. "I've seen him take down a rogue drake with less aggression."

Mathieu didn't answer. He moved across the training yard to the low stone bench near the edge of the clearing, peeled off his outer shirt with a wince, and grabbed the canteen resting in the shadow of the armory wall. The water was lukewarm and tasted faintly of tin, but he drank deeply, letting the coolness chase the heat from his blood.

He wiped a forearm across his brow, then looked up to find the other three watching him.

Laurent leaned casually against a wooden post, one brow arched. Élodie stood beside him, still holding her practice sword, though she seemed to have forgotten it entirely. Thorne hovered nearby, arms crossed, his usual dry amusement tempered by something close to concern.

Mathieu exhaled.

"I got lost in the castle last night," he said. "Not wandering. Properly lost. For hours."

That got their attention. Laurent straightened.

"It spat me out in a place I'd never seen before," he continued. "She called it the Moonlit Courtyard. She being the Queen, because she was also there."

Élodie's brows lifted.

"We talked," he went on. "Then we ended up sneaking through the halls and raiding the kitchen."

Laurent made a low, appreciative sound. "So, secret garden meetings and midnight snacks. Gods, you do move quickly."

Mathieu didn't rise to the bait.

Because now came the hard part.

But before he could speak, Thorne let out a quiet breath and stepped forward, rubbing the back of his neck.

"They came creeping in just past midnight," he said, half to Élodie and Laurent, half to the gravel. "She was barefoot. Laughing. He looked like he'd just stolen the moon."

Mathieu blinked. "I—what?"

Thorne held up a hand. "Don't get me wrong. You two looked... like you were having fun. Like you'd gotten away with something you weren't supposed to do. Like a pair of children caught sneaking sugar from the pantry."

Élodie tilted her head, smirking. "That actually tracks."

But then Thorne's smile faded. He looked at Mathieu fully now, eyes steady, voice quieter.

"I'm sorry," he said. "I was duty-bound to tell Renaud. He's her commander. She was supposed to be in her chambers. I didn't want to—" He broke off, then added, "But I couldn't not tell him."

Mathieu nodded once, his expression unreadable.

"You did your job," he said. "No harm in that."

But the muscle in his jaw ticked all the same.

Thorne dragged a hand through his sweat-damp hair. "Honestly, I had no idea he'd react like that. I've never seen him lose his temper like that—not even when Laurent swapped his sword for a dulled training blade during inspection week."

Laurent held up both hands in mock innocence. "In my defense, it was hilarious."

Mathieu didn't smile. He stared at the ground for a beat, then muttered to Thorne, "You've never seen him react like what? Like he's half in love with her and I encroached on his territory by having some cheese and bread with her?"

There was a pause.

Then Élodie snorted. "Oh, he is fully in love with her. Renaud's been in love with her since his first day as her royal guard. But to be fair—" she shrugged, glancing sideways at Laurent, "—pretty much everyone who meets her is."

Laurent clutched his chest. "Speak for yourself. I am immune to royal charm."

"You're not immune to anything in a silk nightgown," Thorne said under his breath.

Laurent winked. "You're not wrong."

Thorne's expression sobered, the teasing fading from his face like mist in the morning sun. "He may be in love with her, sure. But Renaud is the most loyal, duty-bound man I've ever known. He'd die before he let it show. And he'll bury those feelings a thousand times because he knows his job is keeping her safe."

He paused, rubbing at the back of his neck. "Whatever he felt back there—it wasn't jealousy. It was fear. And guilt. Because she's all he has left to protect."

Élodie glanced sideways at Mathieu, curiosity flickering behind her eyes. "So... what were you doing all those hours you were 'lost'?" Her tone was casual, but her gaze was sharp.

Mathieu didn't answer right away. Instead, he dropped onto the bench beside his canteen and leaned forward, resting his forearms on his knees. One by one, the others followed—Thorne, Élodie, then Laurent with theatrical reluctance, like he was settling in for a bedtime story he wasn't sure he wanted to hear.

They were all eye-level now. Still a little breathless. Still carrying the shadow of Renaud's rage. But something had shifted. The air was cooler, quieter. Expectant.

Mathieu twisted the cap from his canteen, took a drink, and stared into the distance for a beat before speaking.

"I wasn't trying to find her," he said. "I really was lost. Eldrenoire shut every door I tried. Halls folded in on themselves. Paintings I'd passed minutes before vanished. It wasn't just confusing—it was deliberate. Like it wanted me disoriented."

Laurent arched a brow. "Sounds like most of my romantic entanglements."

Thorne elbowed him, but Élodie just waved a hand. "Let him finish."

Mathieu's jaw tightened. "Eventually, the castle spat me out into a courtyard I'd never seen before. Overgrown, beautiful. Quiet. At its center was this reflecting pool that looked like it could show you the beginning or end of the world, depending on when you looked."

"She was there," Mathieu continued. "The queen. I didn't mean to interrupt her, but..."

"And that's when you made your move?" Laurent smirked.

Mathieu shot him a look. "Then we talked," he said. "Really talked."

A long pause. Then, finally, "And later that night in the kitchens, I told her about Alaric."

Laurent's teasing slipped away. Élodie leaned in slightly. Even Thorne straightened.

"You saw him?" she asked.

"In a place full of mirrors," Mathieu said. "I'd wandered into some hidden corridor I've never seen before. Full of reflections that weren't mine. Memories. Regrets. Things I've done. Things I didn't want to see."

The silence stretched.

"And Alaric was there. Waiting. Said the castle didn't know what to make of me." His voice dropped. "He called me a name."

"What?" Thorne asked, brows furrowing.

Mathieu looked at each of them in turn.

"He said that Eldrenoire called me *Wyrdbound*."

"Wyrdbound."

The word fell like a stone into still water, and no one moved. Even the birds in the trees above seemed to quiet, as if the castle itself were listening.

"Wyrdbound?" Laurent said. "Sounds like a particularly moody bard's stage name."

Mathieu gave him a flat look.

"It's not just a name," Élodie said slowly, eyes narrowing. "It's legend. Old legend. From the Veil Isles, I think. My grandmother used to tell stories—something about fate choosing someone to... unravel a curse?"

"Or die trying," Thorne added grimly. "I've heard similar bedtime stories as a child. They're always tragic."

Mathieu gave a short, humorless huff. "That seems about right."

"What else did Alaric say?" Élodie asked. "He never gives more than he wants to. But if the castle named you, that means something."

Mathieu looked down at his hands for a long moment, then said, "He said the name means someone whose fate wasn't chosen—but inherited. Someone bound to destiny but not ruled by it. He said I don't fit the castle's design... that I might be the flaw in the curse."

The others exchanged glances.

Laurent whistled low. "Well, that explains why Renaud looked ready to throttle you with his bare hands."

Thorne leaned back slightly, folding his arms. "He's not wrong to be cautious. If the curse is meant to preserve the queen's suffering, and you're the crack in that—then you're a threat to everything this place is built to protect."

"Or maybe not a threat," Élodie said softly. "Maybe a chance..."

That hung there for a beat.

Mathieu looked toward the castle, where sunlight glinted off the high spires and ivy wound itself like veins through the stone—and saw Margot heading their way across the lawn, a woven basket swinging on her hip.

"Is it just me," Laurent muttered, "or does she always walk like she knows more than you do?"

"She probably does," Élodie replied under her breath.

Margot reached them, her braids pinned up in her usual polished coils, smile easy but eyes keen. She handed the basket to Thorne with a small, practiced flourish.

"Your midnight breakfast," she said. "Figured you'd need something before collapsing like a tragic hero."

Thorne took the basket with a grateful grunt, but before he could reply, she cast a glance around at the rest of them. "You all look like you're trying to solve the kingdom's biggest riddle."

The silence that followed wasn't long—but it was heavy. Telling.

Eyes flicked between them. A flicker of shared understanding. Agreement passed without a word.

Whatever they'd discussed, it stayed between the four of them.

Laurent recovered first, stretching lazily with an exaggerated yawn. "Don't mind us. Just debating the moral complexities of dueling shirtless."

Margot gave him a withering look. "So, the usual."

"And lunch is in the kitchens," she added, already turning to go. "Assuming none of you are too morally complex to eat."

Thorne set his basket on the grass, stretched once, and without fanfare, shifted.

Antlers first. Then hooves. Then fur as black as midnight rippling down his flanks.

The black stag stood tall and regal in the clearing, sunlight caught in the white streak that curved along his left side. He dipped his head, hooked the basket with one horn, and trotted off toward the barracks with all the dignity of a knight leaving court.

Mathieu watched him go, arms crossed loosely over his chest.

"I will never," he muttered, "get used to that."

Élodie snorted. "You get used to everything in Eldrenoire. Eventually."

CHAPTER 18

Améliane

The leaves beyond the library window had turned from gold to rust.

A month ago, the vines curling up Eldrenoire's stone walls had still clung to summer. Now, they whispered of frost, their edges curling like old parchment, their hues deepening into the burnished copper of a dying season. It was subtle—everything in the castle was—but Améliane had learned to mark time in shadows and softness. In the way the light hit the floorboards. In the scent of cold beginning to thread through the air, faint and earthy.

It had been nearly five months since the stranger arrived.

And Valmont had vanished from the ledgers.

She frowned down at the ancient book sprawled open before her, its spine cracked and ink faded with age. The parchment smelled of dust and something older—memory, perhaps. Her fingers drifted over a passage in Belmaran script, the ink too faint to make out entirely, but she knew what it said.

Valmont. Once a proud kingdom in the Northern Reaches. A place known for its warriors and fortified cliffs. Not a trading partner—too isolated—but an ally, once. And now...

Gone. Not destroyed. Not footnoted with battle dates or annexation.

Just *gone*.

Struck from the records.

The queen leaned back in her carved wooden chair, stretching with a quiet sigh as her silk sleeves whispered against polished arms worn smooth by time. She had been here for hours—since before dawn—taking both breakfast and lunch amidst the parchment and dust. Footnotes led her down winding paths through crumbling tomes and forgotten ledgers, some untouched since the days before the curse fell.

Cassien's voice lingered in her mind from his last visit, "*The scribes no longer list Valmont among the Four Northerlies. It's as though it never existed.*"

Her thoughts drifted to Mathieu—not for the first time that morning.

She'd asked him nothing about his homeland. He had volunteered even less. But there was something about the way he spoke—clipped but articulate. The way he studied things before speaking, as though weighing every word like a man who once had to be diplomatic by necessity, not choice.

She tapped the edge of the book with a fingernail. A slow, rhythmic sound in the vast hush of the library.

And then the door creaked.

Not loud. Just enough to draw her head up.

The space had many entrances—two main ones from the upper galleries, one side door from the west hall, and a hidden passage behind the bookcase in the far corner that only the cursed court ever used.

The one that opened now was none of those. It was the south door—the one that never opened. The one even the castle had seemed to forget about, until this morning.

And standing in the threshold, blinking at her in mild surprise, was Mathieu.

His hair was tousled, the dark waves sprinkled with grey falling in a way that looked almost intentional—too careless to be careless. His shirt hung open at the collar, sleeves rolled to the forearms, the fabric rumpled with the ease of a man who hadn't bothered with mirrors. There was a quiet intensity in his stride, like he hadn't meant to find her—but now that he had, he wasn't leaving.

He stepped inside, the door closing behind him without a sound.

Mathieu glanced at the books, then at her, and said with a half-smile, "I was headed for the kitchens in search of some tea, but the castle decided I needed a detour."

Améliane simply gestured to the low table beside her, where a fresh tea service sat, steam curling from the silver spout.

"Then you've arrived exactly where you were meant to be." She paused just long enough to arch a brow. "Though if your idea of a shortcut is detouring through two locked corridors and a turning stairwell, I question your sense of direction."

Mathieu walked to the table, inspecting the teacups with mock solemnity. "I prefer to think of it as... creative wayfinding."

He poured a cup without waiting for permission, then took a sip and winced. "Chamomile. The castle's idea of a joke, clearly."

"Or a hint," she said dryly, "that you might benefit from a bit of calm."

He gave her a look over the rim of the cup. "You wound me, Your Majesty. I'm the very image of serenity."

"Then perhaps it's serenity that should be worried."

That earned a soft huff of laughter. She didn't smile, but her eyes gleamed with the amusement she refused to voice.

The moment held. Not strained. Not tense. Just... quiet. And new.

Then, without a word, she rose from the table and crossed to one of the far shelves, scanning the spines until she found what she was looking for.

Or tried to.

The book was just out of reach. She lifted onto her toes, fingertips brushing the leather binding as her skirts shifted around her legs. She was almost there—almost—

A warm hand settled gently at her waist.

Améliane froze.

Mathieu's body was behind hers, solid and steady, heat radiating through the thin layers of silk and air. His other hand reached past her, plucking the book free with casual ease. His breath stirred a strand of hair near her temple.

"Let me," he said softly.

She didn't move.

Couldn't.

The hand at her waist wasn't possessive, just balanced. Anchoring her. But the contact—after so long without it—sent sparks skittering across her skin. She was suddenly, acutely aware of everything: the brush of his knuckles as he handed her the book, the way her back barely touched his chest, the warmth that pulsed in the narrow space between them.

She turned slowly.

He was close. Too close. And he wasn't moving away.

Neither was she.

For a beat, neither of them spoke.

Then he glanced down at the book in her hands—and something in his expression shifted.

"Valmont," he said, the name a low murmur. "You're researching my graveyard."

They returned to the chairs by the hearth, the silence between them no longer awkward, but heavy with something unspoken. Améliane poured him another cup of tea without asking, her fingers steady even as her pulse remained uneven.

Mathieu glanced down at the cover of the book again, "Why are you researching Valmont?"

Améliane didn't answer right away. She lifted her teacup, sipped slowly, then set it back down with care.

"You remember," she said, "when I told you Cassien brings me the news of the outside world and that Valmont had vanished from Belmara's ledgers?"

Mathieu cringed slightly, but nodded.

"During his last visit, he said something that's been clawing at the back of my mind ever since." She leaned forward, her elbows resting lightly on her knees. "He said, 'The scribes no longer list Valmont among the Four Northerlies. It's as though it never existed.'"

Mathieu blinked. "Erased?"

She nodded once. "From ledgers. Trade logs. Diplomatic records. Even the maps." Her voice dipping into something grim and thoughtful. "I'm trying to remember what I can about Valmont as it was—before the curse exiled me here. Borders. Treaties. Lineages. Anything that might hint at what could justify such a vanishing."

His throat bobbed as he swallowed. "And have you?"

"No," she admitted, glancing toward the shelves. "Valmont wasn't a kingdom I dealt with often. It was self-contained. Fortified. Difficult to navigate, politically. But respected. Feared, even. No one wipes out a place like that without blood."

Mathieu let out a soft breath and settled back in the chair, a book balanced on one knee. The firelight caught on his profile, casting shadows beneath the sharp line of his jaw.

"It wasn't always like that," he said. "Valmont, I mean. It had teeth, sure. But there was more to it than steel and stone." He stared into the fire for a moment, then added, "I grew up there. My mother grew lavender in our courtyard. Said it kept the peace. I thought she was crazy until I realized I slept better when it bloomed."

Améliane's expression didn't shift, but surprise flickered in her eyes.

Mathieu's gaze stayed fixed on the flames, the firelight painting his face in gold and shadow. He was still for a long moment, so long Améliane thought he might not continue.

"Surprising, I know, that I wasn't always a wanderer," he said finally, with a sad smile. "I had a home once. A life."

She said nothing, only waited.

"My father died of age. My mother not long after—grief, I think, though no one ever said it aloud. My older brother took the mantle after them. He was the one born for it—sharp, noble, full of speeches and certainty. He led well. Until the war came."

Something in his voice caught there, but he pushed through.

"The Rothgarians were brutal. Calculated. They struck fast and hard, and we weren't ready. My brother was killed in the first wave, and suddenly everything I thought I was... became something else. One minute, I was commanding battalions in the hills. The next, I was expected to be the man of my house."

His mouth twisted, bitter.

"I was always better with a blade than a council. I knew how to win a battle, not charm politicians. But there wasn't time to argue with succession. There was barely time to breathe."

He exhaled and leaned forward, elbows on his knees.

"We lost the final battle before it even began. They drew us out—burned our stores, collapsed our outer wall with a weapon I still don't fully understand. My men died fast, most of them never seeing the flag fall. I fought until I couldn't stand. And then..." He rubbed the back of his neck, jaw clenched. "I was taken after that."

Améliane's breath caught, but she didn't interrupt.

"They didn't need to kill me," he said. "They just needed me quiet. Forgotten. I was their symbol—so they made an example. Shackles. A cell. Questions I didn't answer. Days that bled into each other—literally and figuratively. Eventually I stopped hoping to be found."

He didn't look at her, not yet.

"But I did escape. Slipped through a guard rotation on a supply run. Killed the man holding the keys. After that..." He lifted a shoulder. "I ran. I've been running ever since."

There was a silence—deep and unflinching—before he added, more quietly, "My wife died the day I was captured. Tess. She wasn't supposed to be near the front, but the capital was breached. She was carrying our child."

Améliane's eyes went soft with something too deep for sympathy—recognition, perhaps. A shared grief.

"I never got to bury them," Mathieu finished, voice rough.

He finally turned his gaze to hers. And in it, she saw the truth he hadn't spoken—not titles or names, but the weight of loss worn into his bones.

Mathieu stood, the quiet motion of it somehow heavier than footsteps. He set the book down on the edge of the table—careful, deliberate—and pressed the heel of his hand to one eye as if he could scrub the memory away. Then the other. No tears fell, but the weight of them hung on his lashes.

He turned from her, walking toward the shelves—toward the order and distraction of old spines and dust-heavy parchment. Somewhere, between the soft sound of his boots and the flicker of the fire behind him, he put his hands on the shelves and let his head bow, just slightly. A man trying to find steadiness in something that didn't sway.

Améliane rose slowly.

She didn't speak. Didn't announce herself or fill the silence with platitudes. She simply crossed the room, the soft fall of her robes whispering across the stones. When she reached him, she hesitated just long enough to give him the chance to step away.

He didn't.

So she reached out and laid a hand on his bare forearm. Her fingers curved against his skin—cool, deliberate, and uncharacteristically bold. The first touch she had ever offered him. The first tether, fragile and terrifying.

She didn't speak right away.

Instead, she let the silence breathe between them—let his grief settle without crowding it. Then, quietly, as if offering a truth instead of a comfort, she said, "I know what it means to lose the life you were meant to live."

He didn't interrupt, and so she continued—quiet, but certain.

"I had a home once, too. My parents were doting and the halls of Miralys were always full of laughter. We lost my mother when my sister was little, and my father left us a few years later. My brother—when he died, I was next in line. Not because anyone wanted me there—just because I was next in line."

Her hand stayed on his arm, and he didn't move.

"Belmara had never had a queen," she went on. "They called me a figurehead. A placeholder. I was twenty-eight when I took the throne. I'd spent my whole life preparing to be the contingency plan and still... nothing prepared me for what came next."

Her eyes darkened, but not with fear—with memory.

"The court split in two. Half shouted that I was unfit. The other half thought it. I hoped I could win them over with time. With strength. With fairness. And then..." She swallowed. "Then I married Edric."

His name landed like a dropped coin—soft, but sharp.

"I thought I loved him," she said. "And maybe, once, I did. He was clever. Beautiful. Devoted in all the ways I thought mattered. But he didn't want to serve beside me. He wanted to rule in my place. And when he couldn't have that, he found another way."

Mathieu's brow furrowed. "The curse."

She nodded. "He made a bargain with dark magic. Convinced others to turn against me. Used the people I trusted to trap me inside this castle. He made the world forget I had ever even existed."

Her fingers tightened just slightly on his arm.

"So yes," she said. "I understand loss."

Mathieu turned toward her fully now, the firelight catching in his eyes. She didn't drop her hand.

"You're not alone in your grief," she said. "And neither am I."

For a moment, neither of them moved.

Améliane's hand lingered on his arm, her fingers brushing lightly against the skin just beneath the rolled cuff of his sleeve. The warmth of him bled into her palm, steady and real, and the silence between them softened—no longer heavy, just... close.

Mathieu looked down at her hand, then back at her. His eyes weren't guarded the way they'd been when he first arrived in Eldrenoire. They were open now. Wounded, yes. But open.

"You don't speak like a queen," he said quietly.

She arched a brow, but didn't pull away. "How should a queen speak?"

"Like someone who still believes she's above the rest of us."

Her smile curved, just slightly. "You think I've given up?"

"I think you've learned how to bleed in private."

That stole the air between them.

He stepped in closer, not looming, not bold—but like someone drawn by gravity he no longer meant to resist. They stood nearly chest to chest now, the faint space between them crackling like a held breath as she tipped her chin up to look at him. Her hand slid slowly down his arm until it rested just above his wrist, where his pulse beat strong and sure.

"And you," she said softly, "don't speak like a man trying to escape."

He swallowed. "Maybe I'm not."

The fire crackled behind them. His gaze flicked to her mouth, then back to her eyes. She didn't move.

Neither did he.

But the pull was there—undeniable, bone-deep. A magnetic thread winding tighter between them with every heartbeat.

Her breath caught, just slightly, as he leaned in—slow, reverent, like he was giving her every chance to stop him.

And she didn't.

Not until—

A heavy book crashed to the floor behind them.

Mathieu reacted on instinct, a soldier's reflex forged by war and loss. He moved fast, a hand at her waist as he stepped in front of her, shielding her with his body.

The silence that followed was punctuated only by the soft creak of a hidden panel still swinging open behind the far bookcase.

They both turned just in time to catch a glimpse—a pale, bushy tail slipping around the corner, vanishing through the passage used only by the cursed shifters.

Mathieu straightened slowly, his expression caught somewhere between amusement and disbelief. He looked back at her, one brow raised.

"Your Highness," he said, voice dry, "should I be concerned about your rodent problem?"

Améliane blinked, still a touch breathless. Then—despite everything, or maybe because of it—she laughed.

"Eldrenoire has many problems," she said, still smiling. "That might be the least of them."

Améliane's laughter lingered between them for one precious heartbeat as she stepped back, smoothing invisible wrinkles from her gown as though that might erase what had nearly happened.

Mathieu said nothing, but the look he gave her was warm. Understanding. The sort of look that suggested he wasn't going to press—but he wasn't going to forget, either.

They moved in quiet agreement back toward the fire. The tea had gone cold, but neither seemed to mind. Améliane reached for the book he'd set down earlier, her fingers brushing the spine just as one of the main doors to the library opened.

Renaud strode in, every inch of him coiled in that particular blend of discipline and disapproval he'd perfected over decades of command. His cloak was half-fastened, sword at his side, and his jaw was already ticking when he took in the scene: the two of them alone, again, in the waning golden light.

He didn't speak at first. He didn't have to.

"Commander," Améliane said, lifting her chin with queenly calm, though the faintest color touched her cheeks. "Is something wrong?"

"Cassien has arrived," Renaud said, voice clipped.

She blinked. "This late?"

"That's what I said." He looked between them, the weight of his gaze pausing on Mathieu a second longer than necessary. "And he came with quite the story."

They filed out without another word—Améliane first, all regal composure; Renaud at her side like the shadow of duty itself; and Mathieu a step behind, quiet, unreadable.

The door swung shut with a soft click.

And then, the library shifted.

A breeze with no source stirred the pages of an open book. The candle flames flickered blue for a breath, casting long, skewed shadows that stretched the wrong way across the floor.

Books that had been neatly shelved now sat stacked in strange, teetering towers on the reading table.

The fireplace hissed, a whisper curling up through the chimney like smoke shaped into syllables no human tongue could parse.

The castle itself was watching. And it had begun to take interest.

CHAPTER 19

Améliane

The sun had barely begun to rise, but Améliane was already dressed.

A soft mist clung to the windows of her sitting room, blurring the jungle beyond into shades of green and gold. Somewhere beyond the haze, the parrots were just beginning their morning chatter—but within Eldrenoire's grounds, all was unnaturally quiet. As if the castle, too, was waiting.

She stood by the tall windows, her arms crossed over the bodice of her gown, fingers drumming lightly against silk. The color was dark plum today—commanding, sober—chosen not for fashion but for armor. Her outer rooms were immaculate, the fire newly stoked, the tea untouched on the low table. She had been up for hours. Pacing. Thinking. Waiting.

Renaud had filled her in the night before—after Mathieu had left to dine with Laurent, Élodie, and Margot. The information had been brief, grim, and lacking in detail.

"Cassien crossed the Belmaran border during a skirmish," Renaud had said, jaw tight with frustration. "He made it out, but only barely."

Barely. That word had sunk its teeth into her and refused to let go.

Sabine had tended his wounds—minor, thank the gods—but by the time he'd arrived, night had already fallen, and she had no desire to summon him when his breath still stank of pain and fatigue. Instead, she had given orders that he be taken to his old guest suite, the one beneath the east tower.

Her eyes flicked again toward the corridor that led to the sitting room's double doors, where Renaud was due to appear at any moment. He would not delay—he never did. Which meant that if he wasn't here already, it was because Cassien was still dressing, still bandaging bruises, or still catching his breath from whatever hell he'd had to outrun to reach them.

Her hand drifted to the small table near the window where her court notes lay open. She didn't look at them. Couldn't. Not until she had the truth.

Because something was wrong.

She could feel it.

The castle was too still. The halls too hushed. The air held the kind of hush that came not before a storm, but after one—when the world pretended calm because it hadn't yet tallied the damage.

And it wasn't just the castle.

Cassien had never arrived late in the evening before. Not in all the years since her exile.

A knock came—three firm raps against the carved double doors.

Améliane turned from the window just as Renaud entered, posture crisp, expression unreadable. Behind him, Cassien followed, moving a touch slower than usual. His right shoulder was wrapped in fresh linen beneath his cloak, and though his gait was steady, it held the stiffness of someone who had not yet healed.

"Majesty," Cassien said with a slight bow, the edges of his coat dusted with travel and tension.

Améliane moved toward him at once, her concern only partially veiled by royal composure. "You should still be in bed."

Cassien gave a faint, tired smile. "And leave you to speculate without answers? Hardly."

She studied him more closely—he looked older today. Not just from the wounds, but from something weightier behind his eyes. "Renaud told me there was a skirmish."

"Near the border town of Ghyrell," Cassien confirmed, voice low and even. "I had planned to avoid it altogether, but Rothgar's forces have been crossing deeper into Belmaran territory than expected. The soldiers in Ghyrell... they weren't ready. I passed through just before the worst of it."

Améliane's brows knit. "How close were you?"

"Close enough that I earned a blade across the arm and a bruised rib," he said wryly. "Sabine says I'll live. I offered to show her the wound, but she muttered something about old men and self-inflicted idiocy."

Renaud snorted quietly behind him. "That sounds about right."

Cassien's gaze flicked toward the fire for a moment, then back to the queen. "But the town suffered. Ghyrell was small—mostly traders, a few outer garrisons. It's gone now."

"Gone?" Améliane's voice dropped.

"Burned. There was no time to evacuate. They weren't expecting an attack so deep into the valley." His jaw tightened. "It wasn't just a raid. It was a warning."

Silence settled over the room.

Renaud crossed to stand beside the hearth, folding his arms. "They're probing. Testing our borders for weakness."

"They're not your borders anymore," Cassien said, though his voice wasn't unkind. Just... heavy.

Améliane moved toward the sitting area, gesturing for Cassien to follow. "Then let's speak of what is mine. Sit, if you're able."

Cassien nodded once and lowered himself into the nearest chair, his every motion careful. "I didn't come empty-handed," he said. "There's news. More than last time."

Améliane glanced at Renaud, who took up his usual post—one pace behind her left shoulder, silent and vigilant.

"Then let's hear it," she said. "All of it."

He reached into the inner pocket of his coat and retrieved a scroll wrapped in crimson velvet—its seal gleaming gold, stamped with Edric's sigil: a serpent coiled in endless loops, its eyes twin pinpricks of malice.

Cassien extended it with both hands.

"Per His Majesty's command," he said dryly, "the weekly report from Belmara."

Améliane took it without flinching. She cracked the wax with a swift twist, the serpent splitting neatly in two. The scroll unfurled in her hands with a whisper of silk and paper.

Cassien straightened and adopted his courtier's tone—smooth, dispassionate, a man reciting half-truths polished for public consumption.

"Belmara prospers," he began, "and the crown thrives."

Renaud shifted behind her in his routine search for eavesdroppers with a sound that could have been a scoff—or the beginning of a growl.

"The harvest festival in Virelle was a rousing success. Temple offerings exceeded expectation, and several High Priests have declared it the most spiritually abundant season in a decade."

Améliane's expression didn't change, but her fingers curled slightly at the edge of the parchment.

"The Queen's sister, Her Royal Highness Elyra, has returned to court with her child. Celebrations in the capital included a naming ceremony in the Temple of Ailone, fireworks over the river, and a parade of scholars through the central square."

Cassien flicked a glance at Renaud, then continued without missing a beat.

"Trade with the Ordréan Empire remains favorable. Their Empress sends blessings and an ornamental dove carved from starwood—an emblem, His Majesty notes, of peace and enduring friendship."

This time, Améliane did snort, softly.

Cassien let the corner of his mouth twitch before regaining his composure. "The king has also decreed the refurbishment of the Solenne estate to accommodate new visiting dignitaries. Renovations are underway under the guidance of Master Architect Eron Vess." He lifted his gaze briefly. "The very same architect who once restored your ancestral villa in Sorelle."

The name landed like a pebble dropped in deep water—just enough to ripple the surface, nothing more.

"And finally," Cassien said, his voice turning just faintly drier, "His Majesty sends his hopes for your continued health and spiritual enlightenment. He reminds you that isolation is a gift when accepted in grace. That peace lies not in freedom, but in understanding one's limits."

Améliane rolled the scroll back up with smooth, deliberate precision and set it aside on the table.

"Do you think he practices those lines in front of a mirror," she asked, "or does he just whisper them to himself while feeding the doves he keeps locked in his study?"

Cassien bowed his head. "I believe he prefers mirrors, Your Majesty. The doves bite."

Renaud let out a soft breath through his nose that might have been a laugh—if one were feeling generous.

Améliane folded her hands. "And now that we've heard the performance," she said, her voice quieter, sharper, "tell me what he didn't have the scribes write."

Cassien's gaze darkened. His tone dropped, no longer that of the king's obedient courier—but the queen's secret ally.

"The truth," he said, "is far less poetic."

Améliane leaned forward, her elbows resting lightly on her knees, every inch of her poised but alert. Renaud stood at her back, perimeter check complete.

Cassien stepped closer, lowering his voice, "The rebellion deepens. Not in the open—not yet—but in the undercurrents. Symbols scrawled on alley walls. Meetings whispered in shadow. And in dreams passed from one Seer to another like coals from a dying fire."

"Dreams?" Améliane echoed, brow furrowed.

Cassien nodded. "The Seers are awakening. Not organized, not led—but drawn together by something older than memory. And the more that remember, the less hold Edric has on them."

He withdrew a folded scrap of parchment from his sleeve. It was creased and faded at the edges—no seal, no insignia, nothing to mark it as important.

Améliane took it, careful and deliberate. Ink marked the center—elegant but rough: a version of the moonlit tidelily, rendered in swift, mirrored strokes. Her sigil.

Not just remembered. Reclaimed.

"They call it the Moonlit Bloom now," Cassien said softly. "A symbol of the rightful queen. It's being chalked on doors in the old quarter. Passed in notes. Painted beneath bridges where guards don't patrol."

Her fingers tightened slightly.

Renaud's voice was quiet steel. "How far has this spread?"

Cassien met his gaze. "Farther than Edric expected. Too far to erase without causing more questions. The meeting place in the old quarter is drawing more each week. They continue to call it 'The Return.'"

Améliane closed her eyes briefly. "Do we know who leads it?"

Cassien shook his head. "Not yet. Whoever it is, they're careful. Strategic. And they've begun gathering those with true Sight."

He hesitated, then added, "One of them—an older Seer from the southern provinces—had a dream three nights ago. She's never spoken prophecy before, but this one..." His voice dropped lower. "She saw something called the Wyrdbound."

Améliane's breath caught.

Cassien watched her carefully. "That name means something, then."

She nodded. "The castle gave it to him. To Mathieu. On a night he nearly didn't come back after getting lost in the halls."

Cassien exhaled slowly. "Then it's more than a title. More than a dream."

"What did the Seer see?" Renaud asked.

Cassien's brow furrowed. "Fragments only. Fire, shadow, a sword against stone. But she named him. Wyrdbound. Said he bore a flaw the curse couldn't contain. That he was the fracture through which fate would bleed."

A silence settled. Not of disbelief—but recognition. The kind that came when a distant threat stepped into view.

"Edric doesn't know about the dream," Cassien said. "Not yet. But he senses the change. He's sent word to one of his court mages to monitor the arcane tremors near Eldrenoire. And he's begun asking questions."

He turned his gaze to Améliane.

"About the curse. About you. And about him."

Améliane's spine straightened. "He knows about Mathieu."

Cassien nodded once. "He knows there's someone else here. An outsider. A variable he didn't account for. And Edric... he's not waiting for answers. He's searching for the sorcerer who cast the original curse."

Renaud swore under his breath.

"If he finds him," Cassien said, "he may try to reinforce the spell—or unmake it in a way that serves him. He could send someone here. Not just to observe. To intervene."

Améliane's voice turned cold. "To remove Mathieu."

Cassien's reply was quiet. "Or you. If the curse is fraying, Edric won't risk letting it unravel on its own. Not if it costs him the throne."

The fire cracked loudly, spitting sparks like a warning neither of them needed.

Améliane stood, the parchment with the Moonlit Bloom still clutched in her fingers.

Améliane folded the parchment and slipped it into the pocket at her hip—close, protected. "You'll need to travel swiftly," she said, her voice already shifting into command. "Avoid the main crossings near Aronne. Rothgar may have eyes there."

Cassien stood with a wince, but didn't argue. "I'll take the long road through Khyreth's Pass. There's less cover, but likely fewer patrols."

Renaud retrieved Cassien's cloak from the stand near the door and draped it over the man's shoulders with a firm pat. "Margot packed you provisions. Stay ahead of the snow."

Cassien inclined his head, then turned back to Améliane. His eyes lingered for just a moment—steady, loyal, resolute.

"You're not forgotten," he said softly. "None of you."

Améliane nodded once, the weight of it landing behind her ribs.

Renaud opened the door with one gloved hand and handed Cassien a sack of coin. The mist had burned off, allowing the corridor windows to sparkle with sharp morning clarity. Cassien stepped through it without looking back.

The door clicked shut behind him.

Silence followed.

Until it didn't.

A voice rose from the corner of the room, quiet as breath and twice as unsettling.

"Miralys will not greet him kindly."

Améliane turned sharply. Alaric stood where no one had stood a moment before—beside the fire, as if he'd always been there, fingers laced loosely behind his back.

Renaud's hand went to the hilt at his side, but stopped short. One didn't draw steel on shadows.

The Keeper tilted his head slightly, eyes flicking toward the door Cassien had just passed through.

"The path he takes will stir echoes," Alaric murmured, almost to himself. "And when the wind reaches Miralys, the Black Keep will feel it."

Améliane narrowed her gaze. "Are you saying he's in danger?"

Alaric's smile was faint and without warmth. "I'm saying the past does not enjoy being disturbed. Especially not where its throne still sits empty."

With that, he turned—flickering like a candle's last breath—and was gone.

The fire popped once in the grate.

Améliane said nothing.

Renaud didn't ask.

They both stood in silence, as if listening for footsteps that no longer echoed.

CHAPTER 20

Mathieu

T he knock came just as he was pulling his tunic over his head.

Not a loud knock—more of a polite tap-tap followed by the familiar squeak of a tray being steadied outside his door. He frowned in the mirror, smoothing the tunic down and running a hand through his hair once, uselessly, before striding to open it.

Margot stood there, smiling like sunshine bottled and corked.

"Good morning, my lord," she said, her voice all airy charm. "A note from Her Majesty." She held out a folded parchment atop a silver tray.

Mathieu raised a brow. "You're very formal this morning, Margot."

She dipped in a graceful curtsy. "It is a formal day."

He accepted the note, eyes skeptically scanning her just a moment longer than necessary. Her dress was pristine, her golden curls tucked into a neat braid, and her fox-bright eyes sparkled with something unreadable. She wasn't usually this polished for a delivery. Or this... rehearsed.

"I was just headed to the training yard," he said, gesturing with the parchment. "Should I be worried?"

Her laugh was soft and tinkling. "Not unless you hate fine wine, too much lace, and sitting next to a queen."

That gave him pause.

She grinned, pleased by his reaction. "It's the yearly... shall we say... commemoration of our imprisonment. A tradition of sorts. You'll enjoy it." She tilted her head, the curls of her braid catching the light. "Everyone does."

He flicked the seal open and scanned the contents. An invitation written in Améliane's hand—formally worded, yet unmistakably personal. It invited him to join her that evening in the great hall for a formal dinner. A single line at the end, written in smaller script, read:

Your seat is to my left. Don't be late.

Mathieu let out a breath through his nose. "And if I prefer sparring with Thorne to polite conversation and lace?"

Margot gave him a knowing smile and a wink. "Then I hope you like your roast with a side of bruises and shame."

With another curtsy, she turned and vanished down the hall, her soft slippers making no sound at all on the stones.

Mathieu stared after her for a beat longer. Then he looked back down at the invitation.

To my left.

That was no small thing in a court—even one trapped inside a cursed castle.

And he wasn't entirely sure what it meant.

But as he tucked the parchment into his belt and turned down the hall toward the training yard, he had a feeling Thorne's sword wouldn't be the only thing keeping him on edge today.

Mathieu made his way through the east wing corridor, boots echoing softly on stone, the queen's note still tucked in his belt.

The castle was already shifting.

Not in the eerie, sentient way he'd come to expect—but in the human way. The alive way. Hallways were busier than usual. Shadows moved with purpose instead of listlessness. Servants bustled in and out of chambers, arms full of polished silver and folded linens and candlesticks tall enough to double as spears.

He dodged one such servant at the top of the stairs, offering a muttered apology as she scurried past, balancing a tray of wine glasses that chimed like bells with every hurried step.

Another servant swept by with an armful of garlands—lavender, moonvine, and something pale and trailing he didn't recognize. They left a heady scent in their wake, all spice and ghostly sweetness.

"Apologies, sir!" came a voice just before two more darted around the corner, hauling a pair of towering flower arrangements between them like an obstacle course set by a drunk god. Mathieu backpedaled just in time to avoid a direct collision with a spray of pale hydrangeas.

"Are we expecting a royal wedding or a mild floral coup?" he called after them, but they were already gone.

The corridor emptied for a moment, leaving only silence and the faint flutter of ribboned drapery behind him. Even the castle itself seemed to be holding its breath.

Mathieu exhaled and pushed open the courtyard door, stepping into the morning light and toward the sparring yard where he could, at least for the next hour, trade laced dinner invitations for the weight of a practice blade.

And maybe figure out why sitting at a queen's left hand suddenly felt more dangerous than going to war.

The air in the courtyard had turned sharp, edged with the kind of chill that stung the lungs and whispered of snow. Not here, not yet—but close. Somewhere just past the horizon, winter was sharpening its teeth.

Mathieu rolled his shoulders as he crossed the gravel toward the sparring ring, spotting Thorne already waiting with two practice blades and a look that suggested trouble—or at the very least, bruises.

"You're early," Mathieu said by way of greeting.

Thorne tossed one of the blades toward him, which he caught without breaking stride.

"No, you're late," Thorne countered. "Which is basically treason."

Mathieu twirled the hilt once in his hand, then stepped into the ring. "Where are the others? I expected at least one sarcastic commentary from Laurent before my second cup of tea."

Thorne stretched his neck until it cracked. "Laurent saw the sky this morning and declared it 'hostile.' Refused to step foot outside."

Mathieu glanced up—grey clouds gathering like wool over the peaks. "Looks like it might snow."

"Exactly," Thorne said, already circling. "Laurent doesn't do wet weather. Claims it ruins his hair."

"I suppose his loyalty has limits."

"Definitely. Especially when atmospheric moisture is involved."

Mathieu snorted and swung first. Thorne blocked with ease, and the rhythm began—step, strike, pivot. A dance of steel and muscle, their breath visible in the morning air.

"So," Thorne said, ducking a wide sweep and countering with a jab, "I heard you've been summoned."

"To dinner. Not the gallows."

"Same thing, depending on the guest list."

Mathieu's brow lifted. "You planning to attend?"

"Wouldn't miss it," Thorne said. "It's the one night a year when the queen lets everyone drink decent wine and pretend they aren't all cursed and trapped in a magical prison."

"A celebration of shared misery."

Thorne grinned. "Exactly. It's tradition."

Mathieu blocked, twisted, and feinted left—earning a surprised grunt from Thorne as the blade grazed his shoulder.

"I've been here long enough to know one thing," Mathieu said, steadying his stance. "Nothing about this place is just tradition."

Thorne reset his grip and tilted his head. "No. But it is something like family."

Mathieu didn't answer right away. He simply raised his blade again—and waited for the next strike.

Their blades met again with a sharp clap, the clash echoing off the courtyard's ivy-clad walls. Neither man spoke for a few breaths, focused on footwork and timing, until Mathieu shifted his weight and asked, "What exactly should I expect tonight?"

Thorne parried, then arched a brow. "Aside from the emotional minefield that is any formal event involving Renaud, Laurent's wine commentary, and Margot trying to charm everyone within breathing range?"

"Yes," Mathieu said drily. "Aside from that."

Thorne dropped his blade slightly—not out of carelessness, but to lean in conspiratorially. "The annual dinner isn't a celebration. It's an anti-celebration. A way of saying, 'Yes, we're cursed, but at least we look fabulous doing it.' There's wine, food, courtly dancing if someone gets drunk enough to suggest it—but mostly it's for show. It reminds us who we were before... all this."

Mathieu absorbed that, circling slowly. "And how should I behave?"

"Like yourself. But less stabby." Thorne grinned, then tilted his head. "Though, knowing you, that might still mean someone ends up bleeding."

Mathieu gave him a look, then added casually, "Margot delivered my invitation this morning. Apparently, I've been asked to sit at the queen's left."

Thorne paused mid-step.

"You're joking."

Mathieu shook his head once.

Thorne let out a low whistle. "That's significant."

"Why?"

Thorne lowered his blade slightly, eyes narrowing—not in suspicion, but consideration.

"Renaud always sits to her right," he said slowly. "But no one sits on her left."

Mathieu tilted his head. "No one?"

"Not in years." Thorne hesitated, then added, "Bastian didn't even have a chance to sit there."

Mathieu caught the name like a blade mid-flight. "Bastian."

He let his guard drop a hair. "I've heard that name before. When I lunched with Laurent, Élodie, and Margot—they mentioned him. But no one would say who he was. Or where he is now."

Thorne looked away, adjusting his grip on the hilt, the air between them suddenly heavier.

"He was..." Thorne exhaled through his nose. "Important."

"To her?" Mathieu asked.

A nod.

"Was he court? A consort? A general?"

Thorne gave a tight smile—one that didn't reach his eyes. "Depends on who you ask. Some would say all three. Others would say none of those things mattered once he left."

"Left?" Mathieu echoed, though his tone said he doubted it was that simple.

Thorne didn't answer directly. He raised his blade again, motioning for the spar to resume. "It's not a story for me to share."

"But it is a story," Mathieu said, stepping back into position. "One I imagine the castle hasn't forgotten."

Thorne's blade met his again with a sharp clang, and this time, there was a different kind of weight behind the blow.

"No," he said. "It hasn't."

They exchanged a few more blows in silence before Thorne stepped back, lowering his blade.

"If you want the full tale," he said, meeting Mathieu's gaze, "the Queen will have to tell you that story."

The first flake landed on the back of Mathieu's hand—soft, weightless, and gone in an instant.

He glanced up just as the clouds split wider overhead, releasing a slow, steady fall of white that dusted the training yard like a whispered curse.

Thorne caught one on his lashes and blinked it away with a groan. "Well, that's my cue."

Mathieu lowered his blade, already feeling the chill sinking through the light fabric of his shirt. "Snow doesn't agree with you?"

"Not when it's this damp," Thorne grumbled, raking a hand through his red hair. "I'm going to swing by the kitchens and beg for something fried. Then it's a nap until someone shouts that it's dinner time."

Mathieu sheathed his practice blade. "See you at the Queen's anti-party, then."

Thorne smirked as he turned toward the covered archway. "Try not to wear black. Everyone wears black. Be bold."

And with that, he disappeared into the swirling flurries, muttering something about biscuits and frostbite.

Mathieu took the long way back inside, pausing under the eaves of the eastern wing as the snow began to fall more heavily. It was quiet in the way only Eldrenoire ever was—like the air itself was listening.

By the time he reached his chambers, his fingers were cold and his shoulders damp. He stripped quickly, swapping his practice clothes for a warm tunic, trousers, and a worn wool vest that smelled faintly of lavender from the wardrobe sachets someone kept replenishing.

He stepped back into the hallway with a specific destination in mind: the library.

And this time, the castle let him go.

No detours. No shifting corridors. No looping back to where he'd started with a wall where a door used to be.

He paused once on the second-floor landing, peering down the grand staircase where the sconces flickered low and gold. Somewhere in the depths, he could hear servants preparing the Great Hall—clattering silver, hurried whispers, the scent of beeswax and fire-roasted meat beginning to drift upward.

But the path before him stayed clear.

The corridor to the library stretched ahead in familiar silence, and with each step, his theory felt more and more certain.

Eldrenoire wasn't random. It wasn't just a trickster.

It was aware.

When he wandered for wandering's sake—when he sought solitude, or peace, or even just a warm place to think—the castle gave him what he needed. Doors opened. Fires lit. Passages unfolded.

But when he asked too many questions... when he reached for doors marked by silence or walked corridors the others avoided...

Then it twisted. Confused him. Moved the walls when he wasn't looking.

It didn't trap him. It warned him.

Mathieu stopped just outside the tall library doors and laid a hand against the dark wood.

The door opened easily. The castle was letting him in. For now.

The library greeted him like an old confidante—grand, quiet, and faintly amused.

As soon as he spoke aloud— "I *want to know how a curse like Eldrenoire works*"—the shelves began to respond.

Books shifted. Pages fluttered. A ladder slid a few feet down the far track of its own volition, stopping beneath a high shelf with an audible click. Titles he hadn't noticed before gleamed invitingly in the afternoon light: *Arcane Locks and Living Walls, Bindings of Flesh and Stone, Curses Woven by Blood.*

Within minutes, he was surrounded.

The long reading table beneath the western window became his outpost. Stacks grew beside him in every direction, each spine older and more brittle than the last. The fireplace at his back crackled dutifully, and the ever-shifting light outside faded into irrelevance as he scoured chapter after chapter for clues. Not just about curses—but about *this* curse. About the way the castle moved. The way it listened. The way it... *cared*, in its own peculiar, haunting fashion.

Most of the texts were academic. Dry. A few veered toward superstition—old wives' tales about curses inherited through lineage, places that grew sentient from sorrow. One theory, scrawled in the margins of a tattered grimoire, claimed that curses rooted in betrayal often gained awareness of their own, "as *if memory itself had been weaponized.*"

That felt... close.

But not close enough.

None of it explained Eldrenoire's choices. Why some doors opened and others didn't. Why it seemed to favor certain rooms. Certain *people*.

Why it hadn't let *him* die.

He looked up at some point, blinking against the sudden ache behind his eyes. The light had changed—the warm gold of midafternoon now tilted, thinner, cooler. The fire had burned low. He rubbed a hand across his jaw, surprised to find stubble there.

Gods, how long had he been reading?

His stomach answered before his mind could.

The door creaked behind him.

"Well, well," came Laurent's drawl. "I see the rumors are true. The Wyrdbound can be contained—as long as you bury him in dusty tomes."

Mathieu looked up to find Laurent sauntering in, a smug grin on his face and a snow-dusted cloak slung carelessly over one shoulder. Élodie trailed behind him with a much more generous expression—and a large tray in hand.

"I told him you'd forgotten to eat," she said, crossing the room with a smile. "So we brought provisions."

Mathieu blinked at the bread and slices of meat piled high on a plate Élodie pulled from the large tray. It was warm. Fresh. Smelled faintly of rosemary and something smoked.

"I—thank you." He reached for it as if someone might take it back.

Laurent dropped into a chair with a sigh that managed to sound both exhausted and theatrical. "You missed lunch. Again. Margot says you're worse than the Queen."

"She misses lunch?"

"She *forgets* lunch," Élodie said. "You *skip* it."

Mathieu took a grateful bite, too hungry to defend himself properly.

Laurent leaned back, propping his boots on the nearest chair and scanning the books stacked on the table. "What are we looking for?"

"Information about the curse.... why sometimes I can move freely through the halls and other times I get lost for hours," Matthieu said around the bread in his mouth.

Laurent raised one arched brow. "So? Find anything enlightening? Are we cursed by love? Betrayal? An angry squirrel with magic?"

"Still narrowing it down," Mathieu said, chewing. "But I'm starting to think the castle might be listening more than it lets on."

"Oh, it's listening," Élodie said, glancing at the nearest candelabra. "It just has very selective hearing."

Mathieu paused mid-bite. "So I've gathered."

Laurent leaned forward, snagging a nearby book and flipping it open with one hand while reaching for a second chair to prop his feet on with the other. "So, what exactly are we trying to figure out? How to break the curse? Or just how to keep the castle from spinning us around like a drunk uncle at a wedding?"

Mathieu smirked. "Both would be nice. But right now, I'm just trying to understand what we're dealing with. Most of these texts are either too general or too metaphorical."

Élodie distributed the teacups from the tray and pulled a chair up beside him, already scanning the titles in his stack. "That's because no one writes about living curses in detail. Too dangerous. The ones that develop... personality tend to object to being studied."

Laurent arched a brow. "Sounds like the Queen."

Mathieu let out a soft laugh, surprised at how easily it escaped. "She's easier to read than these books."

"I'll pretend I didn't hear that," Élodie said, pulling one tome closer. "Here, this one's about sentient architecture. Might have something useful."

They settled into a rhythm—Mathieu reading aloud sections that seemed relevant, Élodie flipping through indexes with the speed of a scholar, and Laurent occasionally interrupting to declare a theory that was either surprisingly insightful or completely absurd.

"Maybe the castle's alive because someone loved it too much," he offered at one point, sprawled halfway down his chair like a bored cat. "Or maybe it's possessed by the ghost of a particularly fussy butler."

"Laurent," Élodie warned without looking up, "you're not helping."

"I'm helping *morale*," he said, smug.

They worked like that for the better part of an hour, the library filling with quiet murmurs, the rustle of pages, and the occasional clink of their teacups.

Mathieu found himself oddly... at ease. Surrounded by books, yes—but also by something else. Something warmer. These people—this cursed, strange, loyal court—they were becoming more than fellow prisoners.

After almost eight months at Eldrenoire, they were becoming *people he trusted*.

As the light outside dimmed and snow began to fall in earnest beyond the arched windows, Élodie stretched and closed her book with a snap.

"We should go," she said gently. "The dinner's in a couple of hours. If we show up late, Renaud will assign us to table polishing duty for the next week."

Laurent groaned. "Again? My hands just recovered."

Mathieu stood as well, tucking one of the more promising texts under his arm. "Thanks. For the food. And the help."

"Anytime, Wyrdbound," Élodie said, smiling.

Laurent paused at the door. "Don't be late tonight. The Queen's got a seat waiting for you, after all."

He winked—then vanished around the corner, cloak flaring dramatically.

Élodie just rolled her eyes and followed.

Mathieu stayed a moment longer, looking around at the library—the books, the table, the candelabras that seemed to flicker with knowing light.

Then he said quietly, "What are you?"

The flames danced higher but gave no answer.

Mathieu left the library just as the bells chimed the quarter hour. Snow had gathered along the outer sill, a quiet hush laid over the castle like a woolen blanket. He moved through the halls with ease—no turning staircases, no doors that vanished when approached. Eldrenoire let him pass.

Which meant, once again, it wanted him to go.

He arrived at his chambers without a single wrong turn and pushed open the door to find something new waiting for him.

A rolling rack stood near the fireplace, glinting slightly in the low light. It was made of wrought iron twisted into curving vines, and hanging from it was a collection of finely tailored clothing—garments he definitely hadn't owned yesterday.

Atop the rack's polished brass rail was a note. Folded, cream-colored parchment sealed with a tiny wax fox.

He sighed before even opening it.

> *Monsieur Mathieu,*
>
> *I figured you might want something more appropriate to wear to dinner. The queen is gracious, but she's not blind. Do try not to embarrass yourself.*
>
> *—Margot*

He huffed a laugh. Sarcasm, weaponized into stationery.

Still, he approached the rack, fingers trailing lightly over the fabrics. There were three outfits: all sharp, elegant, and quietly expensive.

The first was a rich charcoal ensemble with a high-collared tunic that buttoned asymmetrically across the chest, offset by a midnight-blue sash. It was refined, minimal, and felt like something a general might wear if invited to a royal court.

The second was full ceremonial—silver-trimmed black, deep cuffs, a standing collar stiff enough to slice bread. Beautiful. Uncomfortable. No chance.

The third caught him by surprise. Deep forest green with gold accents—trimmed in thread so fine it shimmered when it caught the light. The cut was formal but not rigid: a tailored jacket with fitted sleeves, brass buttons down the front, and faint embroidery along the hem that looked like curling leaves—or was it waves? A subtle nod, maybe, to the coastal kingdom of Belmara. There was even a soft cream shirt beneath it with ties at the throat instead of buttons. A touch of softness in the midst of strength.

Mathieu stared at it a long moment.

It was the kind of thing he wouldn't have touched, even a few months ago. Not his color. Not his style. Not his life.

But now?

He reached for the jacket and shrugged into it. The fit was perfect, of course. Eldrenoire didn't guess.

He fastened the cuffs and ran a hand down the jacket's front, pausing at the curve of the embroidery.

It felt...right. Not because it suited him.

Because he knew the queen would like it. And that, more than anything, surprised him.

The bath was already waiting.

Steam drifted through his chamber like breath from the stone itself, curling around the corners of the tub as if the castle had drawn it for him the moment he chose his evening attire. The water was hot, perfumed faintly with juniper and something darker—cedar, maybe, or smoke. Not overwhelming. Just enough to feel... intentional.

Mathieu sank into it with a sigh that escaped before he could stop it.

The heat worked its way through his muscles, loosening knots he hadn't realized he was carrying. The sparring. The hours hunched over books. The weight of secrets he hadn't yet decided how to share.

When he emerged, the mirror over the basin showed him a man he recognized—but sharper. More focused. He had filled out with months of good food and physical activity. Mathieu trimmed his beard close to his jaw, keeping the edges clean and the shape tight. He looked at his reflection again deciding he looked healthy and strong for a man of forty-two years, though the grey at his temples certainly showed more now.

A tray had been left beside the basin, lined with glass bottles—half a dozen scents, each labeled in looping script. One smelled of citrus and salt. Another of cinnamon and cloves. But one, near the back, stopped him.

He uncorked the bottle and closed his eyes.

A scent like aged sandalwood, warmed leather, and something distant— the sharp edge of mountain air before a storm. It wasn't sweet. It wasn't bright. It was anchored, clean, and quietly dangerous.

It smelled like memory. Like a man returning to a place that should've forgotten him.

He dabbed it across his neck, his wrists. Paused at the last second to press a thumb to the inside of his jacket's collar.

Then he stood. Ready. Not for war. But for something far more treacherous. Dinner.

After an unobstructed walk through the halls of the Black Keep, he arrived to find the Great Hall transformed.

Mathieu paused in the arched entryway, taking in the full weight of the spectacle. It was the same cavernous room where he'd first arrived half-dead, the same hall that had felt too large, too quiet, too burdened with ghosts. But tonight, it glittered like something out of a different lifetime.

Hundreds of candles floated in glass spheres above the tables, casting warm, golden light that danced across the high stone walls and made the stained-glass windows shimmer like jewels. The long banquet table—usually bare—was draped in violet and silver velvet, embroidered with the crest of the castle itself: an ancient tree with roots twisted in knot-work, its branches reaching skyward. Flower arrangements spilled down the length of the table in waves—deep crimson lilies, moon-colored roses, vines of ivy and curling mistleaf—and servants moved among them lighting smaller candles in mirrored holders.

The scent of roasted meats, spiced wine, and something sugary drifted through the air, mingling with music played softly by a trio of instrumentalists tucked into the far alcove. Their violins and harp wove a melody both mournful and lovely.

It was, in every sense, a feast.

But not a celebration.

A servant greeted him with a practiced bow. She was young, with her dark hair pulled into a tight twist and her uniform crisp despite the hall's warmth. "Sir Mathieu," she said, without surprise. "You're expected. This way, please."

She led him along the edge of the hall, past rows of side tables already filled with members of the cursed court. Some wore formal attire; others had clearly pulled together the best pieces they could. All of them had a peculiar air about them—not fear, not exactly. Reverence, perhaps. A strange, hushed anticipation.

Élodie was resplendent in emerald green, her hair pulled back in braids that wove together like a crown. She leaned over occasionally to murmur something to Thorne, who sat at her other side. He had cleaned up surprisingly well. His usual scowl was absent, replaced by an almost awkward sort of polish. His jacket was hunter green with black buttons, collar pressed sharp enough to cut. He looked like he belonged here, in a way that made Mathieu wonder how many versions of Thorne there really were.

Renaud stood beside the Queen's empty chair at the head of the table, speaking to one of the footmen in hushed tones. His formal attire was black as ever, trimmed in silver thread and polished buttons. A ceremonial sword hung at his hip, and his posture was stiff with something more than duty. He didn't look at Mathieu, but Mathieu felt the weight of his awareness anyway.

The servant gestured to the empty seat just beside the Queen's—to her left.

"Your place, sir."

Mathieu nodded, thanked her, and took his seat.

Around him, conversation ebbed and flowed. A murmur of nervous laughter rose from a nearby group. Laurent's voice lifted briefly above the music as he recited something that sounded vaguely scandalous to two nobles Mathieu didn't recognize. Margot, looking radiant in a gown of pale gold with a ribbon at her throat, snorted into her wine.

Mathieu let it all wash over him.

He should have felt like an outsider. Instead, he felt—watched. And strangely, not unwelcome.

He adjusted his cuffs, let his gaze roam the hall again.

Mathieu glanced down the long table—his seat just one away from the Commander of the Queen's Guard. Renaud sat with the same carved-from-stone posture he always seemed to wear like a uniform. He hadn't looked in Mathieu's direction once since the latter arrived.

Mathieu, never one to resist testing the edges of a silent room, leaned slightly toward him.

"Commander," he said evenly. "Enjoying the ambiance?"

Renaud's jaw ticked. A slow turn of the head. "It's a dinner," he replied. "Not an ambiance."

Mathieu smiled faintly. "And here I was hoping for a shared moment."

Renaud arched a brow, unimpressed. "You'll find I'm not often in the mood for moments."

"I've noticed," Mathieu said, then lifted his wineglass in a brief, ironic salute before taking a sip.

Renaud didn't return it, but he didn't bristle either. Which, by his standards, might as well have been an embrace.

And then the room changed.

Not with trumpets or fanfare—but with something more subtle. More commanding.

A hush rolled through the Great Hall like a change in the wind. Conversations paused. Laughter softened. Even the candles seemed to steady their flickering as the tall double doors at the far end of the room swung open.

Améliane entered without heralds or announcement.

She didn't need them.

She descended the staircase with the kind of composure that made lesser queens look like jesters in borrowed crowns. Her gown was a deep, burnished gold—off the shoulder, fitted through the waist, then flaring into folds of silk that caught the light like molten metal. It shimmered as she walked, shifting between dusk and starlight.

Her chestnut hair, usually pinned or braided, had been left down for the occasion. It cascaded over her shoulders in soft, deliberate waves, each one catching the golden glow of the chandeliers. Atop her brow rested a delicate golden diadem—slender and understated, but intricate in its design. Tiny, glinting flowers were worked into the circlet's band. Flowers that Mathieu, unaware of their significance, found strangely familiar.

She was not trying to be beautiful.

She simply was.

The hall bowed as one.

Mathieu rose with the others, his gaze fixed on her as she made her way down the aisle between the tables—every step measured, every breath of silk and shadow carrying the weight of rule.

When she reached the dais, Renaud pulled out her chair at the head of the table without a word. She inclined her head to him and then—her eyes flicked to Mathieu.

Just briefly.

But it was enough to catch him off guard. Because the look she gave him wasn't cold or distant or even guarded.

It was warm.

Like a secret shared across candlelight.

And as she sat, and the music resumed and wine was poured again, Mathieu realized something unsettling.

He wasn't nervous about sitting beside a queen. He was nervous about impressing the woman.

They didn't speak at first.

Not when the soup course was set before them in delicate porcelain bowls rimmed in gold. Not when the wine was refreshed or the candles flickered higher in their sconces.

But he could feel her beside him—radiating heat and calm in equal measure.

It was strange, he thought. He had dined beside generals and killers. Shared firelight with kings and traitors. But this—this quiet proximity to a woman in golden silk, who carried a whole kingdom in her spine—felt more dangerous than any battlefield.

He turned toward her slightly, and when she looked up from her spoon, he offered a quiet, sincere, "You look beautiful."

Améliane blinked, just once.

Then—unexpectedly—she looked down, the edge of a smile tugging at her mouth.

"Thank you," she said. Softly. Almost like she wasn't used to hearing it.

Mathieu tilted his head. "Was that... shyness, Your Majesty?"

Her gaze snapped back up, dry now. "Don't make me revoke your invitation."

"There it is," he murmured with a grin, "I was starting to worry."

She huffed, a near-laugh into her wineglass.

He leaned in just a touch, voice low and warm. "I've seen you command a room with a glare. But tonight... you didn't need to command anything. You just walked in, and the world followed."

That earned him a look. The kind she usually reserved for people who said things far too well and far too truthfully.

And yet, she didn't deflect. Not this time.

"Careful," she said, sipping her wine. "Flattery might get you fed."

Mathieu glanced down at the elegant arrangement of roasted venison and herb-crusted root vegetables being served. "It's working already."

"Good. Eat while you can. The dessert is Renaud's favorite, and he fights dirty."

To his left, the Commander didn't so much as blink.

"Renaud," Améliane added, tilting her head without looking, "stop staring at the sconces and pretend to have a conversation."

"I am," he replied, deadpan. "Just not with him."

Mathieu arched a brow. "This is the warmest welcome I've received from him all month."

Renaud sipped his wine without a flicker of expression. "Don't get used to it."

"Stars," Améliane muttered under her breath, "I surround myself with charmers."

Mathieu chuckled, and the warmth in his chest settled deeper. There was something about this—about the banter, the shared glances, the undercurrent of something more—that made him feel... steady.

As if for a moment, he wasn't a man on the run or a ghost of a fallen kingdom.

He was just a man at a table, sitting beside a queen in gold. And the night was young.

The main course dwindled in quiet bites and murmured praise. Laughter rolled from the lower tables, where Laurent was dramatically recounting some long-suffering tale to Thorne and Élodie. Someone had retrieved a lute. Someone else had already started on their second bottle of wine.

At the high table, Améliane dabbed her lips with her napkin and turned to him with a look that could have been casual—if her eyes weren't so watchful.

"And how did you spend your day, Wyrdbound?"

Mathieu smiled faintly. "Aside from being late to sparring, disappointing Thorne, and nearly getting brained by a flower arrangement on the way out the door?"

She raised a brow. "I assume that wasn't on purpose."

"Mostly not. Though the flower arrangement was deeply offended."

She gave the smallest of smiles. "And after that?"

He leaned back a little, letting the candlelight cast shadows across the curve of her shoulder. "I spent the day in the library. Curses, mostly."

That piqued her interest. "Researching yourself again?"

He shrugged. "Researching the castle. It's starting to feel like I only make it to where I'm going when it lets me."

"Eldrenoire prefers clear intentions," she said, reaching for her wine. "If your motives are vague, the hallways will be too."

He tilted his head. "Was that poetic or literal?"

"Yes."

He laughed, soft and warm. "You're impossible."

She took a sip of wine, then turned slightly toward him. "And what did the books tell you?"

"That I don't know nearly enough," he admitted. "About curses. About magic. About... this place. They told me that most magic has rules. Boundaries. But this one... this curse feels like it has a mind of its own."

Her expression shifted—just for a second.

But before she could speak, his voice dipped just enough to be heard by her alone, "What about you? How was your day?"

"I spent the morning reviewing the week's schedules," she said smoothly, "and the afternoon pretending I wasn't counting the hours until the wine was served."

Before he could press further, a shadow leaned in behind him.

"More wine, my lord?" Margot's voice was soft and musical, her hand already moving to refill his glass.

Mathieu glanced up, offering a polite nod. "Thank you."

She lingered just a second longer than necessary, smiling sweetly as she adjusted the bottle.

"It suits you," she said gently.

Mathieu blinked. "Pardon?"

"The seat," she said, stepping back with a little curtsy. "It suits you."

He studied her for a moment—trying to read the kindness in her eyes, or the angle of her smile.

"Thank you," he said slowly. "That's kind of you."

Her smile brightened. "I hope you enjoy the evening. It's rare the Queen lets the castle feel like a court again."

Then she slipped away, her skirts whispering across the stone like a secret.

Mathieu watched her go.

When he turned back, Améliane was watching him.

"Is she always that friendly?" he asked.

The queen's lips curved. "Margot is many things. Friendly is only one of them."

He didn't ask what the others were.

The dessert was a spiced plum tart—warm, flaky, and served with a drizzle of golden honey and cream. It melted on the tongue, and paired with the heady wine still flowing, it loosened even the stiffest shoulders in the room.

The musicians struck a new tune—something lively, plucked from the strings of a zither and chased by a bright-fluted pipe. A few of the younger footmen who had finished their service were already pulled onto the floor by giggling kitchen maids. Even Thorne, cheeks ruddy from wine and laughter, had been swept into a spin by Élodie, who danced like a woman with fire in her blood and nothing left to prove.

Mathieu watched them with a small, private smile.

Then he glanced toward Renaud.

The commander was no longer seated. He stood now behind the queen's chair, hands folded neatly, expression unreadable. But his eyes missed nothing.

Mathieu could feel the tension radiating from him—each burst of laughter from the dancing crowd, each pair of spinning bodies, seemed to set his shoulders tighter. The wine had loosened the room—but not Renaud.

And in that moment, something shifted.

The music swelled. The dancers clapped in rhythm. And Renaud, ever vigilant, was pulled slightly back by the need to observe the full hall. His line of sight still clear. But his ears? Less so.

Mathieu leaned in—just a fraction—and refilled Améliane's wine glass with a steady hand.

"Careful," she said, watching him from the corner of her eye. "That's the third time you've refilled me."

He raised his own glass. "I'm just trying to keep pace."

She sipped, lips just brushing the rim. "And how's that going?"

"Terribly," he admitted, swirling the garnet liquid. "But at least I'm sitting in the best seat."

Her brow arched. "Is that so?"

Mathieu matched her expression with a quiet, amused one of his own. "The left of the Queen. Seems significant."

"Hmmm."

She didn't elaborate.

So he pressed—lightly.

"Is this an honor reserved for wandering fugitives and would-be researchers of curses?" he asked.

She turned her head toward him slowly, the movement graceful and deliberate.

"Something like that."

Her voice was soft, and her eyes sparkled mischievous.

Mathieu smiled into his glass and said, "Regardless... thank you for the invitation."

"You should thank Margot," she said, setting her glass down with care. "She was the one who suggested you might require a place of dignity."

Mathieu nearly choked. "Margot suggested—?"

She smiled at his disbelief. "Don't look so alarmed. She's not always looking for ways to get under your skin."

He tilted his head. "Just most of the time?"

Améliane leaned in slightly, her voice just above the music. "Margot plays many roles. Some of them she even plays well."

He studied her a moment—eyes dark, thoughtful. "And what role do you want me to play?"

Her answer was a long moment in coming.

Then, "That remains to be seen."

The music played well into the night.

By the time the last tart had been devoured and the final chords from the string quartet faded into the stone rafters, the Great Hall had transformed into something softer. The candles had burned low, the wine flowed freer, and laughter had thickened the air like perfume. Bodies swayed in slower rhythms now, and even the more reserved courtiers had loosened enough to allow smiles and easy touches.

The Queen remained at the head table, regal and relaxed, sipping slowly from her glass as Mathieu sat beside her, their earlier banter giving way to the kind of quiet comfort that surprised them both.

Laurent had long since disappeared with a poet from the kitchens, murmuring something about needing inspiration. Margot had offered a final, suspiciously sweet smile to them all before drifting into the crowd. Élodie, for her part, had been halfway through another dance when Thorne—gloriously, unrepentantly drunk—attempted to bow to her mid-spin and nearly toppled into a tray of empty glasses.

"You," Thorne said to Élodie, voice slurred but full of feeling, "are the fiercest, most terrifying woman in this castle, and I would fight a thousand cursed tigers for one more dance with you."

Élodie burst into laughter, catching him around the waist to keep him from crumpling like a paper swan. "You'd trip over your own antlers, darling."

Renaud appeared like a stormcloud, his glare sharp enough to cut glass. "You're done," he growled, grabbing Thorne's other arm.

"I was just—"

"You were embarrassing yourself," Renaud snapped, hoisting him upright.

"I regret nothing!" Thorne declared to the rafters.

"Yes," Élodie said cheerfully, "and you'll regret that tomorrow."

With Renaud and Élodie dragging Thorne between them from the room—one annoyed, the other amused—the Queen turned slightly toward Mathieu.

And for the first time that evening, they were alone.

Servants had begun clearing the tables, gathering goblets and sweeping away flower petals and crumbs. The hall echoed now with the quieter sounds of tired feet and hushed voices.

Mathieu stood, grabbed the half-finished bottle of wine from the table, and held it up in offering.

Améliane arched a brow.

"Terrace?" he said.

She rose without a word.

Together, they stepped out onto the stone terrace as moonlight spilled silver across the courtyard and the snow fell softly, silently, onto the garden below.

Behind them, the servants cleaned. Before them, the castle exhaled.

And between them, the bottle of wine promised one last conversation beneath the stars before the evening ended.

CHAPTER 21

Améliane

The stars shone like silver dust scattered across black velvet as she stepped out onto the terrace, the hem of her gown whispering along the stone. Behind her, Mathieu followed, wine bottle in hand, his silhouette tall and steady in the flickering torchlight.

Eldrenoire, ever watchful, seemed to breathe around them.

Snow still fell in the gardens beyond—soft, slow, and silent—but not a single flake touched the terrace. Warmth cocooned the stone expanse like a held breath. The air was balmy, faintly perfumed with spice and firewood, and no breeze stirred the Queen's hair. Above them, the sky was impossibly clear, as if the castle itself had created a carved a hole in the snowstorm just for them.

The musicians continued playing from within the hall, the melody gentle, like the memory of a song rather than the song itself. Servants moved in hushed, choreographed precision inside, clearing goblets and stacking silver, their movements blurred by the glass.

Améliane closed her eyes for a moment. This night had taken something from her—but it had also given something back. And she wasn't sure yet which part weighed more.

"So," Mathieu said, his voice low and smooth behind her, "how did I do?"

She turned to find him watching her, wine sloshing gently in the bottle he held. His coat—dark green with golden embroidery—caught the starlight and made him look almost regal.

"You didn't trip, spill wine, or offend Renaud more than usual," she said. "I suppose that counts as a success."

He smirked raising his glass in a mock salute.

"Tonight was beautiful," he said, softer now. "Strange, but beautiful."

She nodded once. "That's the curse of the night."

"And the purpose?"

Améliane moved to the edge of the terrace, resting one hand on the stone balustrade as she looked out over the snow-covered gardens. The moon hung low above the trees, full and luminous.

"It began seven years ago," she said. "Everyone was broken. Disoriented. Grieving the lives they'd lost. I hosted a feast that first winter to lift spirits—but no one could pretend it was a celebration. So I called it what it was. A remembrance. A refusal to forget who we were before the curse, and who we might be again."

Mathieu leaned beside her, shoulder not quite brushing hers. "It doesn't feel like mourning."

"Because it's not," she said. "Not anymore. Now, it's defiance."

He was quiet for a moment, watching the snow drift just beyond their invisible bubble. "You carry it well," he said. "The weight. The memory."

She let out a breath that might have been a laugh. "Some days it carries me."

Mathieu didn't push. He simply stood beside her, quiet and steady, the wine warming between them like a shared secret.

And for one small moment, Améliane allowed herself to believe the snow globe Eldrenoire had created around them on the terrace wouldn't crack.

She glanced sideways at him, wineglass still cradled in one hand.

The moonlight softened everything out here—cast the terrace in silver and hush, turned his sharp edges into something almost sculptural. His jacket caught the light in glimmers of green and gold, but it wasn't the embroidery that drew her gaze. It was the solid warmth of him beside her. The way his shoulders shifted slightly as he leaned on the railing. The way the wind tousled the dark strands of his hair, revealing that streak of grey at his temples—there was something noble in the way it caught the light.

Her gaze drifted lower. That square jaw, now defined by a neatly trimmed beard that suited him far too well. A warrior's face, yes—but one refined by time. Earned, not inherited.

He turned slightly, and she didn't look away fast enough.

Mathieu caught her watching him and smiled. Not the smirk he offered Renaud, or the teasing grin he reserved for Laurent—but something quieter. Warmer. Something that reached into her chest and tapped once, softly, like a question.

"Would you dance with me?" he asked, voice low.

She blinked. "Now?"

He nodded toward the open space near the archway, where the snow refused to fall and the light flickered gold against the stones. Where the music still played, distant and tender, like a memory they hadn't lived yet.

She arched a brow. "You had all evening to ask. Why now?"

His smile didn't falter. But it changed.

"I wasn't going to ask you to dance in front of everyone," he said, voice velvet and gravel. "That would've made it a performance."

He turned toward her fully now, setting his glass aside on the ledge.

"I'm asking now because there's no one watching. No court. No audience. Just us. And I want to spend time with you, Améliane—not your crown. Just you."

The way he said her name—not 'Your Majesty,' not 'Queen'—sent a flutter down her spine that had nothing to do with the wine.

She stared at him, at the way the firelight from inside caught the gold in his hazel eyes. At the way he waited—open, but unpressing.

And for one dangerous, beautiful moment, she let herself want him.

Just enough to say, very softly, "All right."

Mathieu offered his hand in quiet invitation.

She slipped hers into his.

He drew her toward the center of the terrace where the stones were dry and warm beneath their feet, the air encased in Eldrenoire's magic—a bubble of impossible comfort surrounded by winter's hush.

The music drifted from inside the hall—slower now, softer. A waltz played gently on strings and harp, as if the castle had chosen it just for them.

Mathieu's hand slid to her waist, the other cradling hers with care. No pressure. No presumption. Just a quiet invitation for her to come closer.

She did.

And as they began to move in time to the music, Améliane let herself notice.

She noticed how easily they moved together, how his frame fit around hers with surprising grace, how he slowed his steps to match her rhythm without a word.

He smelled of sandalwood and something else—something wild and crisp, like distant mountains or storm-swept stone. And gods, it had been so long since someone touched her like this. Not out of obligation. Not out of command. But because they wanted to be close.

Mathieu's hand tightened slightly at her waist, a gentle reminder that he was here, that she was not dancing alone.

Her breath hitched. She hoped he didn't notice.

His gaze flicked to hers, unreadable and deep. She looked away, just for a moment—because looking at him too long felt like walking a tightrope in silk slippers.

The song went on. And for a few stolen minutes, she forgot about the curse. About the rebellion. About the ache of lost time and the weight of too many secrets.

Here, with his hand in hers, with his warmth pressed gently against her side, she remembered what it felt like to simply exist.

To be held.

And perhaps, just maybe... to be wanted.

"You dance well," she said softly, as if surprised.

He gave a quiet huff of a laugh. "I appreciate that. I've been told I look like a bear trying not to step on anyone."

She arched a brow, amused. "Who told you that?"

"My cousin," he said, smiling faintly. "When I was fifteen. At a harvest ball. I stepped on her twice and elbowed her date in the nose."

Améliane laughed—a warm, full sound that curled around them like the music. "Charming."

"She never let me live it down," he added. "But... I practiced. Over the years. Dancing was expected. Politics in disguise."

She tilted her head. "And yet, you said you didn't ask me to dance in there because you didn't want to make a spectacle."

"I didn't." His voice dipped. "That wasn't for them. This... is just for us."

That quiet sincerity—the ease of it, the truth of it—unraveled something behind her ribs.

The music carried on, the terrace glowing soft and gold. The castle seemed to hold its breath around them.

"What about you?" he asked gently. "Did you dance often? Before..."

He didn't finish the sentence. He didn't have to.

She exhaled. "Not as much as I should have. Not as much as I wanted to. Ruling leaves little time for waltzes."

He gave a soft murmur of agreement. "And yet you move like you were born to it."

"I was trained," she said with a smirk. "Every noble girl is. If I'd known it would someday lead to dancing in a snow globe with a man called Wyrdbound, I might've paid more attention."

Mathieu laughed low in his chest, the sound deep and steady. "I think I like that version of fate better."

They danced a little longer. No need to speak. Just motion and breath and the warmth of closeness.

But then he said, quieter now, "I used to be good at silence."

She glanced up at him.

"But lately," he continued, "I find myself wanting to fill it. With small truths. Even if they don't matter."

She studied him for a moment. "Then tell me one."

He looked down at her hand in his. "I used to wish I'd been born invisible."

She blinked. "Why?"

"It would've made leaving easier," he said simply. "Made failure quieter."

Améliane was silent for a beat, then said, "Small truth for small truth."

He looked at her.

"I used to braid my own hair because it gave me something to do with my hands while I told the rest of me to hold it together."

His gaze softened. "You don't have to explain."

"I wasn't going to," she said, a touch of steel in her voice. But it melted into something gentler as she added, "It's strange. What lingers."

He nodded. "And what doesn't."

The music slowed.

Without quite realizing it, she eased closer, the space between them narrowing like breath in winter air.

And then—deliberate now—she placed her cheek against his chest.

He stilled, just for a moment.

Then his arm curled tighter around her, hand sliding gently up her back until his palm rested between her shoulder blades, warm and steady. He said nothing. Just held her as the stars shimmered above them and the snow fell in silence just beyond the edge of the terrace.

They stayed like that, swaying slowly in the golden hush, with nothing to prove and no one to watch.

Just two people, battered and remade, wrapped in warmth and old music—and for the first time in far too long, not entirely alone.

The music faded into its final notes—something soft and aching, like the memory of laughter.

Améliane didn't move. Her cheek still rested against his chest, her breath slow and even. Mathieu didn't let go, his hand splayed over her back like he might be able to hold the moment still.

For just a breath longer, it worked.

And then—

"A beautiful evening."

Renaud's voice, cool and composed, cut through the quiet like a blade sheathed in velvet.

Améliane tensed slightly in Mathieu's arms before she pulled back, slow and graceful, as if she hadn't been caught wrapped in his arms. Her face betrayed nothing.

Mathieu, on the other hand, didn't bother hiding his annoyance.

Renaud stood at the edge of the terrace, his black coat catching the low light, silver embroidery gleaming faintly along the cuffs. His expression was unreadable, but his eyes missed nothing.

"I'm ready to escort you back to your rooms, Majesty," he said with a crisp nod.

There was no accusation in his tone. Just duty, cloaked in steel.

Améliane gave him a small, measured smile. "Of course. Thank you, Commander."

She turned back to Mathieu with a softer look—one that lingered in her eyes longer than it probably should have.

"Good night," she said.

Mathieu inclined his head. "Until tomorrow."

Then, with the bottle of wine still half-full on the terrace table and snow brushing softly against the magic that held the cold at bay, he watched her retreat.

Renaud walked two paces behind her. Always the shadow. Always the sword.

But even shadows had eyes.

Chapter 22

Mathieu

The terrace felt colder the moment she left.

Not in temperature—Eldrenoire still held its invisible bubble of warmth around the stones, still shielded him from the falling snow just beyond the edge—but in *presence*. In the shape she'd left behind.

He watched her retreat, Renaud two steps behind her like a closing door.

The queen's silhouette was straight-backed and regal, her golden gown catching stray threads of candlelight as it disappeared into the hall. But he knew what she looked like up close now. Not just beautiful—but *human*. The way her eyes crinkled at the corners when she smiled. The way her breath had slowed to match his. The way she'd let herself *rest*, even if only for a moment.

Mathieu didn't move.

The music had stopped, the wine was going warm in the bottle beside him, and the servants were clearing the remnants of the feast with muted efficiency. But all of that faded into a soft, irrelevant hush.

All he could feel was the echo of her voice—low and wry and *honest* for once, stripped of courtly sharpness—still rang in his ears like a thread he didn't know he'd been following.

He ran a hand through his hair, stared out at the garden.

He almost wished he *hadn't* stumbled through Eldrenoire's gates all those months ago. Not because he regretted it. But because now—after the dancing, after the closeness, after *her*—he couldn't go back to before.

It had been easier not to feel this. Easier to wander, to fight, to stay sharp and distant. Easier to be alone.

He closed his eyes, exhaled slowly, and pressed the heel of one hand to his chest like he might be able to press the memory back in. Contain it.

But it was too late for that. The damage was done.

He didn't know how long he stood there.

Eventually, the last of the servants vanished from the Great Hall, the terrace doors swung closed behind him, and Eldrenoire's warmth faded from the stones like breath from glass.

The walk back to his chambers was unimpeded—no shifting corridors, no sudden turns. But the castle was *silent* now. Not the usual kind of hush that settled like dust after dusk, but something more deliberate.

Even the sconces burned low, their flames barely flickering, as if reluctant to break whatever tension hung thick in the air.

He turned the final corner toward his wing—and paused.

A voice.

Low, angry, and unmistakable.

Renaud.

The sound was distant, echoing down the corridor just far enough away that he couldn't make out the words—but close enough that the *tone* carried.

Sharp. Frustrated. Cutting.

There was a second voice too, quieter but unyielding.

Améliane.

Mathieu froze, one hand against the stone wall. He didn't try to listen harder.

He already knew what it was about.

He exhaled, slow and even, and moved on.

When he entered his chambers, the door clicked softly shut behind him. The fire was lit, the bed turned down, and a cup of warm tea had been placed on the table near the hearth.

He removed the jacket he'd worn and hung it neatly over the back of the chair—forest green and gold catching the light.

His fingers trailed over the embroidery and stilled at the place where her cheek had rested.

He could still feel it.

The memory of her weight, her trust, the way she'd leaned into him without ceremony or fear. It was maddening, that softness. That *honesty*.

He stepped back, paced once toward the hearth.

Then again.

He grabbed a book from the shelf—some ancient tome on ancient warfare—and tossed it open on the table. Read a line. Closed it.

Too loud.

He turned to his blade, half-drawn it from its sheath, then shoved it back with a dull *clang*.

Too violent.

He poured another glass of wine from the half-finished bottle he'd brought with him. Set it down untouched.

Too *futile*.

The fire crackled behind him as he braced the heels of his hands to the table and stared down at the empty pages of his own thoughts.

He'd spent years burying things.

Shoving them deep beneath strategy and survival, behind battle plans and running boots. Letting time and distance do what grief and guilt never could.

He hadn't expected her to be the one to dig them up.

Not a queen cursed into silence for almost a decade. Not a woman with a spine of iron and eyes that saw too much. And definitely not someone who could make him feel like he wanted to stay.

Stay.

That word hit harder than anything else.

He hadn't wanted to stay anywhere in a long time. The irony that he was trapped yet wanted to stay was not lost on him.

Outside, the wind picked up. A shutter groaned somewhere along the western wing.

He sat heavily in the chair by the fire, wine untouched, eyes locked on the flames.

It had been years since he let his thoughts drift *backward*. Most days, they marched forward out of sheer necessity, like soldiers toward a war he hadn't won.

But tonight... staring into the fire cracked open something old.

Not the memory of the fire itself—he'd already relived that horror in the Mirror Hall, seen Tess and their unborn child crushed beneath flame and stone as clearly as if it were happening again. He didn't need the crackling hearth to remind him. That moment was etched into his bones.

What haunted him now was something quieter. Memories of Tess and the note she had tucked into his boots all those years ago as he prepared to face the Rothgarian forces on the frigid plains of Valmont.

You'll be a good father, she'd written. *Even if you don't know how.*

He'd loved her in a way one loves a companion on a long, shared road. Respect. Duty. Affection that deepened with time but never ignited.

He'd mourned her loss because Tess was *good*. Because she had deserved better than him, better than the hand fate dealt her. Because she had believed in the kingdom he hadn't wanted.

But nothing he felt for Tess had ever come close to what Améliane made him feel.

Like he *couldn't look away*. Like her voice could steady his hands and her silence could undo him. Like the thought of her returning to her rooms with Renaud had made him feel... *unmoored*.

Mathieu stood slowly, crossing the room toward the tall mirror near the hearth.

The glass was old—slightly warped, ringed in tarnished gold—but it still reflected the man who stood before it.

He didn't look like the boy who had married a stranger out of duty.

He didn't look like the soldier who had buried his grief under steel and strategy.

He looked like someone who wanted *more*. Someone who had let a woman in.

Someone who, despite his better judgment, was falling in love with a queen who danced in a snow globe of magic, who carried the weight of her lost kingdom like it was stitched into her spine, and who made him feel seen in a way that had nothing to do with thrones or titles.

A slow breath left his lungs. He didn't know when it had started. But somewhere between the night they had stolen cake in the kitchen and the waltz on the terrace, it had happened.

He was falling for her.

And the most terrifying part?

He wasn't sure if that was a gift... or a curse.

CHAPTER 23

Améliane

The jasmine was waiting for her again.

One pristine bloom—white as bone, delicate as breath—resting on the polished surface of her nightstand. Its petals hadn't wilted. Its scent was freshly bloomed.

And it hadn't been there when she went to sleep.

Améliane shot upright, breath catching in her throat. Her elbow struck the edge of the nightstand hard enough to send her empty water glass skittering across the surface and crash to the floor.

The noise echoed like an alarm through her chambers.

The door burst open an instant later, Renaud already halfway inside with his sword half-drawn, eyes scanning for threats. He took in the overturned glass, the Queen clutching the blanket to her chest, and then—

The flower.

His expression shifted from readiness to ice.

"You're hurt," he said, already crossing the room.

"I'm fine," she snapped, tossing the blanket aside and sliding off the bed. "But I'm going to start nailing the windows and doors shut if this keeps happening."

Renaud ignored the remark. He crouched beside the nightstand, eyes narrowing at the bloom. He didn't touch it.

His nostrils flared.

"There's a scent," he said.

She turned sharply toward him. "What kind of scent?"

"Faint," he muttered. "But distinct. Jasmine, obviously... and something else."

He sniffed again, eyes narrowing. "Margot."

Améliane blinked. "You're certain?"

"Her perfume. Or something very close to it. Either she's been near this flower, or she delivered it."

Améliane exhaled, pinching the bridge of her nose. "First you suspected Mathieu. Now Margot. Who's next, Thorne? Perhaps Élodie brought it in for the aesthetic."

Renaud rose, eyes sharp. "I'm not accusing. I'm observing."

"You're spiraling," she corrected, already walking to the balcony doors and throwing them open. The air was cold, and the garden below was still blanketed in snow, pristine and untouched. No footprints. No signs of anyone entering or leaving.

The silence hung a beat too long.

Then Renaud's voice, low and roughened by something deeper than cold, snapped the air like a drawn blade.

"This isn't just another of the Black Keep's mysteries, Améliane. It's not a misplaced letter or a shifting hallway. Someone is toying with you. Watching you."

She turned from the window, brows drawn. "And you've already decided who, haven't you?"

His jaw clenched. "You treat him like he's one of us."

"He *is* one of us."

"He's not." Renaud's tone sharpened. "You've never treated any stranger this way. Not the ones who wandered in lost. Not the ones who begged for sanctuary. Not even—"

"Don't say his name," she warned.

He pressed on. "You let Mathieu in. You trust him. You *dance* with him."

The words landed heavy between them.

Her eyes narrowed. "This is about a dance?"

"This is about *you*," he said, louder now, voice cracking against the stone walls. "You're different around him. We all see it."

She stepped forward, chin tilted high. "He *is* different. Eldrenoire knows it. Alaric knows it. Even Laurent, Élodie, Margot, Thorne—*they* know it."

He took a step toward her. "And if he's not what he seems? If he's part of something worse? You think Alaric's riddles will protect you? That a castle with a mood will keep you safe?"

"I think," she said, voice trembling with the effort to stay calm, "that you're angry because I let someone in."

His expression didn't change. But his silence did.

She exhaled slowly, crossing her arms to steady herself against the cold and the ache crawling up her spine.

"You care," she said more quietly. "I know that. You've always cared. But this... this is too much."

A beat. A blink. And in that space, the hurt bloomed across his face before he could hide it.

Not rage. Not frustration. Just pain.

Renaud turned away, jaw clenched, his broad shoulders tight with restraint as he moved to stand before the hearth.

The fire cast flickering shadows across the sharp lines of his face—cheekbones carved by discipline, a jaw marked by tension, and eyes the color of winter sky. Eyes that had seen war, death, betrayal... and her. Always her.

His steel-grey hair caught the light like tempered iron, short and precise, never a strand out of place. A soldier's cut. Even now, in silence, he held himself like a shield—rigid, ready, alone.

The flames danced across the scar at his temple, the thin white line cutting through his right brow, earned before the curse. Before Eldrenoire.

He didn't flinch when she approached. But he didn't move either.

Améliane came to a stop behind him. For a moment, she simply looked at him—the way he filled the space, unmoving and immense, the tension radiating off of him like heat.

Then she reached out and placed a hand gently on his shoulder.

The fabric beneath her palm was warm, coarse with wear. She felt the muscle beneath it tighten, then slowly—slowly—release.

"Renaud," she said softly, "you are my sword and my shield. My oldest friend. The one who never left—even when it would've been easier."

He didn't turn. But his head dipped slightly, as if the weight of her words settled somewhere heavy in his chest.

"I trust you with my life," she went on. "Not because of duty. Not because of the years. But because I know that if the world were on fire... you'd still stand beside me in the ashes."

Her voice faltered just slightly, but she steadied it with a breath.

"We've built something here, you and me. Not a kingdom. Not a court. But a kind of family. And I know I haven't always made that easy. I know I ask more than I should. But you've never let me fall."

Her fingers tightened ever so slightly on his shoulder.

"You will never lose me. Not to him. Not to the curse. Not to anything."

He still didn't speak.

But after a moment, he brought one hand up and covered hers—rough, battle-scarred fingers closing gently over her much smaller ones.

And for the first time in weeks, the fire didn't feel like it was the only thing keeping her warm.

Renaud gave her hand one final, firm squeeze before letting go.

"My apologies," he said, voice low, rough-edged with fatigue. "I'm not at my best."

She gave him a knowing look. "You were on shift last night."

He nodded once. "Thorne was in no condition to stand guard after... well." His mouth twitched, not quite a smile. "Let's just say I didn't trust him not to serenade the torches."

Améliane let out a quiet laugh. "He did have a rather poetic evening."

"He tried to duel a coat rack," Renaud said flatly. "With a dinner spoon."

That broke her composure. She pressed her fingers to her lips to stifle a grin.

Renaud's shoulders softened. "I took his post outside your door. I wasn't going to leave you unprotected."

She sobered at that. "You never do."

A pause stretched between them, quiet and full of the things they didn't need to say.

"I've asked my third to escort you today," he continued, voice gentler now. "Just until I've had a few hours of sleep. She'll remain unobtrusive."

"You've more than earned rest," she said. "Thank you."

He gave a tight nod. "Before I go, I want to speak with Margot. Alone."

Améliane lifted a brow. "Renaud..."

"I won't accuse," he said, though his tone suggested otherwise. "But I will have answers. Her scent near that flower isn't a coincidence."

She exhaled, eyes soft. "Just don't scare her."

"I'll try," he said. "No promises."

She shook her head and stepped back with a wry smile. "Go. Sleep. You're no use to me dead on your feet."

He inclined his head, the familiar formality returning as he turned toward the door.

Then—hesitating at the threshold—he looked back once more. "You'll be safe?"

"I always am," she said softly. "Because of you."

That stilled him for just a breath. And then he was gone, the door clicking quietly behind him.

Alone again, Améliane lingered a moment longer, glancing toward the single bloom of jasmine on her nightstand.

Still there. Still white. Still perfectly wrong.

She didn't touch it.

Instead, she dressed quickly before Élodie had a chance to come fuss over her—choosing a deep blue gown with warm sleeves and silver detailing at the cuffs—and twisted her hair into a low knot without much thought.

The castle was waking slowly around her. Time to see how badly it regretted the night before.

She stepped into the corridor and headed downstairs, ready to face the aftermath of a too-lavish evening in a too-cursed court.

The halls were quiet, but not empty.

Améliane descended the curved staircase slowly, her slippered feet making no sound against the polished stone. Sunlight poured in through the tall windows, filtered through frost-laced panes that turned it soft and golden. The scent of last night's revelry had faded—no lingering wine, no perfume, no smoke from roasted meats. Only beeswax polish and fresh air remained.

When she reached the bottom step and turned toward the Grand Hall, she paused.

Impeccable.

Not a single overturned goblet. Not a single wilted garland or stray ribbon or forgotten shoe. The velvet table runners had been pressed. The candles were gone. The stone gleamed.

The celebration might as well have been a dream.

But the court? The court had most definitely not fared as well.

The first sign was a small brown rabbit, curled up in a sunbeam just off the entryway, ears twitching in sleep.

Then came the lynx, tail draped over its nose, purring faintly beside a bench.

A stag lay half-tucked beneath the base of a grand tapestry, antlers tilted at a precarious angle. Not far beyond, a marmot was snoring—actually snoring—beneath the frame of a decorative suit of armor.

And in the middle of the Great Hall's entrance, sprawled gloriously across a velvet-upholstered bench, was a large red fox with one back leg twitching in dream.

Améliane crossed her arms, a small smile tugging at her mouth.

"Gods," said a voice behind her, low and cautious. "Should I be worried?"

She jumped—only a fraction—but enough that she spun around with a hand at her throat.

Mathieu stood just a few paces away, hands raised slightly in mock apology. His hair was tousled, and he still wore the same boots from the night before, though his coat had been swapped for something softer—navy wool with a high collar, unbuttoned at the throat. His eyes, however, were wide as saucers as he took in the menagerie spread out before them.

Améliane's smile widened. "You startled me."

"You?" he said, glancing from her to the fox to the half-visible antlers sticking out from behind the tapestry. "That's rich. I walked into what looks like a taxidermist's fever dream."

She laughed, the sound bouncing gently off the clean stone. "You get used to it."

He stepped closer, lowering his voice like the animals might wake and demand an explanation. "Should I be more afraid? I feel like I should be more afraid."

"Don't be," she said, eyes dancing. "Being hungover in your animal form makes the symptoms pass faster. Shifting burns through the worst of it."

Mathieu blinked, glancing again at the fox—who let out a soft, tipsy whine and rolled over onto its back.

He gave a slow shake of his head. "You're all mad."

"We're cursed," she said, turning back toward the Grand Hall. "It's a fine line."

And with that, she stepped over the rabbit and made her way deeper into the castle, the scent of winter sunshine and hangover regret following in her wake.

Footsteps padded quietly behind her.

Améliane didn't need to glance over her shoulder to know who followed. She could feel him there—like a shadow made of sunlight and sarcasm.

Sure enough, after a few beats Mathieu said casually, "You know, for someone who drank a bottle of wine and danced under a magic snow globe, you look fresh as a spring daisy this morning."

She smirked. "Are you suggesting I didn't overindulge?"

"I'm suggesting I may have miscalculated," he replied. "You drank like a Queen and woke like a nun. Meanwhile, I'm fairly certain I slept with one boot still on."

She let out a low laugh, glancing at him as they walked side by side. "You didn't have to keep refilling my glass."

"I didn't refill it. I *topped it off*. There's a difference."

"Ah, of course," she said. "Sommelier-level precision."

They passed a cluster of tangled blankets near the base of the staircase—probably once a wolf or a lynx, now just a very hungover courtier disguised as upholstery.

"I was on my way to the barracks," Mathieu said. "Going to see if Thorne woke up in time to be late for our morning sparring session."

She snorted softly. "If he's lucky, he's still unconscious. If he's unlucky, he's awake with a headache the size of the Veil Isles."

Mathieu gave her a sidelong look. "And you?"

"I'm headed to the kitchens," she said, lifting her chin. "For tea. Hot, strong, and capable of keeping my royal temper in check."

"Well," he said, stretching the word with mock solemnity, "I have time for tea."

She raised a brow. "Did I invite you?"

"You didn't say I *couldn't* come."

"A technicality," she murmured, already turning down the hall.

"And you love a technicality," he said, following without hesitation.

The kitchen corridor was pleasantly warm, the scent of fresh bread wafting toward them like a peace offering. Améliane pushed the swinging door open—

And stopped.

So did Mathieu.

At the far corner of the long, rustic kitchen table, nestled beneath the glow of morning light streaming through the windows, sat a midnight-black panther and a large hawk.

The panther looked supremely unbothered, her head resting on crossed paws, eyes half-lidded in contented recovery. The hawk, perched on the back of a kitchen chair, preened lazily, golden feathers catching the sunlight like fire-kissed coins.

They were facing the hearth, unmoving—except for the occasional twitch of a feathery wing and a low, rumbling purr that vibrated through the stones.

Mathieu blinked.

Améliane pressed her lips together.

"I know the hawk is Laurent. Shall I assume," Mathieu said softly, "that the panther is Élodie?"

"Terrifying, isn't she?" she confirmed.

The panther cracked one vivid green eye open at the sound of voices and let out a low, indulgent huff. Beside her, the hawk shifted his talons and tilted his head, glacial eyes narrowing with familiar mischief.

Before Mathieu could comment, the shimmer of magic filled the room—soft and sudden, like sunlight bending through water. In the space of a blink, fur and feathers became skin and silk.

Élodie straightened first, her long braid falling over one shoulder, the high collar of her green tunic slightly askew. She didn't seem bothered in the least. "Majesty," she said smoothly, dipping her head.

Laurent stood next, utterly unruffled. His shirt, somehow, was only half-buttoned and still managed to look deliberate. He raked one hand through tousled golden curls, gave a slow blink, and said, "We were just... meditating."

Améliane folded her arms. "On the kitchen table?"

Laurent placed a hand over his heart. "Some of my best thoughts happen over bread and regret."

The kitchen door swung again, and two young servants entered—then froze upon spotting the Queen, Mathieu, and two freshly human courtiers in the middle of their hearth. One of them made a small squeaking sound.

"Majesty!" the older of the two gasped, dipping into a clumsy curtsy. "We didn't know—you—we weren't expecting—"

"At ease," Améliane said, lips twitching. "We're only here for tea. Possibly scones. And maybe to judge each other's hangovers."

The younger servant vanished in a blur of motion, presumably to summon enough tea to drown a small army. The other nodded so fast her cap nearly fell off and hurried toward the sideboard.

Laurent sank into a proper chair this time, "I knew following my instincts would pay off. Tea with the Queen herself—what an honor for us lowly creatures."

Améliane arched a brow as she took her own seat. "Last I checked, you were nobility."

"Only when it suits me," he said, pouring himself water from the pitcher and eyeing it like it had betrayed him. "And only until I'm offered something better."

"Such as?" Élodie asked, settling beside him, calm and predatory as ever.

Laurent sighed. "Power. Pastries. Someone else's title."

"Then you're in luck," Mathieu said dryly. "You've got pastries on the way."

Améliane sipped her tea—one of the servants had already poured hers, bless their terrified little hearts—and said, "And you? Still on your way to sparring practice, or have we tempted you to defect?"

Mathieu grinned. "Depends on the scones."

The table fell into a warm, easy rhythm as the servants returned with a tray full of steaming teapots, fruit preserves, and baskets of warm, crumbling scones. The morning sun filtered through the windows, casting long golden rays across the table. The kitchen smelled of cinnamon and relief.

Élodie reached for a scone, slicing it neatly and layering it with jam like it was a formal exercise. "Well," she said casually, "the Grand Hall looked perfect this morning. Not a single flower petal out of place."

Laurent leaned in, stealing the other half of her scone. "Unlike half the people who danced there. I stepped over at least one unconscious fox and two very hungover badgers on my way here."

Mathieu chuckled, picking up a warm scone and breaking it open. "Did you two actually stay for the cleanup or just shift into your animal forms and hide in the kitchens?"

"I'm offended," Laurent said, hand to his chest.

"We absolutely hid in the kitchens," Élodie added, deadpan.

The laughter around the table was soft, familiar—like linen worn soft from use. But then Laurent's tone shifted just enough to draw focus.

"Of course, it wasn't just badgers and foxes talking last night." He reached for the teapot with studied nonchalance. "Word around the Hall is the Wyrdbound made quite the impression."

The table stilled.

Mathieu looked up, a touch too quickly. "What?"

Laurent blinked, feigning innocence. "Everyone's talking about it. The Wyrdbound. You."

Améliane set her cup down, too precisely. "That name shouldn't be circulating."

Laurent arched a brow. "Then perhaps don't give your mysterious guests dramatic prophetic titles if you want them to remain private."

"How did that information leak?" she asked, eyes narrowing.

Laurent raised both hands. "I have no idea. But where there is wine and a truly awful poem about fate whispered in the corridor, word is bound to get out."

Mathieu leaned forward slightly, tension behind his humor. "So you heard this more than once last night?"

"Yep," Laurent said, slicing a scone. "It's spreading. Everyone's wondering what the prophecy means. Why Eldrenoire likes you. Whether or not you're here to break the curse or doom us all." He took a bite. "Opinions are divided."

Before Améliane could speak, the door to the kitchen creaked open and Thorne stumbled in—rumpled, slightly green, and clearly regretting every decision he made after sunset.

"Has anyone seen—" His voice cracked. He cleared his throat and tried again. "Has anyone seen Mathieu?"

He spotted the table and froze mid-step. His gaze snagged on Élodie first, who looked far too amused for anyone with that much sharpness in her gaze.

Thorne flushed a deep red. "Oh. You're all... here."

Laurent didn't even turn. "Good morning, party legend."

"I'm going to die," Thorne muttered, scrubbing a hand over his face. "I woke up under the table in the barracks with a candle in my mouth."

"Romantic," Élodie purred.

"I think Renaud is still mad at me."

"Renaud is *always* mad at you," Laurent said. "You've just leveled up."

Thorne groaned and dropped into the nearest empty chair. "Please, gods. Don't let me remember anything else."

Then his bleary eyes landed on the queen.

He went rigid. "Majesty—" he scrambled upright, knocking his knee into the underside of the table with a solid *thunk* before managing a passable bow that nearly tipped him into a tray of scones. "I—apologies—I didn't realize—"

From the doorway Renaud's replacement for the day crossed her arms and scowled. "Second-in-command, indeed," she muttered.

Thorne winced and stood straighter, trying to conjure dignity from the depths of a hangover. "I—present myself for duty, Your Majesty."

Améliane lifted her teacup, eyes dancing. "At ease, Thorne. I'm only here for the scones, not your honor."

Laurent leaned toward Élodie. "Tragic. He pressed his best shirt and everything."

Élodie sipped her tea without missing a beat. "His best shirt smells like wine and desperation."

Thorne made a sound of pure despair.

Mathieu handed him a scone then leaned back, arms crossed. "You just walked into a very interesting conversation."

Thorne blinked. "What were you talking about?"

Laurent grinned. "You, actually. And the Wyrdbound."

At that, Thorne straightened slightly. "Oh. That. Yeah. Everyone in the barracks is talking about it."

Améliane's eyes snapped to his. "They are?"

"Sure," Thorne said, rubbing his temples. "You call someone Wyrdbound in a place like this, people are going to notice."

The queen and Mathieu exchanged a sharp glance.

The secret was out—and it hadn't come from either of them. She didn't speak. But in the silence that followed, her thoughts flickered to every person who'd heard that name wondering who had let slip the one truth that was never meant to echo.

CHAPTER 24

Améliane

The frost hadn't melted yet.

It glittered across the courtyard stones like powdered glass, catching the early sun in shards of silver. Améliane walked slowly through the arched cloisters, her hands folded behind her back, cloak trailing over the rimed stone. The air bit at her cheeks, but she welcomed the sting—it was honest, at least.

Behind her, the rhythmic tread of boots approached. Predictable. Protective.

"Margot didn't deny it," Renaud said without preamble, dismissing his third as he fell into step beside her. "But she didn't confess either."

Améliane didn't look at him yet. "Go on."

"She said she found a jasmine bloom in her chamber weeks ago. Claimed she thought it was a fluke. That the castle sometimes played tricks." He paused, his tone sharpening. "But she wasn't surprised when I brought it up. Not like she should've been."

Now she looked at him, brow furrowing beneath her winter hood. "So, she knew."

"She knew something." His jaw clenched. "She's either lying, or she's terrified. And I can't decide which is worse."

They passed beneath one of the stone arches, and sunlight spilled in through the slats of a wrought-iron window, casting shadows like bars across the stone floor.

"She wouldn't look me in the eye," Renaud added. "And when I pressed her, she asked me why I cared so much about a flower."

Améliane exhaled, breath fogging in the cold. "Because in Eldrenoire, nothing blooms without consequence."

They walked in silence for a few paces, boots clicking in counterpoint. The garden beyond the cloister was frozen in stillness—no birdsong, no rustling branches. Even the evergreens looked subdued.

Finally, she said, "It's not just the flower."

Renaud glanced over. "There's more?"

She nodded, gaze fixed ahead. "At breakfast... they were talking about the Wyrd-bound."

His step faltered, just enough to notice.

"Laurent claimed it spread during the celebration." She turned to face him fully. "But Thorne confirmed it. It's in the barracks now. Everyone's whispering about it."

Renaud's eyes darkened like storm clouds rolling over steel. "If people are whispering prophecy, someone's priming them to act on it."

"My thoughts exactly." She turned back to the path. "And we don't know who benefits."

He didn't speak right away. The silence stretched taut between them, wound with unspoken tension.

Then, quietly, he said, "We're not just cursed anymore. We're exposed."

The words sank like stones in her gut.

They rounded the bend toward the Hall of Windows—a corridor Améliane had walked a thousand times, with its tall arched panes overlooking the eastern gardens and its row of ivy-carved columns.

But the windows weren't there.

Instead, a smooth bricked wall blocked their path. Seamless. Silent. As if the hallway had never opened to light.

Améliane stopped short. So did Renaud.

"That's not right," she murmured.

The moment she said it, a door appeared in the wall. Not slowly—there was no shimmer of magic, no groaning of stone. Just *there*, sudden and still, made of blackened wood and a tarnished brass handle.

Then it vanished.

Renaud's sword was in his hand before she could blink. "That wasn't the castle."

"I know," she said quietly.

They turned slowly in place—and behind them, the torches lining the corridor flickered once, then twice. The flames recoiled into themselves like breath being drawn in reverse, curling inward until only a faint orange ember remained. The stone walls dimmed. The shadows thickened.

And the warmth—that ever-present hum of Eldrenoire's protective magic—wavered.

She felt it immediately.

It wasn't that the castle had gone cold. It was that she had gone cold within it. Like a blanket being slowly peeled away from her skin.

Eldrenoire had always held her close. Watched over her. Mourned with her. She knew its moods like the shifting of her own bones.

But now... now it felt distant.

Muted. Distracted. Renaud shifted closer, sword raised as his eyes swept the corridor. His breath fogged faintly in the air. "There's a chill," he muttered.

"There shouldn't be." Her voice was too calm. Too flat.

He nodded once, sharp and precise. "Something's pressing in."

She lifted a hand to the nearest stone wall, resting her palm against it like one might touch the shoulder of an old friend.

Nothing.

No warmth. No welcome.

Just silence.

The library was still as a tomb when they entered.

Améliane stepped first, her boots making no sound on the ancient stone. Renaud followed a half-step behind, eyes scanning the shadows between the towering shelves.

The scent of old pages and candle smoke hung heavy in the air. The sconces had burned low, casting long shadows between the shelves. Somewhere in the rafters, a raven croaked once before falling silent.

And there he was.

"He's here," she said quietly.

"I don't like it," Renaud muttered.

"You never do."

They rounded the corner of the inner reading alcove and found him—already waiting.

Alaric sat in a high-backed chair like he had been part of the furniture all along, legs crossed neatly, flipping through his blank book with idle precision. His expression was unreadable. His presence—wrongly serene.

"I've always found the smell of ink comforting," he murmured without looking up. "So many lives pressed into such delicate paper."

"Alaric," Améliane said, voice tight, "the castle's acting strange. It's not responding to me the way it should."

Renaud said nothing, but he didn't sheath his sword.

Alaric glanced up, pale eyes sliding past the Queen and settling briefly on the commander. "You brought your wolf."

"Someone has to guard the backbone of this place," Renaud said flatly. "Even if the walls don't know which way is up anymore."

Alaric's smile was thin and humorless. "Even the spine cracks, Commander. Especially under the weight of unraveling time."

Améliane stepped closer. "The castle's shifting in ways it never has. Torches burning backward. Hallways changing. It felt like..." She hesitated. "Like it forgot me."

"No," Alaric said softly. "Not forgotten. Just distracted."

"By what?"

He closed the book. The sound echoed like a whisper snapped in half.

"There are winds pressing in from outside," he said. "External winds... trying to unmake internal threads."

Améliane and Renaud exchanged a glance. She took another step forward.

"Explain."

Alaric's gaze snapped back to hers, sharp now. "The one who bound the curse—who carved memory into the bones of this castle—is speaking again."

Renaud's hand tightened on his sword hilt.

"Those who were never meant to remember. Those whose memory should've stayed asleep inside history."

"Edric," Améliane said, cold certainty in her voice. "It's Edric. He's searching."

"He isn't searching," Alaric murmured. "He's summoning."

The flames in the nearest sconces sputtered.

"You think he's found the sorcerer?" Renaud asked.

"I think," Alaric said slowly, "that memory is no longer keeping the curse intact. The threads are loosening. The boundaries here are no longer sealed." He looked straight at Améliane. "You feel it, don't you? The castle slipping. Your hold on it fraying."

Her throat tightened. "If the curse is failing, why does it feel worse?"

"Because the curse was holding back more than just you." His voice dropped, each word a quiet knife. "It's holding something else in place. Something that's waking now, because memory is being rewritten."

"Rewritten by who?" Renaud demanded. "Edric?"

Alaric opened the book again—no words, just blank pages, turning. "The spell was bound to remembrance. If someone reshapes the past..."

He looked up, "The future becomes unstable. So does the prison."

Améliane's chest tightened. "The prison?"

Alaric opened his mouth to answer—

And vanished.

No sound. No shimmer. No gust of magic.

Just—gone.

The empty book slid from his lap and hit the floor with a soft thud.

Renaud's sword was drawn in an instant, his back to Améliane. "What the hell—"

"He's gone," she whispered.

Renaud turned toward her, face set like stone. "What do you mean gone?"

She bent slowly, lifting the book from the floor. Its pages were still turning.

"He didn't leave," she murmured. "He was cut *off*."

Renaud stood tense beside her, eyes scanning the room, jaw clenched tight. "Then we're not dealing with just prophecy anymore."

"No," she agreed, gaze fixed on the empty chair. "Something's trying to rewrite the curse. And it's not finished."

They didn't speak as they left the library—only moved, fast and silent, shadows among shadows.

"We're going to the Mirror Hall," Améliane said, the moment the library doors closed behind them.

Renaud gave her a sharp look. "You think he'll be there?"

"I don't know," she admitted. "But if there's anywhere the castle echoes most... it's there."

Alaric's vanishing still hung in the air like a dropped thread—tangible and wrong, the kind of silence that didn't belong in a place built of secrets. Renaud moved at her side like a shadow with a sword, one hand on his hilt and the other hovering as if he expected the castle walls to shift again.

They turned a corner, and the Mirror Hall stretched before them.

The long corridor was colder than the rest of the castle—always had been. It shouldn't have been. The same warming enchantments protected it, but they never seemed to hold.

Here, the temperature bit through velvet and bone, and the flickering torchlight danced too fast in the corners of the tall, gilded frames.

They paused at the threshold.

"I hate this place," Renaud muttered.

"So do I," Améliane said.

They stepped in.

The mirrors lined both sides of the corridor—massive, ornate things, each taller than a man and edged in gold filigree. They did not reflect what they should. Some showed moments that had not happened. Others, things that never would. One flickered endlessly between rain and sunlight, another bore a crack that never reached the surface.

The air inside the hall was thick with tension, like breath held too long.

And then—something shifted.

The mirrors pulsed.

Not visibly, but *inwardly*—a pressure, a presence, like something just beneath the glass had stirred. Améliane felt it low in her chest, in the roots of her spine, like an old name being whispered in a room she didn't remember entering.

One mirror drew her gaze.

It stood near the center of the hall—tall, unblemished, untouched by dust or time. Just an aching stillness, like a lake on the cusp of freezing.

She didn't mean to step toward it. But something tugged—soft and relentless—as if her bones remembered a promise her mind had forgotten. And she did.

"Améliane," Renaud warned, stepping beside her. "Don't—"

Her reflection met her gaze—but it was not *her*.

The queen in the mirror sat on a throne of glistening black stone, crowned in sea-glass—jagged shards shaped into a coronet that shimmered green and blue with moonlight. In her hands, she held a bouquet of moonlit tidelilies, their petals glowing with soft luminescence, wilting at the edges like they'd been pulled from the tide too soon.

At her side stood Mathieu, armored in green and gold, the crest of Valmont and the sigil of Belmara braided together at his shoulder. He looked older, wearier. But he stood tall—proud and battle-worn.

Together, they looked like rulers. A pair forged in war and memory.

But behind them...

A shadowed figure loomed in the blurred background. No face. No form. Just a silhouette behind the throne, watching. *Always watching.*

And all around them—flames.

The castle was burning. Fire licked up the pillars. Embers curled through shattered glass. The sky outside the throne room bled red and black.

The sea-glass crown cracked. The flowers crumbled into ash. And the shadow behind them shifted forward, closer—

The image warped, blurring into molten edges and splintered color.

Then the castle crumbled, stone falling in slow motion, swallowed by vines and fire and time.

Out of the chaos came a voice, soft as wind and sharp as broken promises. "*He must choose.*"

Améliane staggered back. Her breath caught, the echo of the voice still in her skull.

"He must choose," it said again.

The flames were gone. The mirror was dark again. Only her own pale, shaken face stared back.

And then—her knees gave out.

Renaud caught her before she hit the floor, arms braced strong around her waist as she folded to the cold stone beneath the mirror.

"Liane!" His voice broke through the fog. "Breathe."

She did. Slowly. Once. Twice. Her fingers clutched his arm.

"I saw..." Her voice failed.

"I know," he said, even if he didn't. Not really. But he knew enough to hold her steady.

Only she had seen the sea-glass crown. Only she had heard the fire curl around her ribs and whisper through her bones: He must choose.

Renaud didn't let go.

He knelt beside her on the cold stone floor of the Mirror Hall, one arm wrapped firmly around her back, the other braced against the ground. His body was a shield against the cold, the strange magic still humming in the air, the silence that pressed too tightly against the walls.

Améliane leaned into him for just a breath longer, grounding herself in the solid weight of him—his warmth, his steadiness, the thrum of his heartbeat beneath wool and armor.

When she looked up, his eyes found hers—those winter-grey eyes, so often guarded, now wide with concern. There was tension in the tight line of his jaw, strength clenched behind it like a sword barely sheathed.

She drew a breath. "I saw... a vision."

Renaud nodded once, silent, listening.

"I was on a throne," she said, voice still raw. "Crowned in sea-glass. Holding a bouquet of moonlit tidelilies. And Mathieu was beside me."

His brows pulled together. "A coronation?"

"Or a ruin," she whispered. "The castle was burning. Something—someone—was behind us. Watching. Waiting. And then everything collapsed. Fire, stone, time... all of it."

Renaud's grip tightened ever so slightly.

"There was a voice," she continued, staring past him, into the mirror that now showed only their reflection. "It said: *He must choose.*"

They were both quiet.

A torch crackled behind them, its flame dancing strangely in the gilded frame.

Finally, she looked back at him, at the lines of fatigue and worry and relentless loyalty etched into the planes of his face. And despite the ice in her bones and the dread in her chest, she found strength in the steel she saw there—in his jaw, clenched against fear, in his eyes, sharp with unsaid vows.

She exhaled slowly.

"Something is reaching into Eldrenoire," she said, voice like frost laced with fire. "And I don't think we have much time."

CHAPTER 25

Bastian

Bastian had no clue where he was. Not that he remembered, at least.

The small village clung to the edge of the forest like a secret, all crooked chimneys and wind-worn stones, huddled between the border of Belmara and the tangled wilds of Ziraveen. A place people passed through without stopping—unless they were running from something. Or, in Bastian's case, trying to find something the world insisted didn't exist.

He pulled his cloak tighter as he moved down the narrow path that passed for a street, bootheels scuffing against packed earth and frost. The tavern ahead glowed faintly in the dusk—one of only two buildings with lights still burning. He didn't plan to stay long. He never did.

He hadn't stayed anywhere for more than a night since the dreams had started.

At first, they were only flickers. A woman with eyes like storms. A castle draped in ivy and shadow. The scent of a garden, caught on a breeze that made no sense.

Bastian had dismissed them, then. As the half-blood son of a Seer mother and commonborn father, visions were nothing new. They came and went like tides—some true, most noise. But the dreams had grown sharper with time. And heavier.

They began months ago.

He remembered waking one morning gasping for air, the name *"Liane"* on his lips, though he didn't know why it tasted like heartbreak.

The next week, he found himself sketching the outline of a mirror in the margins of a supply ledger. Then a flower. Then her face.

He hadn't known what it meant—only that something inside him was waking up.

And then, days ago, everything shifted. It wasn't gradual. It was a flood. All at once, *he remembered.*

Not just dreams—but memories. Of *her.* Of *Eldrenoire.* Of the price he paid to leave.

The Blood Oath had taken it all—his love, his truth, his very sense of why. It was the only way the cursed castle ever let anyone leave.

Somehow the magic holding those memories under lock and key had cracked. He didn't know how, or why, only that it had happened. And now he remembered everything.

Her name was Améliane. He had once loved her. And he had chosen to forget her.

Bastian had been walking ever since. He was trying to retrace the path back to the cursed castle that shouldn't exist. *That no one remembered.* That he hadn't been able to find, despite knowing it must be near.

But no matter how far he wandered past the borderlands into Ziraveen—through dead villages, overgrown trails, forgotten ruins—Eldrenoire did not appear.

He was being kept out. Or perhaps the path back had never been meant to open again.

So, he'd done the only thing he could. He asked.

He backtracked through Belmaran border towns and everywhere he stopped, he asked about a cursed castle. A queen who vanished. A place wrapped in fog and silence. Most people thought him mad. Others pitied him. One merchant muttered a prayer and left without finishing his drink.

He was drawing attention. He knew it. But he didn't care.

Because now he remembered *her*—not just her face or her voice, but her laugh, her fury, the fire in her gaze when she stood against him in the courtyard the day she watched him disappear through the gates into the jungle.

He remembered what it had meant to love her. And what it had cost him to let her go.

And gods help anyone who tried to keep her hidden now.

He'd taken a room at the only village inn for the night. Its tavern was dim and low-ceilinged, its rafters sagging under the weight of age and smoke. A single hearth glowed at the far end, more ember than flame, casting lazy shadows over half-empty tables and crooked chairs.

Bastian ducked through the doorway after asking questions of willing villagers all afternoon, pausing quickly to scan the room.

Quiet. Empty, save for a pair of elderly farmers murmuring into their stew and a cat curled on the windowsill like it owned the place.

Good.

He crossed to the bar and leaned one elbow against the worn wood. The innkeeper—broad-shouldered and balding, with a bristled grey beard and a scowl that might have been permanent—looked up from polishing a glass.

"Evening," Bastian said. "Whatever's strongest."

The barkeep poured a dark amber liquid into a chipped mug and slid it across the bar. "You've been asking questions," he said without preamble. "About a queen. A castle."

Bastian didn't move, but his grip on the mug tightened.

The barkeep lowered his voice. "Might want to stop doing that."

Bastian met his eyes, quiet steel in his tone. "Why?"

"Because," the innkeeper said, leaning in, "you're not the only one asking those questions now."

The room seemed to still.

"They came in earlier. Three of them," the barkeep continued. "Didn't give names. Didn't take off their hoods. But they were looking for a traveler asking about a cursed place and a woman no one's seen in eight years."

Bastian's pulse thudded once, hard and hot behind his ribs.

The innkeeper straightened, went back to wiping the counter like it hadn't just cracked the air with warning. "Didn't look like the type who ask twice."

There was a long moment of silence between them.

Then Bastian slid a coin across the bar—a thick silver piece, heavy and etched with an old crest.

"Keep the drink," he said. "And forget I was here."

The innkeeper nodded once. "I already have."

Bastian turned on his heel, cloak flaring slightly behind him as he moved for the back door—not the front. He'd learned over the years never to follow the exit closest to the light.

The alley behind the inn was slick with the evening rain, its cobblestones shining faintly under a sliver of moonlight. Bastian moved fast, breath shallow, boots silent. The quiet of the village had changed. It was too quiet now—no wind, no dogs barking in the distance. Even the cat from the windowsill hadn't followed him.

He turned a corner sharply, ducking beneath a low archway overgrown with moss and decay. His hand brushed the hilt of the dagger hidden beneath his coat.

Footsteps echoed behind him.

He froze.

Then they stopped.

He strained to listen, heart pounding in his ears, the sound so loud it felt like it might give him away. He pressed his back to the wall of the narrow passage, body still, barely breathing.

Silence. Too much of it.

He exhaled slowly—then heard it. A shuffle. A scuff of boot on stone. Closer this time.

Bastian spun around.

A figure stepped from the darkness at the far end of the alley—tall, hooded, unmoving. The moment his eyes adjusted, a second figure peeled from the shadows behind him.

Trapped.

He didn't wait. He ran.

The alley twisted sharp to the left, then again to the right, each turn narrower than the last. The buildings leaned inward like they wanted to swallow him whole. The path should've led to the main road—but it didn't. The next corner curved wrong, like the layout of the town had changed behind his back.

Bootsteps followed—more than two now.

They were gaining.

Bastian darted into a side passage barely wide enough for his shoulders. He pressed himself into the shadows, hands braced against wet stone as he forced himself to still his breathing. A rat skittered past his boot.

Closer.

He could hear them now. Voices. Low. Not friendly.

A lantern passed at the mouth of the alley, casting light for half a heartbeat. He didn't breathe.

Then—silence.

He waited fifteen seconds.

Thirty.

He moved.

A wrong step splashed into a shallow puddle, and the sound was deafening.

A shout behind him.

He sprinted again, heart hammering, lungs burning. The night fractured into flickers of torchlight and breath and pounding feet. He was almost clear—he could see the end of the alley, the sliver of light from the main road—

Then someone stepped into the gap.

He swerved.

Too late.

Something slammed into him from the side. A hood yanked down over his head—rough burlap, choking-tight. He thrashed, elbowed back hard, felt a body give—

Then another grabbed his arm. A voice growled in his ear, and then—

A crack.

Pain bloomed behind his eyes, blinding. His knees buckled. The world tilted—and then, nothing.

CHAPTER 26

Améliane

The songbirds had returned.

Améliane lay still beneath the covers, eyes closed, listening to their chorus rising through the open balcony doors—soft trills and warbling calls echoing through the mist-laced morning. The breeze that followed was gentler now, laced with the scent of thawed earth and blooming ivy. Spring had arrived, and with it, a quiet shift in everything.

She opened her eyes slowly. Pale gold light filtered through gauzy curtains. Her room—usually cold and stone-shadowed—felt warmer, softer. Almost like it belonged to someone living, not just surviving.

She sat up, pulling her robe around her shoulders as her bare feet touched the rug. The room was quiet except for the birdsong and the faint creak of ancient beams shifting overhead.

A soft knock at the chamber door was followed by the sound of it opening.

"Élodie, if that's you with a hairbrush, I swear—"

"We brought the combs *and* the pins," Élodie called cheerfully, breezing into the room with a tray balanced on one hand and mischief in her eyes. "You'll thank us later when your hair doesn't look like you were chased by a bear in your sleep."

Margot followed behind her, arms full of silk and velvet. "She wouldn't have been caught. Not with *those* elbows," she said with a grin. "Renaud trained her too well."

Améliane laughed softly and stepped toward the vanity. "You two are unbearable this early."

"We're delightful," Margot said as she began to sort the gowns across the foot of the bed. "Besides, you can't start your day looking like a ghost who lost her crown."

"Charming," the Queen muttered, rolling her eyes as she sat.

Élodie set down the tray and began unpinning the braid Améliane had slept in. "Though for the record, if anyone could *intimidate* in a ghostly state, it'd be you. I'd follow your spectral reign."

"Duly noted. I'll make sure to haunt the Mirror Hall in style."

They laughed—until Margot, still smoothing the fabric of a deep blue gown, said too casually, "Speaking of the Mirror Hall, I suppose the rumors about the Wyrdbound prophecy are true, then."

Élodie froze, her hands still halfway through separating a strand of hair.

Améliane's head snapped up. "What did you say?"

Margot blinked, her smile faltering. "Only that... well, you know. The name. The prophecy. About Mathieu. Isn't that what they're calling him now?"

There was a beat of silence. The air itself seemed to narrow.

Élodie turned slowly, her expression unreadable.

Améliane stood. "The information about the prophecy originating in the Mirror Hall is not court gossip. Not yet."

Margot paled.

"I must've heard it wrong," she said quickly, waving a hand. "Or maybe someone at breakfast said something—I wasn't listening closely—"

Améliane's gaze sharpened. "Who said it?"

"I—I don't know," Margot stammered, her voice too bright. "I was half-asleep, probably imagining it. I've had the oddest dreams lately—"

Her laugh was brittle, and her smile didn't reach her eyes.

"I'll fetch your breakfast," she said suddenly. "I'll make sure the tea's hot. And the scones aren't burnt this time."

She turned too fast and nearly bumped into the doorframe on her way out.

When she was gone, Élodie met Améliane's gaze in the mirror.

"She's not herself," Élodie murmured. "Not for weeks."

Améliane's eyes lingered on the closed door. The room felt colder without Margot in it—but not in the way it should.

The silence stretched on as Élodie smoothed the Queen's sleeve, both women lost in their thoughts about Margot and the cracks that were no longer so easy to ignore.

After an awkward breakfast—during which Margot never returned and Élodie barely spoke—Renaud arrived at the Queen's chambers with his usual quiet efficiency, offering his arm and a nod.

"Walk?" he asked.

She took it without hesitation.

They stepped into the garden, and the castle exhaled around them.

What had once been frost-laced paths and sleeping hedgerows was now a riot of bloom. Spring had unfurled with startling speed, as if Eldrenoire had blinked and forgotten winter. Wildflowers sprawled across the lawn in waves of violet and gold. Vines twisted up stone columns that had been bare just days ago. One of the fountains bubbled so vigorously it spilled onto the path like an overfilled goblet, despite there being no visible source.

"It's too much," Améliane murmured.

Renaud nodded, his gaze scanning the garden with the wariness of a man used to waiting for something to explode. "It's wrong."

They walked slowly down a gravel path that curved beneath arching boughs of honeysuckle already in full bloom. Too soon. Too fast.

"It feels wired," Renaud said. "Like it's vibrating underfoot."

She felt it, too. Not the warmth she usually sensed from the castle, but a kind of static—nervous, jumpy, wrong. Eldrenoire was awake. But not in control.

She glanced at him. "Corridors flickering again?"

"And mirrors," he said grimly. "Doors that vanish. One of the stewards swears he walked into a linen closet and came out in the south tower."

Améliane exhaled, eyes narrowing. "It's accelerating."

"Or unraveling," Renaud offered.

They paused at a low stone wall where ivy had begun to bloom with tiny pale blossoms—flowers that didn't exist anywhere else in the realm. She brushed her fingers over one. It pulsed faintly beneath her touch.

"Margot said something this morning," Améliane said suddenly. "Something she shouldn't have known. About the Mirror Hall. The Wyrdbound."

Renaud's mouth flattened into a line.

"I asked her who told her. She claimed she must've heard it wrong."

"And you didn't believe her."

"No," she said softly. "And I think she knows I didn't."

They stood in silence a moment longer, both watching as a breeze ruffled through the high hedges—and a section of them moved in the opposite direction from the wind.

"We keep this quiet for now," Renaud said. "Until we understand what she's doing, and why."

"Hmmm," she agreed with a nod.

Just then, the sound of footsteps echoed from the eastern path.

A footman approached, his face flushed and his voice brisk with formality. "Your Majesty, Commander—Cassien has returned."

Améliane's heart tightened, "Where is he?"

"Waiting in your sitting room."

"Then let's not keep him waiting," Renaud said.

Améliane entered her sitting room with Renaud at her side, the soft click of the door closing behind them like the sealing of a vault.

Cassien was already standing near the hearth, scroll in hand, his travel cloak damp at the hem and dust streaked along the shoulders. He looked tired. Not weary—from long miles or long nights—but tense, as if the message he carried was something coiled tight beneath his skin.

He bowed the moment he saw her, then offered the scroll in both hands. "Your Majesty."

"The usual?" she asked, unrolling the parchment but not yet reading it.

"Only in form," Cassien said. "With your leave, I'd prefer to skip Edric's carefully crafted stories this time."

Her grey eyes lifted at that, "Permission granted."

Cassien turned his gaze to Renaud briefly, then back to the Queen. "We'll start with Rothgar."

Améliane nodded, bracing herself.

"Scouting parties continue along the eastern border—small excursions, testing the perimeter of Ghyrell's ruins and pushing closer to Belmaran trade routes. There's talk of treaty violations. Nothing official, but whispers carry." His jaw tightened. "If Rothgar's waiting for an excuse, they're nearly done pretending to need one."

She exhaled through her nose.

Cassien's tone darkened. "Edric has found the original sorcerer, Vaeril. The one who bound the curse on Eldrenoire."

The scroll in her hands curled at the edges as her grip tightened.

"He's back in Caeravelle and residing at Miralys," Cassien continued. "No one knows why. Not yet. But it's not good. His kind don't linger without reason."

Améliane swallowed hard. "Does Edric intend to visit Eldrenoire again?"

Cassien nodded once. "He's preparing for it. There's a large shipment of Vorskyr weapons due in the capital any day. I suspect he'll make the trip once they've been received."

Renaud's jaw clenched.

Cassien pressed on. "The Return is growing faster than we expected. Their numbers have doubled since my last report. And the sigil—your sigil—it's everywhere. While they call it the Moonlit Bloom, everyone knows it's your Moonlit Tidelily. They've painted it on doors, etched it in alleyways. It's even appeared on the outer walls of Miralys."

Améliane sat slowly, setting the scroll aside as if it had suddenly become too heavy.

"They're risking everything," she murmured.

"They believe you still live," Cassien said softly. "They believe you'll return. And that belief is spreading. Rapidly."

She looked at him then—truly looked—and something in her expression shifted. Not fear. Not pride. Something older than both. Something aching.

"There's more," Cassien added.

"Of course there is," Renaud muttered rubbing a hand along the sharp edge of his jaw.

Cassien nodded. "A man has been asking questions near the border. He's been traveling from town to town asking about Eldrenoire. About a cursed queen. About the court."

Améliane went still.

"He has very specific details," Cassien said. "Names. Descriptions. Rumors say he's relentless. He's drawn attention. Edric knows. So does the Return."

Renaud took a step closer to her. "Do you think it's—"

"I do," she said quietly, her voice barely above a breath. "Who else could it be?"

Cassien didn't react—his face stayed carefully neutral—but there was a flicker of something in his eyes. "He's heading toward Ziraveen. But if either side reaches him first..."

"I understand," Améliane said.

Silence stretched, weighted and final.

"Thank you, Cassien," she said at last. "For your loyalty."

He bowed again. "Always, Your Majesty."

Then he turned and left without another word.

The moment the door clicked shut behind him, Améliane sank deeper into her chair, elbows braced on her knees, hands clasped tight.

Renaud stood beside her, unmoving.

"So," she said softly, "the world is shifting."

"It's already shifted," he replied.

The castle's hush deepened as they headed toward the library. Améliane walked in thoughtful silence, her skirts brushing the stone floor in steady rhythm. Afternoon sun slanted through high windows, casting long shadows like sundials bleeding toward evening. Renaud kept pace beside her, his presence as steadying as the weight of the castle itself.

"You think it's him," he said at last.

She didn't hesitate. "Yes."

"Bastian."

Her nod was small but certain. "The man Cassien described... He's not asking random questions. He knows too much. He's circling the places closest to Eldrenoire's boundary. It has to be him."

Renaud exhaled slowly, not arguing.

"I need to see the maps," she added. "I think he's trying to find his way back to Eldrenoire. If I can map where he's been I'll know for sure."

He didn't reply, but when they reached the tall doors to the library, he opened one without a word and followed her in.

The space was warmer than usual—sunlight filtering in through the upper arches, catching dust motes that danced like restless ghosts between the shelves. Améliane took a breath, expecting silence.

Instead—murmurs. Voices, low and earnest, from the eastern alcove. She and Renaud exchanged a glance before moving quietly toward the sound.

They rounded the final row and found them: Mathieu, Laurent, Élodie, and Margot seated around a long table cluttered with scrolls and open books. Margot's gaze flicked up first—then quickly dropped again. Élodie's expression was unreadable as always, though her hand froze mid-page. Laurent leaned back lazily in his chair, but the tightness in his jaw betrayed him.

And Mathieu—Mathieu's eyes found hers and didn't look away.

Améliane cleared her throat softly. "I hope I'm not interrupting."

"You're not," Laurent said smoothly, gesturing to the chaos of parchment and worn bindings before them. "Unless you're here to add to the confusion. In which case, we welcome you."

Élodie gave a small nod, her braid falling over one shoulder. "We're trying to understand the curse."

"And what might break it," Mathieu added, voice low and even. "If it can be broken."

Renaud retrieved the maps they'd come for, then took up position by the nearest door, arms crossed as he scanned the room—though not without casting a hard glance toward Margot.

The queen moved closer to the table, eyes briefly scanning the documents. "And what have you found?"

"Nothing conclusive," Élodie said. "But the castle is behaving... differently."

"Corridors shifting more frequently," Mathieu added. "Mirrors showing things that haven't happened yet."

"And dream patterns," Laurent said, his voice quieter now. "Stronger than they've ever been."

Améliane turned to him, sensing the weight behind his words.

"I've been dreaming of leaving," he said, gaze distant. "Not just in sleep, but when I'm awake."

Élodie's expression flickered with something like pain.

"I don't want to leave you," Laurent added quickly, eyes snapping to Améliane's. "But I... feel it. Like a door might open soon, and if I don't take it—" He stopped. Shrugged. "I don't know what happens if I stay."

Améliane didn't move. Didn't breathe.

She had grown used to solitude. To holding the line. But the thought of someone else leaving—of Laurent walking out of her life forever while she remained cursed—stung in ways she hadn't prepared for.

She smiled softly, gracious as a queen and brittle as glass. "If the door opens, you go, Laurent. No matter what."

Mathieu's hand brushed the edge of a scroll, but he wasn't looking at the parchment. He was watching her with unreadable hazel eyes. Carefully. Silently. His presence grounded the room, and yet, somehow, it made the ache sharper.

Margot cleared her throat—too loudly—and rose from the table. "Your Majesty. Would you... like me to have the Solar prepared? We were planning to dine there tonight."

It was the first she'd spoken since they entered. Her voice was pleasant. Her smile was polite. But it didn't reach her eyes.

The queen offered a soft shake of her head. "Another time. I promised Renaud I'd eat like a monarch for once."

Laurent lifted a brow. "Tragic. We were planning to serve questionable soup and dramatic complaints."

"I'm sure the evening will be less colorful without me, but you'll make do" she said with a smile, already turning to go.

Mathieu rose as she passed, but said nothing.

As she and Renaud exited the alcove, the air behind them filled again with the murmur of theories and the weight of secrets.

And though Améliane did not look back, she felt his eyes on her until the library doors closed behind her.

They passed back into the corridor without a word.

The silence between them wasn't uncomfortable—only full. Tension still lingered at the edges of her thoughts, clinging like mist, but it was Renaud who broke it first.

He offered his arm without ceremony.

Améliane slid her hand into the crook of his elbow, grateful for the steadying presence. They walked in step, the soft rustle of her gown the only sound for a while.

"Will you have my dinner brought to my chambers?" she asked quietly. "I want to study the borderland paths."

Renaud didn't speak immediately. Instead, he tucked the maps under his arm and placed his free hand gently over hers, where it rested in the crook of his elbow. A quiet gesture of understanding. Of solidarity.

She didn't need to explain why she wanted to be alone.

He already knew.

When they reached her chambers, he opened the door for her and stood just outside as she stepped through the threshold.

She paused, turning back to meet his gaze.

"I won't be long with the maps," she said softly. "Just a few hours. I just... need some stillness."

"I'll post myself outside until Thorne gets here," he said. "And I'll have your supper sent up."

She gave a tired smile. "Thank you."

Renaud nodded once, the warm weight of his hand still lingering where it had covered hers. Then the door shut quietly between them. And the queen was alone once more.

Hours later the fire had burned low in her hearth. Only the faintest golden glow remained, stretching long shadows across the rug beneath her feet. A mostly untouched dinner tray sat cooling near the map volumes stacked with care beside her armchair.

She'd found the region Cassien mentioned—small border towns clinging to the edge of Ziraveen's wilds. Ones even the old maps barely recorded.

And she was certain now. Bastian. The man asking questions, stirring rumors, hunting for the name she no longer believed anyone remembered. He was trying to come back.

Améliane stood slowly, muscles stiff from sitting too long, and crossed to her writing desk. She reached for the leather-bound book tucked beneath its false bottom, hands steady even as her heart beat faster.

The book had no title. No lock. Only a single page inside—unmarked, waiting.

She sat. Drew the quill. And signed her name.

The ink shimmered as it sank into the page. She waited.

Silence.

No whisper of magic. No shift in the air.

Her brows drew together. She signed again—slower, more deliberate.

Still nothing.

Améliane stood abruptly, pushing the chair back with enough force to make its legs scrape the floor. The magic book lay open on the desk, quiet and inert.

Alaric had never before failed to answer a summoning.

A chill that had nothing to do with the fire's dwindling warmth crept up her spine.

She was not easily shaken. But she was shaken now.

Without thinking, she crossed to the wardrobe and threw her robe around her shoulders. The Moonlight Courtyard. If anywhere could center her—offer clarity in the face of a castle losing its mind—it was there.

But not through the front door.

If she walked into the corridor, Thorne would insist on accompanying her. And she didn't want his concern or his questions.

She needed quiet. Without another thought, she crossed to the tall balcony doors and opened them to the night.

The gardens below were silver-washed under the moon, dappled in shadow and bloom. The vines near the courtyard walls shimmered faintly, too green for this hour.

Améliane stepped onto the balcony, exhaled once—and shifted.

The familiar stretch of bone and breath overtook her. Fur rippled down her limbs, her body condensing into feline form, white and sleek in the moonlight. Her balance enhanced instantly.

She leapt to the outer ledge of the balcony, then padded to the corner of the stone railing. From here, she could reach the narrow lip that ran the edge of the castle.

As she leapt to the next ledge, magic pulsed through the stone beneath her paws.

A wrenching crack split through her form, like a door slamming shut in a storm.

The castle's magic surged. Not warm or protective.

Violent.

It snapped the thread of her transformation. Mid-step, her feline body twisted—bones lengthening, limbs shifting back to human too fast.

She stumbled—no balance, no footing—too far from the balcony to catch herself.

Her fingers clawed at air.

Then—

The world tilted.

And she fell.

Stone blurred past her eyes. Moonlight caught the edges of her robe as it twisted in the wind. A cry tore from her throat—instinct, not strategy.

Then impact.

White-hot pain bloomed across her ribs. Her breath left her in a single, broken sound.

Then silence.

She lay sprawled in the garden path just outside the Moonlight Courtyard, still and crumpled beneath the stars.

And the castle, for the first time in years, said nothing at all.

CHAPTER 27

Mathieu

T he castle wouldn't settle.

Mathieu paced the upper corridor with slow, deliberate steps, his boots echoing faintly against the stone. Torches sputtered oddly behind him, casting shadows that moved too quickly, like they were trying to escape their own flames. He hadn't meant to walk so far—but sleep had refused him. The energy threading through Eldrenoire tonight was off-kilter. Restless. A kind of pressure humming beneath the skin, like a storm trapped behind glass.

After being Eldrenoire's guest for almost a year he could feel the difference. Something was coming. Or unraveling.

He passed beneath an arch where ivy twisted in from the outside, trailing too far into the hall—as if even the plants didn't know their place anymore. He didn't realize how close he'd gotten to the courtyard terrace until the scent of flowers hit him. He stopped.

That's when he heard it.

A sound—quick and sharp. Not loud, but wrong. A muffled cry. A shape falling fast through the air.

He bolted toward the balcony rail.

The courtyard yawned open below, bathed in silver light. The vines had overgrown the stone, climbing in strange directions, flowers blooming in impossible shades. The reflecting pool shimmered like a cracked mirror at the center of the courtyard.

And just to the left of it—something had fallen.

No. Someone.

He didn't think. He ran.

Down the stairs, through the garden gate, cutting through shadows that twisted too long behind him. His breath tore through his lungs, dread already clawing at the back of his mind. The scent of crushed flowers hung in the air, and beneath it—blood.

She lay crumpled on the path, half in shadow.

"Améliane," he choked, falling to his knees beside her.

She stirred, groaning softly, one hand moving toward her ribs.

Alive.

He exhaled, a sound halfway between a curse and a prayer. His hands were on her in an instant—searching, assessing, checking for blood, broken bones, breath. The touch wasn't rough or rushed, though his pulse thundered in his ears. It was reverent. Careful. One hand slid beneath her shoulder, the other gently pressing along her ribcage, fingers seeking damage beneath the layers of silk and velvet.

"Tell me where it hurts," he murmured, his voice low and tight.

"I'm fine," she whispered, trying to sit up.

"You fell from the godsdamned sky," he said, a rough edge in his voice that was terror barely leashed. "You're not fine."

Her breath hitched as his hand brushed the edge of a bruise blooming across her hip. She winced, and his grip faltered.

He gathered her gently into his lap, cradling her like something precious and breakable. Her body curved against his, and she didn't resist this time—just let herself be held, her breath shallow and uneven.

She reached up weakly, trying to push him away. "Mathieu, I'm all right—"

The scent of her filled his lungs—wildflowers and firelight, rain on old stone. His hands trembled slightly as they moved, brushing through her hair, along the line of her arms, pausing at her waist, her back, her jaw. He was touching her everywhere he needed to—nowhere he shouldn't—but the intimacy of it still made the world feel smaller.

His thumb brushed a smear of blood from her temple.

"Don't lie to me right now," he said, softer than before. "Please."

His hand cupped her cheek, the pad of his thumb sweeping gently beneath her eye, searching for bruises. His other hand settled at her waist, anchoring her with barely-there pressure.

Her heartbeat thudded just beneath the hollow of her throat.

Eyes finally lifted to his—storm-grey and glassy, framed by lashes still wet from the shock.

And then—she stilled.

His thumb traced the edge of her cheekbone.

Her lips parted—just slightly—but no words came out.

Everything about him was raw in that moment. His hair fell into his eyes, his chest heaved with breath, his expression carved from worry and something too deep to name. His hands—battle-worn, calloused, scarred—were holding her like she was the softest thing he'd ever touched.

The quiet stretched between them, suspended on the edge of something sharp.

"What were you doing?" he asked, barely audible.

"I needed air," she whispered, though the lie sat heavy in her throat. "I needed quiet."

He didn't argue.

His hand slid from her cheek to the back of her neck, fingers threading gently through her hair, anchoring her.

"I thought I lost you," he said.

And just like that, her defenses cracked.

She didn't sob. Didn't wail or weep.

But the tears came—slow and soundless. Falling like drops of ink into water. Her shoulders trembled once. Then again.

She didn't try to hide it.

She couldn't.

She had held too much for too long. Carried too many crowns. Buried too many screams. And now, wrapped in the arms of a man who wanted nothing from her but truth, it all came loose.

Mathieu didn't say a word.

He only held her tighter, the moonlight casting silver shadows around them, the fountain whispering behind them like a memory they hadn't lived yet.

They didn't move for a long time.

The courtyard held its breath around them, cloaked in moonlight and strange silence. The vines along the walls quivered slightly in the wind, and the fountain whispered just loud enough to remind the world that time still moved.

She sat curled in his lap, the fall forgotten, the ache in her limbs second to the ache behind her ribs.

Her tears were silent, slow, endless.

He didn't shush her. Didn't hush her. Didn't tell her to breathe or tell her it would be all right.

He only stayed—arms around her, hand still cradling the back of her head, fingers tangled loosely in her hair. His thumb traced quiet circles at her waist.

He didn't know if she was crying because the fall had shaken her to the core, or if something deeper had cracked open—something older than pain and more intimate than fear.

After a while, he asked softly, "Did you hit your head?"

She shook her head against his chest.

"Are you hurt? Really hurt?"

"No," she whispered. "Just... bruised."

But still, the tears came.

Mathieu tightened his grip, just enough to keep her tethered. He tilted his head until his mouth was near her temple, breath warming her skin.

"You don't always have to be strong," he murmured. "Not with me."

Something in her body eased. Just slightly. Just enough.

The silence returned, but it was different now. Softer. Shared.

He looked down at her, at the fall of her dark hair against his arm, at the curve of her shoulder under the robe that had slipped halfway off. Her eyes were closed, lashes wet, her breath stuttering in uneven rhythms.

He let himself speak. Quietly. Carefully.

"I came out here because I couldn't sleep," he said. "The castle's too... alive tonight. Too strange. I thought maybe walking would help."

She didn't respond, but she didn't pull away.

"So I walked. Through the gardens. Past the old armor gallery. Down that corridor with the crooked windows where the shadows always move wrong." A faint smile touched his lips. "I've come to love this place, as maddening as it is. Who'd have thought someone who hates being trapped would ever say such a thing?"

He looked down again, brushing a strand of hair from her cheek with one finger.

"The people. The way Thorne always complains too loudly when he enjoys something. The way Laurent pretends not to care but always knows exactly what's wrong. Élodie's silence. Margot's quips. Even Renaud's steel."

Her breathing slowed, deepening.

"And the ghosts. The way they don't haunt—they just... linger. Like they're waiting for something they don't quite understand."

A breeze stirred the edge of her robe.

"I love the garden that blooms too brightly. The mirrors that show only riddles. The library that's always a little bigger than I remember."

His voice dropped lower.

"And you," he said. "I've come to love everything about you."

She froze.

Mathieu didn't flinch.

"I love your strength. Your stubbornness. Your sharp mind. Your sarcasm. The way you carry yourself like a blade wrapped in velvet. The way you listen. The way you fight. The way you'll sneak past guards for a bite of coconut cake in the middle of the night. The way you look at people like you already know the truth."

His thumb traced the hollow beneath her cheekbone.

"And you're beautiful," he added softly, "but that's just the last thing on a very long list."

She opened her eyes.

And in that look—storm-grey, wet with truth—he saw something collapse.

Not her composure or her pride. But the distance.

She sat up slowly in his lap and braced herself with one hand on his chest, the other shaking slightly as it brushed along the edge of his collar.

And then, she told him.

Everything.

Her voice was low and raw, cracking in places, steady in others. The story unraveled like a ribbon—torn, frayed, but still whole. She told him of the coup. Of Edric. Of the betrayal that started not with war, but with whispers. Of the curse that bound her to the castle, and the curse that bound those loyal to her in animal skin and stone halls. She told him of the letters Edric sent, the torment threaded into every word. Of the rebellion born in alleyways and Seer dreams—the Return. Of the blooming tidelily that had become a symbol. A sigil. A prayer.

She told him about Bastian. The man who had proclaimed his love and then left her at Eldrenoire. The man who now, somehow, remembered.

And last, her voice nearly breaking—she told him of Alaric.

Of calling him. And being met with nothing.

Mathieu didn't interrupt. Not once.

He held her, listened, and said not a word.

Not because he didn't know what to say.

But because the way it tumbled out felt too raw, too unpracticed to have been spoken before. And now that she had, the weight of it settled in his chest like fire.

He touched her face again when she finished, fingers trailing lightly along her jaw. Her eyes were red, her mouth trembling, her body still curled against his.

And yet, she had never looked more like a queen.

For one breathless moment, the world held its shape.

The wind quieted. The fountain stilled. Even the garden seemed to lean in, waiting.

Améliane's confession still hung between them—raw and unguarded, as bare as her soul had ever been. And as the weight of what she'd just done settled into her chest, her spine stiffened.

Her eyes darted to his face, reading the aftermath. She saw no mockery. No pity. Only something vast and reverent.

But fear had teeth. And hers were sharp.

She drew back, just a fraction—barely a shift in weight, barely a breath—but it was enough.

Mathieu felt it.

The way her hand hesitated where it lay against his chest. The way her gaze flicked toward the exit, as if the weight of her vulnerability might demand retreat.

He didn't pull her back.

But he caught her hand—fingers wrapping gently around hers.

Not to bind.

To anchor.

His thumb brushed the back of her knuckles. His voice was low, nearly lost in the hush.

"You could tell me a thousand more secrets," he murmured, "and I'd still think the most extraordinary thing about you is the way you never stopped fighting."

She stilled.

He sat up straighter to peer into her eyes, still cradling her hand, his other hand lifting to trace the edge of her jaw.

"But I'll earn the rest," he added, voice brushing over her like velvet. "Every truth. Every scar. Every secret."

She exhaled—shaky, uneven and cast her eyes toward her lap.

He waited.

He didn't move again until her silver eyes met his again—and stayed. Until her breath slowed. Until the barest nod gave him her answer.

Then, slowly, deliberately, he leaned in.

And kissed her.

It wasn't hesitant.

It wasn't careful.

It was the kind of kiss that rewrote stories and carved kingdoms into bone. The kind that started slow—firm and certain, mouth molding to hers like it belonged there—and then deepened, catching fire beneath their skin.

His hands slid up to her face, thumbs framing her cheeks, fingers tangling in her hair. He kissed her like he had memorized the shape of her sadness and wanted to kiss every ghost from her throat. His mouth moved over hers—slow, then faster—like he needed more, needed all of her, like nothing else in the world had ever made sense until this.

Her lips parted on a sigh, and he groaned softly into her mouth as his tongue swept across hers—tasting, coaxing, claiming. He kissed her in a way that consumed her without being possessive or demanding.

Her hands rose without thought, gripping the front of his shirt, fisting in the fabric like a woman drowning in the one thing she needed to breathe. She kissed him back with months of ache and years of silence. With grief. With longing. With a hunger that made her shake.

She shifted in his lap, straddling his thighs as her body pressed to his fully now, fitting against the lines of him like she was made for this moment—this man.

The cold courtyard floor might as well have been made of silk. The night air might as well have been fire.

Nothing mattered but the feel of his mouth on hers.

Nothing mattered but the way his hands slid down her back, gripping her waist, anchoring her in place as if he'd never let her go again. The kiss deepened—wet, hot, desperate. Her teeth scraped his bottom lip and he growled into her mouth, dragging her closer.

And still, it wasn't enough. Could never be enough.

She pulled back just enough to breathe, their foreheads resting together, lips still brushing as they panted into each other's mouths. Their hands trembled where they touched—his on her hips, hers in his hair.

Silence stretched. Not the empty kind. The sacred kind.

Her fingers were still curled in his shirt when the twinge caught her—sharp and sudden, flaring through her side as his hand slid gently beneath her ribs.

She gasped, pulling back with a wince.

Instantly, Mathieu froze. The fire in his eyes doused in one breath, replaced by something sharper. Concern.

"Where?" he asked softly, already scanning her again. "Where did it hit?"

"It's nothing," she said, trying to brush it off, but the moment she shifted, her body disagreed—vividly.

Mathieu's hands returned to her waist, firm and steady.

"I would love nothing more," he murmured, "than to keep kissing you until the sun comes up and the castle walls fall down."

She arched a brow. "That's quite the schedule."

"But," he added, brushing a lock of hair from her face, "if I bring you back injured after being out here alone with you, Renaud will kill me. Slowly. Poetically. Possibly with a monologue."

That earned a snort from her, though it ended in another grimace.

He stood first, then offered both hands.

She took them.

"I'm fine," she muttered, straightening with more pride than grace.

"Mmm," he said, watching her like a hawk. "You're wincing like a heroine in a bad stage play."

They made it to the stairs at the edge of the courtyard, and she was halfway up the first step when her breath caught again, her hand instinctively flying to her ribs.

That was all he needed.

Without hesitation, he swept her into his arms.

Améliane startled, eyes going wide. "Mathieu—"

"I know you can walk," he said easily, shifting her higher in his grip. "You can probably fight off an entire Rothgarian battalion on your own. But this is faster. And I don't feel like hearing Sabine's lecture on 'proper post-trauma transport procedures' at midnight."

She blinked at him, trying not to smile.

"You just enjoy carrying me."

"Obviously."

He started toward the castle, his stride steady despite the stone path and her unimpressed expression.

"This is certainly going to start gossip. I have guards, you know," she said as they passed through the shadowed archway. "A whole cursed court of them."

"And yet," he replied, casting her a sidelong glance, "it's always me finding you after dark in moonlit gardens. I'm beginning to suspect you enjoy the drama."

She bit back a laugh. "Careful. That sounds dangerously like affection."

"Oh no," he said solemnly, "I'm far too dignified for that."

By the time they reached her wing, the torchlight had shifted—glowing low and golden, casting everything in a hush of midnight warmth. He turned the final corner...

And there was Thorne.

Standing sentinel just outside her chamber door, arms crossed, posture perfectly rigid—until he saw them.

His eyes widened. Slowly. Comically.

His gaze flicked from Mathieu's arms to the queen's flushed face, to the bruises blooming at her temple, and back again.

Mathieu didn't break stride.

He stopped at the door, nudged it open with his foot, and carried her inside like it was the most natural thing in the world.

"Thorne," he said over his shoulder, "fetch Sabine, please."

A pause.

"Tell her that apparently cats don't always land on their feet."

Then the door shut behind them with the kind of soft, sovereign finality that made Thorne rethink every life choice that had brought him to this moment.

CHAPTER 28

Améliane

Améliane blinked up at the ceiling as sunlight spilled through the balcony doors and painted warm patterns across her duvet. Somewhere beyond the glass, birds were making a joyful racket, and a breeze stirred the sheer curtains like a sigh.

Her ribs ached, her head throbbed with a dull pulse, and she was fairly certain her right shoulder had bruised in the exact shape of a courtyard cobblestone.

But she was alive. Whole. And after three days of being treated like a cracked vase wrapped in lace and guilt, she was thoroughly done with convalescing.

Sabine had visited twice and left with strict instructions: no heavy movement, no stress, no shifting. As if a queen cursed into a castle could simply choose not to feel stressed.

Her injuries were minor—bruised ribs, a mild concussion, and a strained shoulder—but apparently not minor enough to escape the full force of Renaud's wrath.

She sighed and rolled gingerly onto her side, grimacing at the flare of discomfort. She could still hear the echo of his voice the night after her fall—clipped, cold, and very loud. She was sure the castle's west wing was still vibrating. Poor Thorne had clearly taken the brunt of Renaud's ire judging by the sheepish knock on her door the next morning before he left his post.

Élodie had sat with her that afternoon, brushing her hair and muttering that Renaud should take a walk before he popped a blood vessel. Margot had been more doting than usual—fluffing pillows, straightening linens, and all but forcing second helpings of soup on her with wide, eager eyes and a too-bright smile.

Still, the most constant presence by far had been Mathieu.

He'd only left her room to spar or sleep, and even then, she suspected it was more to appease Renaud than from any true desire to be elsewhere. He brought books—some well-worn, others questionably pilfered from the restricted archives—and read them aloud with a voice so rich and steady she could barely stay awake through the second page. He brought her meals, including contraband sweets and the last slice of coconut cake from the kitchen, which he claimed had survived a small-scale war among the footmen.

He also brought silence—comfortable and unintrusive—the kind she didn't realize she needed until it wrapped around her like a second blanket.

Now, she lay in the soft hush of her room and listened to the faint rustle of pages being turned across the room.

Mathieu was back in the armchair by the hearth, legs sprawled, one boot half-off, the other resting on the table in scandalous defiance of furniture etiquette. He was reading *The History of Symbolic Rulership in the Ordréan Empire* with the bored expression of a man counting the ceiling beams.

She cleared her throat.

He looked up instantly.

"You're hovering again," she said dryly.

"I am providing support," he replied, not missing a beat. "Vital, attentive, and charming support."

"You're three synonyms away from being smothering."

"I haven't offered to spoon-feed you anything in at least a day. That's growth."

She laughed—and regretted it immediately. Her ribs reminded her, sharply, that they were still bruised and unamused.

Mathieu was on his feet in a flash. "Pain?"

"Only when I express joy, apparently," she muttered, clutching her side. "Which you seem determined to provoke."

He crossed the room with careful, measured steps and crouched beside the bed. "Tell me what you need."

"I need," she said, drawing herself upright with slow dignity, "to not spend another hour in this bed."

He opened his mouth. She cut him off.

"And yes, Sabine said I could move around—*gently*. And yes, I'm sore. And no, I'm not planning to scale another wall this week."

"I was going to suggest you should stay here another day."

"And I'm suggesting you get out of my way."

He blinked at her. Then slowly, a grin curved across his lips.

"There she is," he said softly. "I was beginning to wonder if you'd been replaced by a very regal ghost with a low pain tolerance."

She narrowed her eyes. "Careful. I'm still the Queen in these parts."

"Your Highness." He gave a shallow bow, smirk overt and unapologetic.

She swung her legs over the edge of the bed, wincing slightly, but said nothing.

Mathieu didn't offer to help her stand. He only watched, quiet and steady, until she was upright.

Then his eyes did a slow sweep of her—unapologetic, concerned, and altogether too fond.

"Out," she said, pointing to the door. "I need to bathe and dress."

"Of course," he said innocently. "Will you be selecting a gown that inspires fear, awe, or heart palpitations today?"

"Depends on what is on the agenda," she retorted.

He crossed to the door and opened it with a flourish, then turned back once more, expression more serious this time.

"Don't push too hard," he said. "Not today."

"I won't," she promised.

And then—because he was already halfway out the door—she added, "Thank you."

He paused. Looked back at her.

His voice was soft. "Always."

Then he was gone, leaving her alone with her aches, her mirror, and the quiet knowledge that everything was changing.

After her bath and morning routine, Élodie helped her into a gown of midnight blue. The bruise beneath her ribs still flared when she twisted wrong, and her head ached if she stood too fast—but it didn't matter. She was dressed, upright, and determined not to spend another hour buried in quilts while the world continued without her.

Élodie stood behind her, fastening the last clasp at her nape with deft fingers. "You look like yourself again."

Améliane met her eyes in the mirror. "Thank you."

"You smell like yourself again too," Élodie added, with the faintest smirk. "Less healer's salve, more command and threat."

"I'll take that as a compliment."

There was a quiet knock before the door creaked open and Margot entered, carrying a tray of fresh-squeezed juice and pain tonic. "A toast to the resurrection," she chirped, setting the tray down near the writing desk with a practiced grace.

"Good morning," Améliane said, tone even. She kept her expression neutral as she watched Margot's eyes flick toward the carved drawer beneath the desk—just for a second too long.

Margot blinked and smiled. "You're up and radiant. Shall I call it a miracle or a warning to those who hoped to inherit your wardrobe?"

Élodie snorted behind her, but Améliane's eyes narrowed the smallest fraction. "Either way," she said coolly, "someone will be disappointed."

Margot handed her the glass, fingertips brushing Améliane's with feigned casualness. "Sabine said you're healing quickly. I told the kitchen to have proper food sent to the council room. Something without broth or roots."

"Thank you," Améliane said, taking the glass but not drinking.

Élodie helped her with her jewelry, then handed her a slim leather-bound folio. "Briefings for the last four days. Nothing too dramatic, just your typical cursed castle chaos."

Améliane raised a brow. "Which is now apparently... normal."

The three women stepped into the corridor where the sunlight filtered through warped stained glass, spilling fractured patterns across the floor. Somewhere down the hall, the sound of metal clanged—sparring in the courtyard below, likely Thorne and Mathieu. The rhythm was familiar, reassuring.

But the castle was not.

As Renaud escorted them toward the council chamber, the flicker of a torch blinked twice. A door at the end of the hall seemed closer than it had been a moment ago.

Élodie noticed it too. Her fingers brushed the dagger hidden in her skirts.

Renaud paused at the chamber door, posture tense. "No sightings of Alaric," he said immediately, his voice pitched low.

"Still?" Améliane asked.

Renaud shook his head. "I've asked the stewards, the kitchens, and even went to the mirror hall. Twice. He hasn't been seen since—" He glanced at Margot and clamped his jaw shut. "It's been too long."

The next half hour unfolded in orderly efficiency—updates on food stores (stable), linen shortages (unavoidable), and rotating guard duties (adjusted since her fall).

Améliane made note of it all, scribbling in her careful script, circling a few entries for follow-up.

Still, she couldn't shake the itch at the back of her neck—the quiet hum of wrongness threading through the air.

Margot sat quietly for most of the meeting but interjected twice: once to report that the east wing windows had begun frosting again despite the rising temperatures, and again to mention that the green corridor now looped back on itself. "Took me nearly ten minutes to reach the conservatory," she said with a dramatic sigh.

As the meeting concluded Margot rose to her feet, smoothing an invisible wrinkle from her bodice.

"I'll see to the kitchens," she chirped, plucking an empty juice glass from the table. "The cooks can't be trusted not to serve boiled misery if I'm not there to supervise."

Améliane gave a polite nod. "Thank you, Margot."

With a bright smile that was too quick, Margot exited the council room and disappeared down the hallway in the direction of the servants' stairwell.

Améliane turned to Renaud. "Let's speak to the footmen. Prepare them for Edric's inevitable visit. I don't want him wandering around Eldrenoire unaccompanied."

Élodie left to see to the housekeeping staff while Améliane and Renaud moved together down the corridor, passing beneath the stained-glass window of the East Corridor. The light cast fractured bands of violet and amber across the polished stone, pooling around their feet like spilled enchantment.

"Do you think she's figured out we're watching her?" she asked under her breath.

"If she has, she's playing it close," Renaud replied, his eyes scanning every archway and alcove.

The main foyer stood tall and echoing ahead of them, sunbeams slanting through the high windows and catching motes of dust in their path. The three footmen they'd requested were already assembled beneath the staircase, standing in a neat line, expressions alert.

Renaud nodded at them in greeting. "You've all seen what the castle's been doing lately. Doors disappearing. Rooms looping in on themselves. And yet none of that is as unsettling as what we're expecting soon."

"Lord Edric," Améliane said simply.

Their posture stiffened as if on cue.

"We don't know when he will arrive," she continued. "But given the.... changes at Eldrenoire, we expect he will come to inspect it soon. When he does arrive, please ensure he his escorted to the Grand Hall and nowhere else."

"Don't engage unless spoken to," Renaud added. "And even then, you say only what you must."

"We will handle the rest," Améliane finished, her voice like cold steel wrapped in silk.

The footmen nodded solemnly. The tension in the room tightened—

—and then a voice piped up from behind them.

"Oh, are we discussing protocols?"

Améliane turned, her expression smoothing just in time to see Margot sweeping into the foyer with her usual grace... but not a hint of breathlessness. As if she hadn't just hiked across the castle after announcing her errand to the kitchens.

She came to stand just beside them, hands folded, gaze far too interested in the conversation at hand.

Renaud's brow arched slowly, the corner of his mouth ticking downward. "Was lunch not in need of your urgent supervision after all?"

Margot blinked innocently. "Oh, it is. I just thought I'd stop and check if you needed anything else."

"We didn't," he said flatly.

Her smile flickered, just briefly, before she gave a little curtsy and flitted away toward the south corridor.

Renaud muttered something beneath his breath that might have included the word fox.

Améliane's reply was cut off by the unmistakable sound of a heavy door swinging open behind them.

As the footmen scurried back to their usual posts, Mathieu entered the foyer with sunlight at his back and sweat glistening across his chest like a blessing the gods had personally applied. His sparring shirt clung to him like second skin, damp and unbuttoned far enough to hint at things no queen had any business admiring in public. His hair was damp and tousled, his forearms dusted with streaks of dirt and smudged bruises from Thorne's practice blade.

Améliane forgot, briefly, what day it was.

Mathieu spotted her instantly. A grin curled over his mouth like it had been waiting there all morning. "Your Majesty," he said with a slight bow. "Lovely day for terrifying the staff."

"I've missed it," she replied, smothering a smile. "The fear. The trembling. The dramatic salutes."

"I'm sure Renaud showered them with orders and menace during your brief absence," Mathieu said, smirking in the guard's direction—and earning an impressively undignified eye roll in return.

"I was planning to continue my research in the library. If you're interested in joining me—after I bathe, of course. Unless you prefer your parchment accompanied by the scent of victory and mild dehydration," he said, wiping a line of sweat from his brow.

She raised a brow. "I think I'll wait for the scent of soap and decency. Renaud and I have some things to wrap up, but if you're still there after lunch I'll take my tea in the library."

"It's a date," he said, clearly enjoying himself.

He passed by with a wink. Her gaze did not follow him.

Not outwardly.

But inwardly, every step he took reverberated through her like the aftershock of something already too dangerous to name.

Renaud made a sound that could only be described as a long-suffering sigh. "You've spent more time with him this week than you've spent with Élodie in the last month."

"That's not true," she said primly.

"Oh no?" he asked. "Should I start tallying the tea invitations?"

They resumed their path toward the council room, the echo of Mathieu's retreating footsteps fading behind them.

"And Margot," Renaud added, quieter now, "she's everywhere. Always a step behind you. Always showing up like she's meant to be there."

The scent of orange blossom and bergamot greeted them before the library doors even opened.

"Tea's here," Renaud muttered with mock solemnity. "Try to contain your excitement."

Améliane gave him a dry look as he held the door open for her. "Some of us don't derive our energy from grimacing and judgment."

"To each their fuel," he replied.

Inside, the grand library was warm with late afternoon sun. The tall windows threw long beams of gold across the rugs, dust motes drifting lazily through the air like magic caught in pause. The space felt calm, even with the castle's magic humming just beneath the surface like a too-taut string.

Laurent was tucked into an armchair near the hearth, a stack of open books balanced across the arms like a literary barricade. He looked up as they entered, offering a one-handed salute with his teacup.

Mathieu stood behind him at the central table, shirt fresh and sleeves rolled to his elbows as he pored over a spread of arcane diagrams and cursebinding theories. He glanced up at their entrance and straightened, his smile quick and genuine.

"Your Majesty. Commander," he said with a slight nod. "We've only just started boiling the water for tea with the sheer power of scholarly frustration."

"Excellent," Améliane replied, crossing the room slowly. Her ribs still twinged, but she managed to keep her gait smooth. "I do love tea with a hint of magical despair."

From the far door, Élodie appeared with a tray balanced expertly in her hands, Margot trailing behind with a second tiered stand of pastries and tarts. The scent of warm honey and plum jam filled the space as the two women set the service on the low table.

"Lemon scones," Margot said brightly to Laurent. "I know they are not your favorite, but I assume you'll be too polite to send them back."

Laurent murmured something unintelligible reaching for a tart and inspecting it like it might talk back.

Margot lingered for a beat longer than necessary, eyes flicking toward the scrolls on the table—and then, too casually, to the far shelves where the castle's historical ledgers were kept.

"Élodie and I will leave you to your terribly serious research," she said, brushing her hands on her skirt. "Do try not to spill jam on any ancient runes."

As they turned to go, Élodie threw a pointed glare in Laurent's direction.

He sighed, dramatically. "Right. I suppose I'm not welcome anymore, seeing as you have a date."

Améliane's eyes went wide, embarrassment creeping onto her cheeks. "Laurent, of course you're free to stay."

"Oh no," he said, standing with exaggerated grace. "I know a battle line when I see it."
Laurent gave a little bow and followed the others out.

Améliane turned to Renaud, lifting one elegant brow.

He met her gaze, sighed deeply, and gestured toward the door. "I'll be right outside."

She nodded once, and he stepped out, closing the library doors with a quiet *click*.

Améliane lowered herself in the high-backed armchair by the hearth, biting back a wince as a dull ache flared beneath her ribs. The fire crackled softly beside her, casting amber light across the spines of the library's oldest volumes.

She had barely settled when Mathieu returned, carrying a tea tray with far more ceremony than was strictly necessary.

"Your finest infusion, milady," he announced, setting the cup beside her with exaggerated care. "Hand-selected from the darkest corners of the pantry and barely spilled along the way."

She raised a brow. "I'm honored by your restraint."

He grinned and produced a small plate with a single plum tart nestled at its center. "And the crown jewel—rescued from under Élodie's protective ward. She said if I didn't bring it to you, she'd curse my boots to squeak forever."

Améliane let out a soft laugh that caught in her ribs and made her flinch. Mathieu's expression sobered in an instant.

"Still sore?" he asked, crouching beside her, his gaze scanning her face.

"Only when I breathe, bend, sit, stand, or exist," she said dryly, clutching her side. "But I've always been an overachiever."

He smiled faintly. "I'll add suffering with grace to the list. It's getting rather long."

She sipped the tea—strong, spiced, familiar—and eyed him over the rim of the cup. "And what grim tomes are you drowning in today, oh scholarly one? I saw enough of them stacked on the table to ward off lesser men."

Mathieu moved to his own chair across from her, separated only by the small round table. One hand absently turned the corner of a parchment page, though he didn't glance down.

"The structure of the curse," he said. "I'm trying to map it. There are patterns—runes under the stone, mirrored symbols in the hallways, phrases that repeat in the oldest texts. It's like scaffolding... or a cage. Something's holding it all together."

He gestured vaguely around them—not just to the library, but to the castle itself.

"It's not random," he added. "There's a key. A fault line. And I think we're close."

Her smile faltered slightly.

"I know it's hard," she said. "Being trapped here. I understand wanting to leave."

Mathieu looked at her then—truly looked. Not like a man searching for an escape, but one searching for understanding.

"I'm not looking for a way out," he said quietly. "I'm looking for a way through. If I find a door, it's not so I can walk out alone. It's so all of us—your court, your people, *you*—can walk free."

Something flickered behind her eyes. Surprise. Then something softer—wonder, maybe.

She opened her mouth, as if to respond, but stopped short when his hand moved gently across the table.

His thumb brushed the corner of her mouth, catching a stray crumb from the tart she hadn't noticed. The gesture was tender—absurdly so. Soft enough to make her breath still in her lungs.

He didn't pull back immediately.

And she didn't look away.

For a moment, the world narrowed to the space between them. The slant of sunlight on stone. The quiet pop of the fire. The feel of his touch, warm and reverent, against her skin.

Then he dropped his hand, slowly, letting the moment settle like dust in the air.

"Will you tell me again?" he asked. "What happened the day you lost your throne?"

She tensed.

Her gaze drifted from his to the fire, shoulders tightening, breath catching as though the memory had just stepped into the room.

"I don't mean to cause pain," he said gently, his voice low. "But I think it matters. The curse. The castle. You. They're bound together. And if I'm going to help break this, I need to understand what broke first."

He didn't reach for her. Didn't press.

He simply waited, steady as the flame, offering her the one thing no one else had: the space to tell her story—and the promise to stay, even if it burned.

Améliane's fingers traced the delicate rim of her teacup, though she made no move to drink. The silence between them had stretched long—but not awkward. Intentional. Like the stillness before a storm.

"Some of this you already know," she said finally, her voice low. "But not all of it. Not the worst of it."

Mathieu didn't speak. He only waited—patient, steady, a quiet force across the table from her.

She exhaled slowly. "I wasn't born to rule. Not directly, anyway. My brother—Tavian—was meant to wear the crown. I was second-born. The one who studied law, who sat beside my father during court, who knew the ledgers by heart but never expected to sign them."

Her gaze drifted toward the window, where sunlight bled gold through the warped panes.

"Our mother died giving birth to Seresin, my younger sister. I was five. Tavian was already showing signs of illness by then—something brittle in his bones, something that stole his breath when he ran too fast or laughed too hard. My father tried to keep the kingdom stable, but after our mother's death, he unraveled quickly. Some say he died of grief. I think... it was guilt. For surviving her. For not knowing how to raise three children alone—two of them girls in a realm that had never found females particularly useful."

Her voice did not waver. But it hollowed slightly. Sharpened.

"When Tavian died, I was seventeen. Too young, they said. Too inexperienced. Too... female." A bitter smile touched her lips. "But I was next in line for the throne and took the crown anyway."

Mathieu leaned forward slightly, elbows braced on his knees, gaze fixed.

"Eventually I married Edric. I thought marrying him would silence the doubt. He was powerful. Well-connected. A respected war tactician. I believed—naïvely—that giving Belmara a king, even one in name only, would make them accept their Queen."

She laughed once, sharp and without joy. A long pause.

"He resented me for wearing the crown he thought should never have been mine. Thought I'd made a mockery of divine order. He told me once—*women were made to birth kings, not become them.*"

Mathieu's hands curled into fists.

"He played the part well for the first few years. Charming. Supportive. But he was building something beneath the surface. I should've seen it sooner." She shook her head. "He courted the ear of my court—my steward, my chancellor. He preyed on Seresin's insecurities. She always felt... forgotten. I loved her. I never thought she'd turn."

The words were quieter now. Strained. "But she did."

Améliane paused to sip her tea. It had gone cold.

"During the Festival of Dawns—Caeravelle's oldest celebration—Edric arranged for a special midnight ceremony. A tribute to the gods of the sea and sky. Said it would show the people how unified we were. That I should meet him to light the ceremonial flame."

Mathieu straightened slightly. "He used the festival as cover."

She nodded. "The city was drunk on revelry. Music, wine, laughter. They led me to the Seaheart Atrium beneath Miralys—one of our most sacred spaces. That's where he was waiting. With Vaeril."

Mathieu's eyes darkened. "The sorcerer."

She nodded again, slower this time. "Once our kingdom's most gifted mage. But he turned to dark magic in the final years of my father's reign. I had him exiled after my coronation, when he tried to bind weather to a warship fleet. He saw my rule as blasphemy—a perversion of divine law."

"And Edric brought him back."

Améliane's lips pressed into a thin line. "They wanted a curse that wouldn't just imprison me. They wanted one that would erase me. Remove me from memory. Strip my name from statues, from history."

She looked up. "And they succeeded."

Silence fell again—this time heavier. The weight of a stolen life pressed against the walls of the library.

"The curse," she continued, "was Vaeril's masterpiece. He wove it from rage, from memory, from the very bones of Miralys. He made... this place." Her eyes swept the shelves, the firelight. "Eldrenoire is a reflection. A mockery. My home—twisted and frozen in the moment of my undoing."

Mathieu's voice was a rasp. "And your court?"

"Those loyal to me refused to kneel that night. They drew blades. They tried to protect me." Her jaw flexed. "So, the curse took them too—but not just their freedom. Vaeril twisted them. He bound their souls to Eldrenoire and warped their bodies into animal forms—a mockery of their strength, a perversion of their spirits. They hadn't been shifters before. That was his invention. His cruelty." Her voice dropped. "The magic didn't just trap us—it reshaped us. Gave them forms that reflected not who they were, but how the curse wanted them to be seen. Animals in a cage."

"And the rest of the realm?" he asked, voice quiet but taut with fury.

"They forgot. The curse wiped me clean. Only a few could remember—those shielded by proximity or purpose. Cassien, as Edric's appointed liaison to Eldrenoire, had to retain memory to allow Edric to taunt me with his weekly news briefings."

"But the curse was flawed," she continued. "Dark magic always is. It leaves a crack—a flaw. And into that flaw, something ancient might slip."

Her eyes met his.

"I've been doing some research of my own, and I think that 'something' could be you."

Mathieu's brow furrowed, but he didn't speak.

"Alaric called you *Wyrdbound*," she said. "Bound to fate but not ruled by it. You came here by accident, and the curse is unraveling because it didn't account for *you*."

She swallowed. "The seers are also remembering. I think that's another flaw. They forgot briefly when the curse was cast. But now... they dream of me. They draw my sigil at night all around Belmara. They call themselves 'The Return.'"

She sat back. Closed her eyes for a beat.

"This place was meant to be a cage. But the bars are rusting."

And when she opened her eyes again, something in them had changed.

Not just pain, but purpose, too.

A long silence stretched between them, heavy with memory and the low hum of the fire.

Améliane looked down into her half-empty teacup, suddenly very aware of how quiet the castle had become. The air felt thinner, like it was holding its breath.

Then the library door opened with a creak.

Renaud stepped in, boots echoing against the stone, his expression dark with purpose.

His gaze found hers immediately.

"He's here," Renaud said grimly. "Edric. He's just arrived at the gates."

The room fell utterly still. Not even the fire dared crackle.

CHAPTER 29

Améliane

T he trio left the library and walked the length of the corridor in silence—Améliane in the center, Renaud at her right, Mathieu at her left. A triangle of tension and unspoken intent.

The scent of parchment and ink still clung to her robes, but the warmth of the library had vanished the moment Renaud entered with two clipped words, "He's here."

Now, the castle's corridors seemed longer, darker—as if Eldrenoire itself was creating distance from its maker.

"Do they know where to escort him?" she asked, voice even.

"The Great Hall," Renaud replied. "I'm sure he has already summoned the court and is acting like he owns the place."

"He always did have a flair for theatrics," she muttered. "Let him hold court. It changes nothing."

Mathieu walked quietly beside her. But she could feel the storm simmering beneath his silence. Not fear, but something more dangerous. A man gauging the threat of another predator.

"We don't keep him waiting," she said as they neared the grand doors. "The sooner we greet him the sooner he leaves."

Glancing at Mathieu she continued, "Let's let him see exactly what he came for."

She paused just before the entrance. One deep breath. One last moment to gather herself.

She looked again at Mathieu then turned her gaze to Renaud. He gave the smallest nod of readiness. His hand hovered near the hilt of his sword—not to draw, but to remind.

And then the great doors began to open on their own, creaking on magic and memory.

The queen entered first, and her shadows followed close behind.

The Great Hall was already full. Court members lined the walls, standing in dutiful rows beneath the tall windows, bathed in that strange golden light Eldrenoire conjured only for occasions like this—sunlight that never touched the outside world.

At the far end of the room, waiting impatiently, stood Edric.

He turned the moment the doors opened, smiling as if he hadn't orchestrated her downfall, as if he hadn't trapped her in a gilded prison and returned only when it suited him.

"Ah," he said, voice smooth as oiled velvet. "There she is. My Queen."

The words slid over her like cold water. She kept walking.

From the crowd, Élodie stepped forward, moving with the grace of her panther form even in human shape. Laurent followed, languid and amused as ever, his hands clasped behind his back like a man attending a play.

They flanked her just behind Renaud and Mathieu, a silent show of allegiance that did not go unnoticed.

Edric's gaze flicked to them—lingering a beat too long on Mathieu.

"And this," he said, voice honeyed and laced with interest, "must be the stranger I've heard so much about. The man who stumbled through the jungle gates and into your... affections."

Renaud stiffened beside her. The court did not gasp—but Améliane could feel them listening harder. How did he know?

Mathieu inclined his head, polite but unbending. "Mathieu Duran."

Edric's smile widened, but his eyes sharpened. "Duran. Curious name for a man with no past."

"I have a past," Mathieu said evenly. "It just wasn't invited to follow me."

Laurent snorted softly. Edric ignored him.

"And what were you running from," Edric asked, taking a slow, deliberate step closer, "when Eldrenoire so generously offered you sanctuary?"

"Bandits," Mathieu replied without missing a beat. "Jungle's full of them. Or hadn't you heard?"

"Of course," Edric said, amused. "How careless of me."

He circled to the side now, gaze sliding between Renaud and Élodie before returning to Améliane—his smile reserved just for her, the kind that meant danger was coming wrapped in silk.

"Fifteen months," he murmured. "And still here. Eldrenoire usually tires of wanderers far more quickly. Unless..." His eyes settled on Mathieu again. "Unless she finds them interesting."

Mathieu offered a ghost of a smile. "I'm told I grow on people."

"Like moss," Renaud muttered under his breath.

Améliane didn't look at either of them. She kept her attention on Edric—because to look away was to lose ground.

Edric's voice turned light again, for the court's benefit. "It's touching, really. The Queen and her little collection of lost souls. How protective you've all become of one another."

"We were never lost," Élodie said mildly. "Just waiting."

Edric's jaw ticked, but only once. "Of course you were."

He turned again to Mathieu, this time letting the charm drop just enough for the inner circle to feel the chill beneath.

"I do hope you're enjoying your stay, *monsieur Duran*. Do take care not to get too comfortable. The castle has a habit of keeping things... until they break."

Mathieu didn't flinch. "I've been broken before. Came out sharper."

Edric tilted his head, that serpent's smile returning. "Yes... I imagine you did."

Edric's gaze, so far trained on her little circle, suddenly cut across the room—to the line of courtiers at the back of the hall.

It was just a glance. A flicker of attention.

But it was enough. Améliane's eyes narrowed.

He was looking for someone. Or at someone.

When he turned back, that smile returned—serene, satisfied.

"I believe we've all enjoyed this little reunion," he said, his voice rising just enough to carry across the room. "But I'd like a moment alone with my Queen."

Silence fell.

Then, movement—uncertain, hesitant.

Renaud bristled. Élodie's posture shifted just slightly, a hand twitching at her side. Laurent went perfectly still, the glint in his eye sharpening. And beside her, Mathieu's jaw had set into stone.

"No," Renaud said, voice low and unmistakably dangerous.

Améliane didn't look at him. She was watching Edric.

Mathieu's jaw clenched twice before he turned to Renaud. "The Queen can handle herself."

Renaud's eyes flared with something fierce and unspoken. Then he turned to Améliane.

"I'll be just outside the doors," he said. "If you need anything—*anything*—I will come."

She gave a single nod.

The great hall emptied slowly, like a tide receding. One by one, the courtiers filed out—silent, nervous, curious. The echo of footsteps on stone faded, until it was only the two of them.

And the throne.

Edric approached it with deliberate ease, lowering himself into it as if the world belonged beneath him. One elbow draped over the carved armrest; his fingers tapped idly against the gilded wood.

"So formal today," he said. "I almost didn't recognize you. Or perhaps that's just the lighting in this place. It's so... flattering."

Améliane stood tall in front of him. The empty space between them hummed with memory.

"This is tiresome, Edric. What do you want?" she sighed.

He smiled again. "Come now. No preamble? No pleasantries for an old lover?"

"You forfeited pleasantries when you cursed my name from memory."

"Oh, such a dramatic way to put it." He rose slowly from the throne, descending a step. "Besides, I'm only here to check on you. I've heard things."

"From whom?"

A single brow lifted. "Does it matter?"

It did. And they both knew it.

He continued, too smooth, too casual. "Things have been stirring here, haven't they? The castle feels...restless. Even from Miralys, I can sense the tension in its walls."

He stepped lightly down the dais, his boots whispering against the stone. "You've let something in, haven't you, darling?"

Améliane's spine straightened. "Eldrenoire is no longer your concern."

Edric chuckled, low and cold. "Eldrenoire is mine by design. Don't forget, I helped build this little haven of yours." He swept a hand around as if admiring his own twisted masterpiece. "And I'm not the only one concerned. Vaeril agrees the magic is... fraying."

Her lips parted, then pressed into a hard line. "You've spoken to Vaeril."

"I've contracted Vaeril," he said. "To reinforce the Black Keep. He's already begun reweaving the threads that hold this place together. We can't have your court growing bold, now can we?"

"Is that what you think this is?" she asked, fists clenching at her side. "Boldness?"

"I think it's desperation," he replied, eyes glittering. "I think your loyal little beasts are starting to believe in escape. And that makes them dangerous. I want you safe."

She stepped forward once, power in every measured movement. "The only danger here is your arrogance. You imply that we are desperate, but it's you who returned, tail tucked, because you felt this place slipping through your fingers."

His expression darkened. "I came back because you need reminding, Améliane. All of this can end. The curse. The masks you wear to keep your court calm. It ends when you take your place beside me."

"I was supposed to be at your side," she snapped. "And you were supposed to be at mine. I am the heir of Belmara—the only one of us born to rule. You stood beside me and swore loyalty in front of the gods, and the moment you hungered for more, you betrayed it all."

Edric's smile faltered. "A crown shared is still a crown, but you never intended to share."

"Because it was mine!" Her voice rang out, echoing in the golden stillness.

They stood like statues—mirror images warped by power and grief. She didn't notice the flicker of movement behind the throne until Edric's eyes darted, just for a moment, toward the alcove.

And then, she saw them.

Renaud and Mathieu.

Shadowed in the same place where Mathieu had once hidden before. Watching. Listening.

Edric followed her gaze and sighed. "Of course," he drawled, rolling his eyes. "Your audience never tires of drama. Well then. You, your cursed court, and your Wyrdbound can enjoy your forever home. Let's see how long before the walls close in."

The word hit the air like a dropped dagger.

Améliane didn't react, not outwardly. But she locked eyes with Renaud. Then with Mathieu. Made sure they heard it.

Edric turned away, already walking toward the door. But before he reached it, he paused.

Without turning, he said, almost gently, "Don't forget, Améliane… even forgotten queens can bleed."

And then he was gone.

The doors closed with a hiss of magic. The throne sat empty once more.

But the hall was anything but still.

CHAPTER 30

Mathieu

Mathieu closed the door to his chambers and leaned his back against it, exhaling slowly as the echo of Edric's voice finally faded from his ears.

Even forgotten queens can bleed.

The fire burned low. The room was dim and quiet—a sanctuary by design, but no longer a comfort. Not after what he'd just seen.

He shrugged off his shirt and tossed it across the nearest chair. Pacing came next—slow, deliberate. One circuit of the room. Then another.

He was trying to clear his head. It wasn't working.

Edric had known too much.

He hinted at looking into Mathieu's past. He knew that Mathieu had been "affectionate" with the queen. And worst of all—he knew the word *Wyrdbound*. A name that had been circulating with the gossip at Eldrenoire, but how had that piece of information made it to Miralys?

How the hell had Edric learned it?

It had to be someone in the court. Someone here. Feeding him information.

The three of them—he, Renaud, and Améliane—had gathered in the Solar just after Edric left. The conversation had been clipped, quiet, and laced with fury.

"There's no other way," Renaud had said. "He couldn't have guessed. Someone told him."

"And not just about Mathieu," Améliane had added. "He knew too much. The word *Wyrdbound* isn't even known outside this castle."

Mathieu stopped pacing, bracing one hand against the cool stone wall. One thing they had all agreed on was that *someone* was leaking secrets.

And now Edric had contracted Vaeril to reweave the curse.

He ground his teeth. They were running out of time.

Something shifted in the room.

Mathieu didn't hear it—not exactly. But he felt it. Like the air had thickened around his shoulders, like the shadows had drawn closer than they ought to.

He straightened slowly from the wall.

The fire cracked, low and strange. One of the flames bent sideways, as if pulled by a draft that shouldn't exist.

Then the shadows at the far corner of the room twitched.

Not moved. *Twitched*. Like something struggling to take shape.

Mathieu was across the room in two strides. His hand closed around the hilt of his sword, still propped by the hearth from earlier. His fingers tightened.

Another flicker. This time near the hearth.

A shape was trying to manifest—*tall, thin, impossible to focus on*. It pulsed between forms: smoke, shadow, man. Every time the fire flared, it changed.

Then it began to settle.

A pair of dark robes took shape first—billowing, indistinct, moving like they were underwater. Then long, silver-threaded locs, too perfect to be caught by gravity. Eyes like molten gold blinked open, shimmering from the hollows of a not-yet-finished face.

The shape flickered once. Twice. A low sound like pages turning in a forgotten book rose into the air.

And then he was there.

Alaric.

Or... the version of him that remained.

He looked older somehow, despite his agelessness—not in body, but in presence. Like something had drained from him.

His robes hung loose around his lean frame, untouched by the dust of the castle. The air around him shimmered faintly, as if he stood in two places at once.

Mathieu didn't lower his sword.

He only watched. Waited. Because nothing good ever came unannounced in Eldrenoire.

Alaric's form wavered once more and then stilled. The flickering stopped—but the air still crackled around him, like magic stretched too thin over broken glass.

"You are not the first stranger to enter Eldrenoire's gates," Alaric said, voice low and soft. "But you are the first in a long while to ask the right questions."

Mathieu didn't lower his sword, but he did step closer. "What's happening to the castle?"

Alaric's gaze drifted toward the fire. "It is remembering. And forgetting. Unraveling itself and weaving itself anew, over and over, like a spider repairing a web no longer anchored to the world."

Cryptic. Of course.

Mathieu's jaw clenched. "Something's wrong. With Eldrenoire. With the curse. You feel it."

Alaric's eyes returned to him, their golden shimmer dimmer than usual. "Yes."

"I've been trying to understand it," Mathieu said, more insistently now. "The layers. The mirror magic. The pathways that lead nowhere. I've kept notes. Patterns."

Alaric tilted his head. "And what is it you think you're looking for?"

"The flaw," Mathieu said. "Every curse has one. A way out."

Alaric smiled faintly. "Not a way out, warrior. A choice."

Mathieu narrowed his eyes. "A choice?"

"You seek escape," Alaric murmured, stepping slowly toward the fire, his robes whispering against the stone. "But the castle does not open its gates for strength alone. You must sit with yourself. All of yourself. Until you know what must be left behind."

Mathieu felt something cold trickle down his spine.

"Is that why I'm still here?" he asked. "Because I haven't let go of something?"

"You haven't chosen," Alaric said simply. "You're still holding on to everything. Believing you can leave whole."

Mathieu swallowed. "Améliane never told me any of this."

"She cannot," Alaric replied, turning to him fully now. "It is part of the design. Those who enter Eldrenoire must discover the truth on their own. The curse forbids her from speaking it."

Silence settled between them. Then, voice cracking, "What truth?"

Alaric's golden gaze seemed to pierce straight through him. "There is only one way out of Eldrenoire before the gates choose to open."

He stepped closer. "The Blood Oath."

The words fell like a stone into water. Mathieu didn't move.

Alaric continued, his voice quieter now. "A sacred binding. The castle allows it—demands it, when all other paths are closed. But it comes with a price."

"What kind of price?"

"You may leave. But in doing so, you must give up something of yourself," Alaric raised a hand and listed, one by one.

"A memory you cherish.

A soul-fragment you cannot reclaim.

Or a person you love."

Mathieu's breath caught in his throat. "I have to give up a memory, a piece of my soul," His voice dropped. "or someone I love?"

Alaric didn't answer. He didn't need to.

Mathieu took a step back, as if the air had thickened. "And once it's gone... it's gone."

Alaric nodded once. "Irrevocably."

"And if I...?"

"If you choose to forget her," Alaric said, voice almost gentle now, "you will not even remember the color of her eyes."

The fire crackled softly, the only sound between them.

Mathieu said nothing at first. He couldn't.

The Blood Oath. A way out. The very thing he'd been searching for. Right there, within reach.

But the price...

His mind flashed with images—his parents, smiling as they passed him a carved wooden sword when he was barely tall enough to hold it. His mother lighting temple incense on the festival of first harvests. His father teaching him how to bow before the gods and before a foe.

His brother, laughing over spiced wine by a campfire before the last battle. His comrades, dying in the mud of Valmont while he screamed their names. Tess—eyes wide as the crumbling buildings of Valmont fell and he saw her face for the last time.

Could he give up even one of those memories? Even the ones that gutted him?

He'd been shaped by them all. By love. By grief. By guilt.

They were the weight he carried. The measure of the man he'd become.

To give them up would be a dishonor to those he'd lost.

And his soul—

The gods may have felt distant now, but he'd been raised to believe his spirit was a thread in something larger. Something eternal. He couldn't cut that thread. Not even to escape.

Because everything—everything—had led him here.

To her.

Images of Améliane filled his head.

The way she looked when she laughed without meaning to.

The feel of her hand pressed to his chest, steadying both of them.

The haunted pride in her eyes when she stood tall, even while trapped in a place that bent time around her bones.

The castle was offering freedom.

But it would come at the cost of the only thing that made this cursed place bearable.

If he left and forgot her—

He wouldn't even remember the color of her eyes.

And he knew then, with a clarity that burned—she was the thing he could not give up.

He looked up, slowly, and met Alaric's gaze.

"No," he said.

Alaric's expression didn't change. But he dipped his head once in something that might have been reverence... or relief.

"Then you are Wyrdbound indeed."

And as the fire dimmed, Alaric began to fade—not suddenly, but gently, like smoke curling into shadow. One flicker. Another.

And then he was gone.

Chapter 31

Mathieu

The library had never felt so alive.

Tonight it breathed around him, slow and strange. The shelves leaned closer than he remembered. The sconces flickered, not with firelight, but with a kind of glimmering unease, like moonlight bouncing off broken glass.

Even the air felt charged.

Mathieu moved through the rows without fully choosing his path. He couldn't sleep after Alaric's visit. After tossing and turning for hours he finally gave up. Something in the castle tugged at him, subtle as a tide.

He found himself in a wing of the library that he didn't recognize. Narrower. Dustier. The ceiling curved into an arch, its beams draped in spiderwebs so fine they looked like silver thread.

There were mirrors here. Small ones. Shards, really—embedded in the stone between bookcases, their surfaces warped and clouded. Most reflected nothing. A few showed shapes that didn't belong to this world.

One mirror shimmered as he passed it. He turned back.

At first, it was just a warped outline of bookshelves and light. Then the surface rippled. And the image changed.

It didn't show him.

It showed the gate. Shrouded in mist. Lit by flickering magic. Humming, like it was waiting for someone to touch it.

Mathieu's breath caught.

He looked down at the shelf beside the mirror. A book sat there, pressed between two cracked tomes, its spine unmarked. The leather cover looked too new for this part of the library, as though it had been placed here recently. Or had never gathered dust at all.

When he touched it, the mirror stilled. The image vanished. Only his reflection looked back—uneven, blurred at the edges.

He took the book.

It was thinner than it looked. The pages were worn, the ink faded, but something about it felt *unfinished*—as though it were still being written. When he flipped through, some pages appeared blank at first, only for words to appear as his eyes lingered on them.

The castle was letting him read.

The first line that resolved clearly was centered on a page, written in firm, slanted script: *The Mirrorbind reflects, but it does not contain.*

He kept reading. Bits and pieces. Fragments of magical theory. Spellwork marginalia. The original design of the curse—not to imprison, but to *mirror*. To reflect the queen's power back on itself. To isolate threat by illusion, not confinement.

But someone—Vaeril—had twisted it. Hardened it. Made the mirror a prison instead of a veil.

Another passage formed before his eyes, this time inked in the margins: *If the reflection begins to believe itself more real than the world that cast it, the mirror must crack.*

Mathieu's pulse surged.

He turned the page and found more notes. Scribbled lines. Half-translated runes. At the bottom of one page, written sideways and barely visible in the candlelight, a phrase was underlined: *The Wyrdbound bends the curse not by power, but by presence. When the world beyond remembers, and the soul within surrenders, the gate will stir.*

He read it twice.

Then a third time.

When the world beyond remembers...

The Return. The rebellion. The Seers were whispering her name again.

...and the soul within surrenders...

Him. His decision to stay.

It wasn't strength that would open the gate. Not power. Not force. It was memory and choice.

A truth faced, not a battle won.

He turned another page, and a different book fell open beneath it. Somehow, two texts had merged—binding together, grafted by the castle itself. This one was a journal, badly misfiled, its entries a desperate tangle of thoughts from someone who had once tried—and failed—to escape Eldrenoire.

In it, scrawled between panicked notes and broken spells, was a final theory:

The Blood Oath is not the only door. But it is the only one known.

The gate responds to truth. It tests intent. Desire alone is not enough. The gate opens only for those who would walk away... and still choose to stay.

Mathieu sat back on his heels, the book still open in his hands.

His heartbeat roared in his ears.

This was it. This was the flaw he had been hunting, not in the castle—but in the curse itself.

The Mirrorbind wasn't invincible. It was built to reflect what was real—and if what was real refused to be mirrored, it cracked. If the person within held fast to truth, to memory, to love—the mirror couldn't hold them.

But if that truth was a lie...

If someone walked through for the wrong reason...

He didn't want to think about what would happen then.

He stared at the final line of the journal, smudged and nearly illegible.

One walked through with only fear in his heart. The gate did not free him. It fed.

Mathieu closed the book and clutched it tight against his chest.

He had to test it.

Not to leave. Not yet.

But to see if the gate would stir for him.

And if it did—

He needed to make sure no one else tried it blindly. Not before they understood what the mirror demanded.

Hours passed and the candle had burned to a stub.

Ash dusted the table. Parchment lay scattered like fallen leaves, some covered in fresh ink, others etched with runes and mirrored script he'd painstakingly copied from the pages that had only appeared when he stared long enough.

Mathieu sat hunched over the desk, jaw tight, eyes burning. He'd gone over the passages a dozen times—checked the spellwork, cross-referenced every note that hadn't already crumbled in his hands. If this was a lie the castle wanted him to believe, it was elaborate. Consistent. Ancient.

And it aligned too perfectly with what he'd seen. With what he'd *felt*.

The Mirrorbind didn't imprison—it mimicked. It responded. It was always meant to mirror reality, and reality was changing.

The Return was waking the world.

And he—Wyrdbound—was waking the curse.

When he'd chosen to stay...

When he'd resisted the Blood Oath...

The castle had shifted. Subtly. But undeniably.

He picked up the journal again. The misfiled one. The final line stared back at him like a challenge:

The gate opens only for those who would walk away... and still choose to stay.

He exhaled through his nose, dragging a hand through his hair.

There were no more questions.

Only the test.

He gathered the most crucial pages into a leather folio and tucked it beneath the folds of his jacket. His sword belt hung nearby, untouched since he arrived at the library, but he didn't reach for it.

This wasn't a fight. This was a step into something he couldn't undo.

And if he was right... He wouldn't walk through. He'd prove that he *could*—and use that information to determine how to get them *all* out.

Mathieu stood, every movement deliberate. He looked once more at the candle as it guttered and died.

The castle made no move to stop him. It only watched.

The sky had just begun to pale.

That strange hour before sunrise draped the castle grounds in a haze of mist, softening the edges of everything—stone, shadow, memory. The world felt quiet. Hollowed out.

Mathieu stepped through the great doors of Eldrenoire without ceremony, without armor, without sword. Just the leather folio tucked under one arm, and a mind sharpened to a point.

The cold met him like a whisper, settling in his bones.

He moved down the front stairs with careful steps, each one deliberate. He wasn't sneaking. He wasn't fleeing. But something about the air made him keep his head low, his presence small.

He had a fleeting thought—he should have written her a letter. Just in case. But the moment felt too sharp for ink, too uncertain for paper.

The outer courtyard opened ahead, and at the far end stood the gate.

Massive. Mirrored. Watching.

It shimmered faintly, the old magic alive beneath its surface. Not just holding—listening.

His boots were nearly silent against the stone path. The mist curled around him, dampening sound, blurring light. As he neared the threshold where the castle grounds ended and the world beyond might begin, he felt the pressure in the air change—*just slightly*. Like Eldrenoire knew.

He paused a few paces from the gate, heart steady but heavy. The folio in his arm held the truth: The Mirrorbind wasn't absolute. The Wyrdbound could bend it.

This wasn't escape. It was confirmation—of a door that would open for him, if he wished it. But he didn't. Not when staying meant choosing her.

CHAPTER 32

Améliane

S he hadn't slept.

Her eyes had closed. Her body had stilled. But her mind had kept racing, looping through every word Edric had said in that damnable hall, every look he'd cast at Mathieu, at her, at the place he still believed belonged to him.

When the first blush of light began to touch the edge of the sky, she gave up the pretense entirely.

Améliane slipped from the tangle of silk sheets, her bare feet silent on the stone floor. She reached for the velvet robe draped over the chair near her hearth, the one Élodie always insisted she wear, and crossed to the balcony doors.

The glass was cold under her fingertips as she opened them.

And the mist hit her like breath held too long.

It coiled across the courtyard below, thick and low and silver-grey, blurring the edges of statues, smothering the garden paths. The castle grounds were always strange at this hour—caught between the illusion of peace and the truth of its curse. But today, the air felt heavier.

As though something had shifted in the marrow of the place.

She stepped onto the balcony, tightening the robe around her waist with one hand.

And then she saw him.

Mathieu.

A dark shape cutting through the fog, moving with slow, purposeful strides across the courtyard.

Her breath hitched.

He wasn't wandering aimlessly. He had direction. Intent. He passed through the gate of the inner wall and disappeared into the mist beyond.

There was only one place he could be going.

Améliane's pulse surged.

She couldn't see the outer gate from her balcony. Not through this veil. But her heart already knew.

She turned sharply, reentered her chambers, and grabbed her slippers without bothering to change from her nightgown. Améliane flung open the door catching a surprised Thorne off-guard. He looked at her opening his mouth to say something, but she cut him off.

"Stay. Here. Thorne."

His eyes widened. He stepped aside without a word, letting her pass.

The robe clung to her ankles as she hurried, ghostlike, through the corridor and down the winding stairs, her footfalls muffled against ancient rugs.

She pushed open the side door leading to the courtyard. The mist swallowed her.

It curled around her legs and clung to her throat, damp and cold and full of dread.

The garden paths, so carefully tended by cursed hands, were slick with dew. Statues loomed in silhouette; their once-gentle features made harsh by the silver light. Even the air smelled wrong—wet stone and old sorrow.

And still she walked, faster now, arms folded tight around herself.

Because it couldn't be happening again.

Not him.

Her mind, cruel thing that it was, conjured the ghosts she couldn't keep buried.

Edric, kneeling at her coronation, all vows and smiles—before he took her kingdom with a kiss and a lie.

Bastian, brushing a hand against her cheek, swearing he'd stay—*before the Blood Oath took every memory of her from his eyes.*

And now—

Mathieu.

The man who had looked at her like she was real. Like she was more than a queen in a cage.

Walking into the mist.

Leaving.

Her heart pounded beneath the velvet folds of her robe. She couldn't see him now, not clearly, but she knew. Even if this moment was different—her heart refused to believe it.

The fog wrapped tighter around her limbs. The courtyard behind her faded into shadow. And she walked toward what she feared she already knew.

The mist thickened as she crossed the outer courtyard.

It clung to her robe and hair like memory, chilling her through the thin fabric. Each step sent small ripples through the fog at her feet, and her breath came hard and fast—faster than it should have.

By the time she reached the edge of the castle grounds, her slippers were soaked through. The soft hush of her footsteps vanished beneath the gate's looming shadow.

And there he was.

Standing just before the great mirrored gate, his back to her. Still. Tall. Unaware.

His shoulders were broad, set with the kind of tension she'd learned to recognize. Not fear. But something just before it. Anticipation.

His dark hair was damp, the ends curling slightly from the morning dew. Droplets slid along the nape of his neck, down the lines of muscle beneath his shirt—creased, as though he'd slept in it. Or hadn't slept at all.

Under one arm, he carried a thin book and a clutch of loose parchment, corners curled, and ink blurred. She watched him pull the folio free, unfolding the papers with care. He studied the text, eyes flicking between the page and the gate like he was working out an equation only he could see.

Every few seconds, he'd tilt his head—first to one side, then the other—watching the shimmer of magic like he was listening for a secret.

He hadn't noticed her.

And she couldn't move. Couldn't speak.

Her chest rose and fell like she'd run a great distance—though it wasn't the steps that had stolen her breath.

Her hands curled at her sides. His next move shattered what little air she had left.

Mathieu set the book and pages down gently at his feet. Then he stepped forward toward the gate. Slowly, deliberately, he reached out and pushed his hand into the mist.

It disappeared—vanished into the magical shimmer with barely a ripple. And he didn't pull it back. He just stood there, half-touched by another world.

And something inside her cracked. It was the sharp, silent shatter of something she had hoped was stronger.

It landed like a blow to the ribs—sudden, breath-stealing.

She gasped. The sound was soft, but in the quiet of the courtyard, it was everything.

Mathieu jerked—his arm retracting instantly. He turned sharply, eyes wide with surprise.

Their gazes met.

And for the first time, she didn't try to mask it. The heartbreak was there—right there—in her face, no matter how tightly she held her spine.

His lips parted. "Améliane—"

She lifted a hand. Not to stop him physically. But as if she could stop the sound.

"Don't," she said. Her voice was sharp, too sharp. It trembled on the first syllable, then hardened.

Mathieu took a step forward. His expression was twisted with something she couldn't name—confusion, maybe. Regret. Desperation. He tried again.

"Please, just let me expla—"

But she was already shaking her head.

She didn't want to hear it. Couldn't hear it. Not when every word risked might sound like Bastian's. Like Edric's.

She turned away, velvet robe swirling at her ankles.

And when she heard the rustle of him following—

She shifted. The change came like instinct. One breath, one heartbeat, and her human form melted into fur, muscle, speed.

A flash of pale limbs. And she was gone. Gone before he could say another word. Gone before she could listen. Gone, because listening would mean hope.

And hope had broken her before.

She was through the castle grounds and courtyard in the blink of a moment before she shot through the entryway like a silver bolt of lightning.

Élodie had just begun to swing open the great, ornate front doors, allowing a wide-eyed servant to stumble in with an enormous floral arrangement teetering in his arms. Moonblooms, dusk orchids, something thorned.

The wind from Améliane's passage made petals scatter like startled birds.

Élodie turned sharply, lips parting in stunned confusion as the queen—a ball of pale fur and fury—disappeared up the stairs without so much as a sound. Her dark eyes followed the movement with growing alarm.

But Améliane didn't look back.

By the time she reached the top of the stairs, her body shifted again. She transformed mid-stride, devastation and heartbreak crystallizing into flesh and bone. Her robe whipped behind her, her nightgown clinging damply to her legs. She barely registered the cold, the wetness, the way her breath caught in her throat.

Renaud was at the landing, coming from the east corridor, brow furrowed, boots scuffed like he'd been searching for someone.

"I was looking for you," he said as he approached, concern breaking through his usual stoicism. "Thorne said you ran out of your rooms like a woman on her way to put out a fire—"

He stopped short when he saw her face.

Tears brimming. Jaw tight. Fury barely leashed.

His voice softened. "What happened?"

She tried to speak and failed. Swallowed. Tried again.

"I saw him. At the gate."

Renaud's expression darkened instantly.

"I thought he—" she broke off. "He had his arm through it. He was ready to go. Just... walk away."

His eyes searched hers, jaw tightening. "And did he?"

"No," she admitted, barely above a whisper. "Only because he heard me there and turned around."

Renaud didn't reply right away. Together, they walked the rest of the way in silence. When they reached her chamber door, she turned to him.

Her eyes glistened. Her posture was still regal—but just barely.

A quiet understanding passed between them.

Renaud gave a short, respectful nod. Then he stepped aside, opened the door, and gently guided her in with a reassuring hand to the small of her back.

He shut the door behind her with the kind of care people reserve for things already cracked.

She let her back fall against it, the final click echoing in her chest.

Then, slowly, silently, she slid down until she was crumpled on the floor, knees to her chest.

Her breathing was uneven, shallow. Her hands trembled.

Tears were threatening to fall when she heard footsteps. Running.

They pounded down the corridor. Stopped directly outside her door.

"Améliane, please—" Mathieu's voice, raw and breathless through the wooden barrier. "Just listen. I wasn't leaving, I swear to the gods—"

Renaud, "You need to go."

"I'm not going anywhere!" Mathieu snapped. "Let me explain. She saw the wrong thing. I was testing the—"

"You think she hasn't *heard* that before?"

"I'm not Bastian," Mathieu growled. "And I'm *sure as hell* not Edric—"

"You're someone she trusted. And right now? You look too much like the men who made her regret it."

There was a pause.

Then a sudden scuffle. The *thud* of boots. A shove.

The doorknob rattled sharply.

"Améliane—!"

"Don't do this," Renaud warned, voice sharp.

Then—

"Gods, Mathieu—just calm down!" Thorne's voice, suddenly in the mix, followed by a grunt and a scrape of feet. "I'm your friend, remember?"

More struggling.

More heartache she could hear but not bear to witness.

And finally—finally—Renaud's voice, low but deadly quiet, "If you have any respect for her, turn around. And leave. Now."

Silence. Then footsteps.

Fading.

Gone.

Inside, Améliane pushed herself to her feet.

She made it to the chair beside the hearth before her legs gave way again. She curled into the cushions, folding in on herself.

Her heartbeat thundered in her ears.

Her eyes stung.

She was angry.

She was hurt.

But most of all—she was scared she'd been right to never believe in hope.

CHAPTER 33

Bastian

Pain arrived before memory.

A dull, bludgeoning ache behind his eyes. A burn in his ribs every time he inhaled. His mouth tasted of copper and dirt.

Bastian opened his good eye—just one. The other was swollen shut, hot and pulsing with pain. The world around him flickered dimly under a single, swaying lantern, its yellow glow casting long shadows across walls of black stone.

He was on the ground. Cold. Damp. His back pressed against uneven flagstone slick with something he didn't want to identify. His hands were bound behind him—tight, raw rope biting at his wrists. Ankles tied, too.

Not a dungeon. A holding cell.

Temporary. Tactical. Just clean enough to avoid infection. Just filthy enough to make a point.

He rolled his head to the side with a groan. The air smelled of iron and moss and old secrets.

And there, carved into the stone opposite him—deliberate, recent, unmistakable—was a symbol.

A flower. Not soft. Not ornamental. Its form was precise—three jagged petals flaring outward in perfect symmetry, like blades honed for war. A central stem ran sharp and straight, flanked by pointed leaves that mirrored its menace. It was encircled by a broken ring—split at the top and bottom, as if someone had tried to crown it, and failed. Or perhaps they never meant to finish it.

The Moonlit Bloom.

He let out a breath that might have been a laugh.

Of course. He'd heard of The Return and their bastardized Moonlit Tidelily symbol. And apparently, they had heard of him too.

He stared at the flower—graffitied on stone like a prophecy no one asked for—and whispered her name before he could stop himself.

A prayer. A curse. A confession.

Footsteps broke the silence. Slow. Intentional.

Someone was coming.

He tried to sit up and managed half a movement before pain arced through his ribs, knocking the breath from his lungs. Something was broken. Maybe more than one thing.

A door creaked. The hinges protested. A shift in the air told him someone had entered.

Whoever they were... they were here to take something from him.

And judging by the symbol on the wall, they might just try to take everything.

The footsteps stopped just short of his boots, and someone placed a shrouded object in front of him.

He didn't look up at first.

The shift in the air was enough. A presence. Not heavy, but honed.

Then she spoke.

"Name."

A woman's voice. Quiet. Unyielding. Sanded steel wrapped in velvet.

Bastian lifted his head.

She stood beneath the lantern light. Hooded, motionless, flanked by two guards. Her armor was mismatched—leather pauldrons strapped over hardened canvas, reinforced with steel in places that mattered. A fighter's gear. But the clasp at her shoulder bore a sigil—subtle, etched in silver—the same Moonlit Bloom carved into the wall behind him.

She was not a foot soldier. She was something else entirely.

At her nod, one of the guards pulled the shroud back exposing a small mirror.

For a breath, nothing happened.

Just Bastian's reflection—blurred, bloodied, unrecognizable even to himself.

Then the mirror pulsed.

Not with light—but with memory.

The surface shimmered, the way sunlight dances through smoke, and Bastian's reflection flickered—vanished—replaced by images he couldn't stop.

A woman. A crown. Storm light in her eyes.

Améliane.

She wasn't speaking. She didn't have to. The mirror didn't show sound, only feeling.

Bastian inhaled sharply as the images hit him—moments pulled raw from the depths of his soul.

Her laugh, when it was rare and real.

Her hand, slipping from his on the day he left.

The look on her face just before she turned away.

The shimmer of the gate as it swallowed him whole.

The way her name had tasted like ash the moment it was gone from his memory.

The mirror flashed again—violently this time.

Bastian let out a strangled noise, somewhere between a gasp and a curse, jerking away instinctively—but the bindings held him firm.

The woman did not flinch. She only watched. Eyes narrowed. Voice unreadable.

"So," she murmured, lowering the shard a fraction. "You did know her."

Bastian's head fell forward. His throat worked around a bitter laugh.

The mirror's glow faded; its surface dull once more—but the damage was done.

Now she knew exactly what he was worth.

Bastian squinted up. The woman's hair was dark, pulled into a tight, high bun. She had a warrior's face—cut from certainty—and eyes the color of deep water, impossible to look away from and twice as dangerous.

She wore a black cloth mask that covered the lower half of her face. Not to hide—no, this was no coward's veil. It was a symbol. A signal.

She didn't blink.

When she finally spoke again, it was softer.

"You've been asking about the cursed Queen."

A statement. Not a question.

"I ask a lot of things," he rasped.

She crouched in front of him. Not like a threat. Like an executioner waiting for permission.

"Then you'll have been given a lot of answers."

Her preternatural stillness was terrifying. She let the silence stretch—taut as a garrote.

Her gaze fixed on Bastian like he was a map she was learning to read. Every breath he took, every twitch of pain. She catalogued it.

When she finally spoke, it wasn't a question.

"Améliane Morvenne. The Forgotten Queen."

He didn't respond.

She tilted her head slightly. "Is she alive?"

Bastian's jaw tightened.

He was too weak to posture, too wrecked to bluff—but some stubborn fragment of pride flickered behind his swollen eye. He tried to deflect.

"You think I'd be sitting here like this if she weren't?"

A sharp nod.

One of the soldiers moved in.

A punch—clean, cruel—landed square against Bastian's ribs. He stifled a cry, folding forward.

The woman didn't blink.

"What does the castle look like?" she asked.

He laughed—choked on it. "Like a palace dreamt up by a god with a grudge."

"Specifics."

"Gold halls. Shifting doors. Gardens that bloom in unnatural colors. Rooms that remember you. And mirrors—so many damn mirrors."

"And where is it?"

"I don't know," he ground out.

Another strike. His lip split further.

"How did you find it?"

"I didn't. It found me."

She took a step closer.

"Then why did it let you go?"

Silence.

Bastian's breath came ragged now, every inhale like dragging knives through his lungs. He knew what she was doing—keep him talking, keep him hurting, keep him open. And she was good at it. Better than she had any right to be.

Still, he said nothing.

She gave the smallest nod.

The soldiers descended again—this time two at once. One yanked his head back by the hair. The other drove a fist into his gut, then his shoulder, then again.

Pain exploded behind his eyes.

When they finally stepped back, he slumped against the wall, coughing blood.

And then, hoarse and cracked and furious, he spat the words that changed everything.

"She was alive when I left."

A breath. A beat.

"And now that I remember," he growled, "I've been trying to find my way back."

The soldiers stilled. Even the air in the room seemed to pause.

The woman's eyes sharpened—not with cruelty, but with calculation. With hope wrapped in suspicion.

She stepped forward again. The lantern light caught the silver filigree of her pauldron, the glint of worn steel at her hip. She didn't lower herself this time. She looked down at him like she was seeing a door that had been sealed for years—and just cracked open.

"You're trying to find her," she said quietly. "You're trying to find your way back."

Bastian nodded. The blood on his lips said enough. So did the haunted look in his eyes. And the woman staring down at him... she understood the weight of both.

The woman—still nameless—stood completely still.

Then, softly, like she was speaking to a ghost rather than a man broken on a cell floor, she asked, "Why do you remember her?"

Bastian coughed once. His throat was raw. "I could ask you the same thing."

A flicker passed through her eyes. Not amusement. Not quite challenge. Curiosity, maybe. But sharper. Dangerous.

She crouched again—not like before. This time, she lowered herself to his level, resting her elbows on her knees. Eye to eye.

Turquoise eyes met bloodshot green.

"Answer the question."

He let out a slow breath, gathering what strength he had left.

"Because I'm not like the others, I guess," he rasped. "I'm half Seer. My mother saw things before they happened. Dreamed of wars before they broke. She said I'd inherit it. I didn't believe her."

He chuckled, bitterly. Then winced.

"I forgot her. The Queen. Eldrenoire. Everything. The castle took it from me when I chose to leave. I thought I was free." He paused. "But months ago, the dreams started again. Her eyes. Her voice. A flower I couldn't name blooming under a moon that wasn't real."

He swallowed hard, voice cracking.

"And then, one morning... I remembered everything. All of it. Like a dam broke. The jungle. The castle. Her. What I gave up."

He met her gaze evenly, despite the pain.

"I've been searching ever since. I didn't care what I'd have to do or who I'd have to fight. I just—" he cut himself off, jaw clenching. "I just need to find her."

The woman said nothing. She studied him for a long moment, the weight of her silence heavier than any threat.

Then, finally, she nodded.

"You're not our enemy," she said, her voice low but firm. "And you might be useful."

She stood in one smooth movement, sharp as a blade sliding from its sheath.

"I'm Moon's Thorn," she said. "But everyone just calls me Moon."

Bastian blinked. "You're the leader."

A small tilt of her head.

He exhaled a shaky breath. "Why tell me your name? If you're part of a rebellion... shouldn't you be harder to trace?"

The corner of her mouth twitched beneath the mask. Not quite a smile. Something colder.

"Because," she said, turning back to him, "either you'll be useful—and it won't matter. Or you won't be. And we'll dispose of you."

She took a step closer, her steel eyes gleaming, "And it still won't matter."

Then she turned to her soldiers.

"Unbind him."

They hesitated—but only for a second. Rough fingers cut the ropes at his ankles and wrists. Pins and needles exploded across his limbs as blood returned.

He slumped forward, catching himself just in time.

Moon didn't wait.

"Get him cleaned up," she ordered. "I want him coherent. If what he says is true... it's time we find the Queen."

She glanced back once, "And let her know that we haven't forgotten her."

CHAPTER 34

Mathieu

For two days, she'd acted like he didn't exist.

Not with cruelty. That would've been easier. Améliane moved through the castle with her usual composure—sharp-eyed, poised, authoritative—but not once had she looked at him.

Not truly.

Not when he'd tried to intercept her near the Mirror Hall. Not when he'd waited outside the council chambers for hours just in case she passed through. Not when he stood outside the Solar, rehearsing every version of an apology he could think of until his throat went dry.

She hadn't locked herself away. No. She'd gone about her royal business with meticulous calm, speaking to the court, walking the halls, tending to Eldrenoire's strange pulse like she had for the last eight years.

As if he had already left.

And worse—she flinched when he tried to speak to her. Not visibly. Just a shift. A tightening around her mouth. A dart of the eyes. A flicker of retreat buried behind the stiff posture bred into royal blood.

But he saw it every time. And it was undoing him.

He'd tried everything short of banging on her door like a madman. Though gods knew he'd considered it. He even got Renaud to listen. Truly listen. It had taken cornering the man after sparring, chest heaving, soaked in sweat and fury.

"She thought I was leaving. I *wasn't*. I wasn't, Renaud."

He'd told him about the Blood Oath he refused to take, about what he had discovered in the library, and about the hypothesis he was testing.

Mathieu had expected stone in response. What he got was a pause. A quiet pause. A flicker of something that might have been pity.

Renaud had looked at him—really looked at him—and said nothing.

That silence said more than any words.

Mathieu had been pacing ever since. Dogged by Élodie's cool stares and Laurent's relentless needling.

"She ran past Élodie like her hair was on fire," Laurent muttered at breakfast the day before, slumped in a chair like a bird who'd had his wings clipped. "What exactly did you do? She's been in a mood for *days*."

Mathieu had said nothing. Just tightened his grip on the table until the wood groaned.

By now, even Thorne had stopped joking.

And still—nothing from her.

The castle watched. The corridors shifted. The air around Eldrenoire was more wrong than ever—like it was bracing for something. The mirrors in every room had begun humming at odd hours. The halls took longer to traverse. More doors locked behind them than usual.

And Améliane? She moved through it all like it was weather. Inevitable. Untouchable.

He watched her from across the grand hall that morning, issuing orders with the same precision he'd once admired. She didn't even glance his way.

And that was it. That was the moment he knew. He was done waiting for a door that wouldn't open.

If she wouldn't listen while standing—he'd speak kneeling.

If she wouldn't see him in the daylight—he'd bring truth to her in the dark.

And if her chambers were her sanctuary... well.

Then let him scale the walls—if only to prove that he hadn't turned his back. Not on her. Not ever.

Mathieu waited until Eldrenoire was still.

It was after dinner, after the last candle had been snuffed in the halls, and after he'd heard the soft hum of Élodie's laughter trailing down the corridor as she said goodnight to Thorne. The hour where silence pressed in close, and the Black Keep held its breath.

He didn't want an audience. Didn't need one.

But before he tried to scale her walls—both literally and figuratively—he decided to try one more time.

Mathieu walked the upper hallways with slow, careful steps. The sconces flickered in their brackets, throwing soft golden halos onto the stone walls, like the castle itself was watching him pass.

His palm slid along the railing as he approached the wing that held the queen's chambers. Familiar by now, but still dangerous. Renaud's quarters were nearby and if he saw Mathieu there...

Well. He wasn't here to ask permission.

He paused at her door. A place he'd once been invited. Trusted.

Now it was closed to him, like a fortress within the fortress.

Thorne was already there.

The red-haired guard leaned against the wall next to the door, arms folded, expression unreadable. He didn't reach for a weapon. Didn't stand at attention. He simply... looked at Mathieu.

"She doesn't want to see you," he sighed. "Still."

Mathieu nodded once. He hadn't really expected otherwise.

"I just—" he exhaled, rubbed the back of his neck, "I just wanted to talk to her. Figured I would try one more time."

Thorne's gaze softened, just a fraction. The ever-present sarcasm wasn't there tonight. Only something quieter. Sadder.

Thorne studied him for a long moment, then straightened.

"She flinches when your name is said aloud," he said. "Even when no one's looking. But she still asks what time the sun rose today. Still tracks the Mirror Hall shifts. She's keeping herself busy, so she doesn't think about you."

Mathieu's eyebrows lifted. "So, you're saying she's still thinking about me?"

A ghost of a smile graced Thorne's lips as he gave a slow nod.

Then he stepped in front of the door and crossed his arms again, "But you're not going to get through this door tonight."

Mathieu held his gaze. "Didn't plan to."

And with that, he turned on his heel and walked away.

The castle grounds were empty.

Not silent—Eldrenoire was never truly silent—but hushed in a way that made every step feel sacrilegious. The kind of quiet that pressed against the ribs and made a man wonder what the stones themselves might remember.

Mathieu slipped through the side door and out into the open air, breath curling before him in the cool night. The garden had gone still, its flowers bowed as if listening. Even the wind had stilled—until a single droplet of rain touched his cheek.

He looked up.

Another drop fell. Then another.

It was not a downpour. Just a soft, slow drizzle, barely enough to dampen his shoulders. But it was *rain*.

The first he'd seen since setting foot in this cursed place.

He stood there for a long moment, letting it soak in. Cool against his skin. Sharp with promise.

Eldrenoire had not allowed a rainstorm in the year and a half since he had arrived. But tonight, the spell had cracked. The rain was real. The curse was changing.

He exhaled, slow and steady, and walked across the courtyard. The stones beneath his boots slicked with rain, shining faintly in the moonlight. The shadows of statues loomed taller in the storm light, and far above him—her balcony.

The queen's chambers jutted out from the western tower, stone railing wrapped in ivy that shimmered slick with water. The glow of her hearth's fire shone from behind the heavy curtains. No silhouette passed in the glass.

But he knew she was in there. Awake. Pretending not to care.

He tilted his head back, rain streaking his face now, and stared up at the balcony like it was a battlement he meant to take.

No ladder. No stairs. The main entrance was guarded—metaphorically, if not literally. But there were stones. Columns. Cracks.

He had been a king. A warrior. Even an outlaw. But tonight, apparently, he was a gods-damned rock climber.

He shrugged out of his coat allowing it to fall to the ground and let the rain kiss the scars on his arms. The castle watched, but it did not stop him.

Above him, the sky darkened. Lightning flashed in the distance—just once.

He looked up at her window again. Then he placed one hand on the lowest stone of the tower wall and began to climb.

The climb was harder than he'd let himself imagine.

The rain picked up halfway through—still not a storm, but enough to turn the ivy-slicked stones into treacherous footholds. He climbed slowly, deliberately, testing each grip twice before trusting it. His palms burned. His arms ached. More than once, his boot slipped on wet stone, and he dangled breathless above the courtyard, heart hammering like a war drum.

But still—he climbed.

He reached a narrow ledge beneath the balcony and paused, bracing himself against the side of the tower. The rain had soaked him through. His shirt clung to him like a second skin, droplets falling from his lashes. Below, the garden shimmered in the dark, cast in silvery hues by moonlight and magic.

Above him, just out of reach, her balcony.

He exhaled once.

Then launched upward.

Fingers found stone. Legs swung. For one terrifying breath, he slipped—but caught the iron railing and pulled himself over in a rough, graceless heave.

He landed hard on the balcony, chest heaving, hands scraped raw, knees soaked through. The storm had begun in earnest now—rain falling in a steady rhythm, drumming on the railing, on the stone, on the breath between heartbeats.

Her balcony door was closed, its lock intact.

His hand closed around the pick he'd slipped into his pocket hours ago—found collecting dust in a drawer, now called into purpose like it had been waiting.

The lock gave with a soft click. The latch unhooked. And the door creaked open.

Mathieu stepped inside, breath still ragged, rain dripping from his shoulders, his hair, the hem of his soaked trousers. He pushed the curtain aside and froze.

Améliane sat in a chair beside the fire, bare feet tucked beneath her, clad in midnight blue lace. The flames cast soft gold across her skin, catching in the dark waves of her unbound hair. Her nightgown clung to her thighs, the thin straps resting lightly on her shoulders. She looked nothing like the queen who'd stormed past him for two days.

She looked like something he'd dreamed. And feared.

Her gaze was fixed on the flames—lost in some thought too heavy to name.

Then the floor creaked beneath his boots.

She gasped, rising to her feet in one smooth, startled motion. Her eyes snapped to him—wild, afraid.

She didn't recognize him at first.

Because what stood in her doorway wasn't a soldier or even a man she knew. It was a shadow-drenched figure, dripping with rain and desperation, carved from storms and silence.

Améliane's mouth parted, breath hitching in her throat. For one heartbeat—just one—she looked ready to scream, a sound already rising in her chest.

Then he spoke.

"Améliane."

Just her name. Soft and ragged. A plea.

She froze.

Her eyes widened, searching his face—rain-slicked, shadowed, and half-unrecognizable, but his voice... she knew that voice.

Her lips trembled. "Mathieu?"

He nodded once, dripping onto her floors like some half-drowned myth.

She took a step back. "What are you doing—how did you—?"

"I needed you to listen." His voice cracked, thick with cold and something else. "And you weren't going to let me in through the damn door."

"You climbed the castle wall?" she breathed.

"I climbed the castle wall," he agreed with the weary exasperation of a man who'd done exactly that and had no regrets.

Her gaze swept over him—his soaked shirt, the bloodied scrape on his hand, the wet hair clinging to his face. Then her expression changed. Hardened.

"No," she spat, voice low and sharp. "No. You don't get to come in here, looking like that, saying my name like it means something."

"Améliane, I wasn't leaving."

"I saw you!" she snapped. "I saw you reach through the gate; I saw the papers at your feet—I know what I saw."

"You saw a moment in time. Not the truth."

"Mathieu, you were halfway through the gate!"

He stepped forward. She didn't move. But her arms wrapped tighter around herself like a shield.

"I was testing it," he said. "Not escaping. I needed to know if it would open."

Her laugh was bitter and hollow. "How romantic. You *almost* walked into another world, but don't worry—I was research."

"No," he growled, suddenly, finally losing some of the restraint he'd been holding onto for days. "You were the reason I didn't go through."

She flinched. Just barely.

"I didn't reach through it to run," he said. "I needed to know *if* I could. Because *if* I could, then I could find a way to get you and everyone else out, too."

She stared at him. Rainwater continued to trickle down his arms, over his collarbone, onto her polished stone floor.

"I've heard this story before," she whispered. "They all say it. '*I'm here for you.*' And then they leave."

"I didn't," he breathed. "Please *trust me.*" His voice broke. "I would never walk away from you."

Her eyes filled—not with tears, but with something more dangerous. Something brittle.

He took another tentative step towards her. "You flinched. Every time I tried to talk to you, you flinched. That was worse than the door slamming in my face."

She didn't deny it.

He scrubbed a hand through his wet hair, pacing a short, frustrated line in front of her hearth before spinning back. "Améliane, I didn't mean to hurt you. I didn't even know I *could.*"

Her voice rose. "Then maybe you should've tried to understand what it felt like. To see you standing at the one place no one ever comes back from. No warning. You didn't even leave a note."

"I *do* understand." He cringed as the words left his mouth.

She raised her chin. "Do you?"

He stared at her. The fire cracked behind her, casting gold streaks through her chestnut hair, and the storm battered the windows, and she was standing there barefoot, angry, beautiful, and wounded.

"Alaric offered me the Blood Oath."

She froze in stunned silence.

"I could have taken it," he said, louder now. "I could've walked through the gate and forgotten everything—*you* included. He told me that. Said I wouldn't even remember the color of your eyes."

She didn't move.

"I didn't take it," he said, voice suddenly hoarse. "Because I *did* remember. And I couldn't give that up."

Her arms dropped to her sides.

"He told me what it cost. A person you love. A piece of your soul. A memory you cherish. And I looked him in the eye and said no."

Her breath shuddered.

"I stayed," he whispered, voice breaking. "For *you*."

Something in her unraveled. Not all at once. Just a thread. Just enough.

For a moment, neither of them breathed.

The storm murmured against the balcony behind him, tapping rain like secrets against the glass. The fire snapped softly beside her, casting flickering amber across her night-gown, her skin, the line of her collarbone where a scar curved like a forgotten constellation.

And then—

Something shifted.

Not in the room. In her.

Mathieu saw it—just a flicker at first. A flash of doubt breaking. Of understanding blooming in her silver-grey eyes.

Because no one was supposed to know about the Blood Oath.

No one except those the castle had deemed ready.

And if he knew—

It meant everything he'd said was true.

Améliane took one step forward. Then another.

Her head tilted slightly, eyes narrowed as if she were trying to see through him, not just look at him.

Like she was trying to figure out how someone could be so infuriating... and so devastatingly real.

He didn't move. Didn't breathe. Didn't dare interrupt whatever was unfolding in her expression.

And then she was in front of him.

Close enough that he could see every detail he'd been aching to hold again—

The silver sheen of her eyes, always unreadable.

The way her hair had fallen in loose, sleep-tousled waves down her back.

The elegant lines of her face—not untouched by time, but deepened by it.

The soft creases at the corners of her eyes, earned not from worry, but from years of watching, knowing, surviving.

They weren't flaws. They were proof.

Proof that she had *lived*. That she had fought for her place in the world, and lost it, and still stood like a queen.

And gods—she was beautiful. Not in the way stories tried to flatten women into youthful perfection. No.

She was beautiful like a storm rolling in from the sea.

Like iron bent by fire.

Like something you did not survive without scars.

And then—

Her hand rose.

Slow. Hesitant.

She reached out... and touched his face.

Fingertips ghosted along the curve of his jaw, tracing the stubble, the soaked hair clinging to his temple. She touched the scar at his cheekbone, brushed a thumb across his brow.

And all at once, the wall in her eyes collapsed.

He saw it—*felt* it—like something ancient finally giving way.

The hand she'd raised to defend herself opened instead. Her lips parted—not in fury, but in wonder.

And he exhaled, shaky and reverent.

"Liane," he whispered.

It broke something soft and sacred between them.

Because he had never called her that. Not until now.

Améliane breathed his name. Not in anger this time. Not anymore. There was something else now. Something rawer. Unshielded.

He brought his hand up slowly, resting it over hers, holding it there against his cheek. His other hand lifted—tentative—and brushed a strand of hair from her face, tucking it behind her ear with reverence.

"You don't have to forgive me," he said quietly. "I should have told you what I was going to do. But I need you to know. I stayed. I'm staying."

Her gaze didn't leave his. "Why?"

"Because," he said, voice low and hoarse, "you're the only thing in my entire cursed existence that ever felt real."

The air cracked between them—just a breath, just a beat.

And then she moved.

Her lips crashed into his like a spark meeting dry timber—sudden, unstoppable, blazing. She felt perfect, her body molded against his like she had been made for him.

Mathieu answered her with every ounce of restraint he'd held back for weeks, months, lifetimes. His hands slid into her hair, threading through the waves, tipping her head back as her mouth opened and his tongue slipped in to caress hers.

She was fire and fury and velvet, and he was drowning in her.

Her hands tugged at his soaked shirt, pulling it loose from his belt. He stripped it off with a ragged gasp, casting it aside. Her hands roamed across his chest, silken fingertips dragging over old scars and he hardened instantly against her.

Améliane groaned into his mouth as he dipped to claim it again snapping whatever remaining control he had. He scooped her up in one smooth movement and she wrapped her legs around his back hooking him in closer.

Then they were stumbling backward, tangled in each other, mouths never parting as they found the bed in a haze of breath and need. He sank down with her, bracing himself over her as the firelight painted them both in gold and shadow. Mathieu ran his lips down the column of her neck.

She made a sound—half laugh, half gasp—and he felt it against his lips as he kissed the curve of her throat. Her pulse thundered there.

"Tell me to stop," he whispered, forehead pressed to hers, voice trembling with restraint.

"No," she breathed. "Don't you dare."

He kissed her like a prayer he would never speak aloud.

Then Mathieu's hands were at her thighs sliding under the silk hem before pulling it over her head and tossing it to the side. He pulled away to survey her, her body naked from the waist up. Hazel eyes darkened as he dropped his head to her breast and sucked gently before flicking against one pink nipple with his tongue.

She arched beneath him, fingers plunging into his hair and pulling him closer, deeper, needing more. His mouth found her other breast as she grabbed at his waistband. Mathieu shifted enough to let her unclasp the leather belt and his pants fell to the floor.

His mouth crashed back into hers, her bare skin warm against him and his hands traveled down the sides of her body. Thumbs hooking on strings of silk, he pushed the last scrap of material between them slowly down her legs.

Every inch of skin they had laid bare was met with reverence—his hands on her waist, her thighs, the curve of her spine; her nails at his shoulders, her mouth tracing the scar across his ribs.

Mathieu pulled back once more and Améliane let out a short growl of protest that was instantly silenced as he gripped her thighs and pulled her to the edge of the bed. Hooking her legs over his shoulders, he knelt before her.

The first swipe of Mathieu's tongue made her jolt, but her subsequent moan unraveled him completely. One broad forearm pinned her hips to the bed as he devoured her in long strokes.

Her legs were trembling as he licked and kissed his way to the apex of her thighs, but when his tongue slid inside her she bucked once gripping the edge of the bed. Her soft breaths came more quickly as he slid his fingers where his tongue had been, still sucking. When his teeth scraped against her most sensitive bundle of nerves, she bowed off the bed, her climax shattering her completely until she lay half sobbing with pleasure.

Mathieu stood and looked Améliane over giving her a slow, satisfied smile. She reached up, placing hands on either side of his face as her mouth found his, tongues and teeth clashing. Mathieu followed her down resting his forearms on either side of her head as she locked her legs around his back. He nudged at her entrance and paused, giving her one last chance to disengage before he lost himself to her completely.

Those grey eyes met his and he could see the storm building behind them as her fingertips traced down the center of his body before closing slowly around his length.

A puff of breath escaped his lips at her touch, and his gaze locked onto her face as he slid in. Her eyes fluttered close.

Mathieu could hardly think beyond where their bodies were joined, and he stilled inside her giving her time to adjust. When she opened her eyes again, he was staring down at her in wonder.

They came together slowly at first, like they had all the time in the world. Each movement was a promise, each gasp a confession.

"You're beautiful," he said, voice ragged as he pulled out slightly and then thrust back in tortuously slow.

"So are you," she whispered, fingers tracing his bottom lip.

Their rhythm built, not frantic but intense, like a tide swelling to break. With each pounding stroke words gave way to gasps, to moans, to the sharp-edged sound of two people coming undone for each other.

She moved her hips in rhythm with his and he kissed her over and over. She came apart again beneath him—silent, shaking, her whole body curling into him like he was gravity itself. He buried his face in her neck as he pounded into her, hard and fast, dragging out her pleasure until he followed moments later, muffling her name against her skin while he shattered.

They lay in a tangle of limbs and breath and quiet afterglow.

Rain pattered gently against the balcony doors.

Outside, the storm had softened.

Inside, the silence between them was not empty—it was full of everything they had not yet said.

And maybe... just maybe... there was time to say it all.

CHAPTER 35

Améliane

R ain whispered gently against the windowpanes of Eldrenoire, a hushed lullaby she'd never heard before tonight. Eight long, dry years had passed without a single drop, and now the heavens seemed determined to cleanse every stone of the castle.

The gentle rhythm of raindrops blended seamlessly with the quiet crackle of the fire in her hearth, bathing her chambers in a golden glow that danced warmly across their entwined forms.

Améliane allowed herself the rare luxury of complete stillness, her head resting against Mathieu's chest. She listened carefully to the steady cadence of his heartbeat—strong and unwavering, a comforting sound she never expected would soothe her.

One of his hands rested at the small of her back, fingers tracing absent patterns over her skin, igniting a trail of gentle warmth that lingered beneath his touch.

In the glow of the hearth, Mathieu's features appeared softened yet undeniably powerful, shadows and light playing across his scarred skin like ancient poetry.

Améliane's eyes traced each line and mark along his body that mapped the story of his life—the harsh curve of an old scar along his shoulder, the faint silvery threads at his temples that spoke of battles won and lost.

He was not beautiful in the polished, courtly way she'd once found appealing in her youth. No, Mathieu's beauty was raw and real, rugged edges tempered by strength and vulnerability.

His dark hair fell across his brow, tousled from her fingers, and his hazel eyes were half-closed, content yet thoughtful, shifting colors in the firelight—greens flecked with warm gold, browns rich and deep. There was something haunting in the way he stared into the flames, as though seeing beyond the room into memories she could only guess at.

A small crease formed between her brows as she realized she'd never felt this exposed, this utterly seen by another person. Eldrenoire had offered him the Blood Oath, and he'd declined it. Hearing those words was as though he'd unlocked a door she'd sealed shut long ago, and the openness left her feeling both lighter and terrifyingly vulnerable.

"You're thinking loudly again, Your Highness," Mathieu murmured softly, his voice carrying gentle amusement.

His gaze shifted from the flames to her, eyes brightening slightly, attentive and deeply tender.

Améliane lifted her chin just enough to meet his eyes, her lips curving faintly despite herself. "And how exactly does one think loudly, Mathieu?"

He chuckled softly, the sound reverberating gently beneath her ear, sending pleasant warmth through her chest. "When it's you, it's practically deafening. Your silence is full of stories."

She exhaled slowly, a quiet laugh mingling with the gentle sound of the rain. "Perhaps I should work harder at being mysterious."

His fingers paused their gentle tracing, sliding upward to tilt her chin slightly higher, ensuring she looked fully into his gaze. "You are mysterious enough already," he assured her, voice low and filled with sincerity. "But there's a story behind those eyes, and I'd listen if you chose to tell it."

Améliane hesitated, heart tightening in her chest. There was one story she hadn't yet fully shared, a wound she'd long pretended had healed—one that was torn open again when she watched Mathieu stand before the gate to Eldrenoire.

Mathieu had shared so much of himself. He had never turned from her truth, never faltered in his trust. So, she decided it was time to trust him in return.

Drawing a breath to steady the sudden flutter in her chest, she settled herself more comfortably against him, eyes drifting toward the flames. "Have I ever told you about Bastian? The whole story?"

Mathieu's fingers tightened slightly against her waist, not possessively, but as though grounding himself for whatever she was about to say. His voice remained gentle, encouraging. "No, but I'm listening."

Améliane closed her eyes briefly, finding courage in his closeness, in the reassuring warmth of his skin against hers. And slowly, carefully, she began.

"Bastian arrived much like you did—unexpectedly. He was a wanderer, drawn by legends and whispered tales of the Cursed Queen of Eldrenoire. At first, I was wary of him, cautious. But he was charming, passionate, and disarming in ways I hadn't anticipated. He promised me many things—fidelity, hope, freedom—even love."

She paused, swallowing against the tightening in her throat, the memory bitter yet achingly clear.

"For nearly a year, he stayed. We grew close, or at least I believed we did. He told me he loved me, repeatedly, fervently. I never truly believed it—not completely—but I wanted to. I allowed myself to hope, to imagine there might finally be someone strong enough to simply stand beside me."

Her voice trembled slightly, and she hated the weakness it revealed. Mathieu's hand moved soothingly against her back, a silent encouragement to continue.

"When the Blood Oath was offered to him, Bastian was given the same options—forget someone he loved, lose part of himself, or sacrifice something he cherished. He chose to forget me." Her voice dropped to a whisper. "And then, he was gone."

She felt Mathieu's breathing deepen beneath her, absorbing her words with silent strength.

She looked up again, meeting his gaze. "I never loved him, not truly. But his leaving confirmed every fear I'd held—that trust is foolish, that promises are meaningless. And when I saw you standing at the gate, I was certain you would run, just as he had."

Mathieu's eyes softened, no judgment in them, only quiet understanding and compassion. "I'm sorry he did that to you."

She smiled faintly, her heart aching but strangely lighter for the sharing. "It's not pity I want. Just... honesty."

"Then honesty you shall have," Mathieu vowed softly, holding her gaze firmly. "Always."

Mathieu drew a deep, steadying breath, visibly gathering courage. His eyes darkened with intensity, and he gently shifted, corded muscles bunching in his arms as he pushed himself upright. She sat up as well, sensing the shift in his demeanor, watching the shadows dance across the angle of his jaw as he stared deeply into the fire.

"My name isn't Mathieu Duran," he finally said, his voice low and edged with raw emotion. "It's Mathieu Corvalis."

Améliane's breath caught sharply, but she remained silent, her gaze fixed unwaveringly on him. The name echoed in her mind, pulling threads of memory from deep within her. She knew that name—Corvalis. Royal blood of Valmont. But last she had heard, Valmont's king, Mathieu's father, had only recently passed when she'd been exiled. Her pulse quickened as she waited, allowing him the silence he needed to find the words, silently urging him to share the truth he had so carefully hidden.

Mathieu exhaled slowly, eyes never leaving the flickering flames as he began again, his voice roughened by buried pain. "I told you part of the story before," he said softly, shadows of memories clouding his expression. "But I didn't tell you everything. Not the way I should have."

He paused, gathering his thoughts carefully, the silence thickening between them. "My father passed peacefully, after a long life spent leading Valmont through times of peace and prosperity. My mother followed soon after, her heart unable to bear the weight of loss. My older brother—Henri—he was the king Valmont deserved, a natural leader. He could weave speeches that stirred hearts and minds, and he was deeply respected."

Mathieu's voice grew tighter, edged with old grief. "I was the second son, the spare, content to lead armies instead of councils. I thrived in the clarity of battlefields and commands, far from the subtleties of politics. But war cares little for our preferences."

His eyes hardened, staring unseeing into the fire as if the flames could burn away the painful memories. "Rothgar struck without warning, brutal and precise. We weren't ready. Henri died in the first assault, leaving me to pick up a crown I had never wanted. Suddenly, I was the last Corvalis, thrust into leadership while my people looked to me for salvation."

He clenched his fists tightly, jaw muscles working beneath his skin. "I tried. Gods, I tried. But Rothgar was relentless, smarter, crueler. They baited us, burned our supplies, and tore down our walls with strange, terrible machines. My soldiers fell swiftly—men I'd fought beside for years died without even knowing they'd lost."

Mathieu paused again, his breath coming sharper now, visibly shaken. "I fought until I collapsed. Rothgar captured me alive—not out of mercy, but as a tool to break Valmont's spirit. They shackled me, threw me in a cell, and asked questions I refused to answer. Days turned into nights, and my blood marked the passing hours more than the sun ever could."

His voice dropped, rough with emotion. "Eventually, I stopped believing anyone would come. I stopped believing I was worth saving. And when I finally escaped—when I killed the guard and ran—it wasn't freedom I felt, but shame. I took the name Duran, borrowed from Captain Duran—my father's closest friend and my mentor in battle—to bury my past, to hide from those who hunted me."

Finally, he turned to Améliane, his eyes raw with vulnerability. "I've carried this shame every day since. But you deserve to know the truth, Améliane. Every painful piece of it."

Améliane said nothing, her heart aching with the weight of his confession. Slowly, she reached up and gently turned his face toward hers, seeing clearly the deep shame and lingering hurt reflected in his eyes. With a tender resolve, she slid from beneath the silk sheets, carefully straddling his lap. Her hands rose softly to cradle his face, fingers brushing tenderly against his jaw.

She met his gaze briefly, letting the silence speak volumes before leaning forward to press a gentle, lingering kiss to his mouth—a kiss filled with understanding, solidarity, and quiet absolution, washing away the shadow of guilt he'd carried for so long.

The soft whispering of the rain and the occasional pop of the fire were the only sounds as she deepened her chaste kiss to thoroughly claim his mouth. Finally, Améliane leaned back slightly, eyes sparkling softly.

"And here I thought the most scandalous revelation tonight would be mine," she murmured, a playful smile tugging at the corners of her lips.

Mathieu's expression softened into gentle humor, his voice dry yet affectionate. "You've been determined to outshine me since my arrival, Your Majesty."

She arched an elegant eyebrow, her smile deepening. "It seems Eldrenoire is becoming infamous as the worst-kept secret refuge for deposed royalty in all of Caelvarra."

He chuckled softly, the tension visibly easing from his shoulders. "Perhaps we should start charging admission fees."

"An excellent idea," she replied lightly, settling comfortably against his side once more. "We'll have Élodie manage the ledger. She'll frighten away any unwanted visitors with a single glare."

They laughed softly together, the warmth of their shared humor grounding them, bringing a welcome respite from the heaviness of their truths.

After their laughter faded softly into comfortable silence, Améliane lifted her gaze, her expression turning contemplative once more. Her fingers traced slow, gentle circles against Mathieu's chest, hesitating briefly before she voiced the question that had quietly tugged at her thoughts.

"Mathieu," she began softly, her tone careful yet sincere, "if you ever leave Eldrenoire...do you intend to reclaim your throne in Valmont?"

Mathieu's expression grew serious, eyes drifting back to the glowing embers as he considered her question carefully. His chest rose and fell steadily beneath her fingertips as he gathered his thoughts. Finally, he spoke, his voice gentle but tinged with quiet regret.

"No," he admitted softly. " Perhaps that's what weighs on me the most. The crown was never something I desired—not truly. My only wish was for my people's safety and freedom, not to rule over them."

He glanced back at her, eyes earnest. "That's why I feel most guilty—because even now, if I had the chance to reclaim everything, I don't want it."

He reached up, gently brushing a lock of her hair behind her ear, his touch tender, his eyes filled with a quiet sincerity. "If I ever leave this cursed castle, Améliane, it won't be alone. Not ahead of you, not behind you, but by your side. I've worn a crown, fought for a throne, and lost it all. But with you—I don't want a kingdom. I want a partner."

Améliane felt a deep, quiet warmth flood her heart, her throat tightening with the intensity of his vow. Without a word, she placed her hand in his, her gaze steady, filled with trust and quiet promise.

They sat together, bathed in the amber glow of the hearth, united as equals, as the storm raged outside.

CHAPTER 36

S he and Mathieu had aligned their intentions long before he slipped from her rooms in the early morning light, casting a cheeky wink over his shoulder at Thorne—who stood outside, eyes wide. Quiet words, traded between silk sheets, had ensured they would speak with one voice when the time came.

Améliane found Renaud waiting outside her door, expression unreadable and arms folded. She spoke in low tones, sharing everything that was to come in the meeting she had called. He listened without interrupting, his gaze sharpening with every word. No argument followed. Just a clipped nod—acknowledgment, readiness, resolve. When they turned toward the stairs, they moved as one.

The council chambers of Eldrenoire were a study in cruel magnificence. Gold-veined marble gleamed beneath their boots, polished to a mirror shine. Towering windows draped in silks the color of midnight cast fractured light across the room, refracted by chandeliers that hovered in midair—each suspended by unseen magic, glowing with flickering orbs of soft luminescence.

A grand table of carved obsidian stretched the length of the room, inlaid with silver filigree in ancient Belmaran motifs—symbols of sovereignty, heritage, and sacrifice. A queen's table.

Améliane entered first, her gown whispering across the polished floor like a tide returning to shore. Beside her walked Mathieu, tall and composed, his presence familiar yet somehow different in this context. He had never stood beside her here. Not in this way.

Heads turned.

Though each of them knew Mathieu—had eaten beside him, trained with him, argued with him—his presence at the council table drew immediate attention. This was different. This was sanctioned.

Élodie tilted back in her chair, arms crossing, one brow arching with theatrical amusement. Thorne gave the briefest of nods, his face unreadable, gaze fixed somewhere slightly to the left of theirs. Margot smirked—but her fingers twisted once in her lap, a nervous tic no one noticed.

From the far end, Sabine didn't rise. She barely looked up. "About time," she muttered, flicking a speck of dust from her sleeve like the whole thing had interrupted her day.

And then—Laurent. Smiling with maddening serenity as he leaned back in his chair, hands steepled. "Well, well," he murmured. "And here I thought the scandal had peaked before breakfast."

Améliane did not respond to him. Instead, she walked to the head of the table and placed her hands lightly on its surface.

"This is the first time I have asked for all of you to gather," she said evenly, her voice calm but resonant. "And not without reason."

She reached out, placing a hand briefly atop the back of the chair beside her. Mathieu lowered himself into it without hesitation, calm beneath the scrutiny.

"Mathieu has been among us for over a year. You all know him. But what you may not know is that last week, Eldrenoire offered him the Blood Oath."

There was a beat of silence—shock without sound.

"He refused it."

That landed.

Sabine snorted softly. "Well. That'll upset the tapestry of fate."

Laurent uncrossed his legs, his brows lifting in genuine surprise.

Thorne sat straighter.

Even Élodie blinked, her smirk faltering just enough to betray the depth of her reaction.

Améliane let the moment breathe. Then she looked to Mathieu. He said nothing, letting the truth speak for itself.

"He was free to leave," she added. "And he chose to stay."

The chandeliers overhead flickered slightly, a brief hiccup in the magic—an echo of the castle's unease, or its approval. It was always hard to tell.

"That," Améliane said quietly, "makes him different. It makes him someone we can trust."

Her words settled with purpose.

Then, with the weight of her court watching, she stepped back and slowly took her seat—never breaking eye contact, "We've never all sat at this table before. That ends today.

There's much I need to share with you, and whatever truths come out—we face them together."

The silence after Améliane's declaration held for a beat too long—everyone waiting to see where this moment would lead. So many truths had been hidden. Not out of malice. Out of necessity. Until now.

She folded her hands on the table before her. "There are things I've kept from you," she said evenly. "Not because you are unworthy of knowing them—but because the castle itself, and the danger beyond it, made caution a necessity."

Her gaze flicked to Renaud and then to Mathieu, both of whom offered small, almost imperceptible nods. She drew a breath.

"Cassien is not merely Edric's courier," she began. "He is my eyes in Belmara."

Élodie's brows lifted, though her face remained unreadable.

That, at least, struck home.

Sabine's brows lifted. "I always said the man was too charming to just deliver letters."

Laurent stilled, his hand pausing mid-drum against the table. "Well," he murmured. "Isn't that delightfully treasonous."

Margot shifted, visibly rattled, while Thorne's posture didn't change—only the stillness in his gaze betrayed new scrutiny.

"Every report Cassien delivers from Edric is a curated lie," Améliane continued. "However, he also brings me the truth."

She leaned forward slightly, tone steady but grim. "And the truth is this: Edric's grip is slipping. He's losing control."

Renaud nodded subtly, confirming Améliane's statement.

Améliane's voice sharpened. "Cassien says the healer's wing is overflowing. Soldiers return from the border broken and burned. The Rothgarians press harder with each passing month."

Thorne's jaw tightened like a drawn bowstring.

"He also contracted a fleet of ships from Mireath." she added, glancing toward Renaud. "Not allies. Mercenaries. Paid to dock at Belmara's western harbors. No loyalty. No code. Just blood and coin."

Thorne exhaled, slow and deep. "So he's desperate to maintain control."

"He's worse than desperate," Améliane replied. "He's reckless. He struck a deal with the Ordréan Empress—she is providing funding disguised as a diplomatic gesture."

"Why does he need funding?" Élodie asked, her voice quiet now, focused.

"The coffers aren't just thin," Améliane said. "They're gutted. Cassien says Edric's been selling off Crown lands—ancestral holdings, centuries-old estates—all to maintain the illusion of control. He's trading legacy for appearances, draining Belmara dry to keep the throne from crumbling beneath him."

Laurent let out a low whistle and sank back in his chair. "Seems our dear consort is bleeding the kingdom dry and calling it statecraft."

"That's not all," she said. Her fingers tapped once on the obsidian table. "He's importing weapons from Vorskyr. Officially, for defense. Unofficially—he's stockpiling. Armoring the capital. Preparing for something."

Margot paled slightly, and Améliane watched her carefully, though she made no comment.

But it was Élodie who leaned forward, voice calm but sharp. "And the people?"

Améliane's tone shifted. "That's where it begins to change."

She rose with deliberate control, hands braced against the table's edge. "There is unrest in Belmara. Cassien says it simmers—not in the streets, not yet—but in the shadows. And it started with the Seers."

That word alone caused a shift in the room. Even Laurent straightened.

"It began with some remembering things they cannot explain. A story half-forgotten, echoing in visions. They didn't realize it was me—not at first. But they have grown substantially over the last year."

She circled the table as she spoke, letting the weight of it settle on their shoulders, one by one.

"They call the rebellion *The Return*."

Silence.

Not the kind bred of fear, but the kind that clings before lightning strikes.

Élodie's gaze burned across the table—furious, hopeful, afraid.

Thorne bowed his head slightly, reverent.

Sabine stared straight ahead, unmoving, as if holding back something that could not yet be named.

Margot swallowed hard, her fingers frozen mid-twist.

Laurent said nothing—for once—but his eyes were sharper than she'd ever seen them.

Améliane drew herself up. "They've begun painting a version of the Moonlit Tidelily where soldiers don't look- they've taken to calling it the Moonlit Bloom. I don't know who the leader is, but I know they're meeting in the old warehouse district regularly."

She let the silence return. Let them absorb it fully.

And then she said, simply, "The kingdom has not forgotten us. And we won't forget them."

Améliane remained standing, her hands still braced on the obsidian tabletop, but the weight of her next words settled differently in her chest. Heavier. Not just truth now, but theory—one they had discussed in low voices, in firelit corners, in moments stolen between strategy and sleep.

"There's more," she said.

The others looked up, still caught in the wake of *The Return*, but alert now, watching her carefully.

"Renaud, Mathieu, and I have been... observing the changes here. The things we've all noticed happening within Eldrenoire's walls."

The lights above flickered again—softly. A single chandelier hummed and dimmed before surging back to life.

"We all feel it," she went on, her tone level but undeniable. "The flickering lights. The walls that shift when they shouldn't. The new doors. The old ones that vanish. This place was once precise—bound and woven by the curse like thread through a loom. But lately..."

"It frays," Sabine said, voice hard enough to cut. "At the edges."

Thorne gave a small, grunted nod. "Even the patrol routes shift. I thought it was me—until I started mapping it."

"We've watched it closely," Améliane said. "Mathieu, Renaud, and I. And we have a theory. We think it started the moment the world outside began remembering us."

The room drew in, like breath before a blow.

She glanced at Mathieu, then back to the table. "When the rebellion stirred—when The Return took hold, when Seers began to speak our names in dreams and shadows—the magic here... faltered."

Élodie's fingers drummed once, thoughtfully. "The curse is tied to memory."

"Exactly," Améliane said. "That was always part of its design. My people forget me, and I stay trapped. But what happens when they begin to remember?"

Sabine finally spoke, her voice quiet. "It reacts. Or unravels. Or both."

Laurent gave a low whistle.

"That isn't all," Améliane confessed. "You all know Alaric named Mathieu *Wyrd-bound*. The entire castle has been whispering about it ever since. You've all heard the gossip. You've all made your judgments."

She didn't pause for protest. "But we've been watching the pattern. And we believe his presence—his otherness in the eyes of this curse—is amplifying the disruption."

Renaud added, "The castle doesn't know what to do with him."

"It let him in," Améliane said. "It offered him the Blood Oath. He refused. And it didn't drive him mad. It didn't erase him. It let him stay."

Laurent's amber eyes narrowed slightly. "Because he's not part of the curse."

"No," Améliane said. "Because he's the flaw in it."

The silence that followed wasn't stunned—it was measured. The kind that belonged to survivors too practiced at weighing danger against opportunity.

And then Élodie leaned forward, voice cool and certain. "If the castle is breaking... we need to decide whether we're escaping through the cracks—or being buried in them."

Mathieu shifted forward, his arms resting on the edge of the obsidian table, his voice low but clear. "We've been asking the wrong question," he said. "It's not just *why* the castle is changing—it's *how*."

The others turned to him.

"Élodie's right," he continued. "Something is breaking. But it's not just the magic. It's the design."

He looked to Améliane, who gave a slight nod—permission granted.

"I've spent the last eight months in the library," he said. "Most of the books are useless—either enchanted to hide the truth or warped by the spell that holds this place together. But some... bleed through. Fragments. Notations. Reflections."

Laurent lifted a brow. "Reflections?"

Mathieu met his gaze. "The curse that binds this place—something called a *Mirrorbind*—was never meant to imprison. It was designed to reflect. A mimic spell. An echo. Something Vaeril originally theorized to hold magical energy safely. Not suppress it."

Améliane stilled at the name. Renaud's knuckles whitened against the armrest of his chair.

"But Edric twisted it," Mathieu went on. "He and Vaeril corrupted the original spell—turned mimicry into containment. The mirror became a cage."

He tapped the table once. "And buried deep in Vaeril's notes—barely legible, written in mirrored script—I found mention of a failsafe."

He paused. Let the word sink in.

Sabine's eyes narrowed. "What kind of failsafe?"

"A condition," Mathieu said. "If someone inside the mirror world becomes more *real* than their reflection—if they tether themselves to something on both sides, through memory or truth—they can pass through."

Margot looked dubious. "That sounds like theory. Not magic."

"Magic *is* theory, until it works," Mathieu replied evenly.

Then, more softly, "And I think that's why the gate responded to me."

The room hushed again.

Laurent blinked. "The gate?"

Mathieu nodded. "I tested it. Not to leave—but to see if it would react. And it did. It shifted. It shimmered. It knew me."

Élodie's voice, when it came, was soft. "Because you're not sealed here. You were never cursed."

"No," he agreed.

A beat.

"In the margins of an old text, there was reference to a soul—*Wyrdbound*—whose presence causes mirror spells to distort or collapse. The idea is... if that person forms a true tether, grounded in memory and emotion and choice, they can bend the spell without being caught in it."

"A tether," Thorne echoed, frowning.

"A truth," Mathieu said. "Faced and claimed. The gate doesn't open for desire—it opens for surrender. You walk forward with anything less, and the spell unravels you instead."

Élodie watched him carefully. "And you... chose to stay."

"Yes," he said simply. "I could have walked free. I had the choice. But I stayed—because the only way forward is with *you*. Not away from you."

Laurent sat back slowly, his expression unreadable for once. "Gods below," he muttered. "You really are here to break everything."

Mathieu didn't deny it.

"I also found a scrying map," he added. "It was tucked behind a false binding in a ruined ledger. It tracks magical currents across the continent. There's one place glowing now that hadn't in years."

Améliane's breath caught.

"Belmara," Mathieu said. "When the world remembers her name, the curse must yield."

He looked directly at Améliane now, his voice softer. "You are being remembered. *They* are calling you back. And Eldrenoire feels it."

A moment passed. Then two.

"So now we know the truth," Mathieu said breaking the silence. "The Mirrorbind is faltering because we're becoming real again. The Wyrdbound can bend it. The world outside is pushing against it. And the curse was never meant to hold that kind of pressure."

His eyes met each of theirs in turn.

"We're not trapped. Not in the way we thought. But leaving won't come from wanting it. It'll come from facing it."

Another silence fell—but this one buzzed with possibility.

Élodie was the first to break it, her voice dry but with a sliver of wonder. "So... all we have to do is confront our deepest truths, remember who we are, and not get unmade by sentient architecture?"

Laurent groaned. "Someone get me a drink."

For a long moment, no one spoke.

Then, Sabine broke the silence—her voice low and deliberate. "If what you're saying is true... then it means there's a path forward." She didn't sound hopeful exactly, but there was a steadiness in her now. A grounding force.

"We've lived in stasis for eight years," Renaud interjected. "If the castle is reacting, even violently—it means something is changing. And change..." He glanced at Améliane. "Change means choice."

Mathieu inclined his head, a flicker of agreement passing between them for once.

Élodie, meanwhile, leaned forward, hands clasped, her brow furrowed. "But let's not pretend we understand the mechanics. If the spell reacts to truth, then whose truth does it weigh? What happens if someone walks forward convinced they've faced everything—only to be torn apart?"

No one answered.

"It's not just about choosing to stay," she continued. "It's about surrender. That's not a decision—it's a reckoning. And people aren't good at those." She tilted her head slightly, watching Améliane. "Even queens."

Améliane didn't flinch. "Which is why we face it together. Strategically. Carefully."

Across the table, Thorne remained silent, but Améliane could feel his attention like pressure—steady, anchored. He was watching the room, not just the words. Measuring loyalty. Fear. Fault lines.

And that was when Margot spoke.

"Maybe..." Her voice was thin and uncertain, a tremor running beneath the words. "Maybe Edric isn't entirely wrong."

All eyes turned to her.

Margot straightened in her seat, but her shoulders remained hunched, defensive. "I just mean—what if breaking the curse costs more than we're prepared to lose?"

Silence.

Laurent blinked, then leaned back slowly in his chair, lips curving into a smile that didn't reach his eyes. "Well. That's a bold take."

Élodie's gaze narrowed, sharp and cutting. "Would you care to elaborate?"

Margot's fingers twisted in her lap again. "I'm only saying... Eldrenoire is dangerous when it shifts. We all know that. If the curse breaks and we don't control how—what if it takes us with it? What if... what if we're safer here?"

Sabine rolled her eyes. "The curse has tried to kill me twice this week just for rearranging the bandage drawer. I'd take chaos with a purpose over homicidal architecture."

"You mean *controlled*," Thorne said quietly. "Not safe. You think Edric's leash is protection."

"No!" she said quickly. "I mean... I just think we should be careful. That's all."

Améliane's voice was calm, but ice edged. "You're not wrong, Margot. Caution is warranted. But nostalgia for a prison is still captivity."

Margot's eyes darted around the table, her smile brittle. "I wasn't saying—I didn't mean to imply—"

Laurent waved a hand lazily. "Oh, let her dig. It's always entertaining when someone panics mid-monologue."

Renaud didn't laugh. "We'll remember your concerns," he said flatly.

Améliane watched Margot carefully, but let it lie—for now. The room was too volatile for accusations. But the seeds of suspicion had been watered. Again.

She exhaled slowly, then turned back to the table. "We move forward with eyes open. All of us. No one walks to that gate until we're certain. But now, at least, we know there is a gate to walk toward."

The silence that followed Améliane's final statement was heavier than any before it.

But it didn't last.

Laurent finally leaned forward, resting his elbows on the table with uncharacteristic precision. His glacial eyes missed nothing as they swept across the group—measured, razor-sharp.

His usual smirk was gone.

"I'll test it," he said quietly. "Let me go first."

The words dropped like a sword into water—still, then chaos.

"No," Renaud said immediately, voice like iron drawn.

Sabine raised an eyebrow. "You planning to leave a blood sample for study, or just your smug last words?"

"Laurent don't be ridiculous," Élodie snapped, straightening in her chair. "This isn't a parlor dare."

Thorne's voice was quieter, steadier. "You don't know what the gate would do to you."

Mathieu tensed beside Améliane, his jaw tightening. "Laurent—"

"I'm not asking permission," Laurent said, louder this time. His voice cut clean through the protests. "I'm telling you. I'm done waiting for salvation to come knocking."

He stood, pushing his chair back, and the motion seemed to ripple across the chamber.

"For eight years, we've lived like ghosts in velvet," he continued, voice raw with a fervor he rarely showed. "Trapped in splendor. Watching the walls move like we're rats in some gilded maze. I've heard the whispers. I've seen the cracks. You all have. But every time we get close to hope, someone says, 'Wait.' 'Plan.' 'Prepare.'"

He looked directly at Améliane now. "What if there is no preparing for truth? What if this is the moment, and we're too afraid to seize it?"

Améliane's expression was unreadable. She didn't speak.

Laurent's tone softened—just enough to let the weariness bleed through. "I refuse to stay trapped here any longer. I'm tired of playing this eternal waiting game. If there's a chance—any chance—I will take it."

Mathieu stood slowly, hands braced on the table. "The gate doesn't respond to desperation. That's the risk. If you haven't faced what the spell demands—if your reason isn't rooted in truth—"

"It will destroy me?" Laurent finished, with a shrug. "Fine. Maybe that's the cost. Maybe I deserve it."

That silenced even Élodie.

A stillness passed through the room.

"You think you're ready," Améliane said quietly, rising to meet his gaze. "But the gate isn't a test of courage, Laurent. It's a test of reckoning."

He didn't look away.

"Then let it reckon with me."

For the first time, Améliane saw it in his eyes—not charm, not deflection, not performance. Just something fractured. Something that wanted to believe that movement—any movement—was better than standing still in purgatory.

Mathieu stepped forward slightly, voice quieter now. "If you go, we won't stop you. But know this—the gate isn't fooled. Not by cleverness. Not by regret dressed as resolve."

Laurent gave a tight, humorless smile. "Then I suppose we'll see what it thinks of me."

The council chamber buzzed with tension—half outrage, half dread.

Then Améliane stood. The effect was immediate.

The flickering lights steadied. The whispers died in the corners of the room. Even the air itself seemed to still, like the castle paused to listen.

Her voice wasn't raised. It didn't need to be.

"Enough."

Laurent froze mid-step. Élodie fell silent. Sabine sat back down. All eyes turned to her.

Améliane looked across the table—not as a woman caught in debate, but as a queen.

"I do not take your offer lightly, Laurent," she said, her tone calm, but iron clad. "And I do not question your will. You have survived with wit and grace in a place designed to unravel lesser souls."

A flicker of emotion passed behind Laurent's eyes, but he remained still.

She turned, addressing the room now. "Each of you has sacrificed to endure this place. Your loyalty. Your freedom. Your truths. I would not ask more of you—not without cause. But as the world outside begins to remember us the curse will continue to thin. And if there is even a chance... a chance that one of us might find a way through the mirror—then we do not waste it."

Her gaze returned to Laurent, and it softened. Not in weakness, but in understanding.

"But we do not rush it," she said. "Not in desperation. Not in fear."

Laurent's jaw clenched, but he didn't speak.

"You may test the gate," she continued. "But only when we are ready. When every ward is in place. When every contingency has been seen to. When the castle has been watched, measured, and accounted for."

She stepped closer to him now, her steely gaze meeting his.

"And you must understand this: if your truth is not whole—if what drives you is fear, or guilt, or pride—the gate *will* know. And it will not forgive you."

Laurent held her gaze for a long moment. Then—quietly, and without flourish—he bowed his head.

"I understand," he said. "And I accept the risk."

A breath passed through the chamber. Not relief, but readiness. A shift.

Améliane nodded once. "Then we prepare."

And just like that, the waiting was over.

The reckoning had begun.

CHAPTER 37

Mathieu

Améliane and Renaud had ledgers to review and Mathieu, having been gently—but unmistakably—dismissed, took it upon himself to return to the library.

Eldrenoire's magic always felt older in the library, like it was remembering itself slowly through the dust and parchment. Light spilled in slanted columns through high, arched windows, catching the faint shimmer of enchanted ink that curled across open scrolls. The scent was familiar by now—old vellum, cold stone, and something sharp beneath it all, like steel in water.

Mathieu moved between the stacks with practiced ease, ignoring the ache in his shoulders and the sleep he hadn't gotten. There were answers here—half-written, mirrored, tangled in contradiction—but they were answers all the same.

He had three tomes open across the central table, their pages propped open with broken crystal weights. Each was a variation on the same cursework theory—reflections, thresholds, bindings tied to truth rather than power. The Mirrorbind wasn't meant to trap. That much he knew now. The question was whether it could still be unraveled.

Or bent.

Mathieu leaned forward, adjusting a shard of mirror glass he'd laid against the margin of an old spellbook. The letters shifted slightly when seen in reverse, revealing a secondary glyph beneath the ink—one shaped like a spiral cracking at the edge.

He reached for his notes, careful not to disturb the fragile balance of magic humming across the table.

The gate was waiting to open. He just had to find the handle. Figuratively speaking.

A sound—a whisper, really—caught the edge of his awareness.

Not the creak of the bookshelves or the ever-present shiver of enchantment, but something more deliberate. A patter. Light. Soft.

Paws.

Mathieu froze, quill still in hand.

He didn't turn his head right away. Just listened. The silence around him was too deep now, like something was holding its breath.

Then, from the corner of his eye, a flicker of movement.

A pale-gold fox, gliding low along the edge of the shelves.

Margot.

Even in her fox form, she moved like a secret—light-footed, elegant, entirely in control. Her fur caught the ambient glow of the chandeliers above, almost too bright to be real, like the ghost of a flame. He watched her slink between the rows with clear purpose, her snout twitching slightly as she paused, scanned the room.

She didn't see him.

He'd chosen the alcove for its shadowed seclusion, and now it served him well. Tucked behind a towering stack of mirrored runic indexes and half-deciphered grimoires, he stayed still, breath shallow.

She padded forward and shifted in a ripple of magic and light—one beat, and she was human again.

Golden curls. Slender frame. Nervous eyes.

Her expression wasn't afraid. It was alert.

She looked around once more, confirming she was alone.

Then she turned to the scroll cabinet.

Mathieu's brow furrowed.

He'd passed that cabinet a dozen times. Dust-laced, sealed. It hadn't opened in all his months of research. The surface bore carvings too worn to decipher—except for one: a serpent devouring its own tail.

Margot placed her palm against the serpent's eye.

The wood pulsed once, then shifted.

A drawer slid out, silent as a sigh.

Mathieu's stomach dropped.

She reached into her sleeve and produced a folded letter—no seal, no crest. The paper shimmered faintly under the chandelier light; a thin sheen of concealment magic woven into its surface.

She hesitated.

Then placed it inside.

Closed the drawer.

And whispered something—inaudible to him.

Mathieu's pulse pounded in his ears.

Margot stepped back, glanced around one last time—and shifted again. Her fox form vanished in a blur of gold, darting down the southern passage without a sound.

Mathieu moved.

He didn't think. Didn't breathe.

Just launched himself over the nearest bench, skidding along the marble as he rounded the table and sprinted toward the scroll cabinet. His boots echoed like thunder in the high-ceilinged chamber.

The drawer was gone.

Seamless wood. Smooth. Untouched.

"Damn it," he hissed, running both hands along the surface. "No, no—don't shut me out now."

He slapped his palm against the serpent carving. Nothing.

He pressed harder, tried to mimic what she'd done.

Still nothing.

Heart racing, he took a step back, raking a hand through his hair. Something twisted in his chest—rage, maybe. Or worse—recognition.

"Come on, Eldrenoire," he muttered, voice low, trembling at the edge. "You've shown me worse—what's one more truth?"

The cabinet shuddered.

The mirrored inlays rippled. The serpent's eye flashed with silver light, as though winking at him.

With a reluctant groan, the hidden drawer slid open—slow, like it didn't want to give up its secrets.

Inside, the letter sat neatly, exactly where she'd left it. Mathieu stared at it, chest rising and falling. He didn't move right away.

The room felt colder now. Or maybe he'd just stopped trusting the walls. He reached forward, slowly, and picked up the letter. It hummed in his hand—warm, like breath on skin.

And in that instant, he knew. Margot hadn't just been keeping secrets. She'd been sending them.

Mathieu turned it over once. No seal. No signature. Just a fold of parchment that shimmered faintly with concealment runes, pulsing like a second heartbeat.

He didn't try to tear it open. He wasn't that stupid.

Letters like this didn't bleed. They vanished. Or worse, they fought back.

He held it lightly, fingers at the edge. He thought back to Margot during the meeting in the council chambers as he stared at the place where the ink shimmered in defiance.

"You were never going to stay, were you?" he said quietly.

He hadn't meant to speak aloud. But the words came anyway—too tired, too bitter to be false.

The letter shivered in response.

A line of light split the fold down the middle, and the enchantment unraveled like mist curling back into shadow. A whisper of static rippled over his skin, like the castle itself had inhaled.

And then it was just paper.

No longer sealed. No longer hidden.

Mathieu unfolded it slowly, eyes scanning the page.

There was no greeting. No signature. Just tight, hurried script in Margot's precise hand—too controlled for panic, too practiced to be innocent.

> *She knows the curse is fraying.*
> *She knows about the rebellion.*
> *We're running out of time.*
> <u>*You promised I'd be free.*</u>

The last line was underlined—not neatly, but angrily. As though she'd carved it in desperation, trying to bind the truth to something—someone—who'd already started slipping away.

Mathieu stared at the words, the shape of them sinking in like knives between ribs.

He hadn't imagined it. The timing. The secrecy. The way she'd always seemed to be listening even when no one was speaking.

You promised I'd be free.

His grip tightened. Margot wasn't just scared. She was involved.

And she wasn't working alone.

Mathieu didn't think—he moved.

The letter still in his hand, he bolted from the library, boots pounding through Eldrenoire's shifting corridors. The walls whispered as he passed, the castle stirring in uneasy cadence. Hallways lengthened, doors blinked in and out, but he didn't slow. The castle knew where he was going.

It let him through.

He didn't bother knocking when he reached Améliane's chambers—just threw open the door to her sitting room, where the scent of firelight and fresh ink clung to the air. She and Renaud were seated near the hearth, scrolls unfurled on the low table between them.

Both looked up in an instant—Améliane half-rising, Renaud already on his feet.

"Mathieu?" she asked sharply. "What—"

He crossed the space in three strides, holding the letter out like it might burn him.

"She's been sending messages."

Améliane didn't take the letter right away. Her silver gaze flicked to his face first—assessing, measuring. Then, slowly, she accepted the parchment and unfolded it.

Renaud stepped closer, his expression unreadable, but his body taut like a drawn blade.

Mathieu exhaled, dragging a hand through his hair. "I saw her. In the library. She came in fox-shaped—didn't know I was there. Shifted, used some kind of enchantment to open a drawer I didn't even know existed. Slid this inside and vanished again."

He gestured to the letter now open in Améliane's hands.

"I triggered the drawer by accident. Or... not by accident. I don't know. I said something and the cabinet just...responded. Like the castle wanted me to find it."

Améliane's gaze moved over the letter's contents. Slowly. Carefully.

When she looked up again, her expression had shifted. Gone was the calculating queen. What remained was colder.

"*She knows the curse is fraying. She knows about the rebellion.*" Her voice was quiet, but every syllable landed like a falling blade.

She handed the letter to Renaud, who read it with a growing storm behind his eyes.

"I always knew she was desperate," he said, his voice low. "But this? This is betrayal."

"Did you see where she placed it?" Améliane asked, already moving toward the door.

"Yes. I can show you," Mathieu said, already falling in step beside her.

Renaud followed, rolling his shoulders as if preparing for battle. "Let's see what else she's been hiding."

The air in the library felt different when they returned. Colder. As if the castle remembered what had just been uncovered and had no intention of letting the silence smooth it over.

Mathieu led the way back to the scroll cabinet, the soles of his boots scuffing softly over the marble. The shadows had stretched in the hour since he'd left, lengthening like they, too, were listening.

He stopped in front of the cabinet—the one with the faded serpent carved into the base—and gestured toward it.

"Here. She placed the letter inside this drawer. There was no seam at first—nothing to suggest it even opened. Until she pressed her hand to it."

Renaud crouched beside the engraving, fingers brushing over the aged wood. His brow furrowed, but he didn't speak.

Mathieu stepped back, rubbing the back of his neck. "I ran over after she left—sprinted, really. Tried everything to get it open."

Améliane folded her arms, watching him closely.

"And?" she asked.

Mathieu exhaled, gaze flicking toward the glinting veins of mirrored runes embedded in the cabinet. "I said something. Out loud. I wasn't thinking about magic. I was just... pissed."

Renaud straightened slightly, eyes narrowing in interest.

Mathieu gave a half-shrug. "I said, '*Come on, Eldrenoire. You've shown me worse—what's one more secret?*'"

He saw the flicker in Améliane's expression—the faintest ripple of understanding. She didn't speak, but her eyes told him everything.

"And the letter?" Renaud asked.

"I didn't tear it," Mathieu said. "It had this shimmer—some kind of concealment charm woven through it. I've seen similar spells. If I'd forced it open, it might've burned, or vanished."

"Then how did you read it?" Renaud asked, sharp but not accusatory.

Mathieu paused. "I held it. Watched it. Then I said—again, without thinking something about how Margot was never content to stay trapped here.'"

He looked at them both. "And the spell... just faded. Like maybe it recognized the truth? I don't know."

Mathieu ran a hand through his close-cropped hair as Renaud studied him in silence.

Not suspicion. Not challenge. Just... weight. Measuring. Listening. Then he nodded once, slowly.

"Smart," he said. "Or lucky."

"Probably both," Mathieu replied, unable to keep the sarcasm from his voice.

Renaud didn't rise to it but gave a subtle nod. Something shifted between them. Mathieu felt it like the echo of a sword being sheathed instead of drawn. Not forgiveness. But a step toward it.

Mathieu didn't miss the flicker in Améliane's gaze as Renaud nodded. She saw it—the shift in the current. And for all her silence, he could feel her cataloging the moment, like a queen taking stock of where new lines of loyalty had begun to form.

Améliane stepped forward, placing her hand lightly on the edge of the cabinet. Her silver eyes scanned the carving, the faint residue of the spell that had once concealed the drawer.

"She used this place because she believed it would hide her. Because Eldrenoire has always kept our secrets."

Her voice dropped.

"But it's choosing not to anymore. Or maybe it just isn't able to."

They were still standing around the drawer when the fox returned.

Mathieu didn't hear her so much as *feel* her—his head turned instinctively at the soft rustle of paws on marble.

There she was. A pale shimmer near the library's southern archway, pausing just past the threshold.

Margot, fox-formed again, her golden fur catching the light like a drop of sunlight trying not to be seen.

But she was seen.

Renaud straightened, his hand inching toward the hilt at his side.

Améliane's eyes narrowed.

And Margot froze.

Just for a second.

Just long enough to confirm everything.

She shifted in a shimmer of light and limbs, golden curls tumbling down her back, lips already parting in feigned surprise.

"I didn't realize anyone was still here—" she began.

"You left something behind," Mathieu said, voice hard.

He held up the letter.

Margot's eyes darted to it, then to Améliane, then Renaud.

Too fast.

Too guilty.

"I can explain—"

"No," Améliane said, calm as a still sea. "You can't."

Renaud took one step forward, deliberate. "How long?" he asked.

Margot's breath hitched.

"I—It wasn't what you think."

"Then tell us what it was," Mathieu snapped.

She backed away, eyes wide now, the flush draining from her cheeks.

"Edric lied," she blurted. "He promised I'd be free—he said—he said he'd release me if I—if I just—"

"If you just sold us out?" Renaud growled.

Her expression twisted, panic rising like steam.

"I didn't want to stay here forever. You don't know what it's like—not really. Every day, waiting. Hoping. Watching the world forget us—watching you," she spat, eyes locking on Améliane. "You still walk these halls like a queen, while the rest of us rot behind the walls!" Her voice cracked at the end—not rage, not fury. Something closer to fear.

Améliane didn't flinch. "And what did betraying us earn you, Margot? Did it taste like freedom?"

Margot's hands trembled. She turned—and ran.

"Margot!" Mathieu shouted—but she was already moving.

Fox again. Gold and quick and impossible to catch.

She darted between shelves, knocking over a stack of books, then vanished into the east wing's shadowed corridor.

Mathieu was after her instantly—no hesitation. His boots pounded across the floor, coattails flaring.

Renaud followed, silent and deadly, like a blade in pursuit.

Améliane came last, regal even in haste, her gown trailing like storm clouds behind her.

The corridor twisted ahead—one of the newer routes, formed after the last magical quake. Mathieu didn't pause to question it. Eldrenoire was leading them.

Always watching.

Always choosing.

Margot skidded through the last archway.

Mirrors shimmered from floor to ceiling. She was trying to lose them in the Mirror Hall.

Mathieu reached the threshold and stopped for just half a second, breath ragged, heart thundering.

Ahead, Margot's reflection scattered—tenfold, then twenty—as she fled deeper into the illusions, golden fur flickering between endless glass.

Renaud arrived at his shoulder, sword drawn.

Behind them, Améliane's voice cut the air like flint.

"Don't let her disappear!"

And they plunged in.

The Mirror Hall swallowed them whole. Glass stretched in every direction—walls, floor, even the arched ceiling above—reflecting not just their bodies, but their movements, their expressions, their fears. Every step echoed twice, as if the castle itself walked with them.

Mathieu charged forward, skidding around a pillar of polished obsidian, breath ragged in his chest.

"Margot!" he shouted, the name ricocheting off ten thousand versions of his own voice.

Her fox form darted through one reflection, then another—always ahead, always just beyond reach.

But something was wrong.

The glass began to ripple.

The floor shifted—one panel at a time—as if the castle were breathing in reverse. Reflections no longer matched reality. Mathieu saw himself ahead, behind, to the left—and then nowhere at all.

Renaud cursed under his breath, pressing forward, sword still drawn. "It's folding. The hall's folding."

"Margot, stop!" Améliane's voice rang out behind them, clear and commanding. "The castle won't save you!"

It was too late.

They rounded the next corner—and stopped cold.

There, caught in a freestanding mirror at the end of the corridor, was Margot.

No longer fox. No longer running.

She was human again, frozen mid-motion—both hands splayed against the glass, her face twisted in terror. Her mouth opened in a silent scream, but no sound came. Only breathless horror.

The mirror began to shift—subtle at first, then with visible distortion. The edges darkened like oil spreading through water. Her image warped slightly, bending as if submerged beneath waves.

"No—" Améliane reached the mirror just as it started to recede into the wall, as though the glass itself were being absorbed into the castle's skin.

She skidded to her knees beside it, hand pressed against the surface.

Margot's palm was still there on the other side, fingers outstretched. Reaching.

But she was already fading.

Falling backward into countless reflections. Becoming smaller. Distant. Gone.

Améliane stared in stunned silence.

Mathieu stood at her back, chest heaving, unable to look away.

Renaud sheathed his sword with a sound like finality.

"The castle has judged her," he said, voice flat. Cold.

And for once, not a single wall dared echo it.

CHAPTER 38

Bastian

The encampment sprawled like a scar at the edge of Ziraveen. What had once been a scatter of tents and scattered rumors had evolved into a fully functional operation. Canvas pavilions reinforced with spell-threaded cords; training circles drawn in ash and sigils. Supply caravans warded with glamourweave. And at the heart of it all—movement. Intentional, relentless movement. The kind of momentum that signaled war was no longer a question, but a promise.

Bastian kept to the edges.

He always did, even now.

His coat hung looser these days, leather weathered by rain and travel. A thin scar cut through the edge of his jaw—new, angry red beneath the stubble. He hadn't noticed it until someone in camp flinched when they saw him. It wasn't the worst scar. Just the newest.

A half-seer boy paced beside him, barely twenty, chatter spilling out like smoke. What was his name again? Keon? Keren? Something with a *K*. The kid didn't seem to notice—or mind—that Bastian barely replied as he walked.

"Moon says we'll march within the fortnight," the boy said, gesturing toward a line of blacksmiths at work near the edge of the clearing. "Three new blades each, prioritized to the eastern scouts. The Seers are finishing the last of the dampening runes tonight—we can't risk another tracer like what happened near the capital."

Bastian nodded once, hands tucked into the folds of his coat.

Beyond the smiths, he could just make out the shimmer of a concealment barrier—faint as heat haze—threaded between stones and tree roots. Half-trained Shadowbinders sat cross-legged at its edge, eyes glazed with concentration, whispering spells that pulsed faintly beneath the skin of the world.

He remembered when all of this had been rumor. When the rebellion was nothing more than a name whispered in dark taverns and dangerous alleys. *The Return*, they called themselves. But what they'd built here was no longer myth. It was military.

"They've started wearing the sigil again," the boy added, like it was nothing.

Bastian's brow furrowed. "What?"

He pointed to his shoulder where a pale cloth patch had been sewn beneath his scout's sash. A sharp-petaled bloom. Three points like knives. A moonlit tidelily—stylized, clean, defiant.

"Moon says it's time," the boy said. "Says they're remembering again. The Queen, I mean. That it's safe now. Or, well—*necessary*."

Bastian stared at the patch.

He remembered that flower. The first time he'd seen it, it was drawn on a napkin in blood. The next time—carved into a stone wall in a prison cell. Now? It was a banner. A vow.

"They still don't know if she's alive," Bastian said quietly.

The boy shrugged. "Doesn't matter. Some say the rebellion started when she vanished. Others say it started the second Edric tried to make them forget her. Either way—she's the reason they're fighting."

She's the reason I'm still breathing, Bastian thought.

But he didn't say that out loud.

They passed the edge of the command quarter. A tall woman with silver-streaked braids raised a hand in greeting. Another nodded, eyes lingering a little too long. Some still didn't trust him. Others trusted him just enough to keep him close. That was fine. He hadn't earned their trust.

The boy kept talking, pointing out new recruits, new weapons, updates to the runic map Moon had commissioned to track magical activity across Belmara.

Bastian let his mind drift. Ten weeks since they'd cut the ropes from his wrists. Ten weeks since Moon had said "closer," and meant: not yet. And in that time, something had shifted.

They hadn't let him speak, not at first.

Moon had stood in that tent of stitched canvas and shadow and given him nothing. Not a welcome. Not a warning. Just silence. Calculated and patient, like she was waiting to see if he'd hang himself with words he wasn't smart enough to keep.

She'd asked him one question, and he still remembered the way it landed like a test, not an invitation.

"The Blood Oath. What is it, really?"

His voice had come rough then, still hoarse from captivity. "A trap with three teeth. Lose a love. Lose yourself. Or lose what you can't bear to."

Moon hadn't blinked. Just tilted her head slightly.

"And what did you lose?"

He'd lied at first. Told her he didn't remember.

But later, when she tested him again—throwing false names, twisted room layouts, made-up sigils—he broke.

He told her about the shifting halls. About the way the castle changed shape when Améliane was angry, and again when she was grieving. About the Mirror Hall and the Library of Forgotten Knowledge.

And when she handed him the silver comb, wrapped in linen and dust, he hadn't needed to ask where it came from. They'd found it in his pack.

He remembered her hands twisting it into her braid the night before the gate locked itself shut behind him. Remembered how she hadn't cried—just turned away, lips pressed white and silent.

"She didn't even seem surprised," he'd said. "She looked at me like I was just one more person who would forget her."

That was the moment Moon had exhaled.

Not a full breath. Just a shift. Like she'd finally decided he might be worth more alive than dead.

She'd told him then, "*You're not in yet. But you're closer.*"

And that had been enough.

Bastian blinked, the cold post rough beneath his palm as he came back to himself. The clang of a sword meeting a practice dummy snapped the memory's grip, grounding him.

He looked out at the camp—twice as large now as when he first arrived.

Closer, he thought again. And this time, not just to the rebellion. But to her.

Just before Bastian turned back from the concealment barrier, something caught his eye.

A girl—no more than ten—scurried past the edge of the blacksmith circle, carrying a satchel twice her size. Her tunic was patched and soot-smudged, her hair woven into a tight braid down her back.

But what stopped him was the sash slung diagonally across her chest: a hand-stitched patch sewn near her shoulder.

A moonlit tidelily.

The embroidery was uneven, clearly done by someone still learning. One petal curled too far left. The moon behind it was a smudge of pale thread. But it was unmistakable. Not the Moonlit Bloom.

She wore the queen's sigil.

No ceremony. No proclamation. Just a child wearing the symbol of a woman the world had forgotten—like it was the most natural thing in the world.

Bastian went still and watched as the girl darted across the camp, slipping between tents with ease, her braid catching the light like a ribbon of gold.

And something in him—something bruised and bone-deep—shifted.

It had been ten weeks since they'd cut the ropes from his wrists. And now, in a rebel camp strung together with borrowed steel and half-believed dreams, a child wore Améliane's flower like armor.

He let the moment settle before closing his eyes briefly, gathering the memory like a breath.

It had started with a map. Or rather, the absence of one.

Moon had summoned him to the strategy tent, the canvas walls quivering under a storm that hadn't broken yet. A low-burning lantern hissed on the table between them, illuminating half-unfurled parchments—trade routes, troop movements, magical pulse points. One corner bore a blot of blood. Someone else's. Maybe his. He couldn't remember.

"We lost contact with the courier from Kireth," she said. "She was carrying a route manifest. One we can't afford to fall into Edric's hands."

Bastian rubbed a hand across his jaw.

"You think she's dead?" he asked.

"I think she's trapped. Or worse—trying not to be followed."

"And you want someone who knows how to disappear."

Moon didn't smile, but the corner of her mouth twitched in approval.

"You said you used to be good at that," she said. "Let's find out if you still are."

The drop point was a collapsed bridge along the northern merchant trail—one used in better times to cross between Belmara's lowlands and the forested slopes of Ziraveen. The bridge was gone now—swept away in a flood three seasons back—but the stone pylons remained, jagged and moss-covered. They were supposed to meet the courier in the hollow beneath the largest one.

They never did.

Bastian and two scouts—Talon and Iri—had circled the outpost twice, whispering signal chants, glyph flares ready in their palms. Nothing. Not even the birds would sing.

That's when they saw the blood.

A splash across the moss. A trail leading down through the roots.

Iri cursed softly and moved to signal, but Bastian stopped her. "No light. We don't know who's watching."

They followed the trail in silence—through water-slick stones, down into a crevasse barely wide enough for them to move through sideways.

They found the courier just past the bend. Alive, barely. She'd crawled into a hollow, clutching the route manifest tight to her chest. A crossbow bolt had pierced her shoulder, the shaft snapped to avoid notice. She shook when Bastian crouched beside her—but not from fear. From relief.

"They're... still here," she rasped. "Riders. Two of them. They want the map."

Talon's eyes sharpened. Iri readied a sigil and pressed it against the courier's wrist, whispering a stabilizing chant. Bastian took the map and shoved it into the lining of his coat.

Then the first arrow hit.

Iri fell before she could scream—struck through the neck. Talon returned fire, but the second rider was already upon them.

Chaos exploded in a blur of wet leaves and steel.

Bastian didn't run.

He stepped between the attacker and the courier, drew the short blade they'd given him, and met the first strike with raw instinct. It was ugly. Brutal. He'd never been the cleanest fighter—his style was desperation, not art.

The second rider grazed him—across the jaw. He felt the skin split, hot and wet, blurring his vision with pain.

But he didn't fall. Didn't yield.

He knocked one rider off balance, rolled with the weight of the next, and slammed the pommel of his blade into a helmeted jaw. When it was done, three bodies lay dead—and Talon was helping the courier stand.

The three of them got out. Barely.

He had returned to camp trailing blood and rainwater, the courier slumped between him and Talon, Iri noticeably absent. Moon stood waiting outside the ward line, arms crossed, face unreadable.

When Bastian pulled the manifest from his coat—drenched but intact—and held it out without a word, she took it with a single nod.

"You're bleeding," she said, voice flat.

He grinned through cracked lips. "So's the other guy."

She looked at him for a long moment—long enough for the storm to break above them in a crack of thunder.

Then she said, "You're in."

That was it.

No applause. No promotion.

But the way the guards shifted at the camp's edge—the way Talon clapped him on the shoulder without flinching—said more than words ever could.

The edge of his jaw still bore the scar—faded now, but firm beneath his fingertips. He exhaled, shaking off the memory of Iri's funeral pyre as the sounds of camp slowly returned around him.

He stood again at the edge of the camp, watching a young woman sewing Moonlit Bloom patches on tunics.

The rebellion had grown. So had he.

He turned toward the map tent, where Moon would be waiting. It was time to prepare. They had not yet found the way back to Eldrenoire. But when they did—he would be ready.

The council tent was tense with heat and strategy as Bastian pulled back the flap and entered.

Ziraveen's mist kept the air cool and damp, but the dozen bodies packed inside were radiating intent. Maps layered the table at the center, weighted at the corners with daggers and stones etched with runes. Chalk marks, smeared and redrawn, cut across the parchment like veins ready to bleed.

Bastian stood beside Moon—not at her right hand, but near. Close enough that no one questioned his place anymore. He was no longer the prisoner. No longer the stranger. Now he stood shoulder to shoulder with rebels and leaders alike, bearing weight in silence.

Moon's pale arms were folded, her gaze on the map. Her hair was pulled back in a dark knot and her mask hung loose at her neck. One of the Shadowbinders hovered near the perimeter, maintaining the concealment wards. A tension curled around the room like the edge of lightning waiting to strike.

And then—

The flap of the tent flew open.

A scout burst through, cloak damp with mist and breath coming hard. He didn't wait for permission to speak.

"The fog's thinning."

The room stilled. Moon's head lifted first. Then every eye turned to Bastian.

His heart didn't pound. It roared.

He stepped forward. "Where?"

The scout swallowed. "South ridge. Past the hollow with the blackroot trees. The mist is pulling back like it's... being called."

Moon's gaze flicked to Bastian.

"You said you'd find her," she said evenly. "Looks like she's ready to be found."

A murmur ran through the tent. Moon silenced it with a single look.

"We move at first light," she announced. "Quiet. Tracked only by Shadowbinders and Seers. If this is what we've been waiting for—we go in prepared."

A flurry of nods and movement followed. Orders whispered. Steel checked. Magic stirred.

But Bastian didn't move.

He stepped outside instead, past the flap, into the deepening dusk.

The horizon stretched beyond the ridge, and just past the line of trees, he saw it: the mist. Still thick, but shifting. Not lifting, but loosening. Like a veil being peeled back inch by inch. Like a spell growing tired of holding.

He exhaled slowly, the weight of the rebellion and the memory of her settling like armor across his shoulders.

CHAPTER 39

Améliane

Dawn in Eldrenoire was a quiet thing.

Not soft—Eldrenoire didn't know how to be soft—but reverent. The sky beyond the tower spires bruised gently from navy to violet, and the mist that clung to the Shrouded Gardens pulsed like breath, rising and falling with the hush of unseen tides.

Améliane stood on the balcony just outside her chambers, one hand braced on the chilled stone rail, the other curled loosely around a porcelain cup gone cold.

Below, the garden stretched out in hushed silhouette. Marble paths shimmered with dew. The fountain in the center trickled slow, its water darker than it should've been. And beneath the twisted branches of the lunar elms, curled like shadow incarnate, lay Élodie.

Panther-shaped. Still. Watching nothing and everything.

Améliane didn't need to look to know who else lingered nearby. A hawk circled lazily above the western wall—gold-feathered, sharp-eyed, too proud to perch. Laurent. Always circling, even now.

It had been two weeks. Fourteen days since Margot's flight. Thirteen sunrises since the mirror swallowed her whole.

And still, the ache hadn't dulled.

Améliane let her gaze rest on the garden's far edge, where the arch of the moonstone gazebo had begun to crumble. Vines curled upward like fingers, reaching for something long gone. The castle hadn't repaired it. Not yet. Not like it used to.

Another wound it was choosing to leave open.

Margot's absence had reshaped the court. Not in form, but in rhythm. Conversations faltered. Laughter caught on the tongue. Doors appeared where they shouldn't, and hallways grew longer between one breath and the next. Even the chandeliers flickered with a subtle melancholy, their magic dimmer than before.

Eldrenoire was mourning. So were they.

Upon hearing the news, Élodie had shifted at once, slinking through the corridors without a word—and hadn't shed her fur since. Laurent had been even worse—aloof in human form, impossible to reach in flight.

Améliane let them process. They had all loved Margot, in their own ways.

A soft gust stirred Améliane's hair. She tilted her head toward it, welcoming the chill, letting it anchor her to the present.

Behind her, the chamber was still wrapped in shadows. The fire had long since burned down to embers. She'd slipped from the bed an hour earlier, unable to sleep through the strange quiet that had settled over her thoughts.

Mathieu hadn't stirred. He rarely did after nights spent in her arms.

She had left him there, tangled in the linen sheets.

The blankets had fallen to his waist, exposing the scars that traced the ridges of his torso—memories written in skin, each one a price paid. His hand rested over his stomach, loose and unguarded. His dark hair was tousled across the pillow in a way that made him look both fierce and boyish—like a squire dreaming of battle.

She had smiled at the sight of him, warm and unexpected. There were still moments, even now, where she couldn't quite believe he was real. That he'd stayed. That he'd chosen this—her.

The warmth faded now as she looked down into the garden, where Élodie's massive panther form barely rose and fell with breath. Where Laurent's shadow cut slow circles through the mist above the crumbling archway.

They hadn't spoken since Margot's fall. Not truly. But Améliane could feel the shape of their silence—and knew it was a kind of grief. Not just for the friend they had lost. But for the illusions that had died with her.

A soft knock sounded at the chamber door. Three quick taps, polite and expected.

Améliane didn't turn, but she heard the rustle of sheets, followed by the low scrape of a deep voice laced in sleep.

"Come in," Mathieu called.

The door opened with a creak, hinges softened by age and enchantment. She heard the familiar footfalls of Anette, one of the castle's younger maidservants—barely more than a girl, though braver than most soldiers she'd known. Améliane didn't look, but she smiled as she listened to the exchange inside.

"You brought enough for a war council," Mathieu teased gently. "Are you planning to recruit me with pastries?"

A muffled laugh. "The Queen prefers tea with honey and the brioche warm."

"She's training you too well."

"You're the one who keeps stealing the sugared almonds."

"You wound me."

The soft clink of ceramic against silver tray, a bit of shifting cloth, the scent of warm bread and ripe stonefruit wafting toward the balcony.

Améliane let the smile linger.

She heard the door shut again, the latch catching softly. And then the sound she knew best now—his bare feet on cold stone.

Mathieu stepped up behind her, warm from sleep and wholly unbothered by the chill. His arms wrapped around her waist with slow certainty, drawing her back against him until the line of his body curved to hers. She felt his lips brush the place where her neck met her shoulder—a kiss, soft and low, like a secret.

"Morning, Your Majesty," he murmured, voice still rough with sleep.

"You've never once called me that in earnest."

"You like it better when I say it like I'm the only one who's allowed to."

A quiet huff of laughter escaped her.

She leaned back into him, savoring the weight of him behind her. The press of his palm against her stomach. The way he sighed when he breathed her in.

They stood there in silence for a moment, overlooking the mist-veiled gardens—Élodie still curled beneath the trees, Laurent circling like a sentry in the sky.

Mathieu's chin came to rest lightly on her shoulder. "She hasn't shifted in days."

"I know."

"Laurent either?"

"No. Though I saw him land briefly on the parapet yesterday. Looked down at me like I owed him a debt."

"You do," he said. "You owe him the respect of letting him brood dramatically in peace."

She tilted her head, giving him a sideways glance. "Are you saying I should coddle him?"

"I'm saying you should let him win a single argument one of these years. It might shock him back to human form."

Améliane let out a soft, dry laugh. "I'll add it to the list of impossible miracles."

Mathieu's arms tightened briefly, a subtle squeeze. "It's quieter lately."

"Yes," she said, quieter now.

Neither of them said Margot's name. They didn't need to.

After another pause, Améliane gently pulled his hands away and turned in his arms, lifting a brow as she gestured toward his very bare chest.

"You might consider putting on a robe before Renaud gets here. He's tolerating you better these days, but let's not test the limits of diplomacy."

Mathieu grinned, crooked and unrepentant. "You say that like he hasn't already walked in on worse."

"Mathieu—"

"I'm going," he said, pressing a final kiss to her forehead before stepping back. "But you'll miss the view."

She arched a brow. "You assume I haven't committed it to memory."

He laughed, low and warm, and padded toward the bathing chamber, the door swinging shut behind him with a soft thud.

Right on cue, a knock echoed from the chamber door—three measured raps, heavier than the maid's.

Améliane smoothed the edge of her robe and moved into the sitting room, the early morning light filtering through pale curtains, casting gold across the breakfast tray. The smell of honeyed tea and lavender bread greeted her.

She opened the door herself.

Renaud stood straight-backed in a storm-grey tunic; his expression carved from stone, but his eyes softened when he saw her. He dipped his head slightly in greeting.

"Morning."

She gestured him in, voice low. "Come. Mathieu is dressing."

"Thank the gods," he muttered as he stepped inside, glancing once toward the inner chamber and then to the tea.

She motioned toward the seat opposite hers. "Eat something before you growl at someone less forgiving than me."

Renaud took the seat, and for a few breaths, neither of them spoke. The teapot steamed quietly between them. Outside, the castle groaned in its bones, ancient and listening.

Finally, Améliane spoke, voice steady. "I used to believe pain was a thing to endure. Something to push through and forget."

Renaud looked up, brow furrowed.

"But it leaves patterns," she said. "It reshapes how we speak. How we move. How we grieve." Her gaze shifted toward the garden again. "It becomes the shape of memory. And if we're not careful, the shape of legacy."

Renaud reached for his cup, fingers steady. "You're quite introspective this morning. What do you propose we do with those patterns?"

She met his eyes. "Trace it forward."

A pause.

"Make something of it. Make it mean something."

Renaud's gaze flicked toward the balcony, where the shadows of Élodie and Laurent still moved in silence.

Then, quietly, "We already are."

Mathieu had left them just after breakfast, a half-eaten pastry in one hand and a steaming cup of tea in the other. He'd pressed a kiss to Améliane's temple, murmuring something about a promising lead in one of the older tomes and the likelihood that the castle's original boundaries weren't fixed, but fluid. She'd nodded, touched his hand, and watched him vanish down the corridor toward the library with that scholar's gleam in his eye.

That had been an hour ago.

Now, Améliane stood with Renaud in the council chamber, the chill of obsidian beneath her palms grounding her as the chandeliers flickered above with low, unsettled magic. The room had taken on a strange stillness—a pressure in the air that hadn't been there the day before. Or even the hour before.

"The third floor staircase led to the bell tower this morning," Renaud muttered, arms crossed as he paced along the southern arch.

Améliane glanced toward one of the tall, silver-framed mirrors near the chamber's edge. "And the reflections?"

"Gone again," he said grimly. "Last night after sunset. Just darkness. And shapes."

Améliane's jaw tensed. "It's unraveling. We knew this would happen."

"We said it would happen," Renaud corrected. "But are we ready?"

Améliane didn't answer. Her thoughts had been circling the same unspoken fear for days. The curse continued to fray... Margot was gone...how long before Edric sensed it? How long before he came?

Before she could respond, the council doors slammed open with a crack like thunder.

Renaud's hand went to his sword in an instant, stepping forward—

—but he froze as Thorne appeared in the doorway, followed by a familiar figure moving with a limp and a grim set to his jaw.

"Cassien," Améliane whispered.

He was barely upright. His cloak was torn, his boots thick with mud. One arm cradled a sleeping child, while his other held steady the shoulder of his wife, who clutched a second child against her skirts. They looked wrecked—bone-tired, travel-worn, the kind of weary that she'd only ever seen in the faces of refugees fleeing to Belmara from the Frostlands.

And behind them—

A stranger.

A woman.

She moved like a blade unsheathed—tall, steel-eyed, wrapped in a dark coat that bore no sigil. Her hair was braided tight, streaked with silver and war-weathered calm. She didn't look around. She assessed. Silent, alert, unreadable. Standing just behind the family, not as if she were part of them—but guarding them. Watching everything.

Améliane was already moving.

"Cassien!" She crossed the room as he stumbled forward, catching him by the elbow before he could fall. His face crumpled—not with pain, but with the sharp, disbelieving relief of someone who had finally reached safety.

"What happened?" she asked.

Behind her, Renaud hadn't moved—his hand still on the hilt of his sword.

And his eyes on the stranger.

"Who the hell is *that*?" he asked, voice low and ready.

Cassien swayed slightly on his feet, and Améliane tightened her grip on his arm. The boy in his hold stirred with a soft whimper, and his wife—Evelyne, normally so composed—brushed a trembling hand down the back of the little girl beside her, whispering a reassurance that sounded more like prayer than comfort.

"I'm here," Améliane said quietly. "You're safe now. Just tell me what—"

The chamber doors hadn't fully closed when another figure stepped into view.

Mathieu.

Hair tousled, coat thrown hastily over a linen shirt, ink staining one fingertip. He paused just past the threshold, his gaze sweeping the room in a single practiced motion—first to the unfamiliar woman, then to the children, then to Améliane's hand still braced on Cassien's arm.

His expression didn't shift.

But his eyes sharpened.

"The castle told me something was amiss," he murmured, voice low, dry.

Cassien turned toward Mathieu, blinking at him like he hadn't seen him in years. "You're still here," he murmured.

Mathieu raised a brow. "Bit late for that revelation."

Cassien almost smiled—almost. Then he looked at Améliane again, and the weight behind his eyes returned like thunderclouds behind glass.

"Edric knows."

The words sucked the air from the room.

Renaud took a step forward, mouth tightening. "How?"

Cassien ran a hand down his face, and for the first time, they saw just how much he was unraveling—creased clothes, blood at the hem, one sleeve torn at the seam.

"It was the way he said my name," Cassien rasped. "Like he'd been practicing it in the dark."

Améliane felt her breath catch.

"He asked me to deliver a message to the Ordréan emissary," Cassien continued, voice tight, clipped. "Said it was delicate. That I was his most loyal courier." His mouth curled bitterly around the word. "He smiled when he said it. The kind of smile that doesn't reach the eyes. The kind that *knows*."

"Gods," Renaud muttered.

"I left the court within the hour. Didn't even pack. Just took Evelyne and the children and ran."

He drew a ragged breath, and his voice, which had held together like a soldier's shield until now, cracked at the edges.

"We slipped out through the parapets. There's a hidden stair behind the north turret of Miralys—the one used by the falconers in winter. Evelyne knew of it from her brother. We waited until the moon passed behind the spire, then crossed the roofline in silence, praying no one looked up."

He didn't look at Améliane as he said it—he was staring through her now, past her, into the cold memory of stone beneath his boots and the weight of his son's body clutched against his chest as they edged along a wall not meant for escape.

"The outer door was sealed. I had to pry it open with my dagger. Every heartbeat felt like it would give us away."

His voice faltered again, and this time when he blinked, there were tears in his eyes.

"We made it to the center of Caeravelle just before the bells tolled second watch. But the soldiers were everywhere. Someone must've seen us go."

Améliane moved to his side again, one hand light on his arm, steadying. But he wasn't finished.

"We cut through alleyways. Hid behind market stalls. At one point, we had to wade through the city canal to avoid a patrol." His jaw clenched. "My son coughed—just once. I thought it would cost us everything."

Evelyne made a soft sound, nearly a sob, and Améliane reached for her hand, guiding her gently to one of the council chamber chairs. Cassien followed in silence, only for his grip to slip slightly as the weight in his arms shifted.

Before he could stumble, Élodie was suddenly there—barefoot, breathless, human again. Her eyes were red-rimmed, and her braid half-undone, but she moved without hesitation, reaching to take the sleeping boy from Cassien's arms.

"I've got him," she whispered, smoothing a hand over his back. "Rest now."

Cassien's hands dropped to his sides, fingers trembling. He let Améliane guide him to a chair beside Evelyne, who was already cradling their daughter tightly in her lap.

Améliane poured tea from the silver pot that had been sitting, forgotten, on the sideboard. Her own hands were steady, though her throat felt tight. She pressed the warm porcelain cup into Cassien's hands.

He stared at it like he'd never seen tea before.

"It wasn't until the third night that they found us," he said softly. "I thought we were finished. Hooded figures in the shadows. No names. No crests. Just knives and questions. I told Evelyne to run with the children."

He looked up at them all, eyes hollow with the echo of fear.

"I thought we were going to die."

"But you didn't," Renaud said quietly.

"No," Cassien whispered. "Because they weren't Edric's men. They were ours."

A long silence fell across the room.

"They helped us vanish. Moved us from safehouse to safehouse—always at night, never the same route twice. They bled for us. Killed for us. And got us to the eastern pass in one piece."

He looked toward the woman behind him—the one who had yet to speak. She met his gaze with a quiet nod of acknowledgment.

"She met us halfway through the eastern pass," Cassien said, nodding toward the stranger. "Said she'd been watching the roads for anyone fleeing Miralys. Said you'd want to meet her."

"Who is she?" Mathieu asked, his voice like steel in velvet. He had moved to stand just beside Améliane now, shoulders squared—not possessive, but present.

The woman finally stepped forward. She didn't bow. Didn't smile.

Her voice was clear, even, and utterly unshaken.

"My name is Serenya Vale," she said. "Vice General of the Return."

Améliane met her gaze, and in that moment—silver eyes to storm-grey—two forces measured each other.

Neither blinked.

Before either woman could speak, a blur of gold swept through the high windows.

The air stirred sharply as claws scraped against the stone frame, followed by the unmistakable rush of beating wings. A golden hawk shot through the upper arches, sharp-eyed and untamed. Gasps echoed from the guards at the chamber doors.

Serenya moved instantly.

Her hand darted to her hip, steel flashing as she drew a slender dagger in one smooth motion. But before she could throw it, the hawk shimmered mid-air—light bending, feathers dissolving—and Laurent landed on the floor in a graceful roll, laughing as he came up in a crouch.

"Gods," he drawled, unbothered. "I've been a bird for two weeks, and that's the welcome I get?"

Serenya didn't lower the dagger immediately. Her grey eyes flicked to Améliane, then to Cassien, silently asking if this was... normal.

"It's just Laurent," Renaud muttered, rubbing a hand over his face. "You get used to it."

Laurent stretched as he stood, golden curls disheveled from the shift. He wore nothing but loose breeches and the self-satisfaction of someone thoroughly unbothered by reality.

"I heard shouting and thought I'd missed something dramatic." He dropped into the nearest chair without invitation, tossing one leg over the arm.

Améliane didn't dignify him with a reply.

Cassien, still pale, picked up where he'd left off, voice steadier now that his family was seated and safe.

"There's more," he looked to Serenya, then back at the queen.

"More of them are remembering you. Not just flashes or dreams anymore. Full visions."

"And not just Seers," Serenya added, finally sheathing the dagger. "Word is spreading through Belmara. Merchants, scribes, even guards loyal to the old line. Some claim they dreamed of her. Others say they simply... knew. Like waking from a long sleep."

"The Return's grown because of it," Cassien said. "Your name—your sigil—has become something bigger than a memory. It's a symbol now."

Améliane said nothing for a moment. Her chest rose, then fell. She looked at the others—Élodie, silent and pale, still cradling the boy. Laurent, inscrutable behind half-lidded eyes. Renaud, tense but alert. Mathieu, unmoving but present at her side. Thorne, standing guard by the doors.

"Also," Cassien said softly. "Before Edric discovered my betrayal... I overheard something. A conversation between him and Vaeril."

The name brought a chill with it. Cassien leaned forward, voice dropping, "Edric tried to come back."

The silence in the chamber became absolute.

"He tried to breach Eldrenoire's gates. He and Vaeril brought everything they had. Blood sigils. Mirrorwork. Sacrificial rites. Nothing worked."

"Because the curse is fraying," Améliane said. Not a question. A fact.

Cassien nodded. "He couldn't get in. And now he's unraveling. Furious. Desperate. I heard him say..." He swallowed. "I heard him say if the gates wouldn't open for him, he'd tear them down. That if he couldn't get back what was his—"

"He mistook marriage for ownership," Mathieu growled, quiet but firm.

Cassien's gaze flicked to him. "He doesn't see it that way. And he's ready to march. He's mobilizing troops—calling in debts from the northern generals. Whispering to Rothgar's enemies. He wants this place—whole or broken."

"And Rothgar?" Renaud asked.

"They know something's wrong in Belmara. Maybe not what. But they've increased their attacks along the border. They're testing us. They can smell the instability."

The air in the chamber felt thinner, suddenly. Heavier.

Améliane stepped away, mind racing.

And then—

A small voice, sleepy and soft, pierced the silence.

"Is that... the moon Queen?"

Everyone turned.

Cassien's daughter—barely five—was peeking over her mother's lap, wide eyes fixed on Améliane. She blinked once, rubbed her eyes, then smiled.

"You're real," she said, wonder in her voice.

Améliane's throat tightened.

She dropped to her knees before the girl, slow and gentle. The girl reached out, brushing her fingers along the edge of Améliane's robe where the sigil lay embroidered in silver thread.

"You're prettier than my dreams," she whispered.

Evelyne let out a quiet sob, turning her face into her hands.

Améliane smiled and rose slowly, the child's words echoing in her chest like a vow she hadn't dared make aloud.

She looked down at the girl and brushed a curl gently from her brow. "Then let's make sure the dreams mean something," she said quietly. "For all of us."

She turned back to the others, her expression composed but shadowed with thought. Her voice didn't rise, but it carried.

"You came with purpose," she said, eyes settling on the silent woman still standing behind Cassien's family. "And I believe it's time we heard it."

Serenya stepped forward.

Not hesitantly. Not with pride. But with the exact weight of a soldier who knew the cost of every word she was about to speak.

She removed her gloves, finger by finger, tucking them neatly into her belt. Then she clasped her hands behind her back and raised her chin slightly—just enough to meet Améliane's eyes on even ground.

"When the visions first began, they were scattered," she said. "Fragments, really. Half-formed names, broken reflections. A woman we couldn't place. A castle no one remembered. And a flower."

Her gaze swept across the room.

"The Seers were the first to understand. They didn't know your name, Majesty—but they remembered your sorrow. Your fury. Your sacrifice."

Cassien's children had gone quiet. Even the younger boy, newly awake, watched her with wide, blinking eyes.

"And when they began to speak of you, others began to remember. Merchants. Nobles. Midwives. Soldiers." Serenya's voice didn't rise, but it carried like a blade unsheathed. "We used to think memory was a gift. Now we know it's a weapon."

She turned her head, and the firelight caught the silver thread woven into the trim of her coat— a delicate embroidery of a flower with three pointed petals.

"Your moonlit tidelily sigil became the Moonlit Bloom. It became more than a sigil. It became a rallying cry. It became a promise."

A pause. Measured. Intentional.

"We now have operatives in every major province. Spy cells embedded across Belmara and beyond. Vorskyr. Mireath. Even Rothgar. Some are Seers. Others are simply... believers."

She looked to Améliane again, and this time, there was something gentler beneath the steel.

"They believe in the world you once ruled. And the one you still could."

She took a single step forward, the stone floor faintly echoing beneath her boot.

"The Return is no longer a whisper. It's a force. And it stands ready to protect you when you leave this place."

Serenya didn't flinch under their collective scrutiny. If anything, she looked galvanized by it—like she'd spent her life walking through fire and found steel in the ashes.

"Moon's Thorn leads us," she said plainly. "She's the Commander- General of the Return. The spine. The strategist. She doesn't chase thrones or titles—she builds the war that topples them."

Améliane's gaze sharpened. "And you?"

Serenya tilted her chin. "I carry her orders. I lead the forces. When her vision points, I move."

Renaud, ever the tactician, stepped forward, arms crossed. "How many?"

Serenya's answer came without hesitation. "Over nine thousand across the provinces. Trained fighters, informants, couriers, Shadowbinders maintaining the concealment network across three borders. More with each passing moon."

Mathieu whistled low under his breath. "You're not just resisting. You're preparing for siege."

"We're preparing to win," Serenya replied. "And we're doing it with structure. Each cell has its own lead. Each region its own vanguard. We have maps. Stockpiles. Strategic hold points. We've learned from every failure—and from every name Edric tried to erase."

She stepped toward the map table, voice hardening.

"The Moonlit Bloom is not a whisper anymore. It's painted on stones in Caeravelle. Carved into wood in children's hands in Belhollow. Stitched into tunics and banners across border towns. The people are remembering."

Améliane sat, slowly, the words pressing down like weight and lifting like wind all at once. "And you would shelter me."

Serenya nodded. "Not because we worship you. But because your fall broke the world, and your return might fix it. If you escape Eldrenoire, we will hide you, protect you, and ready the nation for what comes next."

Mathieu's voice cut in, low and cool. "You said magic is part of your network."

"We have all types," Serenya confirmed. "Seers guide our vision. Runeformers craft spells into steel and stone. Mirrorweavers manipulate light and reflection—our best spies. Naturebinders keep our outposts alive in places Edric's forces won't go. And Shadowbinders keep us unseen."

Renaud's brow rose slightly. "A full magical corps?"

"Not all trained. Not all born with it. But enough. And we're learning. Every day."

Serenya looked to Améliane again. Her voice, this time, quieted.

"We're ready to help you escape. But when you do, this war will begin in earnest. Edric won't just send shadows next time. He'll send fire."

The room fell still, each of them parsing the gravity of it.

Améliane didn't respond right away. Her gaze remained fixed on Serenya, but something shifted behind her eyes. A flicker of something quieter than fear, but heavier than doubt.

"You shouldn't have come," she said finally. Her voice was calm. Too calm. "You do realize that, don't you? Once you pass through Eldrenoire's gates... you don't leave. Not unless the curse permits it."

Serenya's expression didn't change. But there was something in the way she straightened, a subtle readiness—as though she had expected this and filed the risk away long before stepping foot inside.

"I knew the cost," she said. "I knew it before I stepped through the mist."

"And you still came?" Améliane asked, incredulous.

"I waited in the eastern pass for weeks," Serenya said evenly. "Our spies reported that Edric's messenger had a unique ability. That he was the only one—other than Edric himself—who could purposely find the gate. Turns out the messenger had a name."

Her eyes slid to Cassien, who looked deeply uncomfortable under the sudden attention.

"Luckily, he was in the mood for help," Serenya added. "Otherwise, I would've had to stalk him here and use force if necessary."

Mathieu let out a short breath, somewhere between a huff and a laugh. "Charming."

Serenya didn't blink. "Effective."

Améliane's fingers tightened slightly around the edge of the table.

"And now that you're here?" she asked.

Serenya finally stepped closer—not threateningly, but with purpose.

"Now," she said, "we find out if we can break the curse. Or bend it. Or exploit the fractures before Edric does."

She paused, gaze sweeping the room.

"But I need to know exactly what we're working with."

Her next words came more carefully, deliberate.

"The curse. Its mechanics. Its limits. Its cost. Whatever you know—whatever you suspect—we need to understand it. Together."

She didn't posture. Didn't plead. She asked. And waited.

The air shifted.

Améliane felt it first in the mirrors—those ancient sentinels tucked in the corners of the council chamber, their surfaces shimmering faintly though no candle had flickered, no breeze stirred. A ripple, like breath across water.

Eldrenoire was listening.

Mathieu stepped forward from the archway, a leather-bound journal clutched in one hand, the scent of ink and old vellum clinging to him like second skin. His coat was dusted with ash from the hearth in the library, and his hair still bore the ghost of sleep despite the glint in his eyes.

"The Black Keep knows," he said softly. "And I think it's ready."

Everyone turned to look at him—Renaud, still standing near the door next to Thorne with a hand on the hilt of his sword; Serenya, poised and unreadable; Cassien and

Evelyne, seated close but tense, like they'd forgotten what peace felt like. Even Laurent, half-sprawled in a chair, straightened slightly.

Mathieu crossed to the table and spread his journal open, revealing a page thick with sketched glyphs, mirrorbound sigils, and notations layered in three different inks.

"The Mirrorbind," he began, voice steady, "was never designed to imprison."

"It was built to reflect," Mathieu continued, fingers tracing a symbol—a spiral broken at one edge. "To echo truths. To confront. To hold a person within themselves, not trap them outside the world."

He looked up, eyes sweeping the gathered room. "Which is why it's weakening."

"Three things are pressing against it," Mathieu continued, tapping the parchment for emphasis. "First—me. The Wyrdbound. I don't fully understand what that means yet, but I know this: Eldrenoire lets me go where it shouldn't. Doors open when I speak. Secrets unfold because I ask. The castle doesn't bind me the way it binds others."

He paused, then added, "That's not freedom. It's invitation."

Serenya folded her arms. "And the second pressure?"

"The Return," Mathieu said. "People remember her."

He looked at Améliane as he said it, and she felt the weight of his gaze like a tide pulling against stone.

"They remember the Queen. That puts pressure on the curse from the outside. Memory is a tether, and too many threads have begun to pull."

"And the third?" Laurent asked, voice low.

Mathieu turned the journal around so they could all see.

"The Mirrorbind is rooted in emotional symmetry," he said. "Its magic responds to truth—not power, not strength. But truth. That's why wanderers trapped here are sometimes offered the Blood Oath. The person who stands at the gate and gives something of themselves, faces what they've denied, what they've run from—that person might pass."

He stepped back, letting that settle. The room felt impossibly still.

"But—" he added.

Of course there was a but.

"The curse reacts violently to lies. If you approach the gate for the wrong reasons—selfishness, denial, desperation without reckoning—it fights back. Not with force. With unraveling."

A cold silence fell.

Améliane stepped forward, her voice barely a breath. "What does that mean?"

Mathieu's eyes met hers, and for once, he didn't soften the truth.

"It means the gate doesn't answer to desperation," he said. "Not to fear. Not even to hope."

Mathieu closed the journal with a soft thud that echoed more than it should have.

"It opens only to those who face themselves first. Who carry nothing but the truth when they step forward."

He looked up, voice barely above a whisper now.

"Anything else... and the curse won't let you pass. It'll strip you bare and leave nothing behind."

Silence fell and it was the heavy kind—thick with breath held and meaning unspoken. Even the mirrors along the chamber walls seemed to dim, their reflections softening like they, too, were absorbing the words.

No one moved at first.

Then Élodie stepped forward, green eyes hard.

"So if we're not pure of heart, we die?" she asked, voice edged in disbelief. "That's your theory?"

"No," Mathieu replied calmly. "Not pure. Just... honest. If you go to the gate carrying lies—about who you are, about what you've done—it reacts. It was never built to trap us. But it won't be fooled."

Laurent scoffed from his seat near the hearth. "And who decides what counts as truth? The castle?" He gestured vaguely to the dark stone walls. "Eldrenoire hasn't exactly been impartial."

"It doesn't decide," Mathieu said. "It reveals. The magic is mirrorborn—it doesn't judge you. It reflects you. The judgment is what comes after."

A beat.

Renaud stood slowly, shoulders tense beneath his uniform. "Then what do we do? Line up and confess our sins like schoolchildren and hope the gate deems us worthy?"

"No," Améliane said softly, her voice cutting through the growing noise. "We decide what we carry. And what we're willing to let go of."

That stilled the room again.

Serenya's gaze was sharp. "And if someone's truth is ugly? If they've done things they regret?"

Mathieu didn't look away. "Then they'll need to face it. Not justify it. Not bury it. Just face it."

The fire cracked. A candle guttered.

Thorne broke the silence. "If this works... if the curse really lets us through...is it all at once? Or one at a time?"

"I don't know," Mathieu admitted. "But the spell has always responded to individuals. The court was cursed as a whole—but the gate is personal. I think... we'll have to go one by one."

More murmurs. Someone cursed under their breath. Others turned inward, the weight of what had been said sinking like stones in their gut.

Améliane stood, tall and still, her expression unreadable.

"We've all carried truths we tried to forget," she said. "But if this is our way out... then we'll face them. Together."

Élodie, always the sharpest blade in the sheath, let out a slow breath. "Well," she said, dragging a hand through her hair. "I suppose we should all start sorting out what truths we're afraid to admit."

Thorne grunted. "Shouldn't take more than a decade or two."

A few quiet chuckles rippled through the chamber, brittle and brief—but real.

Laurent's voice broke the silence.

"You said I could be the first," he reminded her, not unkindly. "When Mathieu shared what he'd found. You looked me in the eye and said I could be the one to try."

The words were not a challenge. Not a dare. Just truth, placed gently between them.

Améliane closed her eyes for a breath, the weight of the moment thick on her shoulders. She had been queen long enough to know when resolve couldn't be turned aside. And this—this wasn't impulsiveness. This was conviction.

She looked at him again—truly looked. The exhaustion that clung behind his usual bravado. The quiet determination that burned just beneath his icy gaze.

"I remember what I said," she murmured. "And I meant it. I still do."

Mathieu said nothing, but his hand brushed lightly against hers beneath the table. She took strength from the gesture.

"You'll have your chance," Améliane said at last, her voice low but resolute. "In two days."

A flicker of surprise crossed Laurent's face. "Two? Why not now?"

"We need time," she said. "For Cassien's family to rest. To prepare the rest of the court for what's coming. And for one last dinner, in your honor—should the gate open... or not."

Laurent's bravado softened into something quieter. "You're giving me a farewell party?"

"I'm giving you a promise," she said. "That we won't let you face it alone."

He held her gaze for a moment longer, then inclined his head.

"Two days," he agreed.

CHAPTER 40

Mathieu

The upper corridors of Eldrenoire were quiet—but not empty.

Silence here never meant stillness. The castle breathed in its own way: stone shifting beneath velvet drapes, magic pulsing behind the seams of mirrors. This morning, it was particularly alert. Watchful. The sconces along the east wing flared with soft blue fire as Mathieu passed, though he hadn't touched them. Tapestries that once sagged now hung straight and taut, their edges pinned as if bracing for something.

Even the dust—normally a persistent layer over half-forgotten finery—had vanished from the floors.

Mathieu's boots made no sound as he turned toward the old tower staircase, his steps practiced, his hands tucked into the folds of a worn coat. He knew every creak and curve by now, but the walls still shifted slightly, subtly, like a house adjusting its bones. He didn't flinch. He had long since learned that resistance made the castle restless.

At the landing, he paused.

A mirror hung on the far wall—one that hadn't reflected cleanly in the almost two years he'd been there. Usually, it showed his face distorted and fogged, as if the castle resented his presence. This morning, it was clear.

Unsettlingly so.

He stared into it, expecting the familiar blur. Instead, he saw himself exactly as he was—his favorite coat frayed with use, beard shadowing a jaw carved deeper by worry than time. His own eyes looked back at him, tired and hazel and unblinking.

It felt like a challenge.

He exhaled and turned away, ascending the final spiral into the library.

The scent hit him first—old parchment, melted wax, and salt. Always salt, though no one knew why. Perhaps the castle remembered the sea. Or mourned it.

Books towered in precarious stacks where he'd left them. Scrolls lay unraveled across two tables. The center chamber had become more war room than archive in recent weeks—arcane notations scrawled across chalkboards; incantation fragments tacked to velvet walls with silver pins. He passed them all without stopping.

Instead, he crossed to the western alcove—the one with the broken sun window—and lowered himself into the high-backed chair beneath it. The seat creaked beneath his weight. Not from age, but from familiarity.

He'd sat here often enough for the wood to remember him.

Mathieu pulled a leather-bound volume from the stack beside him. It wasn't one of the cursed ones—not enchanted to bleed ink or erase memory. Just a record of noble lineages, obscure and dry. But it was the first book Améliane had handed him when she asked for his help.

He opened it slowly, fingers lingering over the brittle paper. The ink had faded in places, but one name stood out as clearly as ever. Améliane Morvenne.

He whispered it aloud.

The sound stirred something in the rafters. A soft sigh of wind that wasn't wind at all.

Her name carried weight in this place. It always had.

He leaned back in the chair, resting the book across his knees, and let his eyes drift closed for a moment. He had done what he came to do. The research was complete. The theory had held. The Mirrorbind was weakening, and not by accident.

But knowledge was a safer battlefield. Books didn't bleed. Now the next move belonged to someone else.

To Laurent.

Mathieu's jaw tensed. Of all people to volunteer...

He knew why Laurent had done it. Bravado, yes, but also something older. Something fractured that wore charm like armor. But even knowing that didn't make it easier. If the curse rejected him...

Mathieu scrubbed a hand through his hair and stared at the ceiling, watching faint light filter through the fractured glass above.

The Mirrorbind didn't respond to cleverness—it responded to surrender. Mathieu and Améliane had discussed letting him walk through the gate first, but nothing in their research guaranteed he could return. And with the curse unraveling thread by thread, it was a risk they couldn't afford to take.

And maybe Laurent—messy, volatile, unbreakable Laurent—had surrendered more than any of them realized.

Mathieu didn't know how to protect him from that.

He opened the book again, not to read, but to let the silence hold him. Around him, the library creaked gently in response. The chandelier swayed. A book fell off a shelf in the far corner—but didn't hit the floor. It simply... hovered there, waiting.

And the clock, though silent, had begun to count down.

Mathieu exhaled once through his nose and stood. The others would be gathering soon, and if the castle was listening, it only made sense he be there to hear what came next.

Mathieu walked slowly through the guest wing, hands in his coat pockets, his boots silent against the inlaid marble. Eldrenoire was behaving itself—for now. No flickering lanterns. No shifting stairwells. Just the usual hum of watchfulness that had become the castle's version of serenity.

And then, a sound that stopped him mid-step.

A child's laughter.

High, unguarded, and utterly unfamiliar.

He paused just short of the guest quarters, drawn to the open curve of a shadowed archway. The laughter came again—giggling, soft and tumbling, followed by a quiet shushing and the creak of an old rocking chair.

Mathieu moved closer, positioning himself just beyond the view of the doorway. He wasn't hiding exactly. Just... observing. Thorne would've called it reconnaissance. He called it curiosity with plausible deniability.

The door opened slightly with a soft click. Serenya Vale stepped out—her movements precise, her posture unyielding. She shut the door behind her with a quiet finality, and as she turned, she caught sight of him in the shadows.

Her eyes didn't widen. She didn't flinch.

Behind her, just through the cracked door, he glimpsed Evelyne—barefoot, swaying gently as she hummed to the baby on her shoulder. Cassien sat nearby in a slumped armchair, head tipped back, lips parted in exhausted sleep. Their little girl was curled at his feet, clutching a threadbare plush fox.

It looked... human. Soft, even. And that, more than anything, was unsettling.

Mathieu glanced back at Serenya. "They seem whole. That feels like a miracle in itself."

"They're not," she said, adjusting the strap of her shoulder guard. "But they're here. Sometimes that's all survival means."

He nodded once, silently agreeing, then fell into step beside her as she began walking toward the council chamber.

After a beat of silence, he said, "I figured you for a Seer, not a soldier."

"I have magic, and I am a soldier," she replied without hesitation. "But neither title is what brought me to the Return."

He glanced sideways. "No?"

"I was born in Kireth. The daughter of a stonemason and a tutor," she said, her tone measured and without embellishment. "No noble blood. No great tragedy. Just a quiet life—until Edric's enforcers came hunting for 'unregistered casters.' They took my mother first."

Mathieu's steps slowed slightly. "She had magic?"

"She had knowledge. In Belmara, those are often considered the same crime." She didn't look at him as she said it. "I was seventeen. I ran."

Mathieu didn't try to offer sympathy. He'd learned long ago that people like Serenya didn't need it—or want it.

"So what kind are you?" he asked instead. "Magic, I mean."

Her lips twitched faintly. ". Runeformer. Wards, mostly. I build safe houses, break bindings, reinforce glamours. I'm the reason most of our spies live long enough to report back."

"A specialist," he mused. "Let me guess—you label your maps, keep backup knives, and think sarcasm is a waste of breath?"

This time, she looked at him. "Only when it's not useful."

He grinned. "I'm insulted."

"You'll recover," she said dryly.

They reached the outer corridor just outside the council chamber. The doors were still closed, but voices murmured behind them—Élodie's, possibly Renaud's.

Serenya paused, her gaze flicking down the hall toward the castle's east wing. "It's strange," she said softly. "This place is beautiful. In the way a weapon is beautiful."

Mathieu folded his arms. "It's more than that. Or it wants to be."

She looked at him again, eyes narrowing slightly. "You speak of it like it's sentient."

He didn't deny it. "If you've been here long enough, you stop doubting it."

Another moment passed.

Then, more carefully, she asked, "And you? Why did you stay? If you weren't trapped like the others?"

He hesitated—but only for a moment.

"Because someone had to find the way out," he said. "And because the one person I couldn't leave behind was still here."

Serenya's expression didn't shift, but something in her eyes changed. Not warmth. But recognition.

"You're a fool," she said quietly.

"Absolutely," he agreed. "But the useful kind."

The doors to the chamber opened with a slow groan.

The Hall of Voices had not existed the day before.

Mathieu was sure of it. So was everyone else.

It had appeared sometime after the final strategy session—an arched corridor in the north wing that hadn't opened in years simply... breathed open. Like the castle had been holding its breath and finally exhaled. No one summoned it. No magic key or whispered phrase. Just a hallway where there hadn't been one, and at the end of it—a vaulted chamber built of duskstone and spell-glass, tall enough for the whispers of history to echo back at themselves.

The planning had finished late the night before. Hours of maps and pacing, logistics and late tea. They were in alignment, shockingly so. Even Élodie hadn't argued, and Renaud—though clenched-jawed and conservative—had conceded that if anyone could test the gate, it was Laurent. A fact that clearly gave him ulcers.

They'd tried to summon Alaric when the Hall appeared to no avail. The man—or the creature that wore his skin—remained elusive. And that, perhaps more than anything, set the castle humming.

Now, with midday light slanting through enchanted windows and every surface quietly gleaming as if freshly polished, the cursed court gathered for the first time in years.

They filled the newly revealed Hall of Voices shoulder to shoulder—servants, guards, courtiers, scholars, stable hands, the falconer and his birds perched high in the rafters like silent witnesses. Over a hundred and fifty souls, each one marked by the spell that had trapped them here, each one carrying eight and a half years of quiet longing and deepening dread.

Mathieu stood just behind Améliane and her inner circle, near a pillar etched in sigils he hadn't seen before. Likely protective. Possibly reactive.

He said nothing as Améliane stepped forward. All eyes followed her like compass needles to true north.

She didn't raise her voice. She didn't need to.

Her silver-threaded robe whispered as she moved. Her crown—not the one from Belmara, but a new thing born of this place—sat low over her brow, its mirrored crescent catching the light. She stood not as a victim of the curse that trapped them all here, but as its inevitable unraveling.

"I owe you truth," she said.

Silence settled over the crowd, thick and crystalline.

"For too long, we've endured this curse without understanding it. We have waited. Endured. Adapted. Some of us have disappeared. Others... changed. But no more."

She paused.

"This castle is bound by a spell called a Mirrorbind. It was not meant to imprison—but to reflect. To echo truth. But the man who cursed me—who cursed all of us—twisted it into a prison."

Murmurs rippled. Somewhere, a goblet clinked too loud. A falcon cried above, as if in answer.

Mathieu's gaze swept the room, quietly cataloging the reactions.

Élodie, standing off to Améliane's right, held a porcelain cup between her hands—grip tight enough to crack it if she weren't careful. Her expression was neutral, but her shoulders were set like a blade waiting for use.

Renaud stood to the queen's left, arms crossed, eyes scanning the crowd like a tactician anticipating revolt. The only sign of unease was the way his jaw flexed—tight, then tighter.

Sabine, farther back near the outer arc of the hall, hadn't blinked since Améliane began. Thorne was beside her, eyes narrowed, as though trying to see the spell itself and trace its seams.

And Laurent...

Laurent stood near the dais steps, as if awaiting a cue that had not yet come. His gaze hadn't left Améliane since she began. When she said "twisted," his brow furrowed.

When she said "prison," he flinched. And when her voice broke—just a little, only for a heartbeat—he looked at her like a sword being forged.

Mathieu felt it like a stone dropping into water.

Améliane went on. But her voice, when it returned, had shifted. Not in pitch, but in weight. She was no longer simply sharing a theory. Now she was giving them the truth they had ached for—and the warning they hadn't known to dread.

"You've all felt it," she said. "The castle shifting. The walls growing longer. Mirrors where there weren't mirrors. Doors that shouldn't open. Lights that flicker in time with no rhythm but memory."

A ripple moved through the room—not words. Just recognition. Heads turned. Spines straightened. One of the stable hands near the back muttered something under his breath and clutched his pendant.

"The magic that binds Eldrenoire is no longer static," Améliane continued. "It is waking. Reacting. Not only to us—but to the world beyond these walls."

She paused, letting that hang.

Then she turned slightly, gesturing toward Cassien and the dark-skinned woman standing beside him like shadowed iron.

"This is Cassien Montrel, who served Edric in the capital until it became clear his loyalty lay not with the usurper—but with the truth."

A murmur of recognition rippled—soft, but startled. Mathieu caught someone whispering *the king's messenger?* in disbelief.

"And this," Améliane said, her tone deepening, "is Vice General Serenya Vale, commander of a rebellion that calls itself The Return."

Now came the whispers. Not gasps—but breathless, wide-eyed silence. Mathieu felt the shift. The thrum of curiosity tinged with wonder, with fear.

Améliane spoke over it all, her voice gaining the quiet, devastating clarity of a tide pulling back before it crashes.

"For eight years, we believed the world had forgotten us. That our names were erased. That Edric's spell had buried us beneath time and silence."

She took a breath.

"But the curse is fraying. Because people are remembering."

She let that land.

Mathieu glanced around the hall and noted it: the way two footmen stiffened like they'd forgotten how to breathe. A kitchen maid clutched the back of the person beside her. Someone dropped a cup.

"Outside these walls," Améliane continued, "a movement has risen. Small at first. Carried by Seers—those who dream of the past and wake with names on their tongues that should've been lost. Names like mine. Names like yours."

Someone inhaled sharply. The sound was unmistakably a stifled sob.

"They are remembering Belmara as it was. They are remembering this court. And with every name recalled, every sigil redrawn, every whispered vow to their rebellion symbol, the Moonlit Bloom, the curse weakens."

She turned back toward the dais.

"The Return has spies across every province. Fighters. Scholars. Shadowbinders, Mirrorweavers, Seers. Runeformers who cast protective wards across rebel camps. They wear my sigil in the streets. They deface Edric's statues. They teach children stories of a queen stolen from her throne and a loyal court cursed alongside her."

She looked out across the room, her gaze sharper now. Cutting through awe to strike at bone-deep belief.

"They are waiting for us."

Mathieu's throat felt too tight.

Even he, who had already heard it all, who had helped her shape this message in the long hours of candlelit planning, felt it strike again as if new. Raw. Holy.

"We have not been forgotten," Améliane said, voice low but ringing with promise. "And we are not alone."

The silence that followed was no longer stunned—it was seismic. Not the stillness of fear, but of recognition.

The Hall of Voices, true to its name, had erupted into murmurs. Disbelief. Hope. Anxious dread shaped into tentative questions.

Mathieu watched as a servant whispered something to the woman beside her, who clutched her apron like a lifeline. A stable boy looked openly afraid. One of the footmen was crying.

It was too much, too fast—and not fast enough.

Améliane raised a hand. The stillness that followed her gesture was instant and complete.

"There's more," she said. "And you need to hear it before fear decides what you believe."

She turned slightly, her eyes landing on Mathieu—and for the briefest second, something in him stilled. Not under command. Not from fear. But from the soft ache of being seen.

"Mathieu Duran has spent the better part of the past year buried in Eldrenoire's libraries—most of which were intentionally corrupted or cloaked by the curse. But he found what was meant to stay hidden."

Eyes turned toward him. He did not shift under their weight, but his jaw flexed once, silent acknowledgment.

"The curse that binds this castle is called a Mirrorbind," Améliane said. "As I mentioned before, it was never meant to be a prison. It was meant to reflect. But Edric twisted it into a cage."

A sharp intake of breath across the chamber. In the far corner, a knight who had once served her father gripped the edge of a stone pillar as if to stay upright.

"But reflection has rules," she continued. "And one of them is this: truth cannot be held forever. Eventually, it must shine through."

She turned to the dais, lifting her chin slightly.

"We have learned—through records hidden in mirrored script, through maps and shifting spells—that the gate out of Eldrenoire is tied not to time, or to desire... but to truth. A person who walks to it with a reckoning in their heart, tethered to both the past and present, may pass through."

A new hush fell—deeper this time. Heavy with gravity.

"Not to flee. Not to escape. But to surrender to what is real."

Mathieu watched the realization ripple through the room. And then—because it had to be said—Améliane gave them the final truth.

"Someone has offered to test this theory."

She didn't pause for drama. Only long enough to let the weight settle.

"Laurent Volayne."

There was no gasp, no audible outcry. Just a shift in energy—as though even the air itself had drawn taut with alarm.

Mathieu's eyes sought Laurent across the chamber. He gave the faintest nod to the crowd—no flourish. No speech. Just silent confirmation that yes, this risk would be his.

"He will approach the gate tomorrow morning. And tonight," Améliane went on, her voice softening without losing any of its clarity, "we gather in the Grand Hall for a celebration. Not of certainty. Not of victory. But of choice."

She glanced again toward Laurent.

"We honor the courage of one who will walk forward not to escape—but to face what comes."

The Hall of Voices held still.

Not just with silence. But with something heavier.

Hope.

Real. Terrifying. Fragile.

Mathieu stood among them all, heart heavy with admiration and dread.

And for the first time since he arrived at Eldrenoire, he believed they might actually leave this place.

The Grand Hall had always been beautiful in a way that unnerved—vaulted ceilings etched with constellations no star-map could claim, mirrors inlaid with silver lines that shifted when you weren't looking, and chandeliers that floated without flame, aglow with cold, elegant magic. But tonight, the room was warm.

He lingered near the edge of it, not seated yet, watching as servants poured wine into glass goblets rimmed with silver. The long dining table gleamed beneath the flickering lights—each place set with mismatched finery drawn from different centuries. Platters of roasted game, fruits jeweled in syrup, sugared flowers, and golden pastries lined the table in an opulent display of excess.

None of it was new. He'd seen most of it before in forgotten pantries and sideboards—but Améliane had curated it tonight. Chosen each detail. Crafted the mood like a woman trying to hold back fate with the right pairing of wine and candlelight.

As if enough beauty could rewrite what came next.

He caught sight of her at the far end of the hall—her robe a deep ocean silver, unbelted at the waist, her hair twisted into soft coils that shimmered like moonlight on water. She was speaking with a pair of former knights, one of whom looked like he might cry. And still, she smiled. Gently. Like she saw them not as they were, but as they had been.

As they might be again.

Mathieu's gaze drifted and found Élodie.

She was laughing—*actually* laughing—at something Laurent said, her head tipped back, wine glass half-raised. Thorne, seated beside her, tried not to smile. He failed.

Renaud looked like he'd rather be anywhere else, but made the effort to stay. He sat across from Serenya Vale, and the two of them radiated enough unspoken judgment and cold competence to frost the goblets between them.

Sabine had claimed a seat just beyond them, picking at a plate of figs with surgical precision, her eyes scanning the hall like she was preparing for a diagnosis none of them wanted to hear.

Laurent, as always, was in the center of it all.

Louder than necessary. Sharper than required. Wine already spilling from his second glass as he recounted a truly questionable story involving a cursed harp, a startled goat, and a very patient stable boy. Laughter rolled around him, but Mathieu watched closely. Studied the edge in his voice. The forced brightness.

He wondered what it cost to be that radiant on the eve of walking into the unknown.

Mathieu didn't eat much. He'd filled a plate mostly to avoid questions, but it sat untouched. His attention drifted always to the edges—the weight behind every laugh, the way even the mirrors along the vaulted walls seemed to lean in. Listening.

A shift in light and soft rustle of fabric beside him brought him back to the present. Améliane had crossed the room unnoticed, as only she could. She didn't announce her arrival, didn't draw attention—just slid gracefully into the empty seat at his side, her goblet cradled lightly in her hands.

"You're brooding," she said.

Mathieu didn't look at her. "I'm watching."

"Same thing, with more syllables," she murmured, and took a sip of wine.

He huffed a laugh through his nose. "Careful. Keep talking like that, and someone might realize you actually enjoy my company."

She arched a brow. "Someone might think I've been drinking."

"You *have* been drinking."

"Not enough," she said, then tipped her head slightly to glance at him. "You didn't eat."

"I wasn't hungry."

"You're lying."

"I'm *observing*," he said, leaning back in his chair. "And possibly being slowly unmade by existential dread. It's hard to tell the difference."

That earned a quiet laugh. Not much of one. But real.

They sat in silence for a moment, the soft din of the dinner washing around them.

"You were magnificent," Mathieu said suddenly.

She glanced at him, surprised.

"In the Hall of Voices," he added. "Commanding, eloquent, unnervingly calm. Very regal. I almost bowed."

"You *did* bow," she said.

"Exactly. I blame you entirely."

Her smile didn't fade, but it softened. "Thank you."

More silence. Then—

"He shouldn't be the one to do it," Mathieu said quietly. "We both know that."

"No," she agreed. "But I don't think we could have kept him from trying. And I promised."

Mathieu's jaw tightened. "He makes jokes. Performs for the court. But I've seen what he's hiding under all that charm."

"So have I."

"He's not ready."

"No one is," she said gently. "That's the point."

He looked at her then—really looked. The shadows of the hall danced across her features, softening the lines of grief and steel that had carved themselves into her over the years. But her eyes were clear. Unflinching.

She reached for his hand beneath the table, and her fingers were warm against his.

"I know you want to protect him," she said. "So do I. But this is his truth to face. And his to offer."

Mathieu swallowed hard. "And what if it's a death sentence?"

"Then we will mourn him together," she murmured looking away as her eyes shimmered, glassy but defiant. "And we will fight harder for the rest."

He closed his eyes briefly, then nodded.

"You're too calm," he muttered.

"I'm faking it."

"That makes two of us."

She smiled again, just a hint of it. "You should eat something."

"If I die of anxiety, at least I'll fit in my best coat."

She snorted softly. "You're an idiot."

"I'm kidding. Mostly."

She leaned in, brushing a kiss to the corner of his mouth—soft, fleeting. "Behave."

He smirked. "You're going to have to be more specific. In general? Or just tonight?"

"In public."

He made a show of glancing at the table, then back to her. "Debatable."

"You're impossible," she said, but her thumb traced the edge of his hand. "Try the tart. It's your favorite."

"Am I your favorite?"

"You ask that like you haven't already stolen my bed, my library, and the allegiance of my court."

"So that's a yes."

She rolled her eyes, but the curve of her mouth said everything.

Mathieu exhaled, gaze drifting back to the table where Laurent now spun a story with wild hand gestures and a half-eaten tart in his other hand.

"I hate that it's him," he said.

"I know," she said quietly. "But he deserves to be seen. To be brave. And... to be believed in."

They sat like that a moment longer, hand in hand beneath the table, until Améliane rose—leaving behind the warmth of her palm like an echo.

The room hushed with the ease of long habit. Even now, even here, her court knew when to listen.

Her voice carried, clear but warm.

"We have lived in stillness for eight years," she said. "Some of us have found purpose in that stillness. Some of us have lost pieces of ourselves to it. But tonight... we mark movement."

Her gaze landed on Laurent, who offered her a lazy two-fingered salute in return.

"Tomorrow, we test what has never been tested," she continued. "Not with desperation—but with courage. And not alone—but as a court, as a family, as witnesses to what may come."

Her voice dipped slightly, just enough for intimacy.

"I do not know what the gate will ask of you, Laurent Volayne. I only know what you've already given us."

A long silence followed.

Then she lifted her glass.

"To the brave. To the stubborn. To the ones who walk forward when the rest of us aren't ready."

Mathieu watched her eyes as she looked at Laurent—and saw, for the first time, what she truly felt.

Love. And not just for Laurent—for all of them. This strange, broken court she had shielded and carried, even when she herself was shattered.

Laurent stood, exaggeratedly slow, and hoisted his glass.

"To riddles dressed as queens," he began, smirking. "To castles that hum ominously in their sleep. To cursed courts who are, somehow, more loyal than they are sane."

A few chuckles rippled.

Then his smile softened, and he tipped his glass toward the center of the room.

"To the end of mirrors," he said. "And the start of windows."

The room stilled.

The toast hung in the air like a spell not yet spoken—and Mathieu felt the castle shift. Just a pulse. Just a flicker. But it was there.

Eldrenoire had heard it too. He set his own glass down untouched.

Hope is a dangerous thing to feed a place like this, he thought.

CHAPTER 41

Améliane

D awn had not yet broken, but the sky was already beginning to pale—smudged with lavender and bone-grey at the horizon's edge. The windows of Améliane's chambers remained closed, their sheer curtains stirring with the breath of a castle that never truly slept.

She woke to warmth. Mathieu's body curved behind hers, one arm draped low around her waist, the other folded beneath his head. His breath was steady against the back of her neck, slow and even, his chest rising with a rhythm she had come to know as well as her own.

When she shifted slightly, stretching her legs beneath the coverlet, she felt him stir.

"You're awake," she murmured.

"I never slept," he said, his voice low and rough with fatigue. "You did, though. For almost three hours."

She smiled despite the weight in her chest. "If you're going to mock me, at least do it after I've had tea."

"I wouldn't dream of it," he said solemnly. Then, after a beat, "Well, maybe a little."

She rolled to face him, eyes adjusting slowly to the dim light. He looked tired. Not just from lack of sleep, but from something older. Worn. His dark hair was tousled, a faint scar along his cheekbone catching what little light the room offered.

"I checked everything again," he said, answering the question she hadn't yet asked. "The research. The cadence of the spellwork."

She didn't interrupt.

"Thorne double-checked the binding sequence," he went on. "Élodie looked over all of it...again. Even Sabine and Laurent double-checked what we double-checked."

She reached for his hand beneath the covers, threading their fingers together. He held on tightly.

"It should be me," he whispered, not looking at her. "I'm the one the spell won't touch. The one who doesn't belong here. But that's the problem. The curse doesn't recognize me. It won't test me. And that makes me... useless when it matters most."

"You're not useless," she said firmly. "You're the reason we understand the curse at all."

"That won't matter if he dies," Mathieu said, finally meeting her eyes.

A long silence followed. Neither moved.

Then—soft footsteps outside. A knock on the chamber door.

Élodie's voice, deceptively sweet through the door, "Shall I use the jasmine oil today, Your Majesty?"

Améliane blinked—and laughed. A short, surprised sound that cracked the dread for half a breath.

"You're a menace," she called back.

"You're welcome," came the retort, already fading as Élodie walked away.

Améliane sat up slowly, drawing the covers with her. "Come on," she said to Mathieu. "Before she sends in reinforcements."

He stood with her, stretching briefly before following her to the adjoining chamber.

The bathing room was still and warm, faint steam curling from the sunken tub. Candles flickered in their sconces, casting soft gold across the tile. A robe waited on the bench, along with a tray of oils, soaps, and towels— Élodie's subtle way of managing what she would never say aloud.

Mathieu moved behind her wordlessly and began to unfasten the ties of her robe. His fingers were gentle, reverent, brushing over her bare shoulders as the fabric fell away. He kissed the curve of her spine, slow and deliberate, his hands lingering at her waist.

She turned to face him, drawing his mouth to hers in a kiss that was neither rushed nor hesitant—just anchored. Real.

Then she stepped into the water, sighing softly as the heat wrapped around her.

Mathieu sat on the edge of the tub, arms resting on his knees.

"Why jasmine?" he asked after a pause. "Why do you hate it?"

She didn't answer right away. Instead, she dipped a cloth into the water, ran it over her arms.

"Edric," she said finally.

Mathieu's brow furrowed.

"He used to send bouquets," she continued. "Ridiculously large ones. Always jasmine. Every time we argued. Every time he needed to distract me. Every time he forgot something important, which was often."

Mathieu's voice was quiet. "But you never liked it."

"He never asked," she said. "He assumed. Or he didn't care. It doesn't matter." She paused, fingers tightening on the edge of the tub. "I realized one day that I had married a man who had no idea who I was. Not even the simplest thing. Not even my favorite flower."

Silence stretched between them.

"I remember the garden," he said. "You warned me then. 'Preferably not jasmine,' you said."

Her lips curved. "And you guessed the right answer anyway."

"Orchid," he murmured. "Elegant. Rare. Impossible to impress. Impossible to ignore."

She arched a brow. "Is that a compliment or a complaint?"

"Both," he said, grinning.

She lifted one wet hand from the water and flicked it at him. He grabbed her fingers midair and kissed her knuckles slowly.

"Then I suppose," he said, "I'll have to learn how to keep one alive."

They dressed in near silence, broken only by the rustle of cloth and the soft creak of leather.

Mathieu helped her fasten the final clasp of her gown, his fingers brushing against her back like he wasn't quite ready to stop touching her. She didn't rush him.

When they stepped into the hall, the air already felt heavier. Not with dread exactly, but with the kind of pressure that comes when every moment ticks toward something you can't stop.

The queen's sitting room—once used only for private audiences and political negotiations—had been transformed into something almost domestic. The curtains were drawn back, letting the soft morning light spill across the floor in gold stripes. A long, low table had been set for breakfast. Carafes of tea and mulled cider steamed beside plates of figs and honey-drenched pastries, bowls of stewed fruit, and warm, crusty bread.

Already gathered were the people who mattered most.

Élodie sat cross-legged on a velvet chaise, nursing a cup of something dark and bitter. She looked, for once, mostly rested. Laurent lounged beside her, boots up on the arm of the sofa like he owned the place. Renaud leaned against the mantel, arms folded, watching them with the wary fondness of a man who had long since accepted his inability to keep any of them in check.

Thorne stood behind one of the high-backed chairs, not sitting, not fidgeting. Just watching.

Cassien and Evelyne sat near the window, their children nestled between them. The eldest was tracing something on the fogged-up glass with a fingertip. The youngest lay curled on his mother's lap, still drowsy. Sabine was muttering next to them that sleep would've been a better use of their energy than staging a farewell breakfast for a man too stubborn to be reasonable. But she hadn't left the room. And that, from Sabine, said enough.

And Serenya Vale—sharp-eyed and composed—stood near the threshold, her fingers wrapped around a delicate porcelain cup that seemed utterly at odds with the hard line of her jaw.

As Améliane entered, the room quieted. Not in deference—but in gravity.

"I wasn't aware we'd opened my sitting room to general use," she said lightly, glancing at Élodie.

Renaud's mouth twitched. He looked away before anyone could accuse him of smiling.

Laurent grinned. "It's an execution breakfast, how thoughtful." He leaned over the table, plucking a berry from one of the bowls. "Do we get wine with that or just dry toast and impending doom?"

"Only if you behave," Améliane said, arching a brow.

"I'm already doomed," he replied, popping the berry into his mouth. "Might as well be charming on the way out."

Serenya's gaze slid toward the vaulted ceiling, where light pooled against ancient carvings. "Your castle is remarkable," she said softly. "Not just in design, but in intent. It is rare to see cause and courage share the same space."

Her voice wasn't reverent—but it was respectful.

Cassien didn't speak, but his gaze drifted to his children. His daughter had climbed onto a stool and was pretending it was a ship mast, waving a napkin like a banner. The sight made something in his face tighten—not sorrow, but the quiet kind of ache that lives beside fear.

"They won't remember this place," he said softly, eyes still on his boy. "Not properly. Not the way we do."

Améliane glanced at him. "Would you want them to?"

Cassien's hand curled around his cup. "No," he admitted. "But part of me wishes they could understand it. What you all became here."

"They'll understand," Élodie said, tone dry but not unkind. "Someday. When they ask why you flinch every time you see mist or hear wind whistling through stone."

"Or why their Queen gets twitchy around mirrors," Laurent added cheerfully. "Very normal symptoms of prolonged magical imprisonment, I'm told."

Améliane gave him a look. "That's enough."

"Is it, though?" Laurent raised a brow. "It might be the last time I get to monologue before being vaporized by a mystical gate."

"We've already gone over the details," Renaud said, but not harshly.

"Three times," Thorne corrected, reaching for another slice of bread. "Renaud checked the research again this morning. With Serenya, Sabine, Élodie, and me."

Élodie nodded. "We are as thorough as you are stubborn. You're not walking into this blind, Laurent."

Mathieu leaned back in his chair beside Améliane, arms folded. "You just need to be honest."

"That's the tricky part," Laurent muttered.

There was a lull then—one of those odd, sacred silences that sometimes happens among people who've survived something together. No one rushed to fill it.

Then Laurent cleared his throat. "Do you remember the first time I shifted? It was a few weeks after we had first been sent to Eldrenoire."

The change in the room was immediate—lighter. Curious.

"You mean when you thought you'd grown wings from stress?" Élodie asked.

He held up a finger. "I maintain that was a reasonable conclusion. I woke up midair. I hadn't even had my morning tea."

Améliane tilted her head with a smirk. "You broke two windows."

"And a vase," Renaud added.

Laurent grinned. "And the panic attack Thorne had trying to catch me with that net was truly the stuff of legends."

Thorne didn't rise to the bait. "You nearly impaled yourself on a weathervane."

"Details," Laurent waved a hand. "The point is—I was the first. At least, the first to shift in front of everyone. I remember looking down at my hands and seeing feathers. Golden feathers. It should have terrified me."

"But?" Améliane asked softly.

He looked down at his plate, suddenly quiet.

"But it felt right," he said. "Not because I was meant to be a bird or anything poetic like that. But because—for the first time since the curse—I felt like I had a choice."

A silence followed, weightier now.

Laurent gave a lopsided smile. "Of course, I slammed into the eastern tower ten seconds later. Grace comes later, apparently."

"You've never had grace," Sabine snorted, sipping her drink.

"But I have style," he countered.

Mathieu leaned forward slightly. "You're ready for this."

Laurent met his eyes. "I know."

No bravado this time. Just truth.

Améliane looked around the room, at each of them—her soldiers, her friends, her cursed and chosen few.

"Then let's face this day together," she said quietly. "As we have faced every day before it."

Améliane stepped forward, lifting the delicate glass from her place setting.

"To truth," she said simply. Her voice was steady, "To courage."

Her eyes swept across them—Laurent's irreverent smirk, Renaud's barely concealed tension, Élodie's sharp watchfulness. Serenya's stillness. Sabine's practiced detachment. Cassien's grief. Thorne's quiet, unreadable stare.

"And to each of you."

She raised her glass.

The others followed—some quickly, some with hesitation. But all of them, in the end.

Glasses touched. A soft chorus of porcelain and crystal.

For one fragile moment, there was peace.

At last, with the tea gone cold and morning light deepening to gold-washed certainty, Laurent rose, his chair scraping through the hush that had settled over the table.

"Well," he said, brushing nonexistent crumbs from his sleeves, "it's a beautiful day to tempt death."

No one laughed. But Élodie offered a faint smirk, and even Renaud's lips twitched in reluctant amusement.

Laurent's gaze flicked toward the open window, where sunlight filtered in across the stone like a summons. "Time," he said simply.

And just like that, it was.

They rose as one. Mathieu lingered at Améliane's side for a heartbeat longer, brushing his fingers once over hers, a silent vow. Then he stepped back—just enough to let Laurent take his place.

She felt the shift of it. Not deference. Not distance. Just understanding.

Laurent offered his arm with mock elegance. "Milady?"

Améliane arched a brow but took it, slipping her hand into the crook of his elbow. "Try not to be insufferable."

"I make no promises," he said, smiling with just enough edge to hide everything underneath.

The castle doors—massive, ancient, bound in silver-veined stone—swung open without touch. A groan of welcome. Or warning.

They stepped into sunlight.

Eldrenoire's grounds stretched before them, vast and gleaming with dew. And beyond the steps, gathered in a silent crescent around the main path, waited the court.

Over a hundred and fifty souls.

Some stood in human form—servants and scholars, guards in ceremonial rusted mail, footmen holding feathered helms at their sides. Others crouched or perched in animal shapes—panthers with glinting eyes, wolves with ears laid flat, birds stilling their wings on high ledges. Their silence was not fear, but reverence.

The procession began.

Améliane and Laurent led, followed by Élodie, Renaud, Thorne, Sabine, Cassien and Serenya, and finally Mathieu—watchful, silent, every step weighted.

The path curved gently through the heart of Eldrenoire's gardens, now overgrown with impossible flora. Vines shimmered silver-blue in the light. Pools mirrored the sky too perfectly. And there, at the farthest point—the gate stood.

It loomed at the edge of the world, haloed in mist, tall as a tower and silent as snowfall. A freestanding arch of polished obsidian and moonstone, pulsing faintly, like breath held too long.

Améliane kept her chin high. Her steps even. But Laurent could feel it—the tension in her grip.

He nudged her with his shoulder. "If you cry, I'll be offended."

"I don't cry," she muttered.

He gave her a sidelong look. "You sobbed when we broke the wine barrel in the third cellar."

"That was a twelve-hundred-year-old vintage."

"Exactly," he said. "Tragic."

At the base of the gate, he stopped. Let go of her arm. And turned to face her, straightening into something more formal than she'd seen in years.

A bow.

Deep. Precise. Regal.

The air caught in her throat.

"Laurent," she whispered.

And before she could stop herself, before decorum or fear or pride could interfere—she moved.

Crossed the space between them in two strides and wrapped her arms around him.

He stiffened—just for a moment—then melted into it, pulling her in with that same irreverent grace he always wore like armor.

"You were never just a distraction," she murmured, lips close to his ear. "You were hope. Loud, stubborn, impossible hope. I love you. And I'm proud to be your friend."

Laurent's arms tightened once around her before pulling back. His eyes were shining—but he didn't blink.

"Try not to look too surprised," he said, voice rough. "When you find me drunk in a tavern on the other side."

Then—without waiting for permission or applause or anything else—he turned, faced the gate, and strode purposefully toward it.

The mist thickened as he approached, curling like fingers. The arch pulsed once—then rippled.

A shimmer. A swallow. Then he was gone.

The court held its breath.

For a moment, only silence. It seemed the gate had accepted him.

Then—

A scream.

Raw. Terrified. Human.

It tore through the stillness like a blade, echoing through the courtyard, bouncing off stone and glass until it didn't sound like one voice but many—anguish multiplied.

Gasps broke the silence. Someone sobbed. Élodie flinched beside Renaud. One of the falconers fell to their knees. The shifters stilled mid-breath, tails and wings frozen.

The mirror-gate pulsed.

Once.

And sealed. The shimmer vanished.

No trace. No return. Just the yawning stillness of stone that should not close so easily on a life.

The court stood breathless, watching the place where Laurent had vanished. No one moved.

Not even Améliane.

Because that scream still echoed inside her ribcage—like a bell rung too hard. Like a promise broken mid-word.

In the hush that followed, the castle itself seemed to recoil. The air went brittle. Cold.

And somewhere, high above, a bird cawed in warning.

The silence held. Not peace. Not reverence. The kind of silence that knows exactly what it's lost.

Hope cracks louder than fear when it shatters.

CHAPTER 42

Bastian

The mist hung low, curling around tree trunks like ghost light. It muffled the world, dulled every sound, turned the distant birdsong into something warped and echoing. Bastian crouched at the edge of the trail, fingers pressed to damp earth, scanning the terrain as if the gate might simply step out of hiding.

It didn't.

He rose slowly, stretching the stiffness from his shoulders. His coat was still damp from the night's rain, and the leather along his left sleeve was starting to crack from overuse. He needed a new one. Preferably one not worn during a near-ambush last week.

The rebel war party had made camp just inside the tree line, out of sight from the sky and scattered across the slope like shadows. Tents were low and dark-colored. No fires. No music. No unnecessary chatter. They were too close to something for comfort, even if they didn't yet know what.

Bastian turned toward the nearest command table, where a Seer's hand-drawn map had been pinned beneath stones and damp parchment. It showed a rough sketch of Ziraveen, but more importantly red ink marked past sightings of the gate. Each mark shifted in a spiral, as though it moved with the moon or breath or something else alive.

"Fourth time it's changed in two weeks," he muttered.

He didn't realize Commander Halven had stepped up behind him until he answered.

"And it's thinning," Halven said. "The barrier. It doesn't hold like it used to."

Bastian turned. The commander looked more ghost than man—gaunt from travel, his dark coat splattered with old dirt and leaf rot. He'd returned just a week earlier with news from the pass, his voice ragged from the strain of magic and distance.

"You're sure what you saw was Eldrenoire?" Bastian asked, though they'd gone over it twice already.

Halven's mouth tightened. "I followed Serenya and Cassien to the edge myself. The forest bent around them. The fog opened. And then there was a gate. It flickered and kind of shimmered. But it was there, and then it was gone."

"Did they go through?"

Halven nodded. "Cassien did. With his wife and children. Serenya followed. She turned to look at me just before crossing. Didn't say a word."

"And the gate?"

"Sealed behind them. Vanished again a few hours later."

Bastian stared at the trees beyond the camp, where the veil was thickest and the branches tangled like grasping hands. Somewhere in that haunted wilderness was the way in—and he'd missed it. Again.

"And Cassien?" he asked after a pause. "You said Edric found out."

Halven's face darkened. "He's burning everything down to smoke him out. Raided half the noble houses. Rounded up known sympathizers. Miralys is in chaos. The palace is sealed tight."

"So he's moving."

"He's more than moving. He's gathering legions. We intercepted one of his field messengers near the border—coded orders to begin moving troops east. Toward Ziraveen."

Bastian's stomach dropped.

"So he knows," he said quietly. "He's coming for her."

Halven nodded once. "He intends to secure the Queen. Or destroy her."

Bastian looked down at the map again, then back to the trees. The mist stirred. The wind shifted.

A shadow emerged through the fog—one of their scouts, moving fast and low between the trees. His cloak was damp, face tight with urgency.

"Armed camp," he said without preamble. "North slope, less than a league out. Six to eight men. No banners. Too disciplined for bandits."

Bastian exchanged a look with Halven before turning toward the central tent.

"Find Moon," he said. "We go now. Quiet and fast. I want eyes on them before they see us."

Their march was near silent—no clinking armor, no idle chatter, no missteps. Just the rhythm of boots against moss-soft paths and the whisper of fog threading between the trees like an omen. Bastian walked near the front, a few paces behind Moon, her black cloak parting the fog like a blade.

Around them, the forest breathed uneasily. Trees leaned at impossible angles. Roots coiled like serpents. Even the birds had gone quiet, as though sensing something that man had no language for. Bastian had grown used to the wrongness of Ziraveen's borders, but today... it pressed closer. Like a warning unspoken.

Moon finally spoke, her voice low and crisp. "You still think she made it through?"

"Serenya?" Bastian nodded once. "Halven saw her go in. That's enough for me."

Moon's jaw tightened. "And no word since."

"There's no way to reach her," Bastian said. "Not unless the castle lets her out."

She stopped at a fork in the path, eyes sweeping the terrain with quiet calculation. Behind them, the war party adjusted in silence—ready, waiting, watchful. Their forces were small compared to what Edric commanded, but every rebel here had been trained for this. Bastian had helped see to it.

"Do you think they received her?" Moon asked, softer now. "That she wasn't... seen as a threat?"

"She's with Cassien," Bastian said. "That has to count for something."

Moon gave a single nod, then turned onto the rightward path. The trees were thicker here. The air, heavier. The haze didn't part so much as cling. Bastian followed, signaling the scouts behind them to stay sharp.

"She'll find a way," Moon murmured. "Serenya always does."

"And if she doesn't?"

Moon didn't stop walking. "Then we tear the gate open."

Bastian almost smiled. "So subtle."

"You didn't join this rebellion for subtle," she said. "None of us did."

He didn't argue.

They fell into silence again, the crunch of boots the only sound against the woods' unnatural hush. Bastian's gaze flicked to the rear lines—ranks of rebels moving like shadows between trees. Seers with bandaged eyes. Runeformers with ink-stained fingers. Shadowbinders cloaked in veils that blurred the light around them. Naturebinders with dirt-crusted nails and thorns woven into their sleeves.

Each one chosen. Each one ready.

"We've lost too much already," Moon said after a while, almost to herself. "And Edric's legions aren't waiting. The messages we intercepted were rushed—imprecise. But they point here. To Ziraveen."

"To Eldrenoire," Bastian corrected.

She didn't deny it.

"If he gets there first—" he started.

"He won't," she cut in. "We won't let him."

He felt the conviction in her voice like iron. And yet... the air around them pulsed with a different truth. The forest was shifting again. The mist growing thicker. And still—no gate.

Bastian looked up. The branches overhead formed a lattice of black against the grey sky. The world beyond felt very far away.

"Do you think it knows we're coming?" he asked.

Moon gave him a sidelong look. "The castle?"

He nodded.

She didn't smile. "I hope so."

The scout motioned for them to be quiet and pointed straight ahead.

The scent of smoke reached them before the campsite came into view.

Bastian crouched low behind a gnarled root, the forest rising steeply above a break in the trees. Beside him, Moon pressed into the shadows like she was made of them. Neither moved. Neither breathed too loudly. The scout who'd brought them—a wiry man with patchy stubble and a bow longer than his arm—pointed silently down toward the firelit hollow below.

Rothgarian.

There were at least six of them—mercenaries by the look of their armor, pieced together in mismatched patches of chainmail and leather. One had a red sash looped around his belt, the telltale mark of a bounty-grade hunter. Another had a sword that glimmered faintly with enchantment, though not enough to suggest finesse. They were seasoned, but not cautious.

The men sat close to the flames, boots kicked out, tankards in hand, helmets discarded beside them like afterthoughts. One roasted something over the fire—grouse, maybe. Another leaned back against a log and let out a booming laugh.

"Two years," one slurred. "Two years and still no body."

Bastian stilled.

"Bet the bastard's bones are somewhere in these cursed woods," another said. "If the trees didn't eat him, the mist did."

More laughter.

Moon's expression didn't change, but her fingers flexed against the moss, slow and deliberate.

"You believe all that nonsense?" a younger voice asked. "That he vanished into thin air?"

"Oh, I believe he vanished," the first said. "Vanished like any coward king does when he knows he's beaten."

A pause, followed by the slosh of liquid as someone refilled their tin.

"Still," another added, voice low and half-drunken, "The Rothgarian empire is willing to pay handsomely to find him. Or what's left of him. Man must've mattered more than the stories say."

"Wouldn't be the first royal bastard to play dead," the one with the red sash muttered. "Or maybe he didn't play at all. Maybe the forest swallowed him and left nothing but a memory."

The youngest mercenary gave a nervous laugh. "You think this is where he disappeared?"

"Close enough," said the older man. "Fog rolled in fast that night. Tracker swore he saw footprints stop right in the middle of the trail. No blood. No drag marks. Just gone."

Another pause.

"Not natural," one of them muttered. "Place like this... it remembers."

Moon's gaze flicked to Bastian. No words passed between them—but the air felt tighter. Charged. As if the forest had bristled at being spoken of so carelessly.

Then the red-sashed mercenary leaned back and let out a sharp bark of laughter. "All this for a ghost king."

The others laughed. It was the kind of sound that assumed no one was listening.

Moon whispered, "We go at nightfall."

Bastian nodded once. Then, after a moment, murmured, "Let them finish their wine."

A beat passed. The wind shifted.

"And then we show them what ghosts really look like."

The clearing looked deceptively quiet. Firelight danced across bedrolls and empty mugs. Laughter had faded, replaced by the low murmur of drowsy men. One mercenary snored, another sat sharpening a blade with lazy strokes, the rasp of metal masking the faint shuffle in the trees beyond.

The Return moved like smoke—silent, disciplined, surgical. Shadows peeled away from the treeline as two dozen rebels crept inward, half-shrouded in glamours, their blades wrapped in cloth to muffle any glint. Overhead, a whisper of sigils pulsed through the underbrush, muting footsteps and masking scent.

Bastian flanked right, leading a trio of fighters along a narrow path that curved behind the men's wagons. He didn't speak. He didn't need to. Every movement had been drilled a hundred times. Every hand signal known.

A dull thud broke the silence.

One of their sentries—Daren, a younger fighter from the western cells—staggered forward with a gurgled breath, a blade protruding from his neck. He dropped without a sound.

Everything snapped.

Bastian surged forward, his dagger driving clean into the throat of the mercenary who'd thrown the knife. Blood sprayed in a hot arc across the moss. The man crumpled, twitching.

"Now!" Moon's voice cut through the trees like steel through silk.

The clearing exploded into motion. Runeformers had already sabotaged the mercenaries' weapons with etched traps—one sword erupted in flame as its wielder drew it, another snapped at the hilt. Shadowbinders muttered incantations at the perimeter, weaving silence spells to keep the fight contained.

Bastian didn't fight pretty. He fought fast. Brutal. His blade found ribs and tendons, dropped men before they could turn. One reached for a horn—Bastian's boot met his wrist, and the horn clattered harmlessly to the dirt.

Screams were cut short. Steel met flesh. The firelight turned red.

One mercenary tried to flee, crashing through the brush on the far side. He didn't make it five steps before a silvery sigil flared beneath his boots and shattered his knee mid-stride. A Runeformer calmly stepped from the trees and finished him with a single strike.

It was over in minutes.

Silence fell again, broken only by the crackle of the fire and the low, ragged breaths of the rebels. Not one of the mercenaries remained alive.

Bastian stood in the center, chest heaving, the edge of his blade slick. Across the clearing, Moon knelt beside Daren's body, eyes unreadable.

"A clean death," she said quietly. "Better than most."

Bastian said nothing. He wiped his dagger on a discarded cloak and moved to the nearest camp table. Maps were scattered across it—sketched routes, payment ledgers, and one parchment sealed in red wax.

He slit it open.

The sigil inside was unmistakable.

The Rothgarian emperor.

"Burn them," he said.

The others obeyed. One by one, the documents were tossed into the flames. The wax blistered. The crest curled and blackened. But Bastian stood unmoving, staring at the seal as it turned to ash.

They turned back to the trees, leaving behind only smoldering embers.

Most of the war party had gone quiet back at the camp—some tending to wounds, others polishing blades that no longer needed it. A few sat with their backs to the trees, their expressions blank with exhaustion, lost in the echo of steel and blood.

Bastian sat near the edge of the firelight, arms braced on his knees, the crusted blood on his coat beginning to flake. It wasn't his. Not all of it, anyway.

Across from him, Moon crouched beside a log, her face streaked with ash, hair unbound. Her mask hung loose around her neck, forgotten. She hadn't spoken in a while. But her eyes—they hadn't dulled. Not even after the skirmish.

When she did speak, it was to the fire.

"They shouldn't be here."

Bastian looked up.

"Rothgarian mercenaries," Moon said, her voice low and flint sharp. "Too far south. Too deep into Ziraveen. They weren't just hunting coin."

"No," Bastian agreed. "They were hunting legacy."

She glanced at him, brow lifting slightly.

"They were after someone," Bastian said, voice low. "Called him the exiled king."

Moon's jaw ticked. "Valmont. That's the only one it could be."

Bastian nodded once. "They never said a name. Just that he disappeared near these woods almost two years ago."

Moon was quiet for a beat. Then, "I'd heard he escaped the Rothgarian prisons. Rumors, mostly. Some say he died in the attempt."

Bastian's eyes stayed on the fire, "And Rothgar's still hunting."

Moon exhaled through her nose. "Because if he's alive... he's still a threat."

Bastian's gaze sharpened. "Valmont might be ash. But the bloodline isn't. And the Empire knows it."

"They don't want to bury history," Moon said quietly. "They want to erase it."

The fire snapped, casting long shadows between them.

Bastian leaned back slightly, the heat flickering across his face as he stared into the coals. No more laughter. No more stories from drunk men who thought they understood the price of legacy.

"They're not just hunting ghosts," he said quietly. "They're hunting what ghosts can become."

Moon didn't reply right away. Her gaze was fixed past the flames, toward the mist beyond camp—where the trees were still, and the night pressed close. Her fingers tapped once against her knee, a silent rhythm only she seemed to hear.

"Everything is moving," she said at last. "Edric. The Rothgarian Empire. Even the damn forest." Her voice dipped lower. "And we still haven't found the gate."

"We will," Bastian said. It wasn't bravado—it was something colder. Hungrier.

Moon gave the smallest nod, and for a moment the firelight caught the edges of something near her eyes—weariness, maybe. Or memory.

They sat in silence for a while longer. Around them, the war party had begun to settle. Sentries replaced. Scouts already fanning out again, despite the hour. They were too close now for comfort. Too close to rest.

A breeze stirred the mist. Bastian turned his head toward it, pulse ticking.

The fog hadn't lifted. But it had thinned—just enough to make the dark between trees seem deeper. The air tasted like iron and rain.

Moon straightened. "What is it?"

He didn't answer right away. Instead, he stood and walked to the treeline, boots soft against the moss. The mist swirled around his calves, then settled, like it had been waiting.

"It's different tonight," he said without turning. "The forest feels like it's holding its breath."

"Do you think it knows we're here?"

Bastian hesitated. "Maybe," he murmured.

Moon rose slowly, following his gaze into the dark.

They didn't speak again.

Behind them, the fire crackled low.

And in the quiet beyond the flame, the mist coiled tighter—like something unseen had taken notice.

Like something was listening.

CHAPTER 43

Améliane

The light that woke her wasn't sunlight. Not really.

It filtered through the tall window like spilled silver, catching on dust that hadn't been there yesterday. The air felt heavier than usual—more weighted. More aware. As if the castle had drawn one long, slow breath and still hadn't exhaled.

Beside her, Mathieu lay silent. Awake. Eyes open.

Améliane didn't move. Didn't speak.

Outside, a breeze rattled the shutters softly. A sound that once might have meant nothing—except now, every groan in the stone, every flicker in the chandeliers, every sigh in the velvet drapes felt intentional. Felt like Eldrenoire was not only listening, but mourning.

A week had passed. Maybe more. The days had begun to slip.

She turned her head just enough to see him better—Mathieu, hair tousled, the sheet tangled low on his hips, his gaze fixed on the ceiling like it held a riddle he hadn't solved.

She swallowed. The ache had dulled, but it hadn't left. It pulsed like a slow bruise behind the ribs. Not sharp, just... persistent.

"I thought I would know," she murmured. "If he was gone. I thought I'd feel it."

"You did feel it," Mathieu said gently. "We all did."

Améliane turned her gaze back to the window. The sky beyond looked washed out—neither dawn nor full day, but something in between.

Her throat tightened at the memory of Renaud restraining Thorne to stop him from running through the gate after Laurent.

She closed her eyes. "And yet... no body. No confirmation. Just a scream and a sealed gate."

"That's confirmation enough," he said softly. But even then, his voice lacked conviction.

They were quiet for a time. The kind of quiet that came after a fire burns low and no one knows whether to stoke it or let it die.

Améliane shifted to face him more fully, searching his expression.

"You're sure?" she asked. "You checked everything after I looked it over?"

Mathieu nodded once. "Twice. And Élodie went through the calculations with me again yesterday. Thorne and Sabine added their own interpretation of the scrying layers. Serenya checked the binding echoes."

Her breath trembled on the edge of something unshed. Not quite a tear. Not quite a scream.

"I wish he'd waited," she said.

Mathieu's hand found hers beneath the coverlet. His fingers were warm. Steady.

"He did wait," he said quietly. "He waited eight years."

The words fell between them like a stone dropped into still water.

Outside, the castle shifted again. A mirror blinked out in the corridor beyond the chamber. A portrait frame cracked. Somewhere deep below, a door opened that hadn't been there the day before. Eldrenoire was unraveling.

They rose from bed, the silence between them was not heavy, but deliberate. Measured. Like everything else now.

Améliane stood at the edge of her dressing mirror, her gown half-fastened, the morning light spilling in like a stranger who hadn't asked to be let in. Mathieu moved slowly behind her, lacing the final hooks of her bodice with a soldier's precision. His touch lingered just a moment longer than necessary—palming her spine as if to say I'm here, even if the words no longer helped.

"You've kept your chambers quiet," he said, his voice hushed but warm. "No Élodie hovering. No stealthy footsteps pretending not to eavesdrop. I'm almost offended."

She glanced at him in the mirror. "I gave them another morning off."

He tilted his head, mock-wounded as if to lighten the mood. "But who will tell me which sash makes me look less intimidating?"

Améliane didn't smile—quite—but something softened in her face. "I couldn't ask them to fasten a brooch or smooth my hem while the court crumbles around us."

Mathieu stepped beside her, adjusting the collar of his coat absently as he studied her reflection. "So instead, you conscripted the exiled king with suspiciously nimble fingers."

She angled her head. "Suspiciously nimble, hmm?"

He leaned down, lips brushing just behind her ear. "Don't make me demonstrate."

She sighed through her nose—something close to amusement—but didn't lean away. "We have a library to visit."

"Fine," he said, reaching for her brush. "But at least let me braid your hair. Give me something ceremonial."

Her lips twitched. "If you braid a crown into it, I'm throwing you out the window."

"Noted." He began gathering the dark strands, fingers gentle as he worked. "Just a simple plait. Functional. Dignified."

Améliane closed her eyes for a moment. Let the motion anchor her. His touch, steady. The silence, familiar. Not heavy.

The braid was finished with a simple silver pin—a small moon-shaped clasp Élodie had once tucked into a gift box without explanation. When Mathieu turned her gently toward him, there was something unspoken in his expression. Not grief. Not fear.

Readiness.

"Let's go," she said softly.

Améliane reached for her satchel without a word, slipping the soft leather strap over her shoulder as Mathieu fastened his cloak. Alaric's summoning book lay tucked within—plain, weightless, and yet somehow heavier than anything else she carried. She didn't check to make sure it was still there. She knew it was.

They stepped out of her chambers together, and the door shut behind them with a sound like the sealing of fate—not a click, but a *finality*. The corridor beyond was colder than it had been before dawn. The sconces flickered, casting long shadows across the velvet-lined walls. And the air pressed in close, like the castle itself was leaning down to listen.

They walked in silence. A stretch of hallway turned slightly left where it had once turned right.

A set of twin mirrors reflected different scenes—one showed only their passage, the other blinked once, as if uncertain whether to mirror or to remember.

When they passed the old nursery door, Améliane saw it again ten paces later. Same door. Same scratch in the wood. Twice.

Neither of them commented.

At the base of the eastern stair, a statue that had once wept now stood dry-eyed, its face turned the wrong way.

Still, they said nothing.

Eldrenoire was unmaking itself, and their task remained the same: *stay ahead of the fall*.

The double doors to the library opened before they touched them.

Inside, the air pulsed with warmth and dust and something older than both. The chandelier overhead flickered with low blue light—enchanted to never burn out, though it now dimmed in uneven intervals, as if Eldrenoire's very breath stuttered.

The long table was already occupied. Renaud sat with his arms crossed, eyes sharp, coat slung over the back of his chair like armor at rest. At the end of the table, Élodie perched with quiet purpose, her charcoal-smudged sleeve brushing a stack of open tomes, Sabine seated beside her, muttering incantations under her breath. Thorne leaned against the far bookshelf, face unreadable, a scroll half-unfurled in one hand. Serenya stood at the center, her posture rigid, eyes scanning a page like it might confess its secrets if she just stared hard enough.

And Cassien—older, wearier than he had been even days ago—paced behind them all, his fingers tracing the edge of a yellowing map.

Several maps were pinned in place with ornate daggers driven through their corners. Sigils glowed faintly along the table's edge—remnants of recent spells, or warnings that no one had dared erase.

The table was a battlefield of information. And this, Améliane thought, was her war council.

She stepped forward. "Let's begin."

They gathered around the long table, the hush in the library different now—*not reverent*, but raw. Not a silence of peace, but of restraint. Mourning pressed into the seams of every breath, but no one gave it shape. Not yet.

Mathieu remained standing. His hand hovered above a parchment covered in spiraling script, its edge weighted by an inkwell and a cracked, rune-etched stone.

"The research held," he began, voice calm but clipped at the edges. "Every scrying glyph, every binding rune, every sequence of mirror calculations—we've reviewed them all. Again. And again."

He looked to each of them in turn.

"Nothing was wrong with the magic. The spell responded the way it was designed to. It didn't fail. The curse didn't break."

A pause.

"Laurent... wasn't ready."

The words landed like a breath held too long.

Serenya shifted slightly beside a spread of glowing runes, her tone clinical but not unkind. "The rune echoes detected no external corruption. No trap. No sabotage. His energy pattern didn't fracture or splinter. He wasn't torn apart."

She met Améliane's eyes across the table.

"He was rejected."

Élodie's fist closed around the charcoal she'd been using to mark the margins of her translation. It snapped between her fingers.

"I don't care if it was fair," she said. Her voice was tight, every word wrapped in grief. "It doesn't make it right."

No one answered. The only sound was the flutter of a loose page near the window, stirred by air that had no business moving.

Améliane stared down at her hands, the silver pin at her wrist glinting in the low light.

"He was more than brave," she said softly. "Braver than most men I've known. But the mirror doesn't reward bravery."

She closed her eyes for a heartbeat.

"It demands truth."

The room fell still again.

Renaud's voice, when it came, was low. Measured. A rare offering.

"He walked forward believing he had nothing left to lose," he said. "But he never gave anything up."

Mathieu's gaze flicked toward him—surprised, perhaps, by the insight.

Sabine folded her arms across her chest. "And that," she said, "is what the curse was built to reveal."

The library crackled with the unspoken.

Not judgment. Not blame. But the weight of *truth*, whispered like a curse across each of their shoulders.

Améliane reached into her satchel and drew out a narrow leather-bound book.

The table quieted.

It wasn't large—no grand volume of magic or strategy—but the moment she laid it down between the scrying maps and open tomes, something in the air shifted. The cover was unmarked, its corners softened by years of handling. Yet it pulsed faintly, as if the stitching held more than thread and parchment.

"I've been trying to reach him since before Laurent walked through the gate," she said quietly, running her hand over the worn leather. "To confirm the research. To be certain. But he hasn't answered."

Mathieu stilled beside her. Élodie leaned in slightly. Only Serenya looked confused.

"Him?" she asked. "Who are you calling?"

Améliane didn't look up as she flipped to a page near the middle—past dozens of entries, her name inked over and over in fading script.

"His name is Alaric," she said. "He's part of Eldrenoire. Or perhaps... the part that watches. Listens."

"He's a person?" Serenya asked, eyes narrowing. "Or something else?"

Améliane considered that. "A man, yes. Or at least, he appears as one. He doesn't age. Doesn't eat. Doesn't sleep, so far as we know. He resides in the castle's quietest corners—usually here, in the library—but only when he chooses. You don't find him. He finds you."

Serenya's expression turned skeptical, but she didn't interrupt.

Améliane went on. "He keeps a book with no words. Flips through it as if he can still read what was once there. He speaks in riddles. Never gives us direct answers. But a few months after Mathieu arrived, it was Alaric who told us what he was. Wyrdbound." Her gaze flicked briefly to Mathieu.

"He knew before we did," Mathieu added, his voice low. "Knew what that meant for the curse."

Améliane dipped the quill into ink and poised it over a fresh page. "He's been unreachable since the curse began to fray. But this is where he's always answered before."

She signed her name with slow, practiced precision: ***Améliane Morvenne.***

The ink shimmered once, like moonlight on still water. And vanished.

The candle flames didn't flicker. The air didn't gust. And yet, the shift was immediate.

A hush fell over the library like the exhale of something vast. The light bent—not brighter, not darker, but wrong. It refracted along the polished floor and caught the silver etching of runes in the vaulted ceiling, spiraling toward the hearth.

And there he was. Alaric. Not stepping in. Not manifesting in shadow or smoke. Just... there. As if he'd always been standing at the edge of the firelight, halfway between flame and memory.

But this time, he was wrong.

His form flickered like candlelight on water—translucent around the edges, color draining from his robe and skin until he looked like something recalled from a dream. The shimmer of his eyes—normally gold in the right light—was dimmed to bronze. And the book in his hands, though open, remained motionless.

He did not turn a page.

Améliane rose first. "You saw what happened."

Alaric's gaze lifted to hers slowly. "The mirror does not lie," he said, his voice like something pulled from beneath the surface of deep water. "It only reveals what we refuse to see."

Thorne stepped forward, arms crossed tight. "Was the theory wrong?"

Alaric didn't blink. Didn't move. "The mirror yields to truth. Not fear masked as resolve. Not guilt mistaken for devotion. The gate tests surrender. Nothing else."

A silence bloomed—sharp and precise.

Améliane's hand curled at her side. "And Eldrenoire?"

At that, Alaric turned. His form shimmered again as he faced a mirror set into the library's far wall—one that had not been there when they entered. Its surface was rippling faintly, like a pond disturbed by wind. As Alaric stared into it, his reflection stuttered—splitting into fragments, then merging again.

"It is forgetting itself," he said. "The castle's magic echoes the Queen—but the Queen is changing. As she must. The people remember."

He lifted his gaze toward them all now, eyes catching on each face, weighty and remote.

"Reflections no longer match their sources," he continued. "Doors lead to rooms that no longer exist. Magic has lost its anchor. You must choose what remains—and what must be left behind."

Behind him, the mirror went dark.

Then it lit with a dull sheen, cloudy at first—then sharper. A new image flickered to life.

Not a reflection. A ravine, craggy and deep. Banners caught in the wind—royal blue and silver bearing the crest of Belmara.

A column of soldiers, faceless in steel. Marching. Edric's army.

The room froze.

Mathieu stepped forward instinctively. Élodie's lips parted in a soundless curse. Cassien's shoulders locked like stone.

"It's not real," Améliane whispered. "It's not now."

Alaric looked at her one final time. His body blurred at the edges, barely visible.

"Not yet," he said.

Then he vanished—fading like smoke sucked back into the glass.

For a heartbeat, no one moved.

Then—

"Get everyone," Mathieu said, already striding toward the shelves. "We need the court assembled. Now."

"Seal the halls," Renaud snapped. "No one moves unescorted."

Thorne was muttering calculations under his breath, reaching for the scrying chalk.

Cassien's jaw was clenched, eyes distant. "If the image was real, I know that ravine. They'll reach the border of Ziraveen by dusk. Maybe sooner."

Améliane stood unmoving in the center of it all, her hands still on the leather-bound book, her fingers trembling just slightly.

Mathieu stepped closer, his voice low. "Améliane."

She didn't look up, but she nodded once.

"We leave," she said. Her voice rang clear, stronger than it should have been in that haunted room. Her command cut through the chaos.

"All of us," she added. "Together."

Améliane remained by the hearth, unmoving for a moment longer. Then she turned to the others, her voice low but clear.

"Tell them to bring only what they can carry. No heirlooms. No trunks. Just what is essential."

Cassien nodded solemnly, already reaching for the enchanted map tucked into his belt.

She looked to Renaud, then Thorne, then Serenya as they passed. "In two hours, the court convenes in the Hall of Voices. All of them. Every soul still inside these walls."

The library emptied in a flurry of footsteps and orders.

Renaud was already halfway to the stairs, calling commands over his shoulder. Thorne moved with practiced efficiency, gathering maps and scrying pouches. Serenya's cloak caught the edge of a gust as she vanished into the hall, her stride quick and clipped—unmistakably military.

Améliane just stood there for several long minutes after everyone left. Mathieu touched her arm. She didn't flinch from it.

"We need to pack," he said gently.

She nodded once, eyes still fixed on the place where Alaric had vanished.

Then she turned—and the queen walked out of the library.

CHAPTER 44

Améliane

The walk back to her chambers was not long, but the halls bent twice where they shouldn't have. One door appeared twice. Another vanished entirely. Neither of them spoke of it.

When they finally reached her rooms, Améliane crossed to the wardrobe and opened it with too much force. A cloak fell from the shelf. She reached for it, then fumbled another garment from the edge of the armoire. A small glass jar tipped from her satchel as she turned.

It shattered. She froze.

Mathieu moved at once, crossing to her side and kneeling amid the scattered pieces. His hands were steady as he brushed the fragments into a pile, ignoring the sharp edge that nicked his thumb.

Améliane stood very still, her chest rising too quickly. She hadn't wept. But her mouth trembled.

"I can't—" she started, then stopped.

Mathieu stood and caught her hand.

She looked at him, silver eyes storm-tossed. He drew her close, one arm curling around her waist, the other cradling the back of her head as she leaned into him.

"I should have stopped him," she whispered.

"You couldn't."

"I'm the Queen."

"And he was your friend," he said softly.

They stood like that for a long moment—anchored in silence. When she finally pulled back, her eyes were clearer.

"I want you to go first," she said. "Through the gate. I want to know that you're safe."

Mathieu's expression shifted. Not with surprise. With quiet defiance.

"No."

"Mathieu—"

"No," he said again, firmer this time. "That's not how this ends."

Her jaw tightened, but he raised a hand and brushed her cheek with the backs of his fingers.

"You asked me once why I stayed," he said. "And I didn't know how to answer. Not then."

He drew in a breath. "But I do now."

She watched him closely.

He smiled faintly. "The day I entered the Shrouded Gardens, I saw something. A vision. Captain Duran. My father's right hand. The man who taught me to ride, to fight, to lead." He paused. "To lose. The man who's name I took after my exile."

Améliane stilled.

"He told me something I haven't been able to shake. I didn't understand it until now."

He looked down at her, the light catching in his eyes like golden fire.

"'A man's duty is not to himself.'"

The words settled between them, heavier than anything they'd packed.

"I thought that vision was about Valmont," he said. "But it wasn't. It was about you."

Améliane pressed her hand to his chest, over his heart. "And you think your duty is to die beside me?"

"No," he said gently. "I think my duty is to stand beside you. Especially when it's hardest."

She shook her head—frustrated, touched, heartsick.

And then, quieter, "You know this curse… it wasn't just banishment. It changed us."

He nodded once.

She hesitated. "We weren't like this before."

His brows lifted slightly.

"I've told you before that we weren't shifters," she said. "That part of the curse was Edric's invention."

She crossed to the edge of the bed where her satchel lay and lifted a small silver pin—a moonlit tidelily, its edge sharp as memory.

"Cassien overheard him once, during a messenger run. Edric was laughing—telling some confidant that he chose a cat for me because it was small. Useless. Benign."

Mathieu's jaw tightened.

Améliane looked down. "He thought it was clever. To make me something he never had to fear."

She swallowed.

Mathieu reached for her hand.

"Did you have magic before Eldrenoire?" he asked softly.

Her breath caught. And then she nodded.

"Moonlight. Tide. Reflection. Emotion. That's what it was made of. What I was made of."

She looked at him—not proudly, not desperately, just with quiet truth.

"I could bend light, draw out truth from mirrors and voices and faces. I could feel the currents under people's words. I could move tides with a thought—not oceans, but..." she shrugged. "Enough to matter."

"And now?"

"Now it's silence. I can't hear it. I can't reach it. Because my power was never mine alone—it was tied to the crown. To the land. To the people."

She exhaled. "And when all that was stolen... so was I. Mathieu, even if I make it through the gate, I don't know who I will be."

Mathieu didn't speak.

He simply stepped forward, lifted her hand to his lips, and kissed it—soft, reverent.

Then he rested his forehead to hers.

No promises. No declarations.

Just truth.

And the weight of what still had to be done.

The Hall of Voices looked fuller than the previous week before Laurent's departure—and yet, it had never felt so hollow.

Every member of the cursed court stood gathered beneath the mirrored vaults and constellation-scribed stone. Some in fine coats gone threadbare. Others in silks worn thin from too many seasons. And still others had shifted, trembling, barely holding form. Foxes with tear-bright eyes. Hawks with twitching wings. A bear with one paw clenched tight like it might strike the world for daring to ask this of them.

Améliane stood before them all. Cloak clasped, hair braided, heart steady only because it had no other choice.

Mathieu stood to her left. Renaud, to her right. The others were spread among the front row of the crowd—Élodie, Thorne, Cassien, Serenya, Sabine—each a tether, a truth, a silent show of unity.

But the court... they were afraid. And rightly so.

Améliane took one breath. Then another.

"I've called you here," she said, her voice calm but sure, "because the time has come to try again."

The words echoed. She let them settle.

"Eldrenoire is no longer safe."

A stir among the crowd. Someone muttered something. Another turned in a slow circle, as if suddenly unsure the room behind them would still be there.

Améliane's tone sharpened slightly—not cruel, but clear. "We have prepared. We have waited. We have mourned. And now, we must act."

The murmurs started. Low at first. Doubt blooming like rot in the corners.

"He screamed," someone said.

"He died," another added, voice thick. "We all heard it."

"He was brave," a woman said, "and the gate swallowed him anyway."

"He was the bravest of all of us," someone whispered, and there were nods.

A young footman with ash-colored hair raised his voice over the crowd. "What if the gate rejects us?"

The room buzzed louder.

"No one should be first."

"No one should be next."

"We can't go. Not after that. Not after—"

The voices swelled, and for a moment, Améliane let them. Let them feel their fear. Their grief. Their fury.

She didn't silence them. Not yet.

Because sometimes, a court had to break before it could rise.

Renaud stepped forward.

"All of you," he said, evenly. "Quiet."

The court obeyed. Not out of fear—but out of habit. Trust.

Renaud looked out over the crowd, jaw tight, hands behind his back like a commander reviewing ranks before a storm. "No one here is asking you to forget what happened. No one is asking you not to be afraid. But fear is not a reason to stay in chains."

He turned slightly, looking toward Améliane. "Let the Queen speak."

Améliane exhaled. The silence that followed was total.

"What happened to Laurent was a loss. A blow. To all of us. He was beloved, and brave, and loud in the best possible ways." A tremor passed through her voice, but she did not falter. "But he wasn't rejected because the gate is cruel. He was rejected because the mirror asks for more than courage. It asks for truth."

The room held still.

"I've spoken to Alaric," she continued. "He came to us this morning. Even he was flickering, fading. Eldrenoire is unraveling. It's losing its shape, its memory. Because I—because we—are changing. And the castle cannot hold what it can no longer reflect."

A murmur.

"He confirmed our research. Every glyph. Every rune. Every equation. The theory holds. The path through the gate remains. But only for those who walk with nothing to hide—not from the castle, not from themselves."

She paused.

A woman near the pillar pressed a hand over her heart. A boy clutched the paw of a fox beside him—his brother, maybe.

And still—another voice, cracked and desperate, "But what if it rejects us?"

"Then it will reject you here," Améliane said, quietly. "And you will not face the fire alone."

That silence hurt more than shouting.

She lifted her chin. "Alaric showed us Edric's army. They march toward Ziraveen. Toward this place. He is coming—for me, for you, for all of it. And when he arrives, he will not offer mercy."

The court stilled like prey scenting wolves.

"So, I'll say this plainly," she went on. "I won't force you through that gate. But if you stay—there will be no second chance. This place is collapsing. And Edric will not be merciful. Not to traitors. Not to those who remember my name."

A long, trembling silence. A dog at the edge of the crowd let out a low whine. Somewhere, glass cracked behind a wall.

She looked out over them now, her voice strong. "You have given me your loyalty for eight years. You've followed me through silence, through grief, through cursed seasons and stolen selves. You've made a life here when none should have existed. And I will carry that grace with me until my dying breath."

"I love you," Améliane said softly. "Each and every one of you has been a part of my heart. My history. My home. And now I ask you—" Her voice caught, but only once— "to follow me. Not because I am your Queen, but because I am willing to walk through first."

A pause. A heartbeat.

Then Renaud stepped forward, voice calm and clear. "If you're walking through that gate, Your Majesty..." He turned to face her fully. "Then I'll be just behind you."

The flood broke.

Voices rose—not in argument, but in something closer to readiness. Footsteps shifted. Shifters reformed. People grasped each other's hands.

Élodie wiped her cheek and stepped forward. "Well, if the world is going to end, at least now we know we will be remembered."

From the back, a voice rose—the old falconer, his hair silver, his eyes gleaming. "Then let the gates test us. We have nothing left to hide."

Améliane breathed.

For the first time since Laurent's scream echoed across the stone, she allowed herself to hope.

Mathieu's hand found hers and they moved through the Hall of Voices in solemn procession. For once, Eldrenoire did not resist. The corridors held their shape. The staircases did not shift. It was as if the Black Keep had stilled itself in farewell—offering clarity as a final gift.

When they reached the grand entrance, the doors opened wide without a single word. No summoning spell. No whispered phrase. Just a slow, echoing creak that rolled through the halls of Eldrenoire like the exhale of something ancient giving permission.

The court—her court—moved as one. Slowly, with no fanfare, no trumpets. Just footfalls softened by worn boots and padded paws, by cloaks faded with time and furs matted from the long stretch of captivity. Some had their belongings strapped to their backs. Others carried only what they wore, what they were.

There was no pageantry. No titles called out. No declarations of allegiance.

Just survivors walking toward the unknown.

Améliane stood at the front, Mathieu at her side, his hand clasped around hers like a vow. Renaud followed just behind them, a steady presence anchoring their rear guard. Élodie walked with Thorne, their shoulders brushing. Serenya and Cassien led the outer flanks. Together, they formed something more solid than armor.

They stepped out of Eldrenoire's great hall, down the grand front stair. The air had changed—cooler, clearer, laced with salt and fog. A breeze rolled in across the lawn, and for the first time in years, it didn't feel like mourning. It felt like promise.

The castle did not close its doors behind them. It stood open, watching.

The court poured out in silence. Some walked. Some shifted—hawks with eyes like burnished gold, wolves with silver in their fur, foxes darting between boots. No longer afraid to be seen. No longer fragmented.

Améliane's cloak swept behind her like night given form. Her braid was tight, her spine straight, her shoulders squared—not because she felt brave, but because she refused to falter. Not now.

They passed the reflecting pool. It showed no reflection.

They crossed the garden paths that had once changed with her emotions. Now, they held still. Steady. As if even the magic had chosen to walk beside her, rather than beneath her.

And then—they saw it.

The gate.

It stood at the edge of the glade, where mist gathered like breath between worlds. Its mirrored surface shimmered—not like glass, but like water standing on edge. It pulsed faintly, humming with silver light. The frame was cracked in places now, but the magic held.

Waiting.

Améliane stopped just short of the threshold.

The court behind her slowed, instinctively fanning out, a quiet wave of motion settling into stillness. No one spoke. Even the shifters held their ground.

She turned to face them all.

Her voice, when it came, was not loud. But it carried.

"We were cursed because I lost my crown."

A pause. No one moved.

"But I never lost you."

Her gaze swept over them—foxes and falcons, maids and lords, stable boys and courtiers once wrapped in silks. They met her eyes not with fear now, but something rawer. Truer.

"You stayed. You survived. You remembered. And now I will reclaim what was stolen. Not for vengeance. Not for glory."

She turned back toward the gate.

"But for belonging."

A hush. The kind that came before tides turned.

"Whatever waits on the other side, we go to it together. Not because the castle chose us...but because we chose each other."

The gate shimmered again. The mist thickened. Mathieu's hand tightened around hers in a reassuring squeeze before releasing.

Améliane moved towards those closest to her stopping in front of Sabine first. "You were never afraid to wound me to heal me. Thank you for both."

Sabine's mouth twitched. "Someone had to keep your ribs where they belonged." She reached out, smoothed a nonexistent wrinkle from Améliane's sleeve, then dropped her hand as if nothing had happened.

To Élodie, she offered a quiet embrace. "You were never just my handmaid," she whispered. "You were my mirror. My voice when I had none."

Élodie blinked hard and nodded through tears, her grip fierce and fast before letting go.

She reached for both Cassien and Evelyne's hands. "You have served me without question," she said. "But more than that—you believed in me when I no longer believed in myself."

Cassien bowed his head. Evelyne kissed her hand. Neither spoke. They didn't need to.

Thorne stood straight-backed, silent as always. She placed a hand on his shoulder. "You were the blade I never had to sharpen. The shield I never had to ask for."

His eyes met hers, soft beneath the scar. "You were worth guarding."

Renaud stood still as stone, jaw locked, eyes unreadable. Until she stepped into his arms.

He stiffened—then folded around her like a mountain shifting to protect a single flame.

"You have been my sword," she whispered. "My spine. The best of men in the worst of times."

He cleared his throat roughly but said nothing.

As she pulled away, Renaud turned slightly toward Mathieu. Not fully. Just enough.

"You're not what I expected," he said, voice low.

Mathieu raised a brow. "Disappointed?"

Renaud gave the barest shake of his head. "Relieved."

The space between them filled—not with warmth, but something better: respect.

Then Renaud stepped aside. Améliane turned back, eyes full, shoulders squared.

"Promise me," she whispered as she gripped Mathieu's hands. "If I fall—if I fail—make sure as many as possible get through."

He didn't hesitate. He didn't flinch. He simply took her hand again.

"I'm not going ahead," he said. "And I'm not staying behind. I'll walk beside you, Améliane. Wherever this leads."

She didn't answer with words—only with the weight of her grip, steady as faith.

The gate stood open. Waiting.

They stepped forward. The mist folded around them like memory. The surface resembled a mirror. It rippled—not in rejection, but in recognition. And then it began.

She did not see a question in the mirrored reflection. She saw herself.

First: A girl in moonlight, laughing and free. Not yet a queen. Just a child who wanted to do good.

Then: The cat. Small. Trapped. Watching. That self who had learned that silence was safety, and that sharpness could become armor.

Finally: Herself as she was now—braided, bruised, burning with something too steady to be called rage. A woman who had been broken but was no longer breakable.

She almost stopped. Because she knew that to step forward meant shedding them. Not erasing them—but releasing the illusion that survival had been the end of the story.

The mist pressed inward, curling like breath.

And then she heard it—not aloud, but in the hollow space of her heart:

"If you are not your throne, your curse, or your court—then what remains?"

Mathieu squeezed her hand. Not to guide her. Not to ground her.

But to remind her.

Her answer wasn't spoken aloud.

It pulsed outward like a vow written in blood and tide.

"I REMAIN. AND I AM ENOUGH."

The gate surged.

The mirror parted.

And the light changed.

Not golden. Not royal. But warm.

The mist thinned around her. The air turned green with leaves. The soil was soft beneath her boots. And birdsong—real, untwisted, alive—pierced the silence.

She turned her face to the sun. Eldrenoire did not stop her. It simply let her go.

Far behind her, somewhere, deep within Eldrenoire, Alaric smiled—and vanished like smoke into stone.

She escaped the curse. But the war for Belmara is just beginning.

Book Two of the *Ruined Realms* awaits.

Want more cursed castles, dangerous devotion, and haunted magic?

Join the Cursed Court at **ellewildes.com**

Be the first to know about bonus scenes, secret projects, and release dates.

Let's stay in touch:

TikTok—@ellewildes

Instagram— @ellewildes

The court may be cursed, but the stories don't stop here.

ABOUT THE AUTHOR

Elle Wildes writes romantasy for grown women—stories woven with longing, betrayal, second chances, and the kind of slow-burning magic that leaves a mark. Her worlds are steeped in enchantment and consequence, ruled by women who refuse to be tamed and men who are more haunted than heroic.

A lifelong book lover and former English teacher, Elle holds a bachelor's degree in education, a master's in curriculum and instruction, and is currently completing her doctorate in educational leadership. She now uses everything she's learned about stories, systems, and human nature to craft layered fantasy worlds full of power shifts, emotional reckoning, and just enough kissing to count.

When she's not writing, Elle can be found haunting the fantasy aisle of her local bookstore, making moodboards she swears aren't procrastination, or walking the coastline with a plot twist in her earbuds. She lives on the Texas coast with her husband, who cheers her on, keeps her grounded, and sometimes has to lure her out of Caelvarra with coffee and a reality check.

She writes for the readers who've lived through their own battles—and still believe in magic.